OSTLAND

ALSO BY DAVID THOMAS

Blood Relative

OSTLAND

DAVID THOMAS

Quercus

New York • London

Quercus

New York • London

© 2013 by David Thomas
First published in the United States by Quercus in 2015

ISBN 978-1-62365-696-6

Library of Congress Control Number: 2014954164

Distributed in the United States and Canada by
Hachette Book Group
1290 Avenue of the Americas
New York, NY 10104

Manufactured in the United States

2 4 6 8 10 9 7 5 3 1

www.quercus.com

To Clare

AUTHOR'S NOTE

The story that follows is inspired by actual events that occurred in Germany and Russia between February 1941 and July 1944 and by their resolution in the late 1950s and '60s.

Its subject, Georg Heuser, really existed. He was an officer of the *Kriminalpolizei*, or Criminal Police, and also of the SS. Although I have allowed myself creative license in describing the minutiae of his day-to-day life and personal relationships, the basic facts of Heuser's personal history, his detective work, and his activities in the occupied Russian city of Minsk are all presented as accurately as possible. Similarly, all descriptions of acts of violence, their perpetrators, and their victims are based on factual evidence, including contemporary reports, police photographs and sketches, court records, witness testimonies, and subsequent historical research. Court proceedings and verdicts are also quoted verbatim. For reasons of drama and coherence, however, I have marginally altered the timing and/or sequence of some minor events.

Many characters in this book—including all named criminal offenders and their victims, police witnesses, senior police and Nazi officials, and SS officers in Minsk—are either historical figures or, in a very few cases, fictionalized versions of real people. Others, such as those investigating Heuser's past, including Max Kraus and Paula Siebert, are fictional, but their actions—including the trip to gather evidence in Moscow—are based on real events. Likewise, the women with whom Heuser is romantically involved are all imaginary, but again inspired by specific individuals. Heuser really did have an old girlfriend who traveled from Hamburg to meet him in Berlin in February 1942, and three Jewish siblings lived in the basement of the Lenin House in Minsk and left the city in the manner described in the book. The words and opinions attributed to Heuser himself are also based wherever possible on what he is known to have written and said, or what others said about him. My depiction of Heuser's innermost thoughts and feelings is, of course, entirely imaginary.

In order to make police and SS ranks easier to read and understand, I have anglicized almost all of them, to one degree or another. But for those who are interested in these things, Heuser's wartime police ranks rose from *Hilfskommissar* to *Kriminalkommissar* and eventually *Kriminalrat* (of all Nazi titles the one that surely sounds the most appropriate to a British ear). His corresponding SS ranks were *Untersturmführer*, *Obersturmführer*, and *Hauptsturmführer*.

In German, the name Heuser is pronounced "Hoyzer," so that the first syllable rhymes with "noise." Meanwhile Georg is pronounced with two hard "g's" and separate sounds for the "e" and "o," thus: "Gay-org," to rhyme with "morgue."

David Thomas,
West Sussex, 2013

1

LUDWIGSBURG, WEST GERMANY: JULY 23, 1959

The police chief was naked when they came to arrest him.

"Well, we got him," said Max Kraus, appearing at the office door, his massive figure filling the entire frame. The three investigators waiting for the news responded with a mixture of genuine enthusiasm and semi-sarcastic applause. It was a hot summer's day, so all the windows were open, but Kraus had no trouble making himself heard over the sounds coming in from the street outside: the chatter of the passersby, the clacking of heels on the pavement, and the rumbling of all the new Mercedes, Opels, and Volkswagens produced by a miraculously reborn economy. Somewhere in the distance a radio was playing Elvis Presley singing "A Fool Such as I." Presley himself was just a couple of hundred kilometers away in Friedberg, serving as an armored recon scout in the U.S. army. Fifteen years earlier Uncle Sam had sent his finest young men to invade Germany. Now he sent them to defend it.

"Took their time," muttered one of the investigators, a paunchy, middle-aged man named Andreas Becker. He stubbed his cigarette out with a lazy stab that suggested, accurately, that he was hardly a man to rush things himself. Eight days had gone by since the arrest warrant was issued, but it had taken a full week for the authorities in Rhineland-Pfalz to accept that they had to seize their own chief of detectives. Most of the people making the decision knew him personally, and there had never been anything in his behavior, whether personal or professional, to suggest the slightest impropriety. But the weight of evidence was undeniable and so with heavy hearts they'd given their approval.

"Better late than never," Kraus said, as if it were all the same to him, though all his staff knew that he had been the driving force in the investigation, forcing it through the barriers of official indifference, skepticism, and outright opposition with a mental rigor that could be as overpowering as his physical impact.

"So where did they find the Beagle, anyway?" Becker asked. The police chief had been given his canine nickname by his own detectives as a tribute to his uncanny nose for crime. Kraus and his team had picked it up as a way of referring to their target without alerting anyone that he was under suspicion. Even when the need for a codename had passed, they often still called him the Beagle out of sheer force of habit.

"On vacation in Bad Orb," Kraus replied.

"Very *gemütlich!*" said another of the investigators, Florian Wessel. He was even older than Becker, and this backwater posting was his last before retirement.

"Oh really, is it nice?" asked Paula Siebert. The only woman on the team, and much its youngest member, she'd passed the same law exams as Becker and Wessel; her business cards clearly gave her status as *Dr. Siebert*; and she was just as competent, just as ambitious, and much more hardworking than either of her colleagues. But no matter how many of those cards she handed out, the concept of a female lawyer was still so hard for most people to grasp that she regularly found herself being called "my dear" or even "darling" as she was asked to fetch the coffee and biscuits. And when she put questions to witnesses she was often greeted with absolute incredulity, as if the only possible reason for her presence at an interview was to take shorthand notes.

"Did you know that German women have been allowed to practice law since 1922? That's almost forty years ago!" she'd said to Kraus after one particularly infuriating encounter.

"Yes, but men have been lawyers since Roman times. You can't expect people to change overnight."

"It's just so frustrating sometimes. Even my mother keeps telling me I should give up and find a nice husband. 'Your looks won't last forever, Paula. And no man wants a woman who cares more about her stupid little job than making him happy.' Ach!"

Kraus laughed. "Well, I can't help you find a husband. Or deal with your mother . . . But I do know how good you are at your job, and I'm your boss. So forget what anyone else says, that's what matters."

Paula hoped he was right, but now she was cursing herself. Here they were discussing the arrest of a major suspect and the first thing she asked about was his choice of vacation resort. Little things like that only confirmed people's worst prejudices about empty-headed females.

"Bad Orb?" said Wessel, who seemed only too happy that Paula had for once reacted as he would expect a woman to do. "Yes, very nice. It's in Hesse, right in the middle of the Spessart Nature Park. Lots of scenic views and endless cobbled streets, lined with old, half-timbered houses. You know the sort of thing: steep roofs, wooden beams all painted in different colors, very jolly. So what was our boy up to when they got him?"

"Taking a bath," said Kraus. "The local police burst in and there he was, bobbing about in the water, surrounded by other respectable folk, as hot and pink as a freshly boiled ham."

Even Becker could not help but join in the laughter at the image of the Beagle being caught in such embarrassing circumstances.

Paula thought of the smooth, confident, astonishingly youthful face that looked out in three-quarter profile from his police identity card. Some women might well find it attractive, though she couldn't begin to think of him in those terms herself. Paula was well aware that there was no link between a man's behavior and his external appearance. Even so, it outraged her that the Beagle's skin should have remained so unlined, as though he'd been entirely impervious to everything that he'd seen and done. His eyes were very slightly narrowed, his mouth set with the sort of self-conscious firmness with which an actor or a politician might convey manly strength and determination. He had a fine head of neatly combed and pomaded hair without a trace of gray. Only a slight thickness at the neck and jaw betrayed the softening of middle age.

"I'll say one thing for the sick bastard," continued Kraus. "He has a certain style about him. Apparently he got out of the bath, stark naked and dripping wet, and asked the arresting officer whether he might be allowed to dry himself and put on some clothes before they led him away. So they all had to accompany him back to his hotel room. He got into a smart suit, kissed his wife goodbye, and marched off to the police car with his head held high."

"Do you think he expects to get away with it?" Paula asked.

"Why not?" Kraus replied. "He's always gotten away with it before."

That was certainly true enough. Once the investigators had been put onto the Beagle's trail, they soon realized that there had been plenty of opportunities to catch him in the past. Strauch, for example, had mentioned him in his evidence. But the court stenographer had misspelled the Beagle's name, and so no one had made the connection. Now Strauch was dead and his information had died with him. Rübe had named him too, with the correct spelling, but the lead had never been followed up. Two court psychiatrists had examined Rübe at his trial. One said he had a schizoid personality. The other claimed he was a pathological sexual sadist. Either way, Rübe was crazy. Whatever evidence he gave, no one was likely to accord it the slightest significance.

None of the other guilty men had said a word. A conspiracy of powerful, strong-willed individuals is almost impossible to break as long as they remain united and, above all, silent. But as Kraus liked to say, "If the water keeps rising, eventually the dam will burst." So his tactics were always to keep collecting evidence, increasing pressure, going back again and again until—the first crack in the great concrete wall—one of the group members lost their nerve and started to talk. That was what had happened. A few months earlier they'd arrested Ehrlinger and presented him with evidence he couldn't deny. He'd blabbed, and that had led them to the Beagle.

Kraus looked around at the pitifully small, inexperienced, under-resourced forces at his command. There were only a very few idealists like him who were prepared to sacrifice their careers to work in an organization that was held in as much disregard as this one. The staff had therefore been recruited from those who had nowhere else to go. Paula was twice as good as both her male colleagues put together and yet they still regarded her as their inferior. Kraus wondered how long it would take her to realize that she had no real chance of establishing the kind of career her talent and energy deserved: not before this case had finally been dealt with, he hoped.

He let his people bask in their moment of glory for a few seconds, then his voice took on a tougher, more forceful urgency: "Listen up, ladies and gentlemen, this isn't the end of the case. This is the beginning. We still need evidence that will stand up in court, and that means witnesses, documents, unequivocal facts that no smart-ass defendant can deny. And as you're all only too well aware, absolutely no one will be keen to help you. The Beagle is a brilliant detective. He's admired and respected by every cop, every public prosecutor, every judge, every politician you're ever likely to speak to. Even the journalists like him. So the moment you leave this office, you enter enemy territory."

The door slammed behind him, leaving behind a much more subdued group of investigators.

"He's right, you know," Wessel said. "Some of my old chums at the prosecutor's office look at me with pity, as if I've caught some tragic, disfiguring disease. The others don't even bother to hide their contempt."

"The cops are worse," said Becker. "The moment I tell them I'm working for the ZSL, I can see actual hatred in their eyes. They think we're traitors. They'd happily shoot the lot of us and dump our bodies in the Neckar if they thought that would get the Beagle off the hook."

Suddenly the door swung open and crashed against the office wall. The three lawyers turned around to see Kraus standing there again.

"One more thing," he said. "I've had enough of this Beagle nonsense. The man is the suspect in the biggest criminal case since the creation of the Federal Republic. So let's not pretend he's a jolly little puppy dog. From now on we call him by his real name: Georg Albert Wilhelm Heuser."

2

BERLIN, GERMANY: FEBRUARY 6, 11:35 P.M.– FEBRUARY 7, 8:15 A.M., 1941

Not all the propaganda lied. In those early months of 1941, we truly were the master race. We ruled a European empire that stretched from the Atlantic coast of Brittany in the west, to the Russian border in the east: from the northernmost tip of Norway to the sands of the Sahara Desert. And at the heart of it all was my hometown, the capital of the Reich: Berlin.

Marlene Dietrich used to sing that Berlin was the center of the world, the pearl on the River Spree. But that was when she was still a true Berliner, not a Hollywood movie star who called herself an American. That was when the whole town lit up when the sun went down and you could go to the Haus Vaterland on the Potsdamer Platz, eat dishes from Turkey, Japan, Italy, or Spain and dance to eight different bands in a single evening. In those early months of '41, however, Berlin had become a black pearl at the center of a world war, and the most familiar night music was the wail of the air raid sirens. The lights had all gone out. And in the absolute, impenetrable darkness of the blackout the beasts and demons that lurked in the city's underbelly emerged to stalk their prey.

At twenty-five minutes to midnight on the night of Tuesday, February 6, the worst of them all was strolling down the center aisle of an S-Bahn train—one of the old Type 477s that can still be seen on the network to this day. The smattering of late-night passengers sat on wooden benches topped by metal handrails. There was wood paneling on the walls, with a luggage rack just beneath the ceiling. Each carriage possessed eight sets of sliding doors, four on either side. To us Berliners, a carriage such as this was as familiar as our own front rooms, an environment we hardly even noticed, no more than anyone looked twice at the man now making his way between the seats.

He was not an impressive specimen. He had oyster eyes and a fleshy nose—Jewish-looking, as some back then might have said. A meager little mustache sat above his sullen mouth, and his lower lip was set in a permanent pout of resentful disapproval. He was the illegitimate son of a farmhouse servant called Marie Saga: father unknown. His education was limited, to put it politely. He was twenty-eight years old, in his physical prime, but a broken wrist acquired in a minor accident while serving among the occupying forces in France had rendered him unfit for combat. That was why he'd come back home, after just a few months' military service.

His injury had not, however, prevented him from murdering six women. Another half-dozen had somehow survived being battered, stabbed, and discarded like broken dolls beside the tracks of the very line on which this train was now traveling, or being left for dead in the gardens and allotments near his suburban home. There had been perhaps thirty further assaults: he'd not kept a precise count.

This campaign against the female sex had been going on since 1938—longer than the Führer's own war—but barely two months had passed since the authorities finally woke up to his murderous existence. Now the full weight of the Berlin police had been brought to bear. Thousands of possible suspects had been interviewed. The trains and stations of the S3 line—the killer's particular hunting ground— had been flooded with uniformed officers. The authorities had done their best to keep official coverage of the case to a bare minimum, but rumors still swirled through the city. Everyone was talking about the S-Bahn murderer.

And here he was, at twenty-five minutes before midnight, prowling among the passengers as anonymously as death itself while the train moved out of Karlshorst in the southeastern suburbs and headed toward the city center. There were blackout blinds over the windows, and the only light in the carriage came from a single dim blue bulb that provided just enough illumination to enable people to find their way around, but no more than that. The men and women scattered among the polished wooden benches were hunched and huddled, shivering in clothes whose meager wartime fabrics gave scant protection against the winter weather. Stout boots and thick leather soles were fast becoming a thing of the past. Now the people's footwear was often as cardboard as their food, quite possibly because the same sawdust was used for both. Cold and damp seeped deep into the bones, sapping energy and attentiveness alike. The only time that anyone even marked the killer's passing was when he opened the connecting door between one carriage and another, letting in a freezing blast of snow-dusted air, provoking a few muttered obscenities before he closed the door and entered the next . . . and the next . . . until finally he found what he was looking for.

The woman wasn't particularly young or pretty. She did not conform to any specific character type: this wasn't a man who sought out only whores, schoolgirls, or the elderly as his victims. There was, as we would later discover, one particular quality that this man required from his victims, but even that was secondary to the main thing that interested him about this particular female. She was sitting by herself, alone and unprotected.

He looked around, checking that he hadn't missed any other passengers. He tried to control his mounting excitement like a dog owner desperately clinging to the leash of a running hound as his pulse started to hammer, his breathing grew heavier, and his cock swelled beneath his rough woolen pants. His rage was rising along with his lust. He did not see a respectable woman in front of him, just a filthy, germ-laden infector of men. To him she was the killer, the spreader of death, a criminal who deserved to be punished.

And punish her he would. He bent his right hand behind him, wrapping his fingers around the length of rubber-wrapped copper telephone cable as thick as his wrist that he'd hidden up the sleeve of his jacket. This was the bludgeon with which he had cracked skulls and ended lives. He was practiced in its use and confident in his method. Killing, like anything else, is a skill that improves with repetition, and he'd become very good at what he did.

He took another few paces down the aisle. There were shoulder-high partitions in pairs beside each set of doors, and the killer needed to be sure that no one was concealed on a bench behind one of them.

The discovery that she really was alone came to him as a great relief. It hadn't been easy waiting for the perfect moment when he was free to walk the trains; when the cops were looking somewhere else for once; when there was a solitary woman offering herself up as a sacrifice. But here it was. He did not have to hold back any longer. He could satisfy the urges that had been burning in him unassuaged for more than a month since his last killing.

He stepped toward her and gave a polite cough to signal his presence no more than a couple of meters from where she sat. She looked up and saw him, a man looming over her in a deserted railway carriage in the middle of the night.

Then she smiled.

She suspected nothing. She felt completely safe. Quite calmly she pulled off one glove and then the other to make it easier to rummage in her jacket pocket. And that was when he took one long stride toward her and let the length of cable slide down the back of his arm, slipping through his fingers until he gripped it again at the far end. Now he was raising his arm and as she saw what was in his hand the look on her face changed from complacent security to the first wide-eyed tremor of alarm. He twisted his shoulders, gathering his strength. Her mouth opened to scream in terror, but the scream was silenced before it had left her throat as the bludgeon swung down, smashing through the pathetic defense of her upturned arms and crunching into her skull.

As the bone crumpled beneath the impact of his weapon the killer entered a new, blissful state in which all his senses were heightened. Time slowed down for him so that he was perfectly aware of the effect of every single blow as he brought the telephone cable down again and again. His eyes seemed to cut through the gloom of the half-lit carriage, perceiving every drop of blood spattering from the gaping wound, each strand of hair upon the battered head. He pounded his arm up and down in a vile, destructive parody of masturbation, smashing her long after she'd lost consciousness, even when life itself had left her, until, with a hoarse, ecstatic cry, he achieved his orgasm and the battering finally ceased.

The killer would have loved to linger awhile to savor the pleasure of what he'd done, but there was no time for that. He knew very well how long it took the train to travel between each and every station on the line, and he'd spent too long finding his victim to allow himself even the briefest indulgence now. Instead he had to focus on the disposal of her body.

He placed his weapon on the seat close to where the woman was lolling, head down, battered skull exposed, devoid of any sign of life. Her gloves had fallen onto the carriage floor, so he picked them up and stuffed them into one of his trouser pockets. Then he pulled the woman from her seat onto the floor and reached down to grab the back of the jacket. His intention was to drag her along the floor to the nearest set of doors. But the jacket was made from a heavy, prewar woolen fabric, lined with satin and belted at the waist, and all he succeeded in doing was pulling it away from her body so that it bunched under her armpits, forced her arms over her head and ended up in a cumbersome tangle, half on and half off. Meanwhile her body had barely moved five centimeters.

The killer cursed under his breath, beginning to worry now as the next station drew ever closer. His arrogant composure was fraying badly, giving way to a much more familiar mood of simmering resentment: once again the world was against him.

He wasn't beaten yet, though. He pulled the jacket right off and threw it toward the nearest doors on the left-hand side of the carriage. Now the woman was much easier to handle and it was only a matter of seconds before he'd pulled her to the doors. He dropped her beside the coat as casually as if he were back on the farm, dumping a sack of chicken feed in the barn. The thud of her head and shoulders against the linoleum and the grotesquely distorted expression on her upturned face—one eye wide open, yet sightless; the other barely distinguishable amid the bloody pulp of her ravaged skull—did not register with him at all.

Bracing himself against the piercing gale, the killer pulled on the door handle and heaved the woman's body out into the night. The gloves and coat followed in quick succession. His task complete, he closed the door again, heaved a sigh of relief, took off his cap, and passed a hand over his sweaty brow. He walked back to where the woman had been sitting and picked up the bloodstained cable, which he stuffed back up his sleeve. The next stop was Rummelsburg Depot. When the train arrived he got off and made his way down the deserted platform. No one boarded the carriage he'd just left. No one noticed him as he made his way out. In the blue half-light of the carriage no one spotted any traces of blood against the dark red floor.

The S-Bahn murderer had just struck for the seventh time. And I, meanwhile, was lying in bed, trying and miserably failing to get some sleep.

3

Why is it that the young, who have so much time ahead of them, are in so much more of a hurry than the old? I was a little over two weeks away from my twenty-eighth birthday, an age that seems absurdly youthful and immature to me now. I was about to begin my life as a police detective and had every reason to look forward to a successful, fulfilling career. Yet the excitement with which I anticipated all that my future held in store was mixed, not just with a natural anxiety that I might somehow fail to do as well as I'd hoped and others expected of me, but also with a fear that I was already falling behind. Twenty-eight! My God, that was almost half my life already over. I was practically an old man. And here I was, only just getting started.

What fools we are. How little we appreciate the gifts that are bestowed upon us. Only later, in retrospect, do we look back with the hindsight of all the decades that are lost forever and rue the opportunities we once had and the other, better life we might have led. Not that I was entirely blind to my good fortune. Though my mind was turning over as fast and fruitlessly as a racing car's engine that screams its loudest just as it stands stationary on the starting line, I was still bright enough to know that any other police officer my age would happily have taken my place.

I was due to report to police headquarters at 06:00 to meet my new boss, Wilhelm Lüdtke, head of the Berlin murder squad. He had solved more murder cases than any other detective in the Reich, and I'd been assigned to be his right-hand man—a young Watson, you might say, to his Sherlock Holmes. This apprenticeship of a young detective to a master of the craft was known in the department as a *Mordehe,* or murder-marriage. It was a plum assignment and the honor was made still greater by the fact that I'd be joining Lüdtke midway through the hunt for the infamous S-Bahn murderer—the greatest yet most intractable case of his career.

Like anyone else in my position, I wanted to make the best possible impression on the man who held my future prospects in the palm of his hand. For that I had to be properly rested and in the best possible form. Yet my nervous energy would not allow it, and all I could manage was two or three hours of fitful, semiconscious dozing, disturbed by lurid dreams and interrupted by long, fretful stretches of wakefulness.

Of course, I'd already made my preparations. My shoes had been polished until I could see my reflection in their toe caps. My best winter suit had been cleaned and pressed. My shirt was crisply starched, my underclothes freshly laundered. Whatever other shortcomings he might observe, Lüdtke would find no fault with my appearance or cleanliness.

I was then, as I still am, a perfectionist. It is a trait that was drummed into me by my father. No teacher ever had to correct the grammar or spelling in any piece of homework that I presented: Father had already done so and ensured that, in the event of any mistake, I'd written out the right answer ten times over. I thus learned early in life that there is no point in doing anything unless one does it to the absolute best of one's ability, and I was filled with ambition and determination to succeed.

Just a few days earlier I'd graduated top of my class at the Security Police Leaders' School at Berlin-Charlottenburg, following a training period that had lasted just two years instead of the customary three. The small pile of personal items on my bedside table now contained not just my wallet, my watch, and my identity papers, but also the bronze warrant disk that declared me to be an officer of the Criminal Police, the plainclothes investigative branch of the police service, known to one and all as the Kripo.

My newly acquired status of Assistant Criminal Commissar wasn't my only qualification. In July 1936 I passed my first law exams at the Higher Regional Court in Berlin, and put myself on the road to becoming a full doctor of law. By then, I was already in the process of developing my curriculum vitae to give myself the best possible chance of standing out from my contemporaries. In 1934, a year before such service became compulsory, I volunteered for the Reich Work Service, the organization through which young men were recruited to undertake essential labor for the state. In 1935 I spent the first of three summers training as a reserve sergeant and officer candidate in the Luftwaffe. You will gather, I hope, that self-advancement wasn't my only concern. I wanted to serve my Fatherland, too, a desire that arose directly from the circumstances in which I'd grown up.

I was born on February 27, 1913. By the time I was eighteen months old Germany was at war. I was, of course, far too young to have any real awareness of that first great global conflict. I remember going off to kindergarten, at the age of four or five, with a stomach still empty after little more than a small lump of black bread for my breakfast, knowing that hunger would spend all day nagging and gnawing away at my insides. But I did not understand that the reason I was so famished was that our enemies were blockading Germany, and rations were becoming ever more meager.

Then came the shock that greeted the news of our unconditional surrender. Every grown-up I encountered seemed to be possessed by a stupefied indignation that such a capitulation should have occurred. Again and again people asked one another how such a thing could have been possible when not a single enemy soldier had so much as set foot upon the Fatherland. Constantly I heard talk of betrayal, stabs in the back, and evil conspiracies against us. The precise content of what people said was incomprehensible to me, but the emotions behind the words—the anger, intensity, humiliation, and helplessness—were deeply affecting and disturbing.

One recollection from that period comes from what I now suppose must have been January 1919, just a couple of months after the Armistice. My mother, Margarete, had taken me with her as she scoured the barren shops in search of something for our supper. Suddenly there was a series of sharp, explosive reports. Thinking they came from firecrackers, I squealed with excitement. I pulled my hand from hers and made to run toward the noise. My mother screamed, grabbed me with a roughness I'd never before known from her, and swept me up in her arms, scolding me furiously for being so naughty. Not knowing what I'd done wrong, shocked by the strength of my mother's reaction, and frightened by the panic-stricken terror I could sense in her, I burst out crying and was wailing in her ear as she ran pell-mell to the nearest open door. It led into a rough, workingmen's bar, the kind of place that my mother would never normally have dreamed of entering. But there she was, and plenty of other respectable housewives with her: all of them equally possessed by a fear for which I could see no obvious reason. I looked around, my curiosity outweighing my tears, fascinated by the shabbily dressed ruffians clasping glasses of beer, the heavy pall of cigarette smoke in the air, and the nervous chatter of the womenfolk as they discussed what was happening and debated what to do next. We stayed in that bar for what seemed like an age. After a while, the men and women began to mingle, their spirits suddenly much higher. I remember my mother laughing with an unfamiliar, uninhibited exuberance. When we left it was already dark. My mother returned home with her shopping bag still empty, and I was sent to bed with no more than bread and margarine for my supper.

I need hardly say that the sound that had so alarmed my mother was gunfire. The Bolsheviks of the Spartacus League had taken to the streets of Berlin, hoping to bring the workers out in a general strike and provoke a revolution. In those days my father, Albert Heuser, was a respectable businessman. Even now I can close my eyes and I am back in our apartment in Lichtenberg, pressing my ear to the dining room door, listening to him and his guests compete to see who could summon up the most furious denunciation of the Commies, the Bolshies, and the Reds. I had no idea who these red people were, or what precisely they had done to make all the grown-ups so angry. I just knew that they were very wicked indeed.

And then there were the Jews. I was familiar with their race from my Sunday school classes. They were the people who had demanded the death of our Savior. Now they seemed to be responsible for many of the ills that beset the country. The bankers who controlled the world's money were Jews, but so too were the bankers' greatest opponents, the leaders of the Spartacists and Bolshies who wanted money itself done away with. My father was never an overt anti-Semite, but he did not seem to disagree when others suggested that if one looked hard enough at any of the problems besetting Germany, the hand of the Jew could always be seen at work behind it.

To a small boy, of course, what matters above all is his family. On this score I have no complaints. My parents were no better or worse than anyone else's, I got on perfectly well with my sister, and was happy enough at school. Yet I grew up under the shadow of defeat. We Germans had been forced to confess to our guilt for the war itself, as if our supposed aggression were the sole reason for that terrible conflagration. We were crippled by the burden of paying reparations, though we too had suffered a terrible loss of treasure and young blood. And then, when there simply was no money left to pay the victorious extortionists, we had to watch as the French retaliated by marching into the Rhineland, taking the opportunity of our impotence to kick, punch, and humiliate innocent Germans in the street, even beating them with sticks—in public!—defying the populace to fight back.

The madness of hyperinflation struck when I was only ten. The economics of it all meant nothing to me. I just knew that when the baker wrote out the price for a loaf of bread, it had more zeros than I could count. Things became so crazy that I once made a castle for my toy soldiers out of blocks of worthless deutschmarks and complained vehemently as my mother took them away to feed the fire. The banknotes were worth less than lumps of coal. I quite literally saw my country's finances go up in flames.

After those years of political and economic shame came others of cultural decadence. My God, you should have heard my father going on about "that half-naked black whore" Josephine Baker, when the Negro Revue came to Berlin. Men of his type and generation believed that the whole magnificent heritage of German culture was under threat from a filthy tide of foreign trash. He was shocked at the sight of supposedly respectable girls cutting their hair barely longer than a boy's, wearing dresses that hardly covered their asses, painting their faces, smoking cigarettes, and dancing to the primitive jungle music of jazz. The clubs and cabarets that filled the city in those days he regarded as nothing but meeting places for sodomites, transvestites, and subversives. I can't say that I took him too seriously, although my ears did prick up at the information that Josephine Baker, whoever she might be, was half naked and that there were girls out there, somewhere, dancing in such short skirts!

Then came the Crash of 1929 and our own domestic banking collapse of '31. The flimsy edifice of prosperity and self-confidence that had begun to rise from the ruins of our recent past was swept away. It was as if we had painfully risen to our feet again, only to be knocked back down upon our knees, and with this sudden financial shock came a corresponding blow to social order. My father's business suffered terribly and he was forced to lay off almost all his staff. Once again we found ourselves eating meager rations, but this time it was not because there was any lack of food in the shops: we simply couldn't afford to buy it. In the end, father gave up his business and found a job in the civil service. He exchanged the dream of riches for the assurance of a reliable salary. But because he'd entered the service of the state relatively late in his career, he wasn't able to become a *Beamter*, which is to say a civil servant for life, with guaranteed employment and a generous pension providing the promise of complete security until his dying day. Somehow, he scraped together the money to fund my studies, but his generosity came with regular, firm reminders that this was no act of charity. It was my duty now to work hard and gain the qualifications that would assure me either a career in one of the higher professions, or the *Beamter* status that he'd never achieved.

In the meantime, political enmities had intensified once again and sober debate was giving way to violent extremity. The Nazis' brownshirted SA storm troopers attacked the Communist headquarters. Goebbels and his men fought the Reds on the streets of Neukölln, just across the Spree, a few kilometers from where we lived. Once again my mother was looking out of the windows of our apartment in fear, wondering whether the bloodshed would reach our neighborhood. I didn't like to see her so anxious. I, too, was made uneasy by the unnerving sense that we were teetering on the brink of anarchy. Still, I could also see that this was a struggle that had to be fought, and I knew which side I'd rather see victorious.

I wish to emphasize in the strongest possible way, for reasons that surely need no elaboration, that I was never at any time a member of the National Socialist Party. You don't have to take my word for it: search the Party records, you will find no trace of my name. I cannot quite explain why I didn't sign up. Party membership was by no means obligatory in either the police force or even the SS, but of course it helped smooth one's way. I suppose it was in part a matter of genuine principle. I was reasonably certain that I was going to end up working for the state in some capacity or another, and I believed that a civil servant's loyalty should be to the state itself, rather than any one party of government. I think I also possessed a certain conviction, born in equal parts of naïveté and arrogance, that the quality of my work would be high enough in itself to secure me preferment. And maybe there was an element of calculation, too. I'd grown up with so much political uncertainty and change that no matter what anyone might say about the Thousand-Year Reich, I couldn't imagine anyone staying in power for a decade, let alone a millennium. That being the case, I didn't want to be tied too closely to one political party when the next one came along. I cannot, of course, claim to have had any idea at all of the manner in which Hitler's time in office would end. This was just an instinct, not a very noble one at that, as to where my long-term best interests lay.

Yet I must say that when Adolf Hitler became Chancellor at the end of January 1933, I cheered the massed ranks of the SS and SA as they paraded by torchlight through the streets of Berlin. They made a magnificent sight: marching like Roman legionaries behind vivid scarlet banners emblazoned with white roundels and black swastikas, each standard topped by a proud golden eagle.

No one likes to admit it now, but I was far from being alone. Of course, Berlin still had its share of Lefties. It was an irony of the time that the capital of the Third Reich was one of the most defiantly

Bolshie cities in the land, and there were plenty of fights among my grammar school classmates that echoed the ones in the street. But for most of us the National Socialists represented a promise of pride and strength after too many years of weakness and shame. To a youngster standing on the threshold of manhood, this was an intoxicating prospect. In those early years of his rule, the Führer seemed to be a hero, a superman. And compared with all the blithering, weak-willed old men who had tried to lead the German people over the previous fifteen years, that is precisely what he was. When he took back the Rhineland a little bit of our pride was restored, and it swelled still further when first Austria, then the Sudetenland, and finally all of Czechoslovakia were brought under German control. We had no idea of what was to follow: how could we have? It was utterly inconceivable.

Of course, it is true that the first year of my legal studies coincided with a series of proclamations that radically transformed the legal, political, and social landscape. Opposition parties were banned. Limitations were placed on the rights of Jews and other social undesirables. A whole new view of the law was put forward: a law that acted to the benefit of the National Socialist state and its principles. Yet it is a matter of historical fact that the Spartacists would have taken an equally strong grip on the totality of society had they succeeded in seizing power in 1919. So would the Leftists had they won the election of 1932. The Bolsheviks had already created a totalitarian state in Russia and made no secret of their desire to spread their rule around the world. This was the tenor of the age, the common denominator, if you like, between idealists of both left and right. Our problems were so great, the need for change so urgent, that we simply could not afford to be slowed down by anyone proposing alternative, incorrect solutions.

It was my idealism, too, that made me want to serve my country. A few years ago, when that American, Kennedy, said, "Ask not what your country can do for you, ask what you can do for your country," he was expressing precisely what I felt when, in the spring of 1938, I decided to enter the police service. As a fully qualified police officer I'd almost certainly become a *Beamter*, thereby pleasing my father. Moreover, the law in the abstract did not inspire me. I was convinced that ours was an age and a country in which the most interesting legal tasks would no longer be left to lawyers and judges, but would fall instead to those who were actively engaged in the enforcement of state policy.

I was, as I'd always been, interested above all in the maintenance of public order. I wanted my mother, my sister, and all the other decent, respectable women like them to be able to walk the streets in peace. I wanted hardworking small businessmen and manufacturers like my father to be able to go about their business, free from the threat of communist appropriation. And I wanted to fulfill my parents' dearest wish for me and build a solid career in a secure profession: the world, after all, will always need policemen.

So on December 1, 1938, I began the process of training that would lead me to that college at Charlottenburg. And here I must make a brief observation about the structure of policing in the Reich. To put it at its simplest, the police had been placed under the control of the SS, run by SS-Reichsführer Heinrich Himmler. He in turn created a new organization, the Reich Security Main Office, under the command of SS-General Reinhard Heydrich, into which were placed the three elements of the Security Police, to wit: the Criminal Police (Kripo), the Secret Police (Gestapo), and the Party's own intelligence service, the SD. So to be a detective was effectively to be a member of the SS also, and every Criminal Police rank had its equivalent in the SS. In February 1941, upon my graduation as an Assistant Commissar, I also became a second lieutenant in the SS itself. Nevertheless, though a field-gray SS officer's uniform may have hung in my wardrobe, I was then, as I remained for the rest of my working life, a plainclothes policeman at heart. As with the issue of Party membership, the reasons why I make this point about the SS so clear should be perfectly obvious.

But enough of these distractions: back to my story. Dawn was still almost three hours away, yet I was just about to begin one of the most remarkable days of my entire life. The post I'd worked so hard for awaited me. And the most terrible criminal in all the Reich would soon become my prey.

4

I'd been to "Alex," the police headquarters on Alexanderplatz, many times before, but I was still far from familiar with its labyrinth of stairs and passages; its apparently infinite sequence of doors leading to myriad offices and interrogation chambers; its hidden courtyards and subterranean levels. The place was vast: in the whole city only the old royal palace was bigger. The architect had made a token effort to alleviate its massive redbrick bulk with the addition of towers at each corner, pierced by arches and topped with pointed glass domes. On its external facades the windows were arched, and many were arranged in pairs or triplets, split by marble columns. These gave a slight Renaissance feel to the building, as though it were some grossly oversized descendant of a nobleman's palace in Florence or Rome. This was not, however, a building filled with artistic Michelangelo or da Vinci types. It was more a place of Borgias and Machiavellis, and not just among the criminals either.

Those are, I should say, my reflections in retrospect, rather than the associations that sprang to my mind on that dark February morning as I reported for duty and awaited the arrival of the secretary who would escort me to my new workplace. I brushed a light dusting of snow from the shoulders of my overcoat, stamped my feet to clear my shoes, and sat down on a bench in the lobby. A few minutes went by. The air felt warm and muggy after the raw cold outside. For a moment my eyelids grew heavy, and despite my excitement at the challenge that awaited me I succumbed to a yawn. At that precise moment my guide arrived. She appeared to be younger than me, yet her eyes were ringed with deep, purple-black shadows and regarded me with a look of bone-deep fatigue that seemed to mock my single lost night's sleep. Her skin was sallow, her skirt heavily creased, and her hair roughly plaited, with stray strands sprouting all over her head.

Her scruffy appearance came as something of a shock. It wasn't at all what I'd expected. "What is your name?" I asked.

"Tietmeyer, Assistant Commissar."

"Well then, Tietmeyer, let's get to work."

"Yes, Assistant Commissar." Her voice was utterly devoid of enthusiasm, as if she could barely summon up the energy to speak, let alone carry out her duties. As she slid open the concertina metal door of the elevator and stepped aside to let me through, I asked myself whether a woman like this was really best employed working for the Criminal Police, even as a lowly secretary. She was surely young enough to have spent her teens in the League of German Maidens and must have been told a thousand times that the proper business of a National Socialist woman was running her house, caring for her man, and, above all, producing as many healthy Aryan offspring as possible. Such a life could hardly make her more miserable than this one apparently did. But then, what husband would want a wife so shabby and listless?

Well, that wasn't my concern. My priority was getting off to a good start with Lüdtke. I was thrilled to be meeting him and I wanted him to like me too. So by the time I was following Tietmeyer out of the elevator on the third floor and then proceeding along a bewildering sequence of corridors, I'd already set her shortcomings to one side and was instead imagining my first encounter with the great man.

Should I approach him as a humble student, willing to learn at the master's feet? No, he would surely expect someone more assertive. Better, surely, to come across as a keen, highly trained officer, ready to get on with the job: a man who could be of use to him from the start. I had to be confident without being arrogant; suitably respectful, yet in no way cringing. And so I walked on, rehearsing introductions in my mind, until Tietmeyer finally came to a door bearing a sign that read MURDER SQUAD.

"After you," she said, stepping to one side.

"Thank you," I replied. I turned the handle. I opened the door into the duty room of the most prestigious crime-fighting unit in the entire Reich. And I entered a scene of utter desolation.

The stuffy, airless atmosphere reeked with the stale odor of last night's cigarettes. The desks at which the detectives worked were littered with piles of paper, filthy ashtrays, and empty coffee cups. The wastepaper baskets overflowed with trash. It was all of a piece with Tietmeyer's dishevelment, but I still found it hard to believe that this could be the home of an elite. "Is this where the murder squad works?" I asked.

Tietmeyer looked at me as if she couldn't quite decide whether I was teasing her in some way or was really as stupid as my question suggested. "Yes, of course—this is their squad room."

"Is it always like this?"

She shrugged. "Sometimes," she said. "Often it is much worse."

I was opening my mouth to reply when I heard a sound coming from somewhere in the office. I paused, cocked my head to one side, and frowned as I tried to identify the precise nature of the noise. Yes, there was no mistaking it: someone, somewhere, was snoring.

The source of the disturbance wasn't hard to find. I merely took half a dozen steps to my right and stopped in front of a man slumped unconscious across his desk. His black hair, speckled with strands of steely gray, was greasy and unbrushed, and heavy stubble covered his chin. A thin trail of drool was suspended from his open mouth and the stench of his body odor was matched only by the smell of the schnapps that had dripped from the upended, virtually empty bottle by his side all over the desk and down onto the stained, greasy carpet that covered the floor.

I swung around to face Tietmeyer again. "Who is this . . . this tramp?"

"What tramp?" she asked in a tone of sweet innocence, though a look of pure mischief was twinkling in her eye, bringing life to her face for the first time. "This gentleman here is Commissar Lüdtke. Would you like me to wake him for you?"

My blood ran cold. That wreck of a man was Lüdtke? I was struck by a crushing feeling of disillusionment at seeing the true face of a man I'd been taught to revere as a hero, mixed with embarrassment at having shown myself up in front of Tietmeyer, not to mention a chill dread that the old man might possibly have heard what I'd just said. Drunk and malodorous or not, Lüdtke could end my career before it had even begun.

"Er, no . . . no," I stammered. "That won't be necessary."

"Don't worry, I'm awake anyway."

Lüdtke slowly raised his head from the table. He leaned back in his chair, gave a hacking, phlegm-laden cough, and ran a nicotine-stained hand through his hair.

I stood up straight, came to attention with a click of my heels, and snapped my right arm out in front of me with a loud *"Heil Hitler!"*

Lüdtke pulled himself wearily to his feet and vaguely waved a limp arm in my general direction. *"Heil Hitler,"* he muttered and then slumped back down into a sitting position. He looked blearily up at me: "Don't look so damn disapproving, Heuser. I'm not a tramp, as you call it, out of choice. I'd much rather spend nights in my own bed, with a hot, deep bath, a nice big plate of calf's liver for my dinner, and freshly laundered clothes in the morning. I dare say young Tietmeyer here wouldn't mind the chance to go home at night too. Isn't that so?"

"It would be nice, sir, yes."

"Sadly, such luxuries are even less available to those of us here than they are to the rest of our fellow Berliners. I haven't slept for more than three hours a night since the beginning of December. I haven't left this building in the best part of a week."

"But surely," I began, and then stopped dead, realizing I had no idea what I could possibly say.

"Surely it's not supposed to be like this. Surely we are supposed to proceed in a calm, well-ordered, scientific series of steps, leading to the inevitable apprehension of the criminal. Is that what you meant?" Lüdtke asked.

I frowned. "I suppose so, Commissar."

Lüdtke rubbed his eyes hard, and then blinked several times. "Well suppose again. This is not a classroom at Charlottenburg. This is a murder investigation. And I can't even begin to think about it without a cigarette. Give me one of yours, Heuser, there's a good man."

"I'm . . . I'm sorry, sir, but I'm afraid I don't smoke."

A baffled frown creased Lüdtke's face still further. "Don't smoke? What kind of detectives are they producing these days?"

I felt myself blushing like a schoolgirl. "Well, sir, I find that smoking disagrees with me. As you know, the Führer is very keen on maintaining bodily hygiene and he feels that—"

"Yes, Heuser, I'm aware of his opinions on the subject and I'm sure it does you great credit to follow his lead. Sadly, I come from an older, more traditional generation of policemen and I . . ." Lüdtke paused, summoning up the energy for a weary smile as he saw Tietmeyer standing over him, holding out a cigarette. "Ah, bless you . . ." he sighed.

Lüdtke took the cigarette, then leaned forward as Tietmeyer produced a lighter and placed the flame to his cigarette. He took a deep breath and then exhaled, ignoring my attempts not to cough as the smoke enveloped him.

"My God, what's in these things?" he mused. "Sawdust? Pigeon shit? Not much damn tobacco, that's for sure."

The last few words were all but lost as Lüdtke was hit by another consumptive outburst of coughing. He looked up at me with bleary, watering eyes and then, as if reading my mind, said: "Yes, I know, you're quite right, my bodily hygiene is a disgrace. But when I am working on a case, that's the last thing I worry about. My whole mind is focused on the need to catch the killer and prevent more deaths. Everything, absolutely everything else is forgotten. And this case, this big, fat shit-sausage of a case . . . Ach! Look over there, Heuser . . ."

Lüdtke pointed across the room to the far wall on which a large map of one segment of Berlin's eastern suburbs was pinned. It was covered with small colored flags and pinned threads that radiated from those flags to collections of photographs and drawings that surrounded the map itself. A blackboard, propped on an easel just in front of the wall, was covered with notes in white chalk, interrupted by occasional sweeps of an eraser.

"There, that's our case," the chief of the murder squad said. "Give me five minutes to clean myself up and I'll tell you all about it."

5

It was actually closer to fifteen minutes before Lüdtke returned to the squad room, but the time had been well spent. His transformation was remarkable. His face was clean-shaven, his hair brushed, and his white shirt clean and crisply starched. Now he looked like a detective under whom I could be proud to serve.

Lüdtke's dirty clothes were bundled up in yesterday's shirt. "Take that lot to the laundry," he said, giving it to Tietmeyer. "Then see if you can rustle up a couple of coffees, or whatever they're passing off as coffee this morning, for Heuser and me. And when you've done that, go home. You need a break."

"Thank you, Commissar."

Lüdtke and I may have been police officers, but we were also men, so we both watched Tietmeyer leave the room. There seemed to be a new spring in her step, even the hint of a swing to her hips. For the first time I saw her as a young woman who might almost be deemed attractive.

"She's a good girl, that one," Lüdtke said, and then turned his attention back to me. "Come," he said, leading the way toward the map on the wall. "Welcome to a very sick, benighted corner of the Reich."

Lüdtke paused for a moment, gathering his thoughts. Still chastened by my earlier embarrassment, I waited silently to hear what my boss had to say.

"Now," Lüdtke began, "I'm sure I don't have to tell you how important it is that you familiarize yourself with the details of the case as soon as possible."

"Of course, Commissar." .

"In my view we are dealing with six murders, and at the very least another six serious sexual assaults and attempted murders."

The moment Lüdtke began to speak I was struck for the first time in my life by one of the most intoxicating sensations that anyone can experience: being at the heart of events and privy to secrets that are hidden from everyone else. The S-Bahn murders had been the topic of gossip, third-hand misinformation and wild theorizing from the most humble to the mightiest in Berlin. Even at the Leaders' School, though we had discussed the case incessantly over the past two or three months, none of us had really known what it involved. The realization that I was about to find out was absolutely thrilling. My fatigue, my nerves, and my self-consciousness were all forgotten and my attention was absolute as Lüdtke continued: "These offenses can be divided geographically into two main groups. The first group of attacks, of which only one proved fatal, took place here in the Friedrichsfelde district." He pointed to a cluster of flags in the top left-hand corner of the map. "Do you know the area at all?"

I was delighted to be able to say: "Yes, Commissar, I grew up in Lichtenberg, very close by. When I was a small boy my parents used to take me for walks past all the gardens and allotments there. Many of the little lanes were just dirt tracks. I used to like finding loose stones and kicking them along the road."

I fell silent, uncomfortably aware that my enthusiasm had gotten the better of me. I'd given way to an uncharacteristic display of nostalgia when a simple yes or no would have sufficed. "I'm sorry, Commissar. I didn't mean to say so much."

"That's quite all right, Heuser. And you do not have to call me Commissar every time you say a word to me. We will be talking a lot: it might get wearying. So if I give you a direct order, fine. Otherwise, don't bother."

"Yes . . . Commissar." I waited a second then added: "You gave me an order," by way of explanation.

Lüdtke managed a tired laugh. "So I did! Now, these flags in Friedrichsfelde mark attacks on women, none of them fatal. The first took place on August 13, 1939: Lina Budzinski, age forty-three, hit over the head and stabbed four times in the back. Then four months later on December 14, Hertha Jablinski, twenty-one, stabbed four times in the neck and the head. Then there's a gap, I don't know why, until July 27, 1940, when Gertrud Nieswandt, twenty-six, is stabbed in the neck and the thigh. Less than a month goes by and then Julie Schumacher, forty-one, is attacked in a tunnel here, near Rummelsburg. A man shines a flashlight in her eyes then hits her over the head. All the attacks occurred at night. None of the women, therefore, has been able to give us a detailed description of her assailant. Of course, there is no proof that the man who perpetrated these attacks is the one now known as the S-Bahn murderer, but keep the nature of the attacks in mind: the victims are all women and they are hit over the head or stabbed. As we consider the actual S-Bahn crimes, you will see why both the targets selected and the methods used incline me to believe that we are only talking about one man.

"So now let me take you to the Number 3 S-Bahn line from Rummelsburg, here"—Lüdtke pointed toward a point just below the previous cluster of flags—"to Friedrichshagen, here."

Now his finger was at the bottom-right corner. The railway line traced a diagonal line across the map from one corner to the other, dotted by more flags along the way, indicating scenes of crimes.

"As a local, you will doubtless know all the stations on this stretch: Rummelsburg . . . Rummelsburg Depot . . . Karlshorst . . . Wuhlheide . . . Köpenick . . . Hirschgarten . . . Friedrichshagen . . ."

"Yes, Commissar," I said—the title slipped out automatically. I waited for Lüdtke's rebuke, but he wasn't paying attention to me. He was looking across the room and saying, "Ah . . . the magnificent Miss Tietmeyer has returned."

She approached us bearing a tray on which stood a pot, two mugs, milk, sugar, and a blue packet of French Gitanes. The unmistakable smell of real coffee filled the room like a memory of a bygone age. Lüdtke closed his eyes, breathed in the delicious aroma, and sighed.

"We're in luck," Tietmeyer said. "A black marketeer was arrested last night and all the contraband goods he was selling were seized." A knowing smile played around the corner of her mouth as she placed the tray down on the nearest desk, sweeping a pile of papers out of the way to make room for it. "In order to determine precisely what charges should be brought, it has been decided that experienced senior officers will be required to sample and test the goods in question."

"But there are only two cups," Lüdtke said. "The accuracy of this test would surely be assisted by the help of a woman's sensitive palate. Get yourself a cup, Tietmeyer."

"Thank you, sir!" she said, with a smile that lit up her face, reinforcing the good impression that the sight of her departing backside had already made upon me.

Tietmeyer fetched herself a cup, then served us all. I wondered at the propriety of consuming black-market coffee that was now the property of the state. Officers senior to myself had obviously commandeered it for their own use. But was that a justification for drinking it or did it merely compound the offense?

It wasn't for me, however, to criticize Lüdtke's behavior: not to his face, at any rate. So I said, "This is wonderful, thank you," to Tietmeyer as she handed me my cup, and was intrigued to see the rather startled pleasure that she took in my words and the warm smile with which I'd accompanied them. Perhaps she, like me, was reconsidering her first impression.

We all relaxed, savoring our drinks. For months now it had been virtually impossible to obtain anything that even resembled real coffee. We'd all been making do with an appalling substitute known as *Muckefuck*. It was said to contain malt, barley, acorns, figs, chicory, and even the occasional dandelion root. Anything, in fact, but an actual coffee bean, or a single milligram of caffeine. Now here was this magical brew, and as it slipped down my throat my concerns about its origins seemed absurdly nitpicking and naïve. The Kripo played a vital role in society, working long hours, sometimes in circumstances of great personal danger. Surely they were entitled to enjoy an occasional perk of the job?

For a couple of minutes no one spoke, not daring to break the spell that the coffee had cast. Lüdtke quietly occupied himself transferring the Gitanes from their packet to a battered gunmetal case. That task complete, he emptied his cup in one gulp, placed it back on the tray, and in a businesslike voice made harsher-sounding by the mellow silence that had preceded it said, "Thank you, Tietmeyer. You may go. Drink up, Heuser, we must get back to work."

He returned to the map. This time, there was no stopping to look at Tietmeyer. Lüdtke was all business now.

"The first assault that we know of on the S-Bahn occurred on the night of September 20, 1940, at 23:35 hours. A man attempted to throttle a young woman called Gerda Kargoll in a second-class compartment of the train between Karlshorst and Wuhlheide. The attack was completely unprovoked and there was no sexual element. The man then forced her out of the door of the train, which was moving at approximately sixty kilometers per hour. But Fräulein Kargoll had luck on her side. She wasn't seriously injured by the initial attack. And, even more fortunately, she is by profession a school sports teacher. Thanks to this, she was able to keep her balance, and then roll forward when she hit the ground, minimizing the impact."

"Like a parachutist," I observed, thinking back to my Luftwaffe days.

"Quite so . . . Unfortunately, however, both for Fräulein Kargoll and for us, her nimbleness and agility were so great and her injuries so few that when she first went to the Serious Crime Office and reported the incident, some idiot there refused to believe her story. He accused her of making the whole thing up. He thought she'd had some fight with a boyfriend and just wanted to get him into trouble. So there was no follow-up investigation."

I was appalled. "My God, if anyone had known then . . ."

"Yes, we might have caught this bastard before he killed anyone. But that wasn't the only time we overlooked him. Let's go back to Friedrichsfelde . . . You will doubtless recall from your childhood walks all the small buildings that litter the place. Most of them are just weekend retreats, or a place to go for a bit of fun on a summer's night. But some people live there full-time. On October 4 one of them was found dead, stabbed in the throat, in one of those shacks. That's a picture of the murder scene."

He pointed at a black-and-white photograph pinned to the board next to the map. It showed a woman slumped on her knees amid the detritus of a poor family's kitchen. She was slightly hidden behind a wooden stool, on which a white enameled basin was filled with dirty dishes. Her body was leaning against a large basket that might have contained laundry. Behind it stood a wooden kitchen dresser. The woman's dress was riding up over her stockings. It was drenched in blood, as was the basket behind her. There were blood spatters, too, over the front of the wooden dresser. Her head was horribly tilted to one side, as if it could no longer be supported by her mutilated neck.

"My God," I whispered, thinking of my mother and sister. I felt a fierce determination to ensure that neither they, nor any other women in Berlin, would suffer so terrible a fate.

"Her name was Gerda Ditter," said Lüdtke. "She was a war widow, only twenty, had two little children."

"How awful for them, losing their mother and father so young," I observed.

Lüdtke shrugged. "Perhaps. But you mustn't waste time or mental energy feeling sorry for those children. The best thing you can do for them is to catch the man who orphaned them . . . Now, it was assumed that Frau Ditter had interrupted a robbery. The thief, or thieves, lashed out with a knife and that was the end of her."

"Was anything taken?"

"Good question. No, there was no evidence of any theft, and Frau Ditter lived in such poverty that there was very little of any value to steal. Nevertheless, until very recently no one made any connection between the Ditter killing and the incidents along the S-Bahn, the second of which occurred precisely one month later.

"On November 4 a thirty-year-old woman called Elizabeth Bendorf was beaten about the head and thrown from the train, and this time no one could possibly think she was making it up, because she was lying unconscious on the ground, seriously injured and in desperate need of hospital treatment."

"But she lived?" I asked.

"Yes, this one did."

"Then could she not describe her assailant? And what about the sports teacher. Kargoll? Surely she provided a description."

"We spoke to them both and they were able to give us some information. Both agreed that the man wore a uniform of some kind, with a cap pulled so low over his eyes that they were unable to get a clear sight of his face. But they disagreed on the details of his uniform.

Kargoll thought he was wearing a black jacket without any buttons. Bendorf swore it was blue and with buttons. These differences are not significant: there is almost no light on an S-Bahn train, making colors very difficult to distinguish, and the traumatic nature of the women's experiences clearly affected their memories. But there is something very important about the uniform. Can you tell me what that might be?"

I thought for a moment. It was obvious now that Wilhelm Lüdtke was far from the drooling, drunken tramp he'd seemed on first encounter. I was beginning to understand how he'd acquired such a fine reputation, and I wanted to earn his respect.

"Well, neither woman was alarmed when she first saw the man," I said cautiously. I was relieved to see Lüdtke's silent nod of agreement, encouraging me to say more. "Therefore there must have been something about him that made them trust him. The women saw the uniform and assumed that they were safe."

"Very good, Heuser," Lüdtke said, with a warmth that greatly cheered me. "And who is the most likely person to wear a uniform on the S-Bahn?"

"Someone who works on it?"

"Exactly. So when considering the evidence—just the evidence, alone—where would you look first to find a suspect?"

"Among S-Bahn staff," I said, the logic of my argument leading me to that conclusion before I had time to consider its ideological implications.

"Good man," said Lüdtke. "I thought so too. That is why I had more than three thousand men, out of a total of eight thousand workers, interviewed, without any success. We were unable to isolate any suspects."

"What if the killer does not actually work for the S-Bahn?" I suggested. "Perhaps he stole a uniform, all the better to impersonate a respectable employee."

"That's a possibility. The killer could be an impostor. The women wouldn't know it and would respect the uniform just the same."

"So he could be anyone—a foreign worker, for example. There are tens of thousands of them in the city and few of them have much love for our Fatherland."

"I agree," Lüdtke said. "That is why we have already leafleted many of the largest labor camps in the city, offering rewards for information. Unfortunately none has yet been provided. Nor have there been any reports of stolen S-Bahn uniforms."

"And the Jews? Our instructors at Charlottenburg were always saying that they have an inherently criminal nature."

That wasn't a reflection of my opinions, simply a statement of fact. The entire legal system was predicated on the notion that race, political opinions, and personality types were crucial factors in antisocial behavior.

Lüdtke gave a weary sigh. "My superiors have made the same point, repeatedly, but there is no evidence to suggest any Jewish involvement. Think about it, Heuser: Jews are banned from working on the S-Bahn and find it almost impossible to travel on trains or buses. If a Jew wanted to kill women, wouldn't he do it somewhere else?"

I said nothing. Lüdtke's logic was hard to refute, even if it did diverge so markedly from the racial theories I'd been taught.

Lüdtke had turned back to the map on the wall. "I want to move on to the night of Tuesday, December 3. There were actually two murders that night, and in my opinion our man committed both of them. Neither of the bodies, however, was found until the Wednesday morning. One was in Prinz-Heinrich-Strasse. It was very close to the tracks on the southern side of the line—in other words, near the track leading out of the city—about four hundred meters from Karlshorst station. The victim was a nineteen-year-old girl called Irmgard Frese. She had been sexually assaulted, too, very brutally.

"The second victim was a twenty-six-year-old nurse: Elfriede Franke. Her body was barely two hundred meters away from Frese's, toward the center of the city, on the north side of the railway line. She was lying between the track and a wooden fence approximately two meters high, over which she certainly could not have climbed. So she must have been thrown from a train. She also had injuries to her skull, consistent with being hit over the head. So it was clear that her attacker was the same man who had previously assaulted Bendorf and Kargoll.

"Commissar Zach—he's a good man, you'll meet him soon enough—took initial charge of the investigation because I was already at work on the Prinz-Heinrich-Strasse case. But our police pathologist, Dr. Weimann, conducted the postmortems for both bodies. He established that Irmgard Frese had been killed by blows to the head that were very similar to those suffered by Franke, the nurse. Given the proximity of the two bodies, the timing of their deaths, and the method used to kill them, it was reasonable to suppose that both deaths were the work of the same man. And that man had to have been the S-Bahn murderer."

Once again, Lüdtke's reasoning was impeccable. "What happened next?" I asked.

Lüdtke reached for his cigarette case. "Ah well," he said, lighting up. "The following day Zach and I were summoned to see Bernie Wehner. Nebe and Lobbes were both there too. Even Heydrich was sticking his nose into the case. And that was when things became interesting."

6

Lüdtke had just named four of the most important people in the entire Reich police service. The man he referred to as "Bernie" Wehner ran the Reich Central Office for Capital Crimes. SS-General Arthur Nebe was the head of the Criminal Police. His colleague and great friend Hans Lobbes was head of operations for the Security Police, including the Gestapo and SD. Lobbes was a former head of the Berlin murder squad and a legend to detectives all over the country. His collars included the child-murderer Adolf Seefeldt, alias "Uncle Tick-Tock," who was believed to have killed more than one hundred young boys, and Johann Georg Elser, the subversive who bombed the Bürgerbräukeller in Munich in November 1939 and almost killed the Führer. The one I really wanted to know about, however, was the man who commanded them all.

"What about General Heydrich?" I asked. "Has he made his views clear?"

"Oh yes," Lüdtke replied. "By the time we got to the meeting, Heydrich had already been on the phone to Wehner and Lobbes. He ordered them to solve the case as soon as possible, at all costs. That's when they decided to put me in charge of the investigation."

"What a tremendous honor," I said.

Lüdtke gave a rueful smile. "If I catch the killer, yes. If I don't, it might not be quite such a blessing."

"So what did you do to try and catch him?"

Lüdtke closed his eyes and ran a hand through his hair, as though the very act of answering the question exhausted him. "Everything," he said. "We began the business of interviewing S-Bahn staff. We put officers on trains and station platforms. We went through every single case that might have any connection to these ones. There's been quite an epidemic of sex crimes in the whole area around Rummelsburg, Friedrichsfelde, and Karlshorst over the past couple of years, quite apart from the four cases I mentioned to you. So I ordered all the known perverts rounded up and brought in for interrogation. We went hard at them, no messing around. Didn't get anything useful out of them. But I did come across one interesting report.

"In August last year, a woman was walking through some orchards near Rummelsburg station. A man came up to her and asked her if she wanted to take a walk with him. Only he didn't exactly ask her politely. So she screamed for help, knowing that her husband and brother-in-law were nearby. They pitched up and really laid into the man, but somehow he managed to get away from them and staggered off into the darkness. They couldn't see where he'd gone. Do you know what I think?"

"That this attacker was the S-Bahn murderer?"

"That's certainly a possibility. Suppose he's been doing this for months, abusing women, gradually becoming bolder and more violent over time. Suddenly it goes wrong and for the first time he is the one who gets hurt. So he nurses his wounds and broods over what has just happened. He decides that he can't risk being caught in the act again. He must ensure that his victims cannot call for help. And the best way to do that . . ."

"Is to kill them," I said.

"Exactly. At first, of course, he did not succeed. He'd not perfected his method. But he did not give up. And once he'd succeeded, he acquired a taste for it: a craving, even. The full resources of the Reich's security apparatus were ranged against one man and yet the killings continued."

Lüdtke stabbed a finger at the map on the wall. "Sunday, December 22, the early hours of the morning: Elisabeth Büngener, age thirty, was found by the tracks here, between Friedrichshagen and Rahnsdorf. That location, incidentally, marks the furthest extent of the killer's range to date. Exactly a week later, December 29, he's back on familiar territory. Gertrud Siewert, forty-six, found near Karlshorst. Again, precisely one week goes by and then he kills Hedwig Ebauer, twenty-seven. She's found near Wuhlheide. Ebauer and Büngener were throttled before being thrown from the train. Siewert was brutally beaten over the head. Whatever the method, it's always the same man: week after week after week."

"That was more than a month ago," I said. "But nothing since then?"

"Not that we know of. Maybe we've scared him off. Or he could just be lying low until he feels safe again."

It was now about half past seven in the morning. The office had begun to fill as the rest of Lüdtke's team made their way in to start the working day. A young detective came through the door to the duty room. In total contrast to the all-pervading air of exhaustion and disillusion, he had a wide-eyed, boyish expression and such an innocent, guileless smile, one might almost take him for a simpleton. He called across to a colleague: "Hey, Richter, have you seen that great lump of concrete they're putting up in the middle of the zoo? It's going to be the biggest flak tower the world has ever seen. Forty meters high. Guns all over the place."

Richter appeared to be the older of the two men. He had sharp, beaky features, slicked-back black hair, and a sardonic twist to his mouth. "Hey, Baum, do I look to you like a blind man?" he replied with heavy sarcasm. "Of course I've seen the fucking thing."

Baum's enthusiasm wasn't dented in the slightest. "You know what that flak tower proves? It proves we're the most civilized nation on earth. Who else would go to such trouble to protect a zoo?"

"Well if they do all that for a bunch of animals," said Richter, drily, "think how big the flak towers will be once they start protecting people."

Baum was still laughing as he sat down at his desk, directly opposite Richter. It was obvious that they worked as partners, a kind of double act of village idiot and cynic: the one to lure suspects into a false sense of security, the other to stick in the knife.

"You'd better meet your new colleagues," said Lüdtke. He led me over toward Baum and Richter. The two of them got to their feet as they saw us coming. We exchanged *Heil Hitlers*, handshakes, and brief introductions. There were two other officers in the room. Lüdtke led me to another desk, occupied by a much older officer, and said, "This is Senior Detective Schmidt."

"Call me Papa—everyone else does," said Schmidt, whose portly frame and flushed red cheeks did indeed give him the air of a genial father figure.

Up to now, I'd not detected any suggestion of hostility or even suspicion toward me from the other men. But that changed when Lüdtke brought me to the desk belonging to the only other officer-rank man in the room, Inspector Frei. There was an unmistakable aggression in the way he shouted *"Heil Hitler!"* and almost punched his arm into the air.

Frei's resentment wasn't hard to explain. He was around forty, a dozen years older than me, and held the rank of Criminal Inspector. For the time being, as long as I was a mere Assistant Commissar, he was still senior to me. But I was on a fast track up the service. So long as I performed my duties satisfactorily, I could expect a swift promotion to Commissar. At that point I would outrank an inspector. So from the moment he met me, Frei knew that I, a much younger man, would soon be his superior.

"Good morning, Inspector," I said.

Frei glared at me for a moment and then sneered: "So you're the new murder-marriage boy, eh? Tell me, should I call you Assistant Commissar Heuser, or would you prefer Frau Lüdtke?"

The room fell silent. I could feel the tension as the other men waited to see how I'd respond to Frei's challenge: if I got this wrong I could forget about being accepted by the department. Then it struck me that Frei had done me a great favor. He'd made his hostility far too obvious, far too soon. And the reason he despised me so much was the very same reason I could now afford to retaliate in kind: he had no power to hurt my career.

"You may call me what you wish, Inspector," I said, doing my best to make my voice sound a great deal more relaxed than I felt. "But if I were you I'd bear one thing in mind: it never pays to be rude to the boss's wife."

Baum burst out laughing. Richter looked at me with his mouth twisted into something close to a grin. Papa Schmidt gave me an approving nod of the head, and even Lüdtke appeared to be suppressing a smile. Frei, on the other hand, looked like he wanted to hit me. Perhaps he would have, had the urgent trill of a telephone not suddenly interrupted us.

Richter was the nearest detective. He picked up the receiver, listened for a moment, and then looked up. He held the receiver out toward Lüdtke. "You need to hear this, Commissar," he said.

Lüdtke went over to the phone. He gave his name and listened to what the caller had to say. He muttered, "I see," and gestured to Richter to pass him a notebook and pen. He jammed the receiver between his shoulder and jaw, opened the book, and then spoke into the phone. "Where, exactly, did you say it was?" For the next minute or so he was all attention, writing notes on what he was being told. His only words were terse, simple questions: "And this was when?... What time?... Who else?"

As Lüdtke spoke, the detectives got up from their seats and drew closer to him, as did I, until we were drawn up in a rough semicircle by the desk. Lüdtke put the telephone down. We all knew what was coming next.

"He's killed another woman. She's on the line between Rummelsburg Depot and Karlshorst. Someone get hold of Dr. Weimann. I want him there as soon as possible. We need a photographer, a sketch artist, and an ambulance crew. Also, make sure that all S-Bahn traffic in the area is halted immediately and tell them to cut the power. I don't want any of us getting fried on the line."

Lüdtke pulled out a cigarette, lit it, and took his customary deep lungful of smoke. As he exhaled he looked around, his eyes settling briefly on every one of us before he finally said, "Let's go and see what this bastard's done now."

7

KOBLENZ PRISON AND RAMSTEIN AIR BASE, WEST GERMANY: JULY 21, 1960

Paula Siebert picked up a copy of *Der Spiegel* at the station in Stuttgart, just before she got on her train to Koblenz. There was a picture of John F. Kennedy on the cover and a lengthy profile inside, marking his nomination as the Democratic candidate in the forthcoming U.S. election. She'd seem some of his acceptance speech on the TV news, this idealistic, almost boyish figure talking about the creation of a New Frontier. Kennedy was only forty-three years old, an entirely different generation from the current president, Eisenhower, and a full forty years younger than Konrad Adenauer, Chancellor of Germany: "The Old Man," as everyone called him. His beautiful young wife, Jackie, was pregnant and staying at home during the campaign under doctor's orders, but the way she wore the latest Paris fashions with such a youthful, American élan was the talk of the glossy magazines. Even Paula, who was trying so hard to escape the confines of a traditional woman's life, couldn't help wondering how she could acquire some of that Jackie magic.

There were signs of change everywhere. The Russians and Americans were racing to put a man into space, using rockets that could just as easily destroy the whole world with nuclear bombs. But they weren't quite out of the shadows of the past. Both sides had employed

German scientists to design their missiles with technology developed in the Nazi years. And here Paula was, taking a train back into that same darkness, uncovering crimes that had long been forgotten, disinterring victims long dead.

At the prison she was greeted by the governor, who seemed disappointed, even a little offended, that Kraus had sent a deputy, and a female one at that, to interview his star prisoner. "Of course, I'm sure you understand that Dr. Heuser is not at all like our normal inmates," he said. "He is a man of achievement, of culture. I must say, it is a great pleasure to have someone in my charge with whom I can have an intelligent conversation."

Paula wondered whether the governor would have had such a high opinion of Heuser if he'd been familiar with the evidence that she and her colleagues had been compiling over the past two years. It depressed her to think that the answer might just be yes.

"One of my men will take you to the room where the interview will be conducted," the governor said, escorting her from his office and entrusting her to a guard. They walked through the kind of bleak, infinitely depressing prison warren that had become very familiar to Paula over the past twelve months as the net had widened and more men had been caught in it. The roll call of their names had become engraved on her memory: Dalheimer, Feder, Harder, Kaul, Merbach, Oswald, Schlegel, Stark, von Toll and Wilke. So now they had a total of eleven defendants in all—"like our very own football team," Florian Wessel had joked—all of whom had been arrested and were now being held in a variety of different jails.

The guard held open the door to the interview room and Paula walked in. She was pleased to see that Heuser looked diminished by his year in prison. The harsh fluorescent light of the interview room did nothing to flatter him as he sat in his suit and tie on the far side of a bare wooden table. The formality of his dress struck her as faintly pathetic, a desperate attempt to cling to a status that had long since deserted him. He must have lost a lot of weight, for the suit hung loosely on his frame and all the plump, smooth self-satisfaction had gone from his cheeks, which were drawn and slightly saggy around the jaw. His skin had the gray pallor of a man whose life is lived almost entirely within his cell; his eyes were lined and bloodshot; and his hair had become sparse and colorless around the temples.

"Where is Kraus?" Heuser asked, sounding just as irritable as the governor.

"Dr. Kraus is engaged in other matters today," she said. "He asked me to take his place. My name is Siebert. Today I want to examine the years that led to your appointment as a Criminal Commissar in the Rhineland-Pfalz police."

"As you wish, Fräulein Siebert, though I cannot see what significance any of that has to the false allegations that have been made against me."

"My correct title is Dr. Siebert, Herr Heuser."

"And it's Dr. Heuser, if you don't mind."

"We'll come to that in a moment." Paula watched the flicker of surprise in Heuser's eyes and his momentary frown as he realized he'd been played. She knew he'd be wondering what exactly she meant by "We'll come to that." How much did she know? Heuser was a man who liked always to be in control of any interaction. Well, so did Paula Siebert.

She set out her papers on the table in front of her: an aide-mémoire she had prepared that summarized the known information about Heuser's activities, a large legal notepad, and two pens, for it was always possible that one pen might cease to function.

Paula began: "So, where were you when the war came to an end?"

"Commanding a small battle group in Krems, on the Danube, west of Vienna, fighting the Russians."

"And you were taken prisoner?"

"Oh no, anything but that," Heuser replied. "We all knew we'd be dead men in the Russians' hands. So I thought, I'm a plainclothes policeman. I know about undercover work. Why don't I just go undercover now? I put on civilian clothes and headed west, trying to reach the American sector."

"Are you saying that you deserted your men?"

"No," said Heuser, without any hint of apology or guilt. "By that point it was total chaos, millions of people on the move—soldiers, refugees, people of every nationality. I just lost myself in the crowd, and if my men could do that too, good luck to them."

"And you reached the Americans?"

"Yes."

Paula looked at her notes. "So here's the first thing I don't understand . . . All the Allied forces arrested SS officers as a matter of course. The British and Americans interned them for at least three years after the end of hostilities. But there's no record of your internment. Why not?"

"Because I wasn't ever interned. When I reached the American lines I told them I was an officer in the Luftwaffe. So, I admit it, I told a lie. But it wasn't an absolute lie. After all, as I'm sure you know, I'd spent three summers training with the Luftwaffe before the war and had been a candidate for officer rank. It was hardly the worst deception."

"Well, it wasn't just a question of confusing one military unit with another, was it? If you had been correctly identified, the consequences for you might have been much worse than a few years' internment."

"I don't see why."

"Yes you do. You see exactly why . . ." Paula's mother had always taught her that in order to establish dominance over a dog one must look it directly in the eye and hold the gaze until it backed down. And that was what she did now, keeping her eyes on Heuser, an intent, expressionless stare until she could see he was discomfited, and then she went on. "Tell me where you went next."

Heuser seemed relieved by the question.

"Ahh . . . to Goslar, in the northern Harz mountains. My sister had been evacuated there, so I went to stay with her. That's where I met my wife, Edith—she was Edith Kruger then. Anyway, we seemed to hit it off; we were married in October '45 and we've been together ever since. No children, unfortunately. I think Edith regrets that very much, but it was not to be. There's no point dwelling on disappointments, don't you agree? Count your blessings."

"Blessings? You?"

"Absolutely. When I think of all the things that might have happened to me, all the fine young men I knew who lost their lives, or suffered terrible wounds, not to mention the ones that survived but could never quite fit back into civilian life, why of course I feel blessed."

Paula was disgusted by his shamelessness. She wanted to shout, "You have no right to compare yourself to all the good men and women who died!" But that was not her job in this room, on this occasion, so she calmly went on. "About that civilian life . . . yours was difficult for a few years, was it not?"

Heuser nodded. "It wasn't easy, no. But they were hard times for everyone. We all had to make do as best we could. Edith and I settled down in Ludwigshafen and for a few years, yes, I was as low as I have ever been in my career. I had periods of unemployment and often felt obliged to accept jobs that were well beneath my capabilities. I was a clerk in a transport company in Mutterstadt. I was a junior sales manager for a battery factory in Ludwigshafen itself . . ." he sighed. "Hardly places to inspire one, but I was grateful enough for the work."

"How did you make your way back to the police?"

"Well, after the Federal Republic was founded in '49 it was difficult at first for men of my generation who'd been civil servants in the old days."

"You mean servants of the Third Reich."

"There you are: that was exactly the problem we faced. We were all treated as though we had been Nazis, which many were, I admit, but not me. You can look in every record, every archive, but you will never find my name on any Party roll. I was not a member. Not for a single second."

Heuser's voice had been rising with self-righteous indignation as he spoke, and his body had stiffened and straightened with newfound energy.

"I know that," Paula said, very calmly, watching him almost visibly deflate as he slumped back down in his chair.

"Good . . . good . . . Then maybe you'll ensure that my case is not tainted by any false allegations. These things can sway a jury. I've been involved in enough prosecutions to know that."

"The facts of the case will of course be presented as accurately and fairly as possible. Now, can we get back to your application to join the police?"

"Certainly. In '51 the government realized that it was simply impossible to run the country efficiently if all the men who had any experience were forbidden from being involved. So they said that all those of us who held *Beamter* rank could go back to our old jobs, with a full pension entitlement as if we'd worked throughout the intervening years. That was very generous, I must say."

"So you naturally sought to rejoin the police?"

"That's right."

"But you didn't actually go to work again as a detective until 1954, three years later. Why the delay?"

For the first time, Heuser seemed uneasy. "There were a number of technical and, ah, administrative matters to sort out."

"Really? What kind of matters?"

"Well, for one thing, the old Berlin police headquarters on Alexanderplatz had been bombed flat, so it was impossible to get hold of all my service records. And of course, Alexanderplatz is now in East Berlin, so even if the records had existed, the Commies wouldn't have handed them over."

"Is that why you had to fake your doctorate of law, Herr Heuser— because the original records had been destroyed?"

"I have no idea what you're talking about," he blustered. "What in heaven's name do you mean, 'fake'?"

"Fake, as in falsify . . . as in claiming to be a Doctor of Law on your application to rejoin the police, and using that title ever since, when in fact you are no such thing."

"How dare you make such an outrageous suggestion, young lady! I have been proud to call myself 'Doctor' for the best part of twenty years."

Heuser was angry and showed it. Paula was disgusted, but betrayed no trace of anything except calm, methodical competence.

"Maybe you have," she said. "But you never completed your legal studies and the certificates that you presented to the Rhineland-Pfalz police were fakes. It's true that you were granted your university degree in law on July 27, 1936, in Berlin, but that's only the first stage in qualifying as a lawyer. You didn't complete the others. There's no point denying it. We've checked. Not every record was destroyed, you know."

Some criminals keep arguing that they haven't done anything wrong, even when presented with the evidence that they have. Heuser was smarter than that. Like a general making an orderly retreat, he conceded his initial position, but moved to another line of defense.

"Well, all right, that's true . . . I didn't obtain a doctorate, not in a formal sense."

"What other sense is there? Either one qualifies or one does not."

"In times of peace, maybe. But those times came to an end. I went to be trained as a senior detective at Berlin-Charlottenburg and came top of my class. I then had some considerable success as a detective in Berlin. My superiors deemed that academic and practical experience to be at least the equal of a final set of exams, and I was allowed, officially, to call myself Doctor. Believe me, I would not have dared use that title if it hadn't been approved at the very highest level. General Heydrich wouldn't have stood for one of his junior officers lying about a thing like that."

"Nor, I imagine, would the personnel department of the Rhineland-Pfalz police."

"Well, what was I to do? I could hardly say: 'Heydrich said I could have a doctorate.' He's not exactly a good name to bandy about these days."

"So you lied."

Heuser smiled, his self-assurance somewhat restored. "I prefer to think that I provided an alternative explanation."

"Is that what you've been doing in all your interviews with us: providing an alternative explanation?"

The smile vanished. "I don't have to answer a question like that."

"Not to me, no. But shouldn't you have an answer for your conscience? I was talking to Dalheimer . . ."

Heuser tensed, waiting to hear what his codefendant had said about him.

"Oh, don't worry, he didn't give the game away. Not in any way that would concern the court. But he did make what seemed to me to be a very interesting observation about you, that no matter how tough, how ruthless you might be in carrying out your duties . . ." She looked down at her notes and read: "'he could remain, in dealing with us, always a sensitive person.'"

Heuser shrugged. "How else should I be?"

"Von Toll, too, spoke of you with genuine affection, as a good, loyal friend. And Schlegel—he's still pathetically grateful for the letter of recommendation you wrote on his behalf to Mercedes-Benz. He swears he could never have gotten his job without it."

"Schlegel's a good man. He was applying to be the apprentices' training manager. I knew he had a background in education. I was quite happy to point that out to the relevant parties. What's your point?"

"Very simply that you're not a cold-blooded, emotionless psychopath, incapable of empathy with another human being. You know the difference between right and wrong. Look at von Toll. He's been working for the Red Cross, trying to make amends. Don't you want to do the same? Don't you fear what might happen if you don't? Think of Lütkenhus, killing himself."

"What has that got to do with anything?"

"One of your old comrades committed suicide last July, three days after your arrest. You don't think that's significant?"

"I don't know. I have no idea why Lütkenhus should choose to end his own life and nor do you. Did he leave a note?"

"Not that I'm aware of."

"There you are, then. Believe me, young lady, I have seen plenty of suicides in my time, and the reasons for them are seldom as obvious as you seem to think."

"This one is. He knew that if we'd arrested you, he'd be next. He couldn't bear to live with the shame. And what I can't understand is, how can you? Somewhere inside of you, surely there must be a voice screaming at you to tell the truth, to do good, to be redeemed . . . Isn't there?"

Heuser said nothing. He remained almost motionless at the table. He gave no obvious sign of distress. Yet Paula could see that she had at last penetrated that great wall of denial, detachment, and self-delusion with which Heuser had surrounded himself. He wasn't alone in that, of course. They all did it. But because he was the cleverest and toughest of them all, his defenses had been by far the most effective.

An absolute silence fell upon the room. Time seemed to grind to a halt. Paula told herself to say nothing, but simply to let the intense internal drama—whose only external expressions were the momentary tightenings of Heuser's jaw and lips, the fractional twitches of his skin, the unconscious grip of his hands against the edge of the table, and the burning intensity of his eyes—play out.

Finally he spoke in a dry, desolate rasp: "My conscience is clear. I have no reason to reproach myself. I never did anything"—he paused again for more than a minute, stopping himself more than once on the verge of speaking as he tried to assemble the correct form of words. Then he finally finished his sentence—"for my own profit, or for any motivation other than the desire to do my duty to the best of my ability."

"You can do better than that," Paula said softly. "For the sake of your soul, you have to do better than that."

Again Heuser said nothing, and then, quite unexpectedly he smiled, though there was a wistful sadness in his face and his eyes seemed to be focused on something far away in space and time as he said: "You remind me of someone I used to know: a very beautiful young woman, just like you. She also wanted me to repent . . ."

Paula cleared her throat, disturbed by the intimacy with which he'd spoken, and concentrated fiercely on her notes. "Are you referring to your former colleague, Fräulein . . . ah . . . Tietmeyer?"

Heuser chuckled. "Biene? Heavens no! That poor, sweet girl never thought anything but the best of me. No . . . I was thinking of someone else . . ." His voice dropped to little more than a sigh. "It really doesn't matter who."

Paula now regretted her brief, unplanned moment of insight. She wanted very badly to get the interview back on track. "Very well, then," she said, "we can agree that you returned to the police under false pretenses. Did the men who gave you such glowing references know about your deceit?"

Heuser too seemed relieved to be returning to the main business of their interview. "No . . . but it wasn't relevant anyway. They knew I was a damn good cop. And that's true enough."

"Yes it is. That's why they called you the Beagle."

"Really?" said Heuser, the corners of his mouth twitching in amusement, the skin around his eyes crinkling as the smile spread. "I always thought it was because I had such long floppy ears."

Paula couldn't help it. She laughed. Then she saw that Heuser was smirking like a man who's scored a point and knows it. He'd caught her completely off-guard. She'd thought she'd been ready for everything. It had never occurred to her to be armored against his charm.

"Never again," she told herself, and got back to her interview. "There's no denying your progress once you resumed your career. As one of your former colleagues told us, 'Heuser had sharp elbows.'"

"I've always been an ambitious man. I won't deny it, or apologize for it. Ambition is not an indictable offense, not yet anyway . . . and I dare say you're glad of that too, eh?"

Heuser's confidence was growing. He'd thrown that dart knowing it would hit its target. His malice was as precise as his humor. Paula felt the control she'd been seeking slipping further away from her. She could just imagine the delight Heuser was taking in putting this presumptuous young woman in her place. Well, she'd see about that. She went on. "On May 1, 1954, you joined the Criminal Police in the state of Rhineland-Pfalz with the rank of commissar, and in October were posted to Kaiserslautern. On January 1, 1955, you were made the head of the Criminal Police department there. On May 18 that year, you regained the rank of detective superintendent and two months later were transferred to the criminal investigation office of the state of Rhineland-Pfalz. Within a year you were running that too, initially in an acting capacity and soon after as a formal appointment. By the start of 1958, less than four years after rejoining the police, you were the chief detective in the entire state."

"That's right. And do you know what Herr Wolters, the state interior minister, told the press when I was appointed to that post? He said I had 'incontestable professional skills.' Those were his exact words. You can look them up."

"I already have," said Paula.

"Then why are we wasting time with this grotesque charade? Why have I spent months locked in this damn prison when I should be doing my job, putting real criminals behind bars?"

"Because you are a worse criminal than any of them."

Heuser did not rise to the bait, but remained absolutely, almost exaggeratedly, calm. "Just for your information, Dr. Siebert, I have dedicated my entire life to the maintenance of a lawful, orderly society. The only thing I have ever wanted to be is a policeman. Now, I am feeling fatigued. If you will excuse me, I'd like to go back to my cell."

Heuser rose from his seat, though he made no attempt to step around to Paula's side of the table, instead remaining perfectly still as she gathered up her papers and put them away in her briefcase. When the guard came in, Heuser held out his hands to be cuffed without making the slightest fuss. Only when he'd been marched halfway to the door did he politely say, "Excuse me for a moment," to the guard, then stop, turn, and face Paula again. "There was one other thing I meant to say . . ."

She looked up from her case. "Yes?"

"There is someone else you remind me of."

Paula couldn't help herself, for of all the things in the world about which human beings are curious, they are most curious about themselves.

"Who's that?"

Heuser smiled. "Isn't it obvious? You must be in your late twenties, no? A year or two away from thirty, I'd say. We've already established that you're ambitious, and it's quite obvious that you take your work very seriously, always endeavoring to do your absolute best. I'll make another guess and say that you very much look up to Dr. Kraus: his experience, his wisdom, his absolute focus on the case in front of him, to the exclusion of everything else. Oh yes, this is all very familiar . . ."

And now, too late, Paula realized where he was going as Heuser concluded: "Because you remind me so much . . . of me."

The appointment that had kept Kraus from seeing Heuser was taking place at Ramstein Air Base, the headquarters of the U.S. Air Force in Europe and heart of the huge Kaiserslautern Military Community of more than fifty thousand U.S. personnel. During his own time in Kaiserslautern, Heuser had worked very closely with the American military police, and now Kraus was hoping to get a sense of how he'd been regarded. To this end he was meeting Air Force Lieutenant-General Hank Bradford, the KMC commander tasked with maintaining relations with the local German population.

Before the serious business began, they exchanged polite conversation and Kraus said, "May I ask you a favor, General?"

"Sure, but I can't promise to grant it."

"It's not serious. I was just hoping to go to the PX store and buy some candy. I am, you might say, addicted to Hershey bars."

"Hell, you don't have to buy candy here," Bradford laughed. "We can give you plenty of that. You don't mind me asking, where'd you learn to speak English so well?"

"The same place I got hooked on Hershey's—Texas. I spent a couple of years there when I was younger."

The general narrowed his eyes thoughtfully. "Is that so, the Lone Star state, huh? I guess you could tell me quite a story about that . . ."

Kraus gave a noncommittal shrug.

"Another time, maybe . . ." said Bradford. "So, this man Heuser . . . Now I've got to admit, I wasn't here when he was serving with the local police. I only arrived a few months ago. But I asked around and plenty of people remembered him. Good cop, knew his job, got things done, was what they told me. As you can imagine, with this many men a long way from home we always have issues with vice: women, drugs, pornography, and so forth. Did you serve in the military, Dr. Kraus?"

"Yes, General."

"Then I won't have to give you the details. The point is, you get a lot of dirty cops in that area. But Heuser was as clean as a whistle and real efficient. The local papers called him *Der Prostituiertenjäger*— that means the prostitute hunter, right?"

"Correct."

"So I guess what it amounts to is that no one here has a bad word to say about him. Can you tell me exactly what it is he's supposed to have done? My adjutant told me you were a federal investigator working for an outfit called the ZSL, but when I looked that up, damned if I was any the wiser."

"I don't blame you," said Kraus. "The full title of our agency is the *Zentrale Stelle der Landesjustizverwaltungen zur Aufklärung national-sozialistischer Verbrechen*."

"And what the heck does that mean?"

"It's the Central Office of the State Justice Administrations for the Investigation of Nazi Crimes."

Bradford looked shocked. "Are you telling me this Heuser character was some kind of war criminal?"

"Yes, General, the very worst kind."

8

BERLIN: FEBRUARY 7, 1941,
8:15 A.M.–2:30 P.M.

As a commissar, Lüdtke was entitled to the use of a chauffeur-driven car. A gleaming black Adler Diplomat was waiting for him outside the HQ. It was a fine modern sedan with a long hood flanked by sweeping front-wheel arches and a four-door passenger compartment whose sleek lines reflected the very latest thinking in aerodynamic design. The sight of such a fine vehicle only added to my eager anticipation as I stepped over the running boards and took my place in the rear seat next to Lüdtke. My very first day in the job and I'd already been plunged into the thick of the action. A murder had been committed and the chase was on.

The Adler was more than five meters long, but the scene-of-crime vehicle parked next to it, a massive old Maybach sedan known as the "murder bus," was even bigger. Uniformed constables were loading the Maybach with forensic and photographic equipment as we pulled away from police headquarters and made our way toward Frankfurter Allee, the broad dual-carriageway that sliced almost due east through the city as straight as a Roman road. Lüdtke lit yet another cigarette and looked out at the bustling city. A shabby mass of workers and uniformed personnel scurried to work through a monochrome world of gray skies, white snow, and soot-colored buildings. The shopwindows were half empty and even the advertisements for Fewa detergent and Mouson skin cream on the sides of buses and trams seemed leached of color. Only the vivid red Party flags that flew from countless rooftops, and hung in giant banners down the facades of official buildings, seemed to cut through the winter gloom.

"I was wondering when this would happen," said Lüdtke, quietly. "When he'd do it again."

I didn't know what to say. Now that he was away from the duty room and the bulk of his men, my boss's mood had become downbeat and fatigue seemed to have overwhelmed him once more.

"I shouldn't take it personally," Lüdtke went on. "But I see each death as a direct message. He's telling me that there's nothing I can do to stop him."

"It's not just you, Commissar," I said. "If this man is saying anything, he's saying it to all of us, to the whole of civilized society. He's throwing all our moral standards back in our face. But we will get him. That's inevitable. It's just a matter of time."

"Ah, the optimism of youth . . . Yes, I'm sure we will get him— eventually. But how many more women will have to die first?"

"Perhaps this will be the crime that produces the vital clue," I suggested.

"Let's hope so. We've squeezed every last scrap of evidence from the others and we don't even have a suspect."

I must say, I was surprised, even a little shocked, by Lüdtke's attitude. Trying to frame my words as tactfully as possible, I said: "You're very frank to talk like this, so openly, Commissar. Some people might think you were being defeatist."

Lüdtke's head jerked around and his eyes bored into mine. "I hope I can count on your loyalty—and your discretion, Heuser."

"Of course, Commissar. I . . . I didn't mean to speak out of turn."

He kept his eyes on me for another few seconds, as if reassuring himself that my answer was an honest one, and then relaxed back into the seat again.

"Neither Lobbes nor Nebe would think me defeatist, I can promise you that," he said. "They have both been where I am now, staring at a brick wall, racking their brains for any microscopic clue they might have missed, any connection that hasn't been made. The only ones who do not understand are those who have never done the job, even if they are also our masters."

He reached into his jacket and pulled out his cigarettes. "You're sure I can't tempt you, Heuser?"

"No thank you."

"Ach, we'll have you smoking like a chimney before this case is done, just you mark my words."

Karlshorst was a garden district, just like Friedrichsfelde, with large plots of land divided by streets lined with stark, leafless trees. It was a sparsely populated neighborhood where the snow still lay heavy on the road and scrunched beneath the wheels of the car. But any illusion of peace and quiet was shattered when we reached the railway.

In this area of Berlin a profusion of lines that reached out to the east of the city—to East Prussia, Silesia, Poland, and beyond—joined together like the streams of a mighty river. Friedrichsfelde and Karlshorst were thus like islands of greenery, cut off from the rest of the city by these steel streams.

When the car stopped, we made our way, almost up to our knees in snow, through an orchard toward a small wooden gate. I pushed it open, having to work quite hard to force it through the drift, and we stepped out onto the line. Looking to my left, I saw a road bridge over the railway and beyond it the multiple tracks of a classification yard.

Lüdtke glanced across and observed where I was looking. He pointed past the bridge and the railway toward a line of houses.

"Over there, that's Prinz-Heinrich-Strasse, where the Frese girl was killed. Which means . . ."

He looked to the right, frowning in concentration, and I could see a small knot of uniformed city police, or *Schupo*, clustered around a spot on the line, perhaps fifty meters away. That presumably was where the new body lay. Lüdtke ignored them, however, and began striding alongside the line, through the undisturbed snow that lay thick along the verge between the railway and the wooden fence. I hurried to keep up with him until, without any warning, he came to a sudden stop. The *Schupo* were much closer now. Lüdtke pointed toward them. "How far away would you say they are: fifteen meters?"

"At most . . . maybe even a little less."

"Well, where we are standing now is the exact spot where they found the body of Elfriede Franke. That was more than two months ago. And now the killer dumps another body in virtually the same place. Think about it, Heuser. He must have re-created the Franke murder in every detail. He enjoyed it so much the first time, he wanted to feel exactly the same sensations all over again."

Lüdtke squeezed his eyes shut and shook his head, as if trying to eject the thought from his brain. "All right then," he said. "We'd better go and see how well he copied himself."

9

The S-Bahn operated on the "third-rail" system. In other words, the trains ran on two rails and were powered by the electricity carried by a third. A pair of these third rails ran parallel down the middle of the tracks, between the inbound and outbound lines that they respectively powered. Once again, my eyes were drawn to a splash of red in an essentially black, white, and gray setting, but this time it came from the battered, bloodstained female corpse that lay lengthways in the narrow gap between the two third rails. Had it not been for the stockinged feet that were still more or less intact, it would barely have been possible to distinguish a female human form amid the heap of torn clothes and mangled flesh. Not only had she suffered the assault of the S-Bahn murderer, but her body had been beaten and buffeted to a pulp by any number of passing trains.

I had never before seen the victim of a violent death and I confess that the shock of it was enough to make the blood drain from my face, my head swim, and my guts heave. I turned away and bent over, about to retch. The next thing I knew I heard Lüdtke shout "Move!" and felt a shove in the back that sent me stumbling away across the railway line, almost tripping flat on my face on one of the tracks before I finally came to a halt, doubled up, and then vomited. A thin stream of pale brown liquid stained the snow beneath my feet, and the smell of sick was mingled with a faint scent of the coffee I'd been relishing little more than an hour ago.

My face was flushed and sweaty, as much with embarrassment as from any physical aftereffect of my nausea. As I straightened up and used my clean white handkerchief to wipe the mess from my mouth, I wondered how much contempt the other police would be feeling toward me now: the fancy young graduate from the Leaders' School falling apart at the first sight of blood. I noticed Richter walking toward me and steeled myself. I was his senior officer, so he wouldn't be able to criticize me openly, but I'd already seen enough of him to know that he would be able to convey his feelings well enough by the look in his eyes and the tone of his voice. But when he said, "Don't worry. We all do it, the first time," there was genuine sympathy in his voice.

"Just don't tell Frei I puked the first time I saw a dead body."

"Frei? Ha!" Richter exclaimed. "You think he didn't fill a bucket when he saw his first?"

He reached into his coat and pulled out a silver flask. "Here, have some of this," he said. As he unscrewed the top I caught a whiff of the schnapps inside.

"Thank you, but I shouldn't be drinking. We're on duty," I said.

"Think of it as medicinal, Assistant Commissar," Richter insisted. "You've suffered a shock and schnapps is a well-known cure. Any doctor would surely agree with me. In fact they'd prescribe it."

I took the flask.

Richter was absolutely right about the schnapps. It warmed my aching guts and calmed my nerves. I had a second slug of it and then gave him back his flask. "Why was Commissar Lüdtke so angry?" I asked, as the flask disappeared back inside Richter's coat. "You know, if everyone reacts the same way . . ."

Richter gave me a wry smile. "He didn't mind you being sick. He just didn't want you puking on his crime scene. The Commissar is very particular about things like that. He doesn't like anyone leaving so much as a toe print anywhere near a murder victim."

It was, I thought, a bit late to worry about that. The snow around the woman's body had been trampled flat by the boots of railway workers and members of the *Schupo*. I was about to make a remark to that effect, but thought better of it. Instead I simply said, "I'm sure that Commissar Lüdtke is right to have such a meticulous approach to his work."

"He's the best there is," said Richter, simply. "The very best."

So now I knew for sure, if it wasn't already obvious: however unconventional Lüdtke's methods or behavior might be, he had the absolute loyalty of his men. They didn't mind me taking on the odious Frei, but they would react very differently to any challenge to their boss.

"Anyway," Richter went on, "the Commissar wants us to go up the track and keep an eye on those *Schupo* buffoons. They're supposed to be looking for anything else the killer chucked out of the train." He gave an irritable, contemptuous sigh. "Don't get your hopes up, Assistant Commissar. Half of them couldn't even find their own cocks."

I looked toward where Lüdtke was now standing with a small, well-wrapped man whom I took, from the large, black leather briefcase he was carrying, to be Dr. Weimann, the pathologist. He must have arrived while I was distracted. In front of them a photographer was standing a meter or so from the corpse, his camera to his face. I saw a flash and then he moved, taking great care over where he placed his feet—Lüdtke had obviously gotten him well trained—before finding another angle and taking another shot.

I was so absorbed in watching the process that I quite forgot my own duties until I heard Richter's voice: "Assistant Commissar? I think we should be going."

"Of course . . . of course," I said, walking up the track past Lüdtke, Weimann, and the photographer, then beyond the body itself toward a line of half a dozen *Schupo* men. They were strung out across the track and were stepping very slowly, heads bent, their eyes firmly fixed to the ground in front of them.

We were almost on them when there came a shout from a man in the center of the line. "Here! Here! I've found something!"

"Don't touch it!" I shouted, and barged my way through the line to get close to the man who had shouted.

"There!" he exclaimed, pointing at the gap between the power rails.

I followed the line of his finger and saw a small black glove, unquestionably a woman's, lying on the ground in front of us. Then I looked back at the corpse, which couldn't have been more than seven or eight meters away.

"Well spotted!"

No sooner had I spoken than I noticed something else, barely visible in the shadowy gully between the power rails. "Wait! Nobody move."

I took a couple more paces and then crouched down to get a better look. It was a woman's winter jacket. I felt a sudden shock of pity for the victim. She'd lain all night in the snow without anything to keep her warm. It was an absurd, illogical thought, of course. She'd been dead. What difference did it make? Still, I found myself touched by the pitiful fate she had suffered.

Remembering Lüdtke's words about not allowing oneself to be distracted, I forced any pity to the back of my mind. I summoned Richter. "Tell Commissar Lüdtke about the glove and jacket. He'll probably want photographs. I'm going to carry on with these men and see if we find anything else."

Richter hurried away. I ordered the *Schupo* men on again, making sure that none of them stepped close to the glove or coat. We swept another four hundred meters up the track toward the Rummelsburg Depot, straight into the teeth of an icy wind, before I called a halt to the exercise. The man in charge of the *Schupo* detachment was a grizzled old sergeant. His face lit up when I told him, "You can stop now," only for his expression to turn thunderous when I added, "I want you to go back past the body and check the same distance in the opposite direction. Alert me, or one of my colleagues, if you find anything."

He just managed to squeeze out the words "Yes, sir" between his gritted teeth.

I looked him right in the eye. "A woman has been brutally murdered. We have to find her killer. I don't care how cold we get in the process. And nor should you. Understood?"

"Yes, sir."

"So get your men down there and start looking."

I watched the *Schupo* go, then headed back toward Lüdtke. Weimann was crouched directly over the body, examining the head. He got back to his feet and summoned a pair of stretcher bearers standing nearby. I waited while Lüdtke and Weimann exchanged a few words before telling the Commissar, "We didn't find anything more on the line, but I've got the men searching in the other direction, just in case."

Lüdtke nodded in approval. "Good work." He looked away for a moment and called out, "Richter! Keep an eye on our *Schupo* friends. Tell them to look out for the woman's handbag. That'll be where she kept her identity papers."

Then Lüdtke turned his attention back to me. "As for you, Heuser, you're coming back to Alex with me. Dr. Weimann will begin his examination of the body as soon as possible. We need to be there. And if you thought a corpse was hard to take, just wait till you witness an autopsy."

10

"You're in luck!" declared Dr. Weimann as we walked into his personal domain, the autopsy room at Alex. For the first time in my life I breathed in the unique, chilly odor of the mortuary, a blend of formaldehyde, refrigeration, and decomposition that stays in one's nostrils long after one has left the source of it far behind; a nagging, insistent intimation of mortality.

Weimann had a bloodstained bread knife in his hand. God only knows what he'd been cutting with it: certainly not bread. He was standing by a polished steel table, on which lay the victim's naked body. Her vagina and breasts were displayed with a prostitute's flagrancy, a sight made all the more obscene by the fact that the torso between them had been cleaved open, and two large flaps of fat-lined skin pulled apart, exposing all her internal organs. This poor woman had suffered two brutal violations: first by her murderer and now, in death, by the pathologist. It was impossible to believe that her lifeless carcass, helplessly submitting to the butcher's knife, had been a living, breathing, sentient human being barely twelve hours earlier.

I'd sworn to myself that I'd not embarrass myself a second time as I had by the railway tracks. At least my stomach was now so empty that there was precious little left to vomit. But even so, it was all I could do to stop myself fainting at such a gruesome display.

Weimann stopped himself in his tracks, looked at me over the top of his spectacles, and said, "You look distinctly unwell." He glanced at Lüdtke and said: "Have mercy on the boy. Let him go outside and have a cigarette. He needs it."

"He doesn't smoke."

"Doesn't smoke?" said Weimann incredulously. "What are they teaching these young men nowadays?"

Lüdtke gave a shrug that suggested his helplessness in the face of the absurdities of modern life. "I've been asking myself the same thing . . . Anyway, you said you had good news."

"Ah yes, let me see . . . Where did I put them?" Weimann rummaged around on a small table on which he'd placed his tools and notebook among various other bits of clutter. Then he gave a wordless cry of triumph and held up a small folded document. "Identity papers—I found them in her jacket pocket, along with her S-Bahn ticket. Here . . ."

He held out a small sheaf of papers. Lüdtke looked at me and gave a small jerk of the head in Weimann's direction. Feeling like an idiot—of course it was my job to fetch and carry: I could hardly stand still and watch my boss do it—I went across to the pathologist and took the papers.

"Well?" asked Lüdtke.

I shuffled through the collection of official documents without which no German could leave the house in those days. One was related to her membership in a sports club, another to her employment status and workplace, a third to her trade union membership. The most important of all was her folded, two-page identity card.

"Her name is Johanna Voigt," I told Lüdtke. "She's thirty-eight. Her date of birth was April 13, 1902."

"When we're done here, get someone to track down her next-of-kin," Lüdtke said. "And find out if there's any possible reason anyone might want to do her harm. I know it seems obvious that this was an entirely random attack, but we must at least examine the possibility that she may have known her attacker."

"Yes, Commissar," I said, and turned to go.

Lüdtke put out a hand to stop me. "Not so fast. I said, 'when we're done here.' And we're not yet done. Dr. Weimann still hasn't given us his findings. Doctor?"

"Well, the cause of death needs no explanation. Frau Voigt was hit repeatedly on the head by a heavy blunt object, possibly a club or nightstick. The injuries are entirely consistent with those suffered in the previous S-Bahn killings."

"Any sign of sexual assault?"

"No. I've not yet completed my internal examination. But Frau Voigt's underclothes were all in place and there was no sign of any external bruising or abrasions, which one would expect if there had been an act of forcible sex."

"So Frese is still the only one of his victims he raped." Lüdtke exhaled sharply in a wordless expression of his utter frustration at the impenetrability of the case. "Why do you think that was?" he mused.

"Well, I don't like to speculate . . ." Weimann said.

"Try."

"All right, in that case there are two thoughts that come to my mind. The first concerns the question of opportunity. Frese was attacked on an unlit street. He would only have committed his crime if there were no passersby to witness it. Therefore he might also have had the time required to have sex. On the trains, however, he has to complete the entire business of killing and disposing of his victims in the short journey between one stop and another. Therefore there is no time for anything but the murder itself."

"I agree," Lüdtke nodded. "That is the obvious explanation. But you said you had two. What's the second?"

"Think of Kürten," said Weimann. He was referring to Peter Kürten, the so-called Vampire of Düsseldorf and the man for whom Ernst Gennat, the former director of the Berlin Criminal Police and founder of the murder squad, first coined the term "serial killer." Between February 1929 and May 1930, Kürten committed at least nine murders and seven attempted murders, and more than sixty other crimes of violence, much of it of a sexual nature. The whole country had been transfixed by his death spree, which had also been a case study for us trainees at Charlottenburg. Although Düsseldorf was on the other side of the country, more than five hundred kilometers to the west, Gennat had been called in to assist on the investigation.

"What about him?" asked Lüdtke, who, it occurred to me, must have served under Gennat and perhaps even learned his trade from him.

"Well, Kürten's two favorite means of assault were stabbing and battering, as our man's seem to be. There was a strong sexual motivation for his crimes, too. In fact . . ."

I suddenly realized where Weimann was going. Before I had time to temper my enthusiasm in the presence of my seniors, I blurted out: "Berg!"

Weimann looked at me again. "Ah! The youngster seems to have recovered. Shall we let him have his say?"

"Why not?" said Lüdtke drily.

"The psychiatrist Dr. Karl Berg interviewed Kürten on several occasions prior to his execution," I said. "Kürten told him that he killed because he found it sexually stimulating. Stabbing his victim and seeing the victim's blood were erotic experiences to him. So the act of killing was also in itself the act of sex."

"Quite so," said Weimann. "It's possible, Lüdtke—I put it no more strongly than that—that your S-Bahn murderer may have a very similar motivation to Kürten. We know for certain that he has committed at least one rape. We also have good reason to believe that he has been involved in a number of lesser sexual assaults. Now, as his crimes have escalated in seriousness, he may have discovered that the most satisfying sex act of all does not involve penetration by the penis. We are, therefore, looking in the wrong place. If he, like Kürten, finds killing to be the ultimate erotic act, then these horrific blows to a defenseless woman's head may in themselves have brought her murderer to orgasm."

"My God," I gasped. "What kind of man is this?"

"The kind," said Lüdtke, "that we are paid to catch."

We returned to the duty room. A secretary, brought in to cover for Tietmeyer, had a long list of messages for Lüdtke. While he attended to them I dealt with the matter of the next-of-kin. Papa Schmidt was the only officer still in the room, granted the privilege of staying warm indoors out of respect for his age and long service. I gave him Johanna Voigt's papers. "Commissar Lüdtke wants the family tracked down and interviewed. He needs to know if there's anyone who might have had any reason to kill her."

Schmidt looked surprised. "I thought this was the S-Bahn boy's work."

"That's what Lüdtke thinks, too. He just wants to be certain."

Schmidt nodded. I handed over the papers. As he took them from me he said, "So I'll be the one who has to tell them she's dead."

It was a statement of the obvious, but still it hadn't occurred to me.

"It's all right," said Schmidt. "I'm used to it. Whenever there's a grieving parent who's lost their child or a bride who's just become a widow, they always send Papa to pass on the news. Apparently I have a reassuring appearance."

Before I could reply, Lüdtke came striding across the office. "Come with me—now!" he snapped. He walked away, not waiting for me, so I had to scurry after him. "There's a case-meeting over at the

Prinz-Albrecht-Palais," Lüdtke continued, not even bothering to turn his head in my direction. "We're late."

For the second time in as many minutes I found myself struggling to form a coherent sentence. "But isn't, um . . . isn't that the address of the Reich Security Main Office?"

"That's right," said Lüdtke. "It is. And Heydrich's chairing the meeting."

11

SS-General Reinhard Heydrich, Chief of the Reich Security Main Office, General of Police, Plenipotentiary for the Preparation of the Final Solution of the European Jewish Question, and Deputy Protector of Bohemia and Moravia, was the golden prince of the Third Reich. So when I was summoned to meet him, on that extraordinary day in February 1941, I felt as awestruck at the prospect as if I were entering the presence of royalty, and nothing about the occasion served in any way to disabuse me of that notion.

Heydrich even lived and worked in a palace: the Prinz-Albrecht-Palais, located at 102 Wilhelmstrasse. It had previously belonged to the Prussian royal family and was practically next door to Göring's Air Ministry Building. Himmler's SS headquarters at the old Prinz Albrecht Hotel were just around the corner, as was the Gestapo HQ at 8 Prinz-Albrecht-Strasse. The Reich Chancellery itself was barely two hundred meters away. This was, therefore, the very nerve center of the Nazi establishment, but whereas Göring's ministry was as absurdly oversized as the man himself, and the Führer toiled in one of that fraudulent mountebank Albert Speer's exercises in monumental banality, Heydrich's official residence was infinitely more civilized.

Lüdtke and I arrived in his Adler. The black-uniformed SS guards who examined our papers were two perfectly matched specimens of Aryan perfection, straight from a Leni Riefenstahl documentary. Once we had satisfied them that we were worthy of admission, the barrier rose and we drove through an arched gate, between a matched pair of guardhouses and then around an open square flanked on either side by elegant colonnades. In the middle of the square an expanse of virgin snow covered a sizeable lawn, at the far end of which stood the palace itself, an elegant three-story mansion in the classical style. Its facade comprised two narrow wings and a more massive and richly decorated central block, separated by two much simpler, slightly recessed bays. The drive, which was flanked by decorative stone pots that must have been filled with flowers during the warmer months of the year, curved around the lawn and under a broad wrought-iron canopy that sheltered the front entrance.

As we approached it, Lüdtke reached into one of the side pockets of his suit jacket and pulled out a Party badge, which he now attached to a lapel. After everything he'd said, a Party member was the very last thing I expected Lüdtke to be, but on reflection there was no real reason to be surprised. He was, after all, a senior police officer: why would he not wear that badge? The greater surprise was surely that I, with all my proper Leaders' School attitudes, did not. There was no time to discuss or even think about these ironies, for now we were pulling up beneath the canopy and more uniformed guards were opening the passenger doors.

Lüdtke and I emerged from the car, were greeted by one of Heydrich's adjutants, and led into a splendid hall. The vaulted ceiling and the classical sculptures high up on the far wall, facing the magnificent central staircase, were worthy of a Roman emperor's residence, and light from great chandeliers sparkled off gilt paint so that the whole great room seemed to shine. The splendor of it took my breath away.

Never in all my life had I set foot in a room like this, and there were more to come, for now the adjutant was leading us up the stairs toward the high-ceilinged first floor where the palace's most magnificent chambers were arranged. Before I had time to gather my wits, he was leading us toward a double door that seemed high enough to allow a giraffe to walk through at full stretch and wide enough for an elephant. The door was opened, we were ushered in, and there to greet us was Reinhard Heydrich himself.

Today, if people know of Heydrich it is as an evil psychopath; the most blood-soaked of all the Third Reich's "desk killers"; the planner of the Final Solution to the Jewish question; a man known variously as the Blond Beast, the Butcher of Prague, the Hangman, and even the Evil Young God of Death. But in February 1941, no one of my modest rank had the faintest idea that the wholesale extermination of the Jews had even been contemplated. So there was no reason whatever for me to think that Heydrich was anything other than the heroic figure I took him to be, one to be admired and even emulated—at least as far as my infinitely more meager talents would allow. He was less than a decade older than me, but whereas the ink was barely dry on my graduation certificate, he commanded the entire Security Police apparatus.

And now here he was, coming toward us with a broad, welcoming smile on his face, a tall, slender figure in his gray uniform, with his general's oak leaves on his collar and his breeches tucked into gleaming black boots. Heydrich's official portrait, a drawing widely reproduced in poster form, gave him an almost movie-star glamour, and though it was flattering, I could now see that it wasn't entirely unrealistic. Neatly brushed blond hair, slightly receding at the temples, was swept back from a high forehead that gave him the appearance of an intellectual or an aesthete. His most prominent feature was his nose, which was long and fine-boned, with a hooked profile that may have contributed to the persistent rumors that this, the most ruthless of all persecutors of the Jews, had a taint of Hebrew blood in his veins.

His lips, meanwhile, were surprisingly full, with an almost feminine sensuality.

Heydrich saluted us both, and though we were not in uniform we snapped to attention and produced *Heil Hitler*s that were worthy of the occasion. That formality completed, Heydrich greeted Lüdtke and then remarked: "This is a very bad business. I'd hoped we'd seen the last of these terrible murders."

His voice was surprisingly sympathetic, more as though he were consoling Lüdtke than upbraiding him. But then, Heydrich was what women might call a "charmer." He knew exactly what to say to put a person at ease, win their confidence, and get them on his side. One might, of course, see this simply as manipulation: it is often very difficult to distinguish between the genuinely kind person who wishes to make others feel better and the calculating puppet master who coldly toys with their emotions to satisfy his own ends.

Lüdtke was certainly grateful for the reprieve. "Yes, General," he said. "We had all hoped to have solved the case and apprehended the killer by now."

"Quite so," agreed Heydrich, with just the faintest glimmer of steel beneath the velvet.

Lüdtke stiffened a fraction, sensing the possibility of danger. "May I introduce Heuser, my new Assistant Commissar?" he said, changing the subject.

Heydrich turned his attention on me, narrowing his eyes like an auction-house expert assessing the value of a newly delivered painting and fixing me with a hard, chilly, calculating stare. The inspection lasted only a couple of seconds and then the apparent warmth reappeared.

"Ah yes," he said. "Heuser . . . Top of the class at Charlottenburg, I gather."

"Yes, General," I said, amazed and delighted that he should have known.

"Well then, let me introduce you to your comrades in the Criminal Police who have joined us here today . . ."

Heydrich led us across the room to a table, around which four men were already sitting. He pointed to a thickset man whose ruddy, weather-beaten yeoman's face made him look like the very epitome of the honest, reliable policeman, albeit one who seemed even more exhausted than Lüdtke.

"Perhaps you already know Commissar Zach, a fellow officer from the homicide department?" Heydrich said.

"No, General, we've never met."

"Then let me tell you that Zach has been working around the clock, trying—and until last night succeeding—to keep travelers on the S-Bahn safe from this maniac."

Heydrich gestured toward the next of his guests, unaware that he was picking out the very man who in less than eighteen months' time would be leading the investigation into his own death: "Dr. Wehner here is representing the Central Office for Capital Crimes . . ." Heydrich moved on again: "Chief Superintendent Lobbes, as I'm sure you know, has—with all due respect to the other eminent officers here— more experience of solving major murder cases than anyone else in the Reich. And I'm sure General Nebe needs no introduction."

I saluted frantically, jerking my arm like a windup toy soldier as I tried to acknowledge each of the introductions.

Nebe was forty-six, but looked rather older, perhaps because his hair was already entirely gray. His face bore an expression that was wry, ironic, amused by all the absurdities of human life he saw. As the commander of the entire Criminal Police he was someone I very badly needed to impress, but his character was so enigmatic, his true feelings so hard to read, that it was impossible to know how that might be done. Even now I cannot decide whether he was one of Nazism's most dedicated and deadly followers, one of its most committed opponents, or simply a man who played his own private game and the hell with everyone else.

Of all the higher-ups there, Lobbes had the most impressive record as a policeman, yet he made the least immediate impression upon me. The fashion at the time was for men to clip their hair very severely from the neck to a line several centimeters above the ear. In Lobbes's case this had unfortunate results. He possessed a particularly large, egg-shaped head, atop which a small patch of dark hair perched like a seagull's nest on a high chalk cliff. His face was pouchy, his expression careworn. If one did not know that he was a truly great detective, he might have been taken for a provincial secondary-school headmaster.

These, then, were the men who gathered on this February day in 1941 to discuss the failure of the finest and most experienced police officers in the entire Reich to identify and apprehend a lone murderer. Knowing that I'd be by far the least significant person in the room, I'd resolved upon a simple policy. I'd keep my eyes and ears open and my mouth firmly shut. The men surrounding me had managed to succeed within a system that was unashamedly run on Darwinian lines. Individuals and institutions alike were expected to compete with one another in an unending struggle so that only the fittest would survive. I wanted to see how it was done. Who would try to impose themselves upon the meeting? Who would hold back and let others talk themselves into trouble? And which approach would work best in the long run for me?

No sooner had I taken my place at the table, however, than my plans lay in ruins. For General Heydrich surveyed us all with an affable smile on his face and addressed us as follows: "Well, gentlemen, we have now spent more than three months using every method at our disposal trying to catch this murderer. Seven women have lost their lives. And we have got precisely nowhere. It seems to me we need some fresh thinking, a new perspective upon the case. We need to look at it through eyes that have not spent too long staring at the same blank wall. So, Comrade Heuser . . ."

Heydrich turned to me with his charming smile and his viper eyes and said: "Give us the benefit of your brilliant mind and your youthful energy. Put us tired old men to shame. Tell us what you think about the S-Bahn murderer."

My God! I have been in some nerve-racking situations in my time and seen some terrible things, but I doubt that I have ever, before or since, had a shock quite like the one that Heydrich gave me at that moment.

I felt like a schoolboy who has been daydreaming through a lesson, only to have the teacher point at him and demand a full account of what has just been said. Just as the other children all stare at their unfortunate classmate, so Lüdtke, Zach, Wehner, Lobbes, and Nebe all turned their eyes on me. I remember a couple of their expressions quite clearly. Lobbes seemed genuinely curious about my ability to rise to the challenge. Wehner looked put out, as though he were jealous of the attention being paid to a younger, far junior officer. Nebe, of course, was as inscrutable as a Chinaman.

None of them, however, could help or hurt me now. This was entirely a matter of my ability to say what Heydrich would want to hear. And the first thing to do, surely, was to reassure him that I was sound in my thinking, with views in accordance with accepted official doctrine. Still, I needed to come up with something a little bit more original than simply blurting out: "Yes sir, I think he's a Jew."

So I played for time and began by stating the obvious: "Well, General, it is evident from his actions that this perpetrator has no shred of mercy, decency, or moral propriety about him. The fact that he attacks defenseless women tells us that he is also a coward. The fact that his assaults have frequently contained a sexual element confirms that he adds perversion to his many other degenerate tendencies."

Heydrich had not been offended by any of that, but neither had he been particularly impressed. "Yes, I think we can all agree with every word of that," he said, without much enthusiasm. "Anything else?"

This second chance, I could tell, would also be my last. If I wanted to turn the attention I was receiving to my advantage, I had to do it now. And then I had a moment of extraordinary good fortune, for an idea appeared in my mind so brightly and so spontaneously that I had to force myself not to grin in delight as I said, "Yes, sir, there is something that has occurred to me."

For all my efforts to suppress it, my enthusiasm must have conveyed itself to the other men, for I could feel a sudden change of atmosphere in the room: an entirely new mood of anticipation.

I continued: "Although it seems unlikely that the killer is a man of education and culture, one must admit that he possesses a certain animal cunning. For example, it is common for a murderer to move his victim's body from the scene of the crime. But in this case, it is the scene of the crime that moves. We find the victim lying on the tracks, quite close, one presumes, to the point on the line at which she was killed. He is obliged to dispose of her quickly, after all, before the train reaches its next stop. Yet by the time the woman's body is discovered, the carriage in which she met her death is far away. It may be attached to a different train. It may even be running on a different line. Travelers from across the city will be getting on and off it. So even if by some miracle we were to find this precise carriage, the chances of being able to collect any useful evidence would be very small indeed. This makes it much harder to catch the killer. Whether by accident or design, he has thus devised a very effective method, from his point of view."

"Very interesting, Heuser," said Heydrich, with a satisfying tone of pleasurable surprise. "'It is the scene of the crime that moves . . .' I like that. You have also described the killer's likely characteristics. So tell me, are there any conclusions you can draw from them? For example, in racial terms . . ."

I'd gotten away with one original opinion. Now it was time to toe the Party line. "Yes, General. From everything my instructors taught me, I would say that if one describes a man who lacks morality, or manly courage; who welcomes degeneracy and indecency; who seeks ways to harm good Germans, and yet who possesses, nonetheless, a form of perverted intelligence which displays itself as self-seeking calculation and cunning, then one is describing the Jew."

Heydrich was delighted. "You see! Here is a junior officer, possessed with the clarity of youth, who sees straight to the heart of the matter."

Wehner, Nebe, and Lobbes all nodded in agreement. Zach, it now seemed to me, was too exhausted to care. Lüdtke, however, had a thunderous look on his face. I suddenly realized that in pleasing one master I'd offended another. We both knew that he'd fought against his superiors' attempts to limit the search for the killer to Jews and foreign workers. If I didn't want to make another enemy in the homicide department—and one who could do a great deal more harm to my career than Inspector Frei would ever manage—I needed to make amends, fast. Before anyone else could speak, I said: "Thank you very much indeed, General. I am honored by your kind remarks. But I should also add that while the Jews must be seen as suspects, I fully support the actions of my superior, Commissar Lüdtke, in broadening the search to include other groups, including S-Bahn staff. One must consider every possibility. It is possible that this man's degeneracy arises from causes other than race. He may be a Bolshevik saboteur, for example. His moral sickness may be the result of a physical or mental impairment. Or he may, quite literally, be diseased. Syphilis, I believe, can drive a man insane. Perhaps it might drive him to kill."

This passing afterthought would, in the end, prove to be of far more significance than I could possibly have imagined when I uttered it. For now, however, my immediate concern was Lüdtke. He seemed to have relaxed a little. The look he was giving me was devoid of emotion. He was, at this point, neither an enemy nor a friend. He was also about to have something far more important to think about than me, for Heydrich, having murmured "Thank you, Heuser," turned his attention to Lüdtke and continued: "So, Commissar Lüdtke, you have heard about our man. What do you intend to do about catching him?"

Lüdtke took a deep breath, sighed, looked Heydrich right in the eye, and simply said: "I think we should surrender."

There was uproar in the room. "Disgraceful!" Wehner shouted.

"Good God, man, you can't do that!" Lobbes exclaimed, shocked that a homicide department man should have capitulated so pathetically.

Even Nebe was moved to raise an eyebrow and emit a silent whistle of amazement.

Heydrich, however, retained his composure, though all trace of bonhomie had now disappeared, replaced by a chill as freezing as any snowdrift. "Surrender is never acceptable," he said. "Under any circumstances. So unless you were trying to make some particularly unamusing joke, I'd advise you to come up with something better."

"Perhaps I should explain myself," Lüdtke said. He seemed remarkably unruffled by the outrage he'd provoked. "Let me start by considering what we have done and where it has got us . . ."

"Do we really need to repeat what every single one of us already knows?" Wehner asked testily.

"If you don't mind, General . . ." Lüdtke murmured, glancing at Heydrich.

"Proceed," said Heydrich, holding his fire.

"Very well . . . For the past month we have poured all our energies into this case. And alongside the work of detection, a huge effort has been made to protect passengers on the Number Three line, lone females in particular. Our men are exhausted. Fewer and fewer are either willing or physically able to undertake night shifts. Last night there were less than half as many officers covering the Number Three line as there had been four weeks previously. And that was when the killer chose to strike again.

"So I ask myself: is this a matter of chance? Does the killer just happen to attack when we are weak . . . or does he know precisely what we are doing, when and where we are doing it, and how many people are involved? Heuser here referred to the killer's animal cunning and, yes, he certainly possesses that. But I believe he has something even more valuable: information. I think he knows precisely what we are doing."

"But how?" Wehner asked indignantly. "How could he possibly know our secrets?"

"Because they are not secrets," Lüdtke replied. "They cannot be. We have to coordinate our activities with Reichsbahn officials and stationmasters. They must in turn inform their staff of any planned operations that might affect them as they carry out their duties. So plenty of men in S-Bahn uniforms know when we will be flooding the line with police, and when we will only be supplying a minimal level of protection. And one of these men, I believe, is the killer."

"Suppose he is," said Heydrich. "Why should we simply surrender? That would be like an entire army laying down its weapons in the face of a single enemy."

"I assure you, General, I have no more intention of giving up than you do. But if this man gets to hear what we are doing, let's take advantage of that. Let's feed him false information. Why not call a meeting with the men from the Reichsbahn? Tell them that, regretfully, it is no longer possible to maintain the same police presence on the S-Bahn. We need a formal statement, something like: 'This is a temporary, tactical withdrawal. We are merely pausing to reevaluate our operational procedures.' Of course, none of them will believe us. They will all go back to their offices thinking: 'These useless coppers are giving up the ghost.'"

"But what will we actually be doing?" Heydrich asked.

"It sounds to me," said Nebe, "as though we will be reevaluating our operational procedures."

A ripple of laughter broke the tension around the table.

"Quite so," said Heydrich, allowing himself a brief, indulgent chuckle. "But what form, precisely, will this reevaluation take?"

"Ah, that I don't know—not yet," Lüdtke replied. "As you can imagine, I have not had much time in the past few hours in which to consider matters of strategy. But I can say this. Whatever we do, it will be a very, very long way from any form of surrender. It will be done under conditions of absolute security, with no confidential information whatever being allowed anywhere near any railway employee, no matter how senior. And everything we do—absolutely everything—will work toward the same end."

"Which is?"

"Very simple, General. I want to lure this beast out of the shadows. I want to spot him, hunt him, corner him, and catch him. And then I want to kill him."

"I see," nodded Heydrich, pensively. Then he looked up and addressed the whole table again. "I think we can all agree that the best place for the S-Bahn murderer is beneath the blade of a guillotine . . ."

There was a murmur of agreement from all the men present. Lobbes and Wehner both banged the table to underscore their feelings.

". . . So if that's what you mean by 'surrendering,' Lüdtke, you'd better go ahead and do it."

12

When we got back to Alexanderplatz, Lüdtke did not, as I'd expected, head straight back to the squad room. He didn't even enter the police headquarters at all. Instead he led me away down the road.

"You hungry?" he asked.

So much had happened that I hadn't even thought about food. But the moment Lüdtke asked the question, I realized I was starving. "Yes, very," I replied.

"That makes two of us. Follow me . . ."

We took a ten-minute walk to a small café on Wassmannstrasse. "They know me here," Lüdtke said, "and it's far away enough from Alex that it's not completely overrun by other cops."

Sure enough, as we walked in, Lüdtke was greeted by a hearty cry—"Commissar! How nice to see you, sir!"—from a plump middle-aged woman behind the bar. She came around into the dining area and started fussing over us, making sure we had a nice table and collecting our orders for beer.

"I think we've earned it today, don't you?" Lüdtke said, and I hesitated only for a moment—we were still on duty, after all—before I agreed with him.

The manageress was still hovering over us, with the air of someone with vital news to impart. "We've got something special on the menu today, for our very best customers," she said. "We call it 'Balcony Pig Pie'!"

She looked at us expectantly and Lüdtke played along. "Good heavens, Frau Meissner, what on earth is a balcony pig?"

"It's what they're calling rabbit these days," she said, delightedly. "From all the bunnies people are keeping on the balconies of their apartments. Our son Franz—you remember Franz, don't you, Commissar?—brought us back some lovely bacon from Denmark—he's been serving over there, you know—and we've used some of that, nicely diced, with a couple of rabbits, plenty of potatoes, and a bit of onion, to make a delicious pie. We've only got two slices left, but you're very welcome to them both. I'll do you some turnips to go with it. How does that sound?"

"Like the best meal I've had in a very long time. Thank you, Frau Meissner. We'll both have the pie—is that all right by you, Heuser?"

"Of course."

"My pleasure, Commissar," said Frau Meissner, and she hurried away to get our food.

"She's a good soul," said Lüdtke. "But how about you, Heuser . . . are you a good soul?"

"I don't really know. I try to be, I think. I certainly try to do the right thing."

"Yes," said Lüdtke, lighting a cigarette. "And you try to say the right thing too. That was very clever, the way you handled General Heydrich's question about the S-Bahn murderer." He said the word "clever" as though it were not entirely a compliment. "You told him exactly what you knew he wanted to hear, but then you made sure that I was satisfied too. It makes me wonder how you would answer Heydrich's question if the general himself were not present. What kind of man do you actually think we are trying to find? Forget politics or racial theories. Just get down to the practicalities. Tell me about our killer."

I was saved from having to provide an immediate response by the return of Frau Meissner with our beers. By the time she'd gone, I'd ordered my thoughts and could reply: "I agree with Dr. Weimann, Commissar. I think we are dealing with another Peter Kürten."

"By which you mean?"

"A psychopath, someone who has an addiction to death."

"I agree. So what does he look like, this psychopath?"

"Well, we know he wears a uniform. Other than that, it's hard to say."

"Precisely!" Lüdtke agreed, with an enthusiasm that surprised me. "It's not just hard to say, it's damn well impossible. You see, Heuser, this is where theory and practice disagree. Your tutors at the Leaders' School may have all sorts of ideas about what a criminal looks like, but while they've been teaching and philosophizing, I've been getting on with the tedious, day-to-day task of catching people who kill. And I have discovered, as you will too, in due course, that even the most vicious, sadistic, perverted, monstrous killer can have the annoying habit of looking like a perfectly normal human being. Ah . . . here is Frau Meissner, with our balcony pigs!"

Two plates were put in front of us, heaped with hot pie, proper Teltower Rübchen turnips, and a dark, meaty gravy. We attacked our plates with gusto, washing the excellent food down with our beer until the edge had been taken off our hunger. The pie was as good as Frau Meissner had claimed. Just as there had been something magical about the taste of real coffee that morning, so the sensation of eating real food, with tender meat and good, rich flavors, was so intense as to be almost intoxicating. Reality, however, soon butted back in as Lüdtke cleared his plate, took a good long drink of his beer, put down his glass, and said: "You remember Kürten's last words, of course?"

I swallowed my mouthful of potatoes and pie and said: "Yes. He even regarded his own death with pleasure. He said he hoped that when they cut his head off he would have the time to hear his own blood gurgle from his throat." I shook my head at the very thought of it. "Even to contemplate such evil is inconceivable. One simply cannot imagine what it must be like to be such a person."

"Yet, as you will recall, Frau Kürten described her husband as a good man, who loved children, attended church on a regular basis, and was a loyal member of his trade union. His police photograph shows a respectably dressed citizen with a starched white shirt, a suit, and tie. Our man, too, will probably look like the very last person whom anyone would ever think of as a killer. And as for catching him, well, how was Kürten eventually caught?"

"It was an accident, wasn't it—something to do with a letter?"

"Just so: a wrongly addressed envelope in a dead-letter office was opened in case the letter within contained the sender's address, so that it could be returned. The official happened to read the letter, which was written by a young woman. She described meeting a man in Düsseldorf who had attempted to rape her. The police interviewed her. She gave them the address in Mettmänner Strasse where the attempted rape had occurred. There they found Peter Kürten. Coffee?"

"Yes, please . . . It's incredible, the way the Kürten case ended. After so much time, so many deaths, so much work by the police . . . and what finally gets him is a matter of pure chance."

Lüdtke had been leaning back in his chair, making hand signals to Frau Meissner to indicate that we both wanted coffee. He turned back to me and said: "Chance is what gets almost all of them. But there was something else worth noting in the story of Kürten's capture: something that I should have thought you would have noticed at once."

There was the hint of amusement in Lüdtke's eyes as he said that, as though he was having a little fun at my expense. If so, I wasn't in on the joke.

"I don't understand," I said.

"It was the man in the dead-letter office. He broke the rules. It is one thing to check a correspondent's return address, but it is quite another to read a private letter unless one has the authority to do so. And there's a lesson for you in that. I've noticed you today, the way you reacted to the state of our squad room, or being offered a cup of black-market coffee—even my offer of a beer just now. They all made you uneasy. Correct?"

I couldn't deny it. "I suppose so. It's just . . ." I paused, trying to find words that wouldn't make me seem like a total prig. "Well, it's just not what I expected."

"Because we are the famous Berlin murder squad, who solve ninety-five percent of all our cases, and we should be setting an example?"

"I don't know, I . . ."

"You've been taught to obey the rules. I understand."

Our coffees arrived, smelling of anything but actual coffee. Lüdtke took a sip and grimaced in disgust. He put the cup down with an expression of intense distaste that had still not faded from his face as he looked back at me and said: "You're not in the Leaders' School now, Heuser. You're out in the real world and the rules are different here. Don't get me wrong. I'm not one of those cops who makes himself look good by sending the wrong men to jail when he can't find the right ones. I could have dragged some pathetic, perverted sex offender off the streets, faked the evidence, and paraded him to the world as the S-Bahn murderer. But what good would that have done if the real killer was still out there, ready to strike again? So first, and most importantly, we get the right man. But we use every possible means to get him and to establish his guilt, and if that means bending the rules from time to time, so be it. Was it worth breaking the rules to catch Peter Kürten?"

"Yes, of course."

"Then it's worth it for other killers too. We do what we have to do, and"—Lüdtke looked me in the eye and jabbed his forefinger for emphasis—"we stick together. The squad only works if we can all rely absolutely on one another. I must know that if I give you an order, even if you don't like it, you will obey it without question and never, for one second, betray any doubt to the other men. And those men—not just now, but throughout your career—need to be certain that you never ask anything of them that you wouldn't be willing and able to do yourself. Lead from the front and they will always follow.

"Understand this, Heuser, because this is the key to everything . . . Without unity and solidarity, we have no hope. We live and work on the dark side of the street, where the most wicked, depraved scum of the earth hide in the shadows. So this job of ours takes its toll on us all. You saw the state that Tietmeyer and I were in this morning. You'll see other comrades exhausted, drunk, enraged, or even weeping like children. You'll see them do things you may disapprove of; perhaps even things that disgust you. But as long as they are in the murder squad and you are in the murder squad, you stick together, and whatever you or anyone else may say in the privacy of our squad room, you never, ever show the slightest disloyalty in public. Do you understand me, Heuser?"

There was only one possible answer. So I gave it, and I meant it, too: "Yes, Commissar, absolutely."

Lüdtke nodded. He looked satisfied, as though I had now become, for the first time, one of his men. "Then I'll add one further piece of advice. It's about this ambition that you so clearly possess."

I was about to defend myself, but he put up a hand to silence me. "Don't worry. There's nothing wrong with wanting to get ahead. If you work hard and contribute to the team then you will succeed, and deservedly so. But you have to do it the right way. If all you think about is personal advancement; if the only reason you do anything is to make yourself look good, then, yes, maybe you'll climb, and plot, and stab your way to the top. But you won't have my respect, nor that of anyone you work with, or who works for you. So by all means, think about what's good for Georg Heuser. But think about what's good for the job and the team first."

"I understand, Commissar."

"Good man. So, drink up your coffee and let's get back to work."

13

LUDWIGSBURG:
APRIL–OCTOBER 1961

On April 12, 1961, Yuri Gagarin completed the first manned orbit of the Earth in his *Vostok 1* spacecraft, thereby demonstrating that the Soviet Union was a political, military, and scientific superpower that could match or even surpass the United States. On June 4, at a summit meeting in Vienna with President Kennedy, the Soviet premier Nikita Khrushchev told the American, British, and French occupying powers in Berlin that they had until the end of the year to leave the city. As both sides ramped up their military preparations, the threat of nuclear Armageddon hung over the world like a cloud of psychological fallout.

Life still had to carry on, however, even in the face of imminent oblivion, and for Paula Siebert that meant more preparations for a trial that was still over a year away. The ZSL investigators were now being assisted by special police task forces, staffed by officers known to have no links whatsoever to Nazism. They were conducting interviews across the country, sending a stream of information back to her office, all of which had to be analyzed, assessed, and set against the testimony of other witnesses. She was totally immersed in her work, barely even thinking of a personal life. It was true that she and Kraus went out to dinner once or twice a week after yet another late night at the office, but she told herself that it was just two colleagues sharing a working meal. There was nothing more to it than that.

One evening they found an Italian restaurant still open when everyplace else had closed. The proprietor gave them the same food that he and his staff were about to eat: spaghetti carbonara and a carafe of rough red wine, served in a raffia basket. They talked shop for a while and then, out of nowhere, Paula said: "Do I remind you of Georg Heuser?"

Kraus burst out laughing. "You've got to be joking!"

To his surprise there was not a trace of a smile on her face. "No, I'm absolutely not," Paula said. "Last year when I interviewed him he said that I reminded him of himself. It's been eating at me ever since."

"But you've got nothing in common with him at all."

"That's not true. I'm the same age he was during the war. I'm a lawyer, like him—"

"A qualified lawyer."

Paula smiled. "Yes, I made that point to him too. But even so, I'm ambitious; so was Heuser. I want to do my best, a little bit of a perfectionist, even."

"So are countless young lawyers. Listen, you're the exact opposite of Georg Heuser in every way that matters, and the only reason he could have said such a thing, apart from wanting to hurt you, is because you remind him of what he might have been: a decent, honorable, caring human being."

"Thanks."

"You're welcome," Kraus said. He drank some wine and looked at Paula in a way she'd never seen him do before, as a man appraising a woman. Almost to her surprise she was flattered by his attention.

"Also," Kraus went on, "whereas Georg Heuser is a repulsive middle-aged man with whom I would not share a meal even if I was starving and he was holding the world's largest sausage . . ."

Paula giggled, Kraus grinned back at her, and he was laughing too as he said: "You, on the other hand . . . you are a very beautiful young woman and dining with you is one of the very few pleasures of my increasingly miserable life."

"Miserable? What's the matter?"

"I'm sorry . . . I didn't mean to wreck the mood. Forget it."

"No. There's something bothering you. You can tell me what it is. I don't mind."

Whatever Paula might have expected, Kraus's reply was far more blunt and more shocking: "Barbara kicked me out."

"Why? What have you done?"

"What haven't I done, more like. I've not been at home with my family. I've not paid attention to her or the kids. I've spent all my time on this damn case."

"Doesn't she understand how important this is?"

"Just the opposite; she thinks it's a total waste of time. All her friends are convinced I'm going after decent German men, destroying their reputations and throwing them in jail over issues that should have been forgotten long ago. Frankly, Barbara agrees with them. And I don't even get paid any more money for working all these evenings and weekends."

"But it's not fair to make you choose between your family and your job."

"Barbara would say I've already made that choice myself. If I work when I could be at home. And maybe she's right. I love little Hansi and Gitta with all my heart . . . but I spend my time with men I despise. And I'm not even making a decent case against them. Of course they're guilty, but the bastards know we can't prove it. The witnesses are either all dead, or they're too scared to talk. We need a smoking gun, but God knows where we'll find it."

Paula toyed with her spaghetti. "Maybe Becker and Wessel had the right idea. One of them managed to get another job. The other simply retired."

"So why do we hang on, eh?"

Paula just about managed a little laugh as she said, "What else can I do?"

"I know what your mother would say. Think how happy she'd be if you got down to the job of marrying and making babies."

"How dare you!" Paula cried in mock outrage, laughing genuinely this time.

"But it's the same choice, isn't it?" Kraus said, with a quiet seriousness. "We've both put our work before our personal lives. Why do we do that?"

"Because we can't let them get away with it."

"Why not? After all, Barbara's right, they're all leading decent, respectable lives."

"Because of what they represent."

"Which is?"

Kraus was expecting an argument founded on political morality. And he got the feeling that what she said surprised her as much as it did him.

"They killed my daddy," she said, like the girl she must have been when she'd heard the news. "He died outside Moscow, at a place called Khimki. It was the absolute farthest the army got into Russia. They told us he'd died at our greatest moment of glory, as if that was supposed to make it better . . . I think of him lying there in the snow—his poor, frozen body—when he should have been safe and warm at home with his family, a proper father, kissing his wife and playing games with me. And I don't blame the Russians. I blame the Nazis who started the war and sent him to fight in it . . . So that's why I can't let the things they did be forgotten, whatever my mother says. It would be like forgetting my own father. Like betraying him."

He reached across the table and rested his hand on hers. She didn't move it away, enjoying the feeling of her fingers being swallowed up in his great paw, relishing the tenderness of his touch. She found herself entwining her fingers with his, still with her head down, gazing at the hands on the white tablecloth, not yet ready to look him in the eye again.

Finally she said: "How about you? Why do you do it?"

"Ah, now that's a long story . . ." Kraus leaned back in his chair, his head back, his shirt straining against his shoulders and chest. He thought for a moment and then leaned forward again, putting his elbows on the table.

"I was taken prisoner by the Americans. It was May 13, 1943, the day the Afrika Korps surrendered. We'd been going back and forth across that damn desert for two years, but we couldn't go on any longer, not once the Yanks had come into the fight. They took us across the Atlantic in the same ships they'd used to send their boys to North Africa . . ." Kraus grinned. "Shitting ourselves all the way, terrified we'd be sunk by one of our own U-boats. When we got to America we were sent to Camp Hearne, Texas, way down near the Mexican border. We couldn't believe it. We'd been in the Sahara desert, but this damn place was even hotter!"

"My God, how terrible."

"No, it wasn't too bad at all. The rations were set at two thousand calories a day—I ate better there than at any other time in the whole war. The enlisted men had to work in the fields outside the camp, but it wasn't forced labor. They got paid the same as the local farmhands. I was a noncommissioned officer so I was allowed to study instead. I learned English and began my first law degree. We had a theater, an orchestra, we were even given a daily bottle of beer."

"My God, that sounds like paradise compared with life at home back then! Why did they treat you so well?"

"They were Americans. They had food and drink to spare. And they thought the Afrika Korps were Good Germans. We'd fought an honorable war. General Rommel himself had ordered us not to mistreat any Jews we came across. So the Americans had some respect for us as worthy enemies . . . And then one day in early May '45, just as the war in Europe was ending, everything changed. We went into breakfast and there was half as much food as before. The guards—men we'd gotten to know, that we joked with and shared cigarettes with—were looking at us with hatred and contempt in their eyes. We couldn't understand it. We knew the war was ending. Shouldn't they be more friendly now, not less? Then we were led into the theater. It had a projector for showing movies. The lights went down, the projector came on, and it was a newsreel. American jeeps, driven by GIs just like the ones guarding us, came up to the gates of a camp, and in the middle of the gates were metal letters that said *arbeit macht frei*. Then the gates opened and the jeeps went through and immediately they were surrounded by a host of men and women, some in ordinary clothes, others in striped uniforms, but all of them thin . . . so thin, my God, we couldn't believe it—they were like skeletons . . ."

Kraus pushed away the remains of his spaghetti as if the very sight of it was offensive and went on: "It was Dachau. The Americans had gotten there at the end of April and they wanted us to know what they'd found. The camera showed piles of hundreds, even thousands of dead bodies, all naked and, again, just skin and bone. And there were Germans, in SS uniforms, having to carry these bodies into huge open graves . . . There was a train, too, the death train from Buchenwald: cattle trucks filled with more and more dead bodies . . . The horror of it was . . . indescribable . . ."

His voice tailed away for a moment and then Kraus continued. "We'd heard stories, of course, rumors really, about the killing of the Jews, but how could any sane man even imagine that anything like this could possibly exist? Anyway, from that day on, the Americans hated us . . . So if you want to know why I put my work before my family it's because I love my children, and I don't want them to grow up having to bear the burden of their fathers' and grandfathers' shame. I want us to be redeemed in the eyes of the world. I've already fought for my country once, and now I'm fighting for it again in a different, better way. And nothing that anyone, including my wife, can say will ever convince me otherwise."

After they left the restaurant Paula stopped on the pavement, took Kraus's hands in hers, and looked up at his big, broad face with its silver-streaked beard, its weather-beaten skin, and those deep brown eyes that could be full of gentleness one moment and as black and hard as coal the next.

"We can't breathe a word of this to anyone," she said, knowing there was no need to explain herself.

"For both our sakes," Kraus replied. And so it began.

It was a Sunday morning in August and the air was already warm, the sun slicing through the gaps in the curtains, lighting up the dust motes floating in the air, as Paula lay in bed, watching Kraus sleep. She reached out and traced a finger down his back and smiled as she thought of how he'd taken her to bed. She'd cooked his favorite dish, roast pork, braised cabbage, and dumplings, and had just carried the dirty dishes into her tiny kitchen. She put them in the sink, turned around, and there he was, looking at her with a wicked smile on his face, and before she could say a word he'd put his mouth over hers and kissed her with an intensity that had taken her breath away. While her head was still spinning and at the exact moment when she was beginning to wonder if her legs were still capable of supporting her, he had reached down, lifted her off her feet, and held her in his arms, still kissing her. She felt weightless, helpless and vulnerable to him, and yet absolutely safe. Above all, she felt consumed with sheer physical desire, a passionate hunger that no other man had ever induced in her.

Just thinking about it now made her tingle, and she curled up behind him and draped an arm across him, pressing herself against his body to feel his warmth and breathe in his smell. Kraus grunted, rolled onto his back, and she wrapped her leg around his thigh and nestled her head against his chest. Paula loved the sheer mass of him. He was like a mighty granite cliff and she was the sea, hurling herself against him, knowing that he could withstand anything.

With other lovers she'd always been less than her true self, forever restraining her intelligence and her opinions for fear of undermining their fragile sense of masculine superiority. At work, invariably the lone woman surrounded by men, she had to struggle to find the confidence to make herself heard. If she did speak up, half her concentration was spent pitching her voice at the precise point where she would seem neither meek and feeble, nor shrill and aggressive. Even when she succeeded and got her point across, she had to wait for one of the men to repeat it before anyone would take it seriously.

But Kraus was different. He wanted to know what she thought about things, and took her views seriously enough to argue with her when he disagreed. The first few times he'd done it, Paula had been upset, not wanting to displease him and fearing that a dispute might hurt their relationship. It took time for her to understand that Kraus was actually paying her the compliment of treating her as an equal. He was happy for her to test him. He wanted everything she had to offer. The moment she truly accepted that Kraus could handle her—all of her—it seemed to liberate her physically as well, allowing her to seek pleasure without shame or restraint.

No one on earth could arouse her as he did. And now he was waking up, his arm was snaking down her back, cupping her bottom in his hand and pulling her closer to him, and she was lifting her head to meet him as he brought his lips to hers and the bliss was spreading through her all over again.

Afterward, as they were lying together, basking in the afterglow, Paula said: "Tell me why you love me."

Kraus laughed. "What . . . again? You're like a kid who wants to hear the same bedtime story every night!"

"But it's such a good story. And we are in bed . . ."

"Oh all right then . . ."

Paula snuggled up to him and put her head on his chest, wanting to feel the soft, rumbling resonance of his voice as Kraus spoke.

"I love you for your mind," he said, "which is so fine, so clever and original, but well disciplined when it needs to be. I love you for your heart, which is brave and filled with love and passion and commitment to all the things you believe in—all the people, too."

"Like you," she murmured.

"Mmm . . ."

"What else do you love me for?"

"For your pretty face, even when it's grumpy and frustrated because the world isn't treating you right, and especially when you smile and your eyes light up and suddenly you're like the sun coming out on a cloudy day, making everything seem better. I love all the funny little expressions you have when you think I'm not watching you. I love you because you snore . . ."

"I don't!"

". . . very, very softly and then insist that you don't. I love you when you're getting dressed and even more when you're getting undressed. I love the scent of your hair. And I really love your body. I love feeling your tits in my hands, and the curve of your back, and the line of your legs. I love what's between your legs. And finally, I love . . . your . . . ass!"

As he said the last word he spanked her, once, just hard enough to sting a little, and she squealed in surprise as the momentary pain seemed to heighten all the other, softer sensations she was experiencing, like a dash of chili in a rich, warm stew.

"You beast!" she cried, doing her best to sound outraged. She sat up and straddled him. When she looked down at Kraus's face it was wreathed in a smile of pure contentment. His eyes were fixed on her breasts. "You look fucking great," he said, and then, a moment later, "I could really use a cup of coffee."

"Then get it yourself!"

"How can I? You're on top of me."

Paula rolled off. "Now I'm not."

"Oh, go on . . . I said how much I love you. Don't I deserve some coffee in return?"

Paula sighed. "All right . . . just this once. Because you did say it very nicely . . ."

She got out of bed and walked, still naked, into the kitchen. She sorted out the percolator, lit the gas burner, and waited for the coffee to brew. She thought of going back to bed but knew that if she did, she wouldn't get out again, so decided to stay where she was. There was a transistor radio sitting on the windowsill and Paula switched it on, expecting to hear the usual blend of light classical music and popular songs from her favorite station. Instead there was some kind of news report—a live broadcast, by the sound of it.

She caught something about soldiers and crowds of onlookers, then the reporter's voice rising in volume and pitch as he described a young East German soldier dashing away from the rest of his unit, toward the crowds that had gathered on the western side.

Paula called out to Kraus, "Come here! There's something happening in Berlin—something awful."

And that was how they heard the Berlin Wall go up.

Over the following weeks the fortifications and defenses, all on the East German side, grew more deadly and more complex. The Cold War between the East and West deepened by the day. Soviet newspapers were filled with stories about evil German "revanchists," or revenge seekers, who wanted to attack Russia in retribution for their defeat in 1945, and cartoons in which Germans were represented as fat, pig-faced Nazis.

And then, out of the blue, the breakthrough came. Kraus received a message from the Russian embassy in Bonn informing him that the justice department of the Soviet government was aware of his investigation into Nazi atrocities. Following consultations with the highest levels of the Politburo, it had been decided to offer the assistance of the Russian people to the prosecution of the criminal Heuser and his accomplices. To that end, a cache of documents, seized by the Red Army in July 1944, would be made available for inspection, and any that furthered the case against Heuser could be copied and taken to Germany for use as evidence in the forthcoming trial.

Kraus went straight over to the private office that was one small reward for Paula's loyalty to the case. "Pack your bags! We're going to Moscow!"

"Moscow? But that's impossible. Why would they ever let us in there?"

"Because the Russians have decided to let us have the documents they found when they recaptured the Lenin House. Or to put it another way—"

Paula had to resist the urge to leap up and kiss him. But she could at least finish his sentence. "They're giving us the smoking gun!"

14

BERLIN:
FEBRUARY 7–JULY 3, 1941

It was commonly supposed that the Gestapo were everywhere. The average Berliner had a picture in his or her head of countless thousands of agents on the prowl, constantly looking out for anyone who was in any way disloyal to Party or state. That impression, of course, was very carefully calculated: fear was a useful tool in the maintenance of absolute power. Yet in February 1941 there were just seven hundred Gestapo men covering the entire capital. This relatively small force was able to maintain control over millions of people thanks to the efforts of the people themselves, for in those days betrayal was a way of life. Neighbors, coworkers, friends, and even family members had long been accustomed to reporting one another's slightest infractions. So when, three days after our meeting, Lüdtke issued a public request for any information that might help catch the murderer, it was a heaven-sent opportunity for every snoop in the city.

Hundreds of denunciations poured in to the murder squad. Many simply named the nearest Jew or foreigner they could find. Others took the opportunity to slander anyone against whom they held a particular grudge. A few S-Bahn employees accused their colleagues of suspicious behavior. There were even a number of people who had no particular culprit in mind, but had traveled on the S-Bahn on the date of one murder or another and thought that they might have seen something that could be of assistance to the police.

It was my task to sift through this flood of bile and determine which leads were worth following up. Some correspondents were so obviously malicious, stupid, or plain crazy that they could safely be ignored. Others made claims that were contrary to the known facts. They, too, were dismissed. Others again referred to suspicious individuals or events in parts of Berlin far from Rummelsburg, Karlshorst, and Friedrichsfelde. The concentration of all his attacks in these areas suggested that our man was a local, but it wasn't impossible that he came from another part of the city. So these leads were considered to be lower priority, but not ignored altogether. That still left a very large number of sane, credible correspondents requiring a telephone call, a summons to Alexanderplatz, or a visit from a detective, and it was my responsibility to decide who should get what.

While managing that process, I was also trying to familiarize myself with the case as a whole: not just the general facts that Lüdtke had already described for me, but the vast amount of information that underpinned them. There were, for example, three thousand interviews with S-Bahn staff, all of which I was expected to read. He also wanted me to study shift patterns, trying to find anyone who might have an S-Bahn uniform but wasn't at their post at the times of the various murders. From first thing in the morning until late at night I sat surrounded by files and ledgers, studying, noting, and committing their contents to memory in a way that I'd not had to do since I revised the legal code for my last law exam. Woe betide me if I missed anything, because Lüdtke would grill me at regular intervals. What did I think of so-and-so's personnel file? How many of his free nights matched the murder dates? Who was in a position to get hold of the inside information about our operational plans that the killer seemed to possess?

The other detectives saw this as a form of initiation rite: Lüdtke's way of discovering whether I was willing to take shit without complaining, or was just a stuck-up golden boy from the Leaders' School who thought he was too good for donkeywork. Each man reacted as I might have expected: cheerful banter from Baum, intercut by more cynical mockery from Richter; avuncular sympathy from Schmidt and snide bitterness from Frei, for whom my status as an arrogant fancy-pants was taken as a given. I responded to each of them as positively as I could. I was keen to demonstrate that I was a good team-member, willing to handle my boss's demands and my comrades' banter with equal grace.

Much the best part of the whole process was the chance it gave me to get to know Fräulein Tietmeyer a little better. I discovered that her first name was Sabine and that she was a very different person when she'd been able to get a decent night's sleep. Her hair was washed, the dark rings around her eyes a little lighter, and the smile that I'd only glimpsed that first morning now a much more frequent visitor. She would appear at my desk with armfuls of material from the departmental filing cabinets, which she would exchange for all the papers I'd already dealt with. No matter how tired I was or how much my eyes ached from the endless hours of reading, I'd find myself smiling too with the pleasure of seeing her. I began to depend upon her presence to brighten up my days, and when she took a day off and I had to put up with a replacement secretary, I found the time dragging and my eyes glazing over the pages before me in a way they never did when Sabine, as I now thought of her, was around the place.

She wasn't a beauty in the sense of some perfect, doll-like creature whose entire existence is centered upon the desire she can provoke in men. Her features were quite pronounced—one might almost say handsome rather than pretty—but her eyes were bright and filled with laughter; her smile was warm and always entirely sincere. I never once knew Sabine to adopt a pose or attitude for effect: she had a wonderful honesty that made one trust her at once and without reservation.

Her body was of a piece with her face. By that I mean that she didn't possess an hourglass figure, or tiny, delicate hands and feet. She was instead a tall, slender, athletic sort of girl. In those days the propaganda ministry liked to liven up the weekly newsreels by filming groups of fine German maidens, invariably dressed in short, revealing tunics, doing their exercise routines in the sun: touching their toes, swinging hoops or clubs above their heads, and generally looking like fine breeding stock for red-blooded young Aryan males. Sabine had just that look, or rather she would have if she'd made any effort at all to show herself off.

This was in part a function of the times in which we lived: in an era of shortages, women were encouraged to discard all extravagance and frippery. But it was also Sabine's own response to working in an almost exclusively male environment. She didn't want to spend her days fending off advances and wandering hands, and so tried to present herself as one of the boys. In this, she was only partly successful, since it didn't take any man with red blood very long to work out that there were two long legs and a fine pair of breasts hidden away beneath her less-than-flattering clothes.

I'd been working at the murder squad for two weeks, and had very nearly completed my analysis of the case so far, when I finally plucked up the courage to ask Sabine out on a date. Making sure that there were no other squad members within earshot, I made a direct but rather formal inquiry: "I was wondering if you'd like to have dinner with me on Thursday. I've been lucky enough to book a table at Borchardt and I thought we might also take in a show. People say the *Something Crazy* revue at the Scala Theater is really quite entertaining."

"That's very kind of you to ask, Assistant Commissar," she said, replying with equal correctness. "But I really don't think that would be a good idea." Sabine must have seen my face fall, so she added: "Please don't take this personally. I simply don't wish to confuse my personal and professional lives."

I wasn't going to give up that easily. I was making Fräulein Tietmeyer quite an offer, for Borchardt was one of the smartest restaurants in Berlin, and who didn't love the shows at the Scala?

"Please," I said, looking at her with what I hoped was a friendly, engaging expression. "I've been stuck here at my desk for the past two weeks. I'm in very bad need of some innocent fun."

"Innocent, eh? I'm not so sure about that," she said.

Her tone was skeptical, but I had the feeling I'd made a little ground, so I played my trump card. "And the reason I want to have this fun on Thursday, in particular, is that it's my birthday. Surely you can't allow me to spend my birthday all alone?"

"Oh, I'm sure you're not often alone, a good-looking man like you. I bet you have a little black book just filled with pretty girls' names."

She'd called me good-looking—that was a good sign!

"Of course!" I said, with a smile. "But none of them want to talk to me. They all say that I have become boring with all this work I keep doing. And so, Fräulein Tietmeyer, there's no one left to ask but you."

"So I'm the last resort? That's not very flattering!"

I could tell that she was just about to laugh, and I knew that the moment she did, I'd won.

"On the contrary," I said. "I have told every one of them that I am no longer interested. I only have eyes for another."

Even in those days, I wasn't given to flights of fancy, but for once I made an exception: "Berlin is filled with beautiful women wondering what extraordinary creature has taken their place in my heart. 'Who is this Tietmeyer?' they ask. 'What does she have that we do not?' You may not know this, Fräulein, but you're the talk of the town."

And then she laughed and said: "You had better ask Commissar Lüdtke's permission. He won't know what to do with himself if we're both out of the office."

"I already have," I said. "I always like to plan ahead."

"Yes," she said, "I can tell."

And so we arranged our first evening out. To be honest, I'd never really doubted that Sabine would accept my invitation. I was a good catch, well on the way to the *Beamter* status that would guarantee financial security for life. Above all, I was just about to turn twenty-eight, an age when one has begun to acquire the trappings of a man without entirely losing the glorious optimism of youth. I felt immortal, indestructible. I thought I could conquer anything.

15

Sabine looked wonderful. She may have been standing in the front room of a modest little boarding house, with bare patches on the carpet and fading patterned paper on the wall, but I didn't care. In her dark blue satin cocktail dress, with every line of her body picked out by the glossy material, she took my breath away. "Tonight, Fräulein Tietmeyer, you must be the most beautiful woman in Berlin."

She seemed surprised by the compliment, and as she said, "Thank you," I thought I could detect the trace of a blush beneath her makeup.

Before I could say another word, her landlady, Frau Hartung, came in. Sabine had warned me about her in advance. Indeed, she'd been reluctant to let me collect her from her lodgings for fear of the endless disapproving questions the presence of a man might provoke. "Don't worry," I'd assured her. "I have the perfect way of keeping her sweet."

I came to collect Sabine in the dress uniform of an SS-Second Lieutenant, complete with greatcoat, britches, and riding boots. Frau Hartung had a mean, shrewish face, with a sharp nose and tight little mouth. She was the kind of woman whose only pleasure comes from criticizing others, and I was quite sure that if I called up Gestapo headquarters I'd find a thick file stuffed with her observations—all negative—on her tenants and their associates. But the moment she saw me, she suddenly became almost pathetically solicitous and eager to please. For the first but by no means the last time, I experienced the overwhelming effect—an awestruck combination of admiration and sheer terror—that an SS uniform could induce. Now Sabine faced no disapproval whatsoever. On the contrary, Frau Hartung was as humble as a lady's maid as she helped her young tenant into her coat and fetched her handbag and gloves.

The moment we were through the front door and out of her landlady's earshot (though I'm sure the blackout blinds were twitching as she tried to spy on our departure), Sabine took my arm and burst out laughing. "My God! She'll be treating me like a princess from now on!"

"As will I . . . I've even arranged for a royal carriage."

The blackout was so absolute that it was at first difficult to distinguish anything at all outside. But then I switched on the small flashlight that, like any sensible Berliner, I always carried with me at night. It was absolutely forbidden to shine the light upward, but I was able at least to illuminate the wheels of an unmarked Criminal Police car waiting at the curb a few meters away. "I slipped the driver five reichsmarks and he's ours for the evening," I told Sabine, by way of explanation. "The murder squad has vehicles going in and out at all hours of the night; no one's going to notice."

"And I thought you were the kind who was a stickler for the rules."

"Let's just say I'm learning which ones can be bent. In any case, I have just worked seventeen straight days, for at least twelve hours a day, and that's against the rules too."

The theater was on Lutherstrasse in the Schöneberg district, not far from the Kaufhaus des Westens department store, which all Berliners, then as now, knew as the KaDeWe. It was an extraordinary experience, driving through the city in the blackout. There were few cars around and they all proceeded at little more than a brisk walking pace, their drivers made tentative by the feeble washes of light, not fit to be called beams, emitted by their hooded, slitted headlamps. The only light on the streets themselves came from the traffic lights at intersections, which were also half blinded, and the glows cast on the paving stones by the flashlights of passing pedestrians. It was virtually impossible to distinguish where one was actually going, and the dazzling lights above the theater that had once formed the message ". . . *and evenings at the Scala*" were now all dimmed. So it came as quite a surprise when the driver came to a halt, leaned around to face us, and said: "We're there, sir. I'll be right outside when you need me. One good thing about driving for the Criminal Police: no one ever dares tell you to move."

We stepped out into a crowd of people, milling about beneath the theater awning. Something about the darkness seemed to discourage us all from making any noise, as if enemy bombers might be able to hear as well as see us, so there was very little of the buzz of bright chatter one would normally expect before an evening performance. But then we passed through the heavily curtained front doors and into the foyer and suddenly the whole scene burst into light, color, and sound, like someone switching on the film projector in the middle of a pitch-dark cinema.

We had arrived with only a few minutes to spare. There was just time to drop off our coats, buy a program, and make our way to our seats. The auditorium held three thousand people, and one could easily end up needing binoculars to see the performers, but I'd managed to get us seats quite close to the front. Before us rose the golden pillars that supported the great curve of the proscenium arch. Above, the ceiling was studded with lights like a magical, starlit night, and to either side rose the tiers of boxes filled with eager theatergoers in their evening dresses, uniforms, and double-breasted suits. Then the lights went down, the legendary Scala house band, conducted by Otto Stenzel, struck up the opening chords of "Music! Music! Music!" and the show began.

I daresay that *Something Crazy* would seem like tame stuff today. The ways in which we are entertained have changed so much in recent decades. So it may be hard for those who are not of our generation to imagine Sabine and me roaring with laughter and cheerful applause for a troupe of comedy trapeze artists who kept finding new ways to fall off their swings; a team of trick cyclists who weaved between one another at tremendous speed, with two, three, or even four performers on each bike; a man in a Chaplinesque tramp costume who had amusing ways of playing the xylophone; four Negro minstrels in blackface; and even a horseman in a scarlet riding jacket who performed a dressage routine set to music.

The Scala dancers, however, would have been a sensation in any age. They were called the Hiller Girls and I can see them now, those wonderful creatures opening the show dressed as little toy soldiers, with plumed hats, shiny boots, and toy guns. They marched across the stage in perfect formation, kicking out their long, long legs in a style that was halfway between a goose step and a can-can. The Führer's own bodyguard could not have displayed more immaculate precision.

For their next appearances the dancers appeared as sensuous maidens from a Balinese temple; flirtatious señoritas in much-abbreviated Spanish dresses; and half-naked savages on an undiscovered Pacific isle, who writhed and tumbled in a glorious pattern of bare legs, pert bottoms, slender brown stomachs, and bouncing breasts. In their most spectacular number, each girl was dressed in diaphanous pajamas and placed in her own extravagantly draped and quilted bed, so that the whole stage looked like some extraordinary dormitory, with the beds all arranged in tiers, so that we could see each pretty little maiden as she slept. Then, while the band played an instrumental version of "Smoke Gets in Your Eyes" (given an appropriately Germanized arrangement so as to erase any taint of American Judaism), one particularly beautiful and long-legged dancer came to the front of the stage and performed a graceful series of semi-gymnastic movements: cartwheels, handstands, and various bends and stretches, much to the audience's delight.

Sabine seemed just as entranced by the girls' extravagant costumes, intricate hairstyles, and painted faces as I was. She examined each passing body with the cool, appraising eye that attractive young women apply to their peers and potential rivals. When the show had ended and we were standing in the cloakroom line to collect our coats from a bespectacled grandmotherly lady with a great bun of silver hair atop her head, Sabine insisted on asking me which girl had been my favorite. She was almost disappointed to discover that my recollection of the individual dancers was really quite sketchy, whereas she could describe them all with precise detail and a full account of each one's distinguishing features.

"I wish the S-Bahn witnesses were as observant as you," I said. "We'd have caught the killer long ago!"

"Well I'm very glad that other detectives aren't as unobservant as you," she replied. "You don't seem to have noticed a thing."

"That's because I was only thinking of you," I said, collecting our coats and handing the woman a tip. Having quickly put on my coat, I held up Sabine's and, as she was standing just in front of me, slipping her arms into its sleeves, I told her: "There wasn't a single girl up there who was nearly as lovely as you."

"Don't be mean," she said, turning around and waving a finger at me. "You're just teasing me."

She was right, I had been, or at least I'd thought I was. Now, though, I looked at Sabine and then, quite seriously, replied, "No, I'm really not teasing. I absolutely mean it."

She linked her arm through mine as we walked out under the theater awning and onto Lutherstrasse. She'd done the same, of course, as we had left her lodgings. But this time she nestled her body appreciably closer to mine.

16

Despite the public announcements that we were rethinking our strategy, Zach was still guarding the stations and putting plainclothes detectives onto the trains themselves to mingle with the passengers and keep an eye out for suspicious behavior. Exactly as he had planned, no details of their operations were given to the S-Bahn authorities, but it must have been obvious to any of the railway staff—and all the more so to anyone whose evil intentions might have made him especially watchful—that there were often policemen aboard the trains. Even in civilian clothes we tend to have a certain air about us. Lüdtke's hope was that their presence, and the fact that it was unpredictable, might have some deterrent effect on our killer.

One of the methods Zach employed was to assign female officers to act as bait, like the tethered goats used in India to attract a hungry tiger. This was a task that demanded extreme courage from the women concerned, since they were obliged to travel unaccompanied and to sit whenever possible alone in a carriage. Men were always posted in adjacent carriages to either side, but no one could guarantee that in the event of an attack they would be able to come to the rescue of their female colleague in time. It was for this reason that the first "tethered goats" used on the trains had been male officers in female dress. That experiment had soon been abandoned, since the killer would have had to have been blind not to spot that these were no ordinary ladies. There was thus no alternative but to use the real thing.

One night an officer called Helga Schwab was on duty, alone in a carriage near the rear of a late-night train. On the infamous stretch between Rummelsburg Depot and Karlshorst she saw a man dressed just as the killer's surviving victims had described: in a dark, loose-fitting uniform jacket with a cap pulled low over his eyes. He'd come in through the connecting door at the very far end of the car-riage from where she was sitting. Schwab turned her head away from the man, but kept him under observation out of the corner of her eye as he slowly walked down the aisle toward her. He looked to the right and left as he went, very clearly making sure that she was the only passenger aboard. Schwab felt that paralysis which can strike even the bravest soul at moments of great fear. She had to fight to regain her self-possession as her pulse raced and the first prickles of sweat broke out on her skin. She told herself to remain calm and vigilant.

She had every reason to be fearful. For I wasn't the only man who had marked this date in his diary for a special night out. The S-Bahn murderer had gone hunting. And once again he was taking the No. 3 line.

17

The Scala Theater was destroyed in the early hours of November 23, 1943, in the very same air raid that also demolished the original KaDeWe. By then the war had decisively turned against us and the best that one could hope to eat in any restaurant anywhere in the Reich was a watery, tasteless soup to start with, followed by some colorless agglomeration of gristle and sinew that might once have belonged to a living creature. Next to that, the early months of 1941, however drab they may have seemed when compared with life in peacetime, were like a veritable age of plenty.

When we arrived at Borchardt, once again passing from the cold, bleak blackness of the street outside to the warmth and brilliance of the restaurant's interior, we were led to a cozy little table beside one of the marble columns that supported the ceiling. The waiter moved the table to allow Sabine to slide onto the red banquette beyond it. The banquettes acted as low partitions, dividing the room into small, intimate sections, and they were topped with brass handrails, so that as I settled onto my wooden dining chair I was uncomfortably reminded of an S-Bahn carriage.

Sabine must have seen something change in my expression, for she at once asked: "Is anything the matter?"

"No, it's nothing," I said. "I just thought of something to do with the case. But don't worry, we are certainly not discussing that for a single second."

We ordered a meal that had seemed to symbolize the promise of what our new German empire and its allies might offer us when the war was through: Norwegian lobster on Italian noodles, washed down with French champagne. Both of us handed over our ration cards so that the necessary coupons could be removed. When the first drinks had been poured and I'd offered a toast to Commissar Lüdtke—"For bringing us together"—I made a request to Sabine: "I have now told you twice how beautiful you look tonight. I think it's only fair that you should tell me why you think I'm handsome."

She giggled and toyed with the stem of her champagne glass. "What makes you think that I do?"

"Because you told me one afternoon at Alex. And I always remember vital evidence."

"Oh, and why is this so vital? I'm sure your opinion of yourself is already good enough without me having to make it any better."

I nodded thoughtfully. "I admit, I'm aware of my abilities in certain areas."

"I'm sure!" Sabine laughed again. This time she was just as ready to tease as I was.

"But . . . *but*," I emphasized, "not all areas. So yes, I think I'm a damn good police officer—or that I'll become one, anyway. I'm confident in my intelligence, my hard work, all those boring but necessary qualities. But I've never thought of myself as good-looking."

"Really?" asked Sabine, sounding quite intrigued. "Then what do you think you look like?"

"Normal!" I honestly couldn't think of a better answer. But I tried to expand it a little. "Neat, tidy, respectable . . . I don't know. It's not something I really think about."

"Why not? I don't believe I'm especially vain, but I can't imagine not thinking about my appearance."

"That's because you're a woman. To a man, it's just not important. My priority is my work. So long as my appearance is acceptable to my superiors, that is all that matters."

"But it does matter to you," Sabine pointed out. "Otherwise you wouldn't have asked me about it."

Some men do not like to be challenged by a woman. Personally, I enjoy it. I like to be kept on my toes and I am arrogant enough to believe that I'll always come out on top in the end. So now I laughed and admitted, "Touché! All right then, I suppose this seems like a new thing to me—that someone could see me as more than just a good student or a good worker: that maybe they could see the real person underneath." I paused, realizing that I might be revealing more of myself than I'd intended. "Sorry, I am becoming sentimental."

"Really, Georg, there is no need to apologize."

As ridiculous as it may seem, that was the first time she'd ever called me by my first name. We both seemed to realize it at the same time, and Sabine became a little flustered.

"I'm sorry . . . I didn't mean to be forward. I hope you do not mind me calling you Georg."

"Of course not . . . Sabine."

She smiled. "My friends call me Biene."

"Then Biene it will be, because I very much want us to be friends."

I poured some more champagne and we both took our time to sip it. It had, I think, been evident that there was something between us from the moment I saw her in that dingy living room, but we had both been acting as if we hadn't really noticed what was happening. Now, though, it was coming out into the open, this tricky negotiation between a man and a woman that happens on the way to love.

The food arrived and gave us another excuse not to do anything but enjoy it and make appreciative small talk about the wonderful luxury of eating lobster. I didn't know it at the time, but it would be a decade, at least, before I consumed a meal that even came close to the sheer pleasure of this one. At the time, however, my only concern was the very real possibility that I'd be surviving on stale bread and water for the rest of the month: the evening had so far cost me the best part of three weeks' wages.

Biene was the first to start the conversation again. "I don't understand why people have not thought of you as more than a student or a worker. Surely you must have had other girls in your life—all those beauties in your little black book!"

I smiled and raised my hands a little off the table in a gesture of mock surrender. "I confess, I might have been exaggerating a little when I told you about them."

She responded with mock outrage. "So the beauties of Berlin aren't all in a rage of jealousy, thinking about the mysterious seductress Fräulein Tietmeyer? I've been lied to by a policeman! I'm shocked!"

"Well, I wasn't lying to you in an official capacity."

"Very well then, tell me the truth. Have you had other girls in your life?"

Sometimes the most serious questions are delivered in the most casual manner. In love as in police work, that can be how you obtain the most honest answers.

"I'm not a virgin, if that's what you mean," I replied. "I have certainly had girlfriends, even if they don't fill a whole book. But have I truly fallen in love or had anyone fall in love with me? No, I don't think that I have."

Biene frowned: "How terrible to reach the age of twenty-eight without knowing love. No wonder you want to hear nice things from me. Let me see, then, what can I tell you?" She looked at me thoughtfully, and with such a serious expression that I had to turn away from her gaze. "You are an attractive, handsome man. You are good and tall, which helps. You have nice eyes and strong, even features, too. You look determined and full of purpose, just as a man should. If you were an actor you would be the leading man. If a woman loved you, you would be her hero."

She sat back in her chair. "There! I have been sitting here flattering you, which is not at all what is supposed to happen. You are the gentleman and you are supposed to be flattering me. So I am not going to say another word, and you are going to say wonderful things about me."

"That would be my great pleasure," I assured her. But before I could even start my sweet-talking there was a commotion at the restaurant's front door. The driver was standing there, talking to the maître d'. They both looked across at our table, then the maître d' scurried over to us.

"Excuse me, Assistant Commissar," he said, "but I have an urgent message for you from Commissar Lüdtke. He says you are to return to headquarters at once. There has been a development in the case."

"Thank you," I replied. "Please may I have the bill at once."

The maître d' paused. "Please excuse my presumption, sir, but would the Commissar be referring to the S-Bahn case?"

"Yes, that is correct."

"Then please, accept the meal with the compliments of the house. Everyone in the city is praying for your success. All we ask is that you catch this evil man."

"That's very kind. Rest assured we will do our very best."

So that was one piece of good news. But as I escorted Sabine from the restaurant, I was very much afraid that I was not about to hear another.

18

Helga Schwab had been told that the killer was believed to be posing as a ticket inspector, lulling his victims into a false sense of security and then attacking them when their guard was dropped. She waited for the man to approach her, tensing her muscles so that she was ready to leap from her seat and evade his attack just long enough to allow help to arrive.

Closer he came. All her instincts, as a woman and a police officer, told Schwab that this was the man. Although he affected a relaxed attitude, he seemed to be repressing a much more keyed-up, jumpy, almost feverish personality. Had she not known the things this man was capable of she wouldn't have been particularly alarmed, for he was at most medium height, and—though the loose jacket and poor light made it hard to be sure about this—lightly built. But this was a man who had strangled, stabbed, and bludgeoned his victims to death. He posed a deadly threat. Schwab knew that his weapon had to be hidden on him somewhere. At all costs, she dared not lose sight of his hands, for she would only have a fraction of a second to react to his first aggressive move.

He was only a couple of meters away now, and as she looked up at him she forced her expression into a nervous, ingratiating smile.

He paused for a second, weighing her up. He took a step more toward her . . .

And then, without any warning, he was backing away, muttering: "Excuse me, madam," and hurrying toward one of the sets of doors at the far end of the carriage. It took Schwab a moment to work out what was happening, and then she realized that the train was slowing. They must be entering Karlshorst station. She knew there were some of Zach's men posted among the waiting passengers on the platform, but how would she spot them? Stations, like the trains, were lit so faintly that it was impossible to make out any more than the vague outlines of individual people. As the train slowed to a halt Schwab got up, trying to remain as casual as possible so as not to alarm her suspect. They were both standing by separate sets of doors, which began to slide apart.

The moment they were even fractionally open, the man in the S-Bahn uniform had slipped through them, darted onto the platform, and was making his way between the passengers trying to board the train, moving with a quick, nervy stride that was halfway between walking and running, dodging between the wrought-iron pillars that supported the wooden-beamed roof. The dim blue bulb inside the train cast a faint, spectral half-light over the edge of the platform and Schwab could just see the man's cap getting further away from her as she tried to press her way through the people all around her.

She tried to remember who was on duty at Karlshorst that night. A name came to her and she called it out: "Brandt!"

A flashlight switched on a few meters away. It shone in her direction and she had to screw up her eyes as the beam hit her face. She jabbed a finger down the platform and shouted again: "In the uniform! He's getting away!"

Brandt swung his flashlight in the direction Schwab was pointing and caught sight of the suspect. He appeared to be heading for a set of stairs that ran down from the platform, which stood on a raised viaduct ten meters or so above street level. About a dozen other passengers who had just left the train were doing the same thing. One or two of them were looking around in alarm, sensing that something was wrong. In the carriage next to the one Schwab had just left, one of the detectives who was supposed to be standing guard over her had realized that she was now on the station platform, and was trying to make his way off the train. But he was too late. The doors were closing again. The train was about to pull out.

Schwab had reached into her handbag and found her own flashlight. She shone it toward Brandt and he pointed toward the stairs. She nodded in acknowledgment. The two flashlight beams swung across the platform like searchlights, back toward the suspect . . .

And he had gone. Vanished into thin air.

Brandt and Schwab were standing alone on the fast-emptying platform. Brandt shouted over the noise of the departing train: "Police!"

The people on the stairs stopped as one and turned to face him. Brandt pointed his flashlight at them. Schwab was still sweeping hers from side to side, hoping to catch sight of the suspect.

"Has anyone seen a man in a uniform?" Brandt called out. "Black jacket, black cap. He was on the platform, right here, a moment ago!"

A man on the stairs pointed toward the empty darkness where the train had been standing a few moments ago. "He went that way—onto the tracks!"

Brandt and Schwab raced to the edge of the platform. Schwab heard something, a scuffing sound followed by a quick, involuntary exclamation of pain. She aimed her flashlight toward it and caught a flicker of movement. "Over there!" she shouted. But whoever it was out there evaded her beam.

Brandt jumped down onto the tracks. "Come on!" he shouted. "He must have gone this way!"

Brandt started jogging back up the tracks toward Rummelsburg Depot, in the direction the train had just come from.

Moving more tentatively, Schwab lowered herself onto the track. Brandt was up ahead of her, his flashlight pointing just a few meters in front of him to light his way across the railway ties. To their left a second set of tracks ran parallel to the ones they were on. Just then Schwab heard or perhaps just sensed something: a humming vibration coming down the tracks, followed by a distant clattering sound coming from behind her. It took her a moment to work out what it was.

"Train!" she yelled. "Brandt! Watch out! It's a train!"

Brandt stopped dead. The clattering was louder now—much louder. Schwab swung around and pointed her flashlight back down the tracks. An S-Bahn train was heading straight toward them, a huge dark shadow bearing down at tremendous speed.

Schwab had proved her courage well enough already that night, but she couldn't prevent the scream of utter terror as she stood helpless in the path of the train.

It sped by on the track to her left, so close that the rush of air almost knocked her off her feet. When it had gone she heard a nervous laugh from up ahead. "Phew! That was close!" Brandt exclaimed, the forced laughter in his voice barely disguising the fact that he'd been just as frightened.

"It's no good," she said. "We'll never find him out here. He probably knows these tracks like the back of his hand, and we have no idea where we're going."

Brandt sighed. "You're probably right. And the next train from Rummelsburg Depot will be coming along the line we're on any minute from now. Damn it! We were so close to him!"

"Count yourself lucky, Brandt," Schwab muttered under her breath. "You weren't half as close as me." Then she spoke up more clearly. "Come on, then. Back to the station before we both get flattened."

It was my job to interview Helga Schwab when she returned to the station. Papa Schmidt had been doing the same with Brandt. We compared both accounts and wrote up an incident report, which we checked with the officers concerned and then handed over to Lüdtke.

Schwab and Brandt were both angry and bitterly frustrated at their failure to catch the killer. "You are not to blame," Lüdtke assured them. "I have had months to catch him and have not come anywhere near doing so. You at least came close."

Yet a pall of depression seemed to settle over the murder squad in the days and weeks that followed. We had been offered a chance, however fleeting, and failed to make good on it. Now the only thing that we could do was hope we would get another before one more woman paid for our failure, just as the seven before her had done.

19

Winter slowly warmed into spring. The snow melted, the first buds appeared on the trees, the seasons changed. But the S-Bahn murderer was still out there somewhere, and still as elusive and as mysterious as ever. There was another late-night encounter in a deserted carriage: this time at Erkner, the terminus of the No. 3 line. A guard was doing a final check on an empty train that was about to be shunted into the sidings for the night when he disturbed a man dressed in dark clothes. The guard called the alarm and chased the man across the tracks. Shots were fired. But once again the man, and surely we can say that it was the killer himself, disappeared into the pitch-black night.

More weeks went by and there was no further sign of him. One month after another passed without an attack. Now we began to ask ourselves whether we had finally chased him away from the S-Bahn, and, if so, were we merely shifting the problem somewhere else? Or had he disappeared from the city altogether? It was perfectly possible that he'd been called up for service in the armed forces, but we dared not assume that the killing spree was over. We had to keep patrolling the trains, guarding the stations, and going through the information we had in our possession again and again, reading the files until they became as deeply engraved in our memories as ancient inscriptions on a stone monument.

Lüdtke was convinced that the murderer had to be, or have been, an S-Bahn worker in the Rummelsburg area. Geographically it sat at the heart of both of the killer's areas of operations: the gardens and allotments of Friedrichsfelde and the trains of the No. 3 lines. Administratively it had been at the heart of all our police operations on the S-Bahn: a place where the killer would be able to monitor what we were up to and adapt his plans accordingly. And it was also one of the busiest sections of the entire Berlin rail network: a great complex of lines, junctions, sidings, and signal boxes, where crowds of workers came and went all the time, and one man could easily lose himself in the crowd of people or the web of intersecting tracks.

In circumstances such as these, when all seems hopeless, there is nothing for a junior officer to do but trust in his superiors, obey their orders, and work to the maximum of his ability. That was there-fore what I did. By sheer hard work, Lüdtke and I cross-referenced the working hours and known movements of hundreds of S-Bahn employees, and came up with a list of eight who might have been able to commit the seven murders and six serious but nonfatal assaults that we had connected with the S-Bahn murderer.

It was hugely tempting to bring them all in and try to interro-gate or if necessary beat a confession out of them. The problem was that every one of the eight had already been interviewed at length without saying anything that had given rise to any suspicion. Nor had anyone else given any evidence that might incriminate any of the eight. There was thus no good reason for us to detain them, and even if we had done so, we had no material to work with during an interrogation. A police officer, like a prosecutor, is always in a much stronger position if he already knows the answer to the question he is asking. It is one thing to make a man admit to a truth that you have already discovered for yourself. It is quite another to take pot-shots in the dark, hoping that you are lucky enough to strike a target.

We were, therefore, completely impotent until something else happened that gave us something more to work on. And then something did happen, and it made not a blind bit of difference. Another woman was hit on the head and sexually assaulted in Friedrichsfelde. Luckily for her, she survived. Unluckily for us, the blow dazed her so badly that she was unable to remember anything of the incident, or her assailant. Once again we had nothing to tell our increasingly impatient masters at the Reich Security Main Office, and we could only be grateful they had so much else on their minds that they didn't have the time to take a more active interest in our case.

Something was up. All through April, May, and June, Criminal Police officers were disappearing from Alex and transferring to a mysterious training center at an old border police college in East Prussia. There they worked under circumstances of total secrecy. Whatever was happening there, it went all the way to the very top, because Arthur Nebe himself was involved. He'd been offered some sort of new command. Apparently he'd done everything he could to avoid it, but Heydrich was insistent. He needed his very best officers for this task, whatever it was, and even a man of Nebe's exalted status could not say no.

On June 22, 1941, we discovered what all the fuss was about. For that was the day that Operation Barbarossa began: the invasion of Russia, the single biggest undertaking in the entire history of warfare. The Wehrmacht launched the greatest of all its blitzkriegs and smashed through Stalin's Red Army with even more devastating success than it had through the British and French a year earlier. In the wake of our armies came a second wave of invaders, four SS task forces known as Einsatzgruppen, and lettered A to D. Their officers were almost all drawn from the Criminal Police, Gestapo, and SD, while their lower ranks tended to comprise uniformed police officers, many of them middle-aged and therefore too old to fight in the army itself, organized into so-called police battalions.

We assumed their job was to carry out the police work that was bound to be needed as we occupied the vast new territories that were falling into our hands, seemingly by the hour. Biene and I, like men and women all across Germany, sat enthralled as the newsreels showed our Panzer divisions smashing through Russian defenses, while the infantry rounded up hordes of defeated Soviet prisoners of war. The numbers were so vast as to be almost meaningless: thousands of enemy tanks destroyed; tens of thousands of their men killed; hundreds of thousands captured.

We were shown the desperate panic measures of the fleeing Bolsheviks as they set fire to their own crops and cities; the ugly and pathetic forms of the subhuman Slavs we had defeated; and the hooked noses and deceitful expressions of the Jews who populated the vast spaces of Russia that would now be opened up for colonization by healthy, civilized Germans. Yet although we rejoiced at the victories won by our brave soldiers and airmen, Biene and I weren't too concerned by the politics that lay behind the Russian campaign. We were too busy falling in love.

She remained insistent that none of this should ever be apparent from our day-to-day conduct in the office. Lüdtke knew of our blossoming relationship, but we somehow managed to keep it secret from everyone else. In this we had been greatly helped by the sudden ending to our first date. The police driver had taken me back to Alex and Biene to her boardinghouse. At no time had we behaved as anything other than colleagues on a friendly but perfectly proper evening out. There had thus been very little for even the most imaginative gossips to work on, particularly when Biene was, if anything, rather cooler to me in public than before.

By the beginning of July the Berlin murder squad appeared becalmed. One by one, officers were drifting away to other, more immediate cases as the S-Bahn murders seemed fated to be forever unresolved. After months of overwork, we even had time to waste on idle conversation. Baum had somehow convinced himself that he was going to get a transfer to Paris, and could spend hours describing the apartment he would get himself and the beautiful Parisian women with silk stockings and scented skin who would join him there to make love, drink champagne, and nibble on foie gras.

Then the killer struck again.

In the early hours of July 3 the body of a thirty-five-year-old woman called Frieda Koziol was discovered on a path through an area of allotments in Friedrichsfelde. She'd been smashed over the head and raped. Suddenly the higher-ups at the Reich Security Main Office were paying attention again. They wanted action now.

By the end of the day, all eight of Lüdtke's suspects were in detention. If one of them wasn't the S-Bahn murderer, we had nowhere else to go.

20

LUDWIGSBURG AND MOSCOW: OCTOBER 1961

A senior Foreign Office official came to see Kraus and Siebert to dissuade them from traveling to Moscow. He was tall, thin, silver-haired, and dressed in a gray suit whose perfect fit and impeccably understated cut was surely the work of a London tailor. His name was Klaus Graf von Schenk und Lichtenburg, and he looked at them with the same lordly disdain with which his ancestors must have regarded the peasants on their aristocratic estates.

"We are, as you know, in a state of crisis, possibly on the brink of another war, and there are many people who believe that your visit to Moscow will play into Russian hands," he said. "The Soviets would not have contemplated opening up their files to you unless they saw an advantage in it for them. Clearly they think that the information they are giving you will serve to discredit our nation. If you have any love whatsoever for your Fatherland, you should think twice and ask yourself: Is this trip really necessary? Must we place ourselves in debt to the Soviet Union? And do we really want to assist our enemies?"

Kraus was an old socialist at heart. He had no time for titles and fancy names. "Forgive me, Herr Lichtenburg, if I ignore your warning. I have spent the past three years being told why I shouldn't do the work I do, and not one of the many arguments made against me has persuaded me to stop. If the Russians are stupid enough to think that

I'm in any way helping their cause, good luck to them. All I care about is that the papers they're giving us might just make it easier to achieve a successful prosecution and lock guilty men behind bars. In the meantime, I'm leading an official, federal investigation into indicted criminals and I need no further justification than that."

"Very well, then, I can see there is no purpose in trying to dissuade you," Lichtenburg conceded. "But if you must go to Moscow, there are things you need to know."

"Go ahead. I'm all ears."

Now Lichtenburg dropped the diplomatic rhetoric and spoke with the blunt, pragmatic assurance of a man who knows his subject. "Bear in mind, above all, that you will be under observation at all times: night and day, awake and asleep. You will have a minder who will probably be introduced to you as an official from the Ministry of Justice. Assume that he is a KGB agent. Assume, too, that he is not the only person watching you wherever you go. Your hotel rooms will be bugged. The table in the hotel restaurant will be bugged. The offices where you work will be bugged."

"Sounds like old times," Kraus observed.

"Actually, that's not a bad comparison. Just imagine the Gestapo are watching you. Trust no one. Suspect everyone. And assume that anyone who approaches you is doing so under orders. Never accept a drink from anyone, especially an attractive member of the opposite sex. It is distressingly common for foreigners to be drugged, knocked unconscious, photographed in a compromising position, and then blackmailed. Likewise, you may well be approached by someone, usually an elderly man, claiming to have been given permission to emigrate so that he can join his family in Australia, or wherever. He will explain that he requires foreign currency for his journey and offer to exchange rubles for your coins at a very generous rate. Foreign currency dealing is absolutely illegal in Russia. If you hand over so much as a single coin, you will be arrested and threatened with a lengthy jail sentence unless you cooperate with the Soviet authorities."

"I don't think I'm likely to be giving old Russians my money!" Kraus joked.

"This is no laughing matter, Dr. Kraus. This happens. There is nothing remotely amusing about being in a KGB cell in Lubyanka Square, facing ten years in a Siberian labor camp."

"What should we expect from the city itself?" Paula asked, feeling the tension between the two men returning and wanting to move things on.

"I'll tell you something about Moscow that you won't find in any guidebook," Lichtenburg replied. "As you drive in from the airport, you'll pass mile upon mile of apartment blocks. None of them is more than ten years old, but many are already falling apart. That's because they were built by Russians. The best new blocks in Moscow—the ones reserved for senior Party officials and foreign diplomats—do not fall apart. You know why? Because they were built by Germans. Captured soldiers, taken during the war on the Eastern Front, who . . ." Lichtenburg stopped in midsentence. Paula was looking at him with an expression of utter desolation.

"I'm so sorry, Dr. Siebert," he said, with genuine remorse. "I didn't mean to upset you. Here . . ." He took the silk handkerchief from his breast pocket and offered it to her.

"No thank you . . . You're very kind but I'll be all right. It's just, well, my father was killed very close to Moscow—during the war, I mean . . ."

"Then you should be glad for him that his end was swift," said Lichtenburg. "The men who were captured were condemned to a hellish existence. Many died within weeks or a few months of captivity. Others lasted years. The lucky ones finally came home, broken men most of them. But there are more still in Russia, thousands, maybe tens of thousands of them, and try as we might, we cannot get them back. The Russians hate us. They will never forgive us and they would stick you both in one of their camps without a second thought. So I feel obliged to repeat my first advice: do not go to Moscow. And if you insist on going, spend every second of your time there in fear. That, I would suggest, is the best way of ensuring that you come back home again, safe and sound."

Sheremetyevo International Airport was less than two years old, yet it had already acquired the tatty, drab, gray patina that Paula would soon come to associate with the Soviet capital. Their baggage was brought to them by a porter and inspected with a thoroughness bordering on paranoia by the customs men. As each item of her clothing, underwear included, was fingered and examined, Paula felt an almost physical sense of violation. They had been on Russian soil for less than an hour but already she understood that, far from being absurd exaggerations, Lichtenburg's warnings were no more than the simple truth. Two people met them: a Soviet official from the Ministry of Justice, who introduced himself as Poliakov, and Neumann, a representative from the West German embassy. "I'll just come with you to the hotel," Neumann said with forced breeziness. "Make sure you're both settled in properly."

It was a cold, dark, damp autumn day and they drove in on a road that was as wide as an autobahn, yet almost empty of traffic. A few kilometers from the airport they passed some kind of installation, like a modern art sculpture: great clusters of concrete beams, gathered on either side of the road, like the skeletons of giant, brutalist wigwams.

"What on earth is that?" Paula asked.

Poliakov twisted around from the front passenger seat. There was a smug smile on his face, and he made no attempt to hide the triumphal pleasure in his voice as he said, "That is the Khimki War Memorial.

Those are tank traps and they mark the furthest point reached by the fascist forces in the Great Patriotic War. This is where we held them and smashed them. We never took another backward step from here, all the way to Berlin."

The blood drained from Paula's face. She heard a rushing sound in her ears and her vision blurred. Neumann was sitting next to her, in the middle of the rear seat. She grabbed his arm and gasped, "Please, tell him to stop the car."

A brief argument ensued; Neumann was plainly trying to relay Paula's request and Poliakov was refusing it. The driver slowed the car, not sure what to do. Though Paula couldn't understand a word of the Russian in which the two men were shouting at one another, she could detect something in Poliakov's voice apart from anger: fear. This was not part of the plan, not allowed for in his orders, and he was patently terrified of giving in to the Germans' request. But a distressed woman, on the point of fainting, has a certain power in any culture and the car finally pulled into a lay-by. Paula got out and turned back the way they had come, trying to see the memorial. Poliakov immediately tried to follow her but Kraus blocked his way and snarled at Neumann: "Tell this shithead Ivan that her father died here, twenty years ago. She just needs a little time . . ." Kraus clenched his right fist and held it up by his face. "And if she doesn't get it, he'll have this to answer to."

Neumann took a deep breath, gathered his thoughts, and began his negotiation with Poliakov, using a much more conciliatory tone this time.

Paula paid no attention to any of them. She was just staring back down the road at the distant outlines of the tank traps, trying to make sense of it all. Here, on this banal, nondescript stretch of highway, cutting through a drab suburban town, was where her father had lost his life. His body was somewhere nearby, an anonymous bundle of bones beneath the earth, without even a gravestone to mark its presence. She wanted to look so hard at everything around her that somehow she would absorb it all, take it into her and thereby take her father in as well: give his spirit somewhere warm and loving to inhabit. But it didn't happen. The cars and trucks kept rumbling by. The sky stayed the same dreary shade of gray. The men by the car talked with increasingly heated voices and waved their arms in her direction. She made a vow to herself that one day she would return to this grim, uninviting spot, and then she walked back toward the men and said to Neumann: "You can tell him I'm ready to carry on, now."

They reached the fringes of the city itself and the apartment blocks began, just as Lichtenburg had said they would: rank upon rank of identical ten-story buildings, all plagued with the same instant decrepitude as the airport. When they pulled up at a set of traffic lights not far from a group of half a dozen boiler-suited workers mending a hole in the road, it took Paula a second glance to realize that they were all women: strapping but not unattractive blondes, watched over by a single scrawny man standing lazily to one side, smoking a cigarette.

Toward the center of the city Paula saw much bigger buildings: colleges, government departments, and living quarters for the Party elite. All conformed to the same pattern: a squat, foursquare block with a short tower at each corner and a much larger structure rising from the center of its facade. Here three or four towers of decreasing size would be piled one upon the other like the layers of a wedding cake with a spire at the top. The overall effect was halfway between a crudely muscular version of a medieval cathedral and a shrunken Empire State Building, repeated again and again and again across the city.

So much was said about the crushing power of Soviet communism that Paula was surprised above all by how dreary and impoverished Moscow seemed. The people wore ancient coats and felt boots that reminded her of her teens: those years before and immediately after the end of the war when she, like everyone else in a defeated nation, was fed on scraps and dressed in rags and tatters. The new, rich, booming West Germany had left those marks of poverty far behind, but these Muscovites seemed trapped in deprivation. Instead of advertising billboards they had huge political posters, with Party slogans and dour Soviet leaders taking the place of commercial catchphrases and smiling models. There were no bright, colorful shopwindows; no enticing displays of pastries in welcoming cafés. When she walked through city streets at home, she always had an eye out for the way other women presented themselves, silently mocking those who had more money than taste, or admiring the lucky few who could afford beautiful clothes and had the figures to carry them off. But there was none of that here. Perhaps the shock of passing her father's final resting place had made her unduly gloomy, but she felt sure she would have had the same impression whatever her mood: Moscow was simply a city from which all the sensory delight, all the fun, all the pleasure had been knowingly, deliberately removed.

The Russians had put Paula and Kraus up at the Leningradskaya Hotel, yet another huge building with a wedding-cake tower. Poliakov led them into a cavernous foyer, whose high coffered ceiling was supported by marble columns as tall as redwoods, and informed them that they had been given rooms three floors apart. Hers was the lower. When the elevator doors opened, the entire party—Paula, Kraus, Poliakov, Neumann, and a pair of hotel porters—got out and moved en masse toward her room. An old woman was sitting on a wooden chair, strategically positioned so that she could see both the elevators and the staircase. She had a samovar of tea beside her and a notebook on her lap. As they all passed by, Poliakov nodded at her and she began scribbling in her book.

"What's she doing?" Paula whispered to Neumann.

"Watching," the diplomat replied, in an equally low voice. "Everyone who goes in or out of any room will be noted and reported." He grinned at her impishly. "There's another woman just like her on every floor of the hotel. So never try to conduct an illicit affair in a Russian hotel. You'll be found out instantly!"

For a second she wondered if he somehow knew about her and Kraus. Was he warning her off? Then she spotted the look of slight disappointment on his face. He'd been joking and was hoping for a more enthusiastic response. She smiled at him and said: "I'm sorry . . . I'm just a little tired by the journey."

"Of course," he said, his pride satisfied.

The flight had gotten into Moscow shortly after two in the afternoon. By the time they were all settled it was past five. Neumann bade them farewell and they were left in Poliakov's hands. He told them that he would wait in the lobby for an hour while they unpacked, washed, and changed: just long enough, Paula realized, for one or both of them to do something potentially incriminating if they thought they were no longer under observation. They might, for example, have decided to make love, but when she and Kraus were finally alone he simply jerked his head in the direction of the old woman, rolled his eyes, put on an exaggeratedly sad face, and pretended to slit his throat with his finger. Paula giggled and mouthed a little air-kiss in Kraus's direction, loving him for making her laugh and shining a brief ray of sunshine through the clouds that had lowered over her for the past few hours.

At the agreed time, they rejoined Poliakov and were led to a large black Zil limousine that was waiting outside the hotel. Poliakov barked a series of orders to the driver and they set off through Red Square, past the great redbrick walls of the Kremlin, the gaggle of people outside Lenin's mausoleum, and the massed onion domes of St. Basil's Cathedral. After a brief guided tour of central Moscow, they were taken to a performance of *Swan Lake* at the Bolshoi Ballet. All the color missing from the rest of the city was suddenly, gloriously restored in the gold and scarlet interior of the theater and the gorgeous costumes of the performers. And for all the tragedy of the drama, the luscious passion of Tchaikovsky's music combined with the beauty of the ballerinas' movements—their delicate limbs stretching and swaying so gracefully, yet with such absolute precision—to transport Paula far away from the real world and all its troubles.

"I was watching you even more than the dancers," said Kraus as they were leaving. "You were as wide-eyed as a little girl and so completely absorbed." He leaned his great head down toward hers and murmured: "I've never seen you look more beautiful." She treasured those words all evening, basking in their warmth.

They moved on to a restaurant where the Chicken Kiev turned out to be better than she'd expected. The men drank vodka and talked about the war. When Poliakov discovered that Kraus had never set foot on Russian soil, but had only ever killed British and Americans, he decided that he was a splendid fellow and made one toast after another, downing a glass with everyone. Paula had never seen Kraus the worse for wear, no matter how much he drank, but even he was finding it hard to match a Russian's capacity for alcohol. She was glad for once that her gender ruled her out of the competition, and limited herself to a few glasses of sweet Soviet champagne, another of the occasional treats for the senses that the communist system allowed. As she watched the men lose themselves in alcohol she worried that this might all be part of a plot to render Kraus unconscious and open to blackmail, but when the meal ended and they staggered out toward the waiting Zil limousine, arm-in-arm and singing "The Red Flag," she concluded that this was nothing more than a good excuse for a mid-ranking Ministry of Justice official to get very, very drunk at the state's expense.

The following day they got down to work. Poliakov, who seemed remarkably unaffected by the excesses of the night before, took them from the hotel to a virtually identical ministerial building. There they were greeted by the head archivist, a woman introduced as Dr. Sofinskaya, who led them to a meeting room where a number of large ring-bound folders lay stacked on a large table.

"These files were all seized when the Red Army liberated Minsk in July 1944," said Poliakov. Last night's bonhomie had faded from his voice as he continued: "They were found in the SS headquarters and detail the many vile, unforgivable atrocities inflicted by the Nazi fascists on the Russian people. I will leave you now, but Dr. Sofinskaya will remain to assist you. I hope you find what you need."

Kraus and Paula divided up the files and began to work through them. Many of the papers were of no relevance to the forthcoming trial, but every so often Paula came across something that might prove useful and handed it to Sofinskaya to be duplicated. The documents provided absolute proof, if any were needed, that terrible crimes had been committed. Here were office memoranda, written orders, field reports from junior squadleaders, correspondence with Berlin, and detailed train timetables. Yet all of this was dry, impersonal data. Heuser was mentioned in one or two documents, and some even linked him tenuously with the crimes he was accused of, but jurors, and even judges, need their emotions as well as their intellects to be stirred if a criminal case is to be won, and there was, as yet, nothing here to signal what kind of a man they were really dealing with, or to paint the full horror of what he and his codefendants had done.

Paula was beginning to fear that the trip might turn out to be less of a breakthrough than they had hoped when she found a memo, sent from Heuser to a senior official in the local Reichsbahn office, one Saturday morning in May 1942 at the start of the Pentecost holiday weekend. At first, as she skimmed through the contents, only half reading them, it seemed as inconsequential as all the other papers: just a four-point summary of the agreement made at a meeting between one of Heuser's men and the railway official's team. A delivery was due to be made that weekend, and the Reichsbahn had clearly been unwilling to alter their timetable. On the other hand, Heuser's people were adamant that they could not deal with the goods until the end of the holiday weekend. In the end a working compromise had settled the immediate problem, and procedures had been agreed that would prevent its recurrence. The memo ended with the sort of honeyed words that signal peace—however temporary—in any bureaucratic conflict: *"With my special thanks for your consideration and understanding in this matter, Dr. Georg Heuser."*

"Ha! Even his signature is a lie," Paula thought to herself. And then something nagged at her, a single word in the sentence that followed the third bullet-point. She went back to the top of the letter and read it again. Then, as a feeling of physical sickness rose in her stomach at the sight of those poisonous words, she went through it a third time. She read slowly, deliberately, considering the full implications of exactly what Heuser had written and, even more importantly, what he'd left off the page. For hidden between the lines of this everyday piece of office correspondence was a story of suffering that was almost too terrible for her to contemplate, let alone comprehend. Here was a callous, institutionalized indifference to the most fundamental principles of human decency, and was clearly taken for granted by both the sender and recipients of the memorandum.

Paula's personal distress at the reawakened memory of her father's death now vanished from her mind. Her entire concentration was focused on this letter, and now her initial moral outrage was giving way to a hard-nosed legal calculation about its value as a trial document.

She pushed the pieces of paper a few centimeters away from her and raised her eyes. "Come here," she said to Kraus. "I've found something that you really need to see."

21

BERLIN: JULY–OCTOBER 1941

On the morning of July 4, I was in the squad room when a call was put through from the front desk. Biene took it and then came over to me, since I was the only detective around at that moment. "There's a man downstairs who says he used to work at Rummelsburg station. He thinks he might have information about the S-Bahn case," she said. "Do you want me to go and get him? I can have them tell him to put a statement in writing, if you'd prefer."

At this point there was no straw so flimsy that any of us would not grab at it.

"I'll hear what he has to say. Take him to the interview room."

"I'm on my way," said Biene.

A few minutes later she led a scrawny, gray-haired man, with a face battered by an outdoor life and a diet of cigarettes and cheap schnapps, into the interview room. He was carrying a shapeless brown hat, clutched tightly in his fingers, and wore a tatty black suit whose fabric was shiny with decades of wear. His name, he said, was Helmut Schwibs.

"I cleaned the platforms at Rummelsburg, see?" he told me. "Forty-eight years on the S-Bahn, man and boy I was, through the last war and this one. I'm retired now, mind—turned sixty-five in April, and that was it."

"So what is it you want to tell us, Herr Schwibs?"

"Well, it's about this feller used to work at Rummelsburg."

"What was his name?"

"That's just it, I can't remember. I mean, I know the name, it's on the tip of my tongue. Just slipped my mind, is all."

"I see. And what did he do, this unnamed man?"

"He climbed over the fence, didn't he."

I sighed to myself. Had it really come to this? Were we really so desperate that I was wasting time on a foolish old man with a story that made no sense about a man whose name he couldn't remember?

"I don't know if he climbed the fence," I said, trying to summon up the patience to finish the interview, instead of just throwing Schwibs out on his ear, there and then. "That's what I'm hoping you'll tell me. What fence are we talking about?"

"The fence on the side of the track, of course. That's what he jumped over. I asked him what he was doing, bunking off in the middle of a shift, and he said he had this woman and he was going to see her."

A bell in the back of my mind started ringing, telling me to start taking this man seriously. I cannot say why, but I had a strong, instinctive feeling that Schwibs was talking about the killer.

"This man of yours, did he go over the fence at night or in the daytime?"

Schwibs thought for a moment. "I'm pretty certain it was night . . . Yeah, that's right, it must've been, 'cos I only saw him on account of there was a signal lamp and so I could see there was someone there. You know, by the fence."

"How many times did you see this happen?"

"I dunno . . . two or three. I couldn't rightly say."

My next question was a long shot: "Can you remember exactly when these times were?"

Schwibs scratched his silver head with grimy fingernails. "Nah, not really. I don't keep a diary or nothing like that. It was winter though, I reckon."

"A name, Herr Schwibs . . . It really would help us a lot if you could give us a name."

He grunted. He looked around the room, almost as if he were hoping that the name had magically been written on one of the walls, or even the ceiling. He scratched his head again and then used the back of the same hand to wipe his nose on the way down. Then he shook his head. "No, sorry, gone completely. Tell you what though, if I remember, I'll let you know."

Great God Almighty! I came within a whisker of losing my temper, but managed to restrain myself to force out a terse "Thank you, Herr Schwibs, we will look forward to that. You may leave now."

I watched him depart, being led by Biene back down to the entrance. Yet again, there had been the slightest flicker of hope that the killer might finally be emerging from the thick fog of confusion and ignorance that surrounded this case, and yet again he'd disappeared before we could get a good look at his face. He seemed to be mocking us: now you see me, now you don't. All I wanted, more than anything else, was the chance to grab him before he vanished again; to put my hand on his shoulder, feel his physical presence beneath my hand, and tell him: "You're coming with us."

The next two days were occupied with Lüdtke's eight suspects. We questioned them. We spoke to their wives, their coworkers, their bosses, and their known associates. And then we let them go. There was simply no reason to keep them. In seven cases they had alibis, backed up by witnesses that stood up to all our attempts to disprove them. The only man who could not account for his whereabouts at the time of the latest murder was called Paul Ogorzow. I took his statement. He told me that he'd been working late and his wife had been asleep when he'd come home, so she couldn't con-firm that he was lying in bed beside her during the crucial hours between midnight and two. But as any defense lawyer would point out, that only proved that Ogorzow was a thoughtful husband who made sure not to wake his wife. And there was little in any of our other evidence to justify making him a suspect.

I remembered Ogorzow from his file, partly because he was, like me, twenty-eight. He had actually been stopped and questioned at Karlshorst station, back in September 1940, after the initial spate of nonfatal attacks. Further information had been accumulated on him, as it had on a huge number of other men, of course. But the investiga-tion into him had been closed on December 23, 1940, simply because there was no good reason whatsoever to continue it.

Ogorzow had worked for the Reichsbahn since signing on as a laborer in 1934, and his superiors ever since, without exception, had regarded him as hardworking and reliable. He was called up in Janu-ary 1940, served in the invasion of France, and then invalided home in mid-July with a wounded wrist. The injury hadn't prevented him from returning to work on the railways. For the past year, he'd been an assistant signalman at Rummelsburg. The stationmaster there spoke particularly highly of him. Ogorzow, he said, had become a sort of factotum: running errands for him, doing odd jobs, and even making him breakfast from time to time.

His personal life was equally beyond reproach. He married his wife, Gertrude, a former saleswoman, on June 5, 1937. She was two years his junior and already had a daughter from a previous relationship. Ogorzow and Gertrude had a son of their own. Immediately after their marriage the couple lived with Ogorzow's mother, Marie Saga, in her family apartment at 24 Dorotheastrasse, a mid-nineteenth-century building in Karlshorst, near the station. They later moved to a ground-floor apartment of their own in the same building. It had a garden and a small cherry orchard, where Ogorzow liked to pass the time and play with his children.

So here we had a good, honest German workingman. He wasn't particularly tall and had a light build—in that he conformed to the descriptions given by the women who had survived the S-Bahn murderer's attacks. But then, so did a great many men in Berlin. In other respects, however, Ogorzow didn't remotely answer to the picture we had built up of our man. Insofar as the women described their assailant's face, for example, they were agreed that he had a straight nose. Ogorzow had a crooked nose that looked as if it had been broken and then not properly reset.

As if that were not enough to rule him out, he was a sergeant in the SA, having joined the Party in 1931 and the Brownshirts in '32. By definition, a loyal National Socialist was incapable of committing crimes as heinous as these. He'd even taken part in SA operations to guard women in and around the stations on the No. 3 line and on the trains themselves. In short, there was every reason to keep his file closed and none whatsoever to reopen it.

Lüdtke, however, was possessed by one of those obsessions that sometimes strike even the greatest police detectives. Something about Ogorzow had got under his skin. He was convinced that this was our man and wouldn't listen to any counterarguments. I wasn't quite sure then, nor am I any the wiser now, about why Lüdtke felt the way he did. Perhaps it was a simple physical response. For all his golden reputation, Ogorzow didn't look like the picture of Aryan perfection. His face was set into an expression of sullen resentment, as if he were dissatisfied with his lot in life and wanted someone to blame. But how much did he really have to complain about? He'd been born illegitimate in Muntau, East Prussia. His mother was a farm servant who had gotten herself pregnant and his father was never named: the surname Ogorzow came from a subsequent one of his mother's lovers, who adopted young Paul when he was eleven. Illegitimacy carried a stigma, true enough, but his childhood was hardly the violent, sexually abusive hell in which Peter Kürten grew up, and no worse than countless other bastard children have had to cope with. His life now, working in a secure job, far from the front line, and going home every night to his wife and family, was one that millions of German men could only dream of. Yet the fact that he was an irritating, ungrateful little man with a face one wanted to punch hardly gave reasonable grounds to call Paul Ogorzow a criminal.

I did, however, spot another tiny scrap of evidence, though it was utterly circumstantial. There had been a gap in the original Friedrichsfelde attacks between December 1939 and July 1940 that exactly fitted the time Ogorzow was away with the army. I pointed it out to Lüdtke, suggesting it gave us a basis for reopening the investigation into Paul Ogorzow. But then we finally caught a break and the investigation was sent off in a very different direction.

22

Two knee-prints and a set of footprints had been found near Frieda Koziol's body. The footprints consisted only of the soles of the shoes that had made them—no heel marks at all—suggesting that they belonged to someone who was running. The obvious explanation was that the killer had got down on his knees to examine his victim, been disturbed for some reason and then fled the scene of his crime. Find the shoes that made these prints and we would have our man.

The prints led away down the path for fifty meters before they disappeared. We'd tried to pick up the trail beyond that point, but not even our best police dog was able to follow it. But all was not lost, for the footprints bore a distinctive pattern. Our forensics people took a plaster cast and were able to identify the shoe as a Salamander "Podiatrist," size 40, sold in the Salamander shoe company's own stores.

"We've got him!" shouted Lüdtke exultantly, when he heard that news. He knew now that it was just a matter of time and hard work. Anyone buying shoes required special coupons. More than twenty thousand coupons, issued to men in the districts of Berlin surrounding the area in which the killings had occurred, were cross-referenced with coupons used to purchase size 40 Salamander Podiatrist shoes.

A man was found who lived just a hundred meters from the path on which Koziol had been killed.

His shoes exactly matched our plaster cast.

He was a known sex offender.

But he was not Paul Ogorzow.

His name was Hermann Wirtig. He worked as a carpenter, but in his spare time he was a Peeping Tom whose particular pleasure was to creep around the Karlshorst area, looking for women who'd neglected to draw their bedroom curtains, couples making love in the open, or any other glimpse of someone else's sexuality with which he could feed his pathetic fantasies.

Wirtig admitted that he'd stumbled across Koziol's body on the path that night. He even confessed that he'd stuck his hand in his pants and masturbated at the sight of her lying there. But that, he swore, was all he'd done. He'd not even realized she was dead at first: in the darkness it was hard to tell. But once he'd seen the terrible wound to the side of her skull he panicked and ran off as fast as his legs would carry him.

It was very, very tempting to pin the whole S-Bahn case on Wirtig. Any half-decent group of detectives could have beaten a desperate confession out of him—the kind that is given to avoid further punishment—cooked up some evidence, and had him convicted. God knows it would have made our lives easier. The Koziol killing had infuriated Heydrich. Yet another dead woman for the public to talk about and no sign whatsoever of her murderer—it smacked of disorder, incompetence, lack of control: all the things that the Nazi Party despised and feared most. Impatience at the Reich Security Main Office was growing by the hour. Influential voices were starting to suggest that since the Berlin murder squad seemed incapable of doing their jobs, it was time someone else was brought in to do it for them. If that happened, the consequences for those of us who had been seen to fail would not be pleasant. We feared we might find ourselves putting on Waffen-SS uniforms and getting first-row tickets to the Russian Front. And all Lüdtke had to do to make everyone happy was take a man who'd confessed to being in the presence of the murder victim on the night she died and name him as the S-Bahn murderer.

Lüdtke wouldn't do it.

"What would people say, if they saw that this was the way we do things in Germany?" he insisted. And what, he might have added, will people say if we arrest the wrong man and the killings continue?

So back we went to Paul Ogorzow. Through all the months of frustration, the men's loyalty to Lüdtke had remained unshakable. Now, for the first time, it began to be strained as we grew more and more committed to what many of us believed was a wild-goose chase. The only source of any good humor whatsoever was provided by Helmut Schwibs. He'd taken to visiting Alex almost every day and giving us the name of the man who he thought had jumped over the fence. Three times he tried and three times he failed. Two of the men he named adamantly denied doing any such thing, and could prove that they were never on night shifts at Rummelsburg. The third name didn't belong to any S-Bahn worker at all. Baum and Richter began a competition to see if anyone could guess the name that Schwibs would come up with next. *Winston Churchill* was the most popular choice, followed by *Lili Marlene*.

On July 9, Schwibs turned up at Alex for a fifth time. When the call came through to the squad room there was heated debate about whether to let him up again or not. Frei was dead set against it. He regarded Schwibs as nothing more than an absurd distraction from our proper jobs, and for once I could see his point. Baum and Richter, of course, just wanted to find out whom he would name today. In the end it was Lüdtke who sighed: "Oh, what the hell, let's hear what the old fool has to say for himself now."

So Schwibs came up to the squad room and was greeted with a cheery cry from Baum of "Morning, Helmut!" As always, the old man was wearing the same shiny black suit. His hands worked nervously at the felt of his old brown hat as a small crowd of detectives gathered around to discover what today's name would be.

"So, Herr Schwibs, what would you like to tell us?" Lüdtke asked.

Schwibs swallowed hard. He shuffled his feet. "I've got the name," he said. "And this time it's the right one. I know it is."

"And what is this name?" Lüdtke asked.

"Adolf Galland!" Baum shouted, referring to the Luftwaffe's greatest ace.

Schwibs looked appalled. "Oh no, it's not him," he said. "I'd never say nothing bad about a hero like Colonel Galland. Never! I mean I'm a loyal citizen, I . . ."

It was clear that he thought we might at any moment arrest him for treason. Lüdtke flashed a furious look at Baum and then said, "Don't worry, Herr Schwibs. No one seriously thinks you were going to name Galland. So who was it really? Who climbed over that fence?"

The room fell silent. Schwibs said nothing. I feared he'd forgotten what he came here to say. The silence continued—for an eternity, it seemed. Then, at last, Helmut Schwibs gathered his scattered nerves together, took a deep breath and said, "Ogorzow. The man's name was Paul Ogorzow."

In German law, even Nazi German law, a criminal can be arrested only with a warrant issued by a court at the request of a public prosecutor. Of course, in those days we had the power to take political prisoners into so-called protective custody, which is to say, internment without trial in a concentration camp. But for a homicide case such as this, the principles enshrined for decades in the Code of Criminal Procedure still applied, albeit with some adjustments. It took two more days for us to assemble our evidence and have it put before a judge. The case we made against Ogorzow was not a strong one, but in 1941 the National Socialist League of German Jurists ensured that every judge in the land understood the importance of acting in the best interests of the Party and the state, which were effectively one and the same thing. The Party wanted the S-Bahn murderer arrested and convicted as soon as possible. There was a possibility, however distant, that the arrest of Ogorzow would enable this to happen. Therefore we got our warrant.

"I want you to make the arrest," Lüdtke said as we left the courtroom.

I was overwhelmed at the honor, but not quite able to believe it. "Are you sure?" I asked. "After all this time, don't you want to be the one to bring him in?"

Lüdtke shook his head. "No, I want to be the one who makes him admit that he did it. And it'll do you good. You've got to make your first arrest at some point or other. Why not start with a big one? Besides, I need a good night's sleep. I want to be as sharp as a razor when I sit down to interview this man."

There was precious little sleep for me that night. The arrest was carried out on July 12 at four in the morning, the best hour to catch any man at his weakest and most befuddled. I posted men around the building to make sure that Ogorzow couldn't escape, and then rapped hard on the door of his apartment. There was no response. I knocked again. A few more seconds went by and then a woman's sleepy voice called out: "Hang on, I'm coming."

The door opened to reveal Gertrude Ogorzow, knotting the belt of the dressing gown that was covering her otherwise naked body. She was only thirty-nine but looked older: feeding, clothing, and caring for a family were not easy tasks for women in wartime. There was a bicycle behind her, propped up against the wall.

"Is your husband at home?" I asked.

"Of course," she mumbled.

A small boy appeared, peering around the bicycle's rear wheel and wanting to know what was happening. Gertrude shooed him back to his room.

"Where is he, your husband?" I asked.

"The room at the end, on the right," she said, jerking her head toward a door at the far end of the hall.

"Excuse me, please," I said and walked down the hall past the woman and her child, who was still lingering, desperate to see what was going on. I'd not gotten far when Ogorzow himself appeared, dressed in nothing more than a pair of black pants. He was fiddling with the top buttons of his fly, trying to make himself decent. He looked up at me with that dull, surly expression of his and said: "Oh, you . . . What do you want, then?"

"I have a warrant for your arrest. You are charged with the murder of Frieda Koziol and seven other women. You will come with me to Criminal Police headquarters, immediately."

"Why? I've done nothing wrong!"

I ignored his plea. "Get dressed, now."

Two of my men were loitering by the front door, waiting for instructions. I told one of them: "Go with him. Make sure that he doesn't try anything."

Ogorzow and the police officer went into the bedroom. The daughter had now appeared next to her brother, and Gertrude was trying to push them both back into their bedroom. She finally closed the door, snapped an exhausted, infuriated "Now just stay there till I tell you to come out!" and turned to me.

"What the hell is going on?" she said. "My husband is a respectable man. He's been questioned, followed, taken up to Alexanderplatz. Now this. Why won't you leave us alone?"

"We have reason to suspect that he may be involved in a number of very serious crimes," I said, trying to keep my voice calm. I might be a police officer, but she was a woman on the verge of hysteria and I had no intention of driving her any closer. "Please pay attention to me, Frau Ogorzow. My men have orders to seize all of your husband's clothes, shoes, and personal belongings for forensic examination. You will assist them to do this as quickly and efficiently as possible. If you do not cooperate with them, there will be consequences. Do I make myself clear?"

She glared at me, not saying a word.

"I'll ask you again: do you understand what I just told you?"

"Oh yes, I understand that you're taking my Paul. I understand that you want his clothes and all that. But why? That's what I don't understand."

"We have reason to believe that your husband is involved with the S-Bahn murders."

"My husband? Don't be daft! What on earth makes you think that?"

Not a lot, I thought to myself. To Gertrude Ogorzow, however, I said: "I am not at liberty to discuss this matter any further. I repeat: you will please assist my men with all their inquiries. A receipt will be issued to you for any property taken from these premises."

Ogorzow emerged from his bedroom, fully dressed with his hands cuffed. "I'll take him from here," I told the police officer. "Turn this place upside down. I want everything this shit-bag owns over at Alex, fast."

Twenty minutes later, Ogorzow was sitting in a police cell. Lüdtke had left specific instructions that he was not to be allowed to sleep before his interrogation. He could have one tin cup of water, but no food. Nor could he be told anything further about the case, or our case against him. The interrogation would begin at nine o'clock sharp.

23

As Lüdtke's assistant my job was to watch, listen, take notes, and keep my mouth shut. I suppose I'd been hoping for some moment of genius in which my boss would, like the hero of a cheap crime novel, reveal some crucial piece of evidence or brilliant deduction, hitherto kept secret even from his fellow detectives, that would force our man to crack and admit all. Instead, the first session with Ogorzow was a frustrating, even depressing affair.

Lüdtke was dressed quite formally in a smart suit and tie, with his Nazi Party badge in his lapel. He would always make sure to have it clearly visible whenever he was with Ogorzow, a detail whose significance would only become evident several days later. Now he sat down opposite Ogorzow. There was nothing between them on the table. Lüdtke liked to make his connection with suspects as direct and uncluttered as possible.

"You climbed over the fence by Rummelsburg station when you should have been at work," Lüdtke began. "Why did you do that?"

"No, I never," Ogorzow replied, sleepily. He yawned and rubbed his eyes. He didn't just look tired, he seemed bored by the entire proceedings.

"Don't lie to me," Lüdtke told him. He slammed the table, as much as if he were trying to attract Ogorzow's attention as to frighten him into an answer. "We know you went over the fence. You were seen and you know it. So don't act like you don't know what I'm talking about. Why did you go over the fence?"

"I told you. I never went over the fence."

And so it went on . . . and on . . . and on: the same questions, the same denials, again and again, around and around. Soon I felt almost as exhausted and bored as Ogorzow: I'd been up even longer than him, after all. Finally Lüdtke said: "You went over the fence so that you could go and kill innocent women, smash them over the head, isn't that right?"

That was the first time Lüdtke had mentioned the murders, and it produced the first fractional weakening in Ogorzow's resolve.

His voice went up in pitch from a grumpy mumble to a resentful whine: "What do you mean, smash them over the head? What are you talking about?"

"You know what I'm talking about. I'm talking about all the women you killed. After you'd jumped over the fence. Because that's what you did, isn't it? You skived off in the middle of your shift, got over the fence, and went looking for a woman to kill."

"No, that's not what happened at all. I didn't kill nobody."

"But you did go over the fence. So what really happened?"

"You got a cigarette?" Ogorzow asked.

"Of course." Lüdtke took out his gunmetal case. The fancy French cigarettes had all gone long ago. Now he was smoking the same blend of weeds and sawdust as everyone else. He handed Ogorzow a cigarette and lit it for him. Then he waited until Ogorzow had had a couple of puffs before he said: "So, what really happened when you went over the fence?"

Interrogation is like a game of poker. Sometimes the person on the other side of the table keeps their intentions as well hidden as their cards. But then there are times when, for all their efforts, they cannot help but reveal themselves. This was one of those. Ogorzow said nothing, but his face betrayed the calculations he was making as he tried to come up with a story good enough to satisfy our curiosity without causing him serious trouble.

"I saw a woman, that's true, but I didn't do her no harm," he said. "What happened, right, was every day I used to hang the temporary signal lights out on the track. There's houses next to it and there was this woman in one of them, proper tasty she looked and all. She used to hang out her washing most days, right about the time I went by. I reckon she did it deliberately, you know: 'I'm here if you want me.' We gets to talking over the fence and she says her husband's away at the front, in the army. So I says: 'You must get lonely, all alone in that house, without a man around the place.' And she laughs, all flirty like, and, well, that's how it started."

"How what started?"

"What do you think?"

"You began a sexual relationship."

Ogorzow possessed a certain animal cunning, there was no doubt about that. But he was fundamentally very stupid. And one of the signs of his stupidity was his misguided belief that he was actually a very clever, shrewd individual who could run rings around thick-headed policemen. "Ohhh," he said, adopting an exaggerated, mincing tone. "'You began a sexual relationship' . . . Yeah, I nailed her, if that's what you mean. And she was begging me for it, and all."

"So what was her name, this woman who was begging for it?"

A look of alarm crossed Ogorzow's face. "I don't want to tell you that. I mean, if her man finds out he'll kill me."

Lüdtke smiled affably. "Ogorzow, listen to me, and pay attention now. You really don't want to be worrying about the odd angry husband here or there. Think about it. You're sitting in Alex. We're very reasonable men here. We play by the rules. But all I have to do is stick you in a car and send you off to Prinz-Albrecht-Strasse, and once my Gestapo colleagues have taken care of you for a couple of days . . . well, you know how it is down there."

There wasn't a man, woman, or child in Germany who wasn't all too aware of the tortures—real or imagined—that the Gestapo could inflict. Ogorzow was no exception. For the first time he was genuinely scared.

"She's called Kluge," he said. "Frau Elise Kluge."

"There, you see? That wasn't so difficult. And now you can go back to your cell."

Ogorzow was led away. When he was out of sight and earshot, Lüdtke leaned against a wall, his eyes closed, as if exhausted by what had actually been a relatively short interrogation. He took a deep breath, exhaled slowly, then reached for a cigarette of his own.

"He did it, I'm sure he did. I'd bet everything I've got on it," he said, the unlit cigarette in his mouth, speaking as much to himself as to me. "But we don't have him and he knows it." He lit up and drew the smoke deep into his lungs. "I need a confession. God knows how we're going to get it, though."

I waited for a moment while Lüdtke smoked some more, still deep in thought. Then I asked him, "What do you want me to do?"

"Find this Kluge woman. See if his story checks out. And see if you can get any dates off her. Maybe they'll match some of the crimes. Though, come to think of it, we'll be no better off if they do. His defense will just be that he couldn't have killed this or that woman if he was screwing another woman at the same time."

Lüdtke threw his cigarette end onto the interview room floor and stamped on it two or three times, not so much extinguishing as pulverizing it. "I hate this damn case," he muttered, and stalked out, not bothering to see if I was following. After we'd gone another ten meters down the corridor he stopped dead so suddenly that I almost bumped into him.

"And get onto the forensics people. Tell them I need something, anything, that ties Ogorzow to the killings. If they start bleating they need time, remind them that we don't have time. I won't be able to hold Ogorzow unless I can find proper, concrete, reliable evidence against him. So they'd better get it to me. Now!"

I asked Biene to get me an address for a Frau Elise Kluge, living near Rummelsburg station, then went down to the forensic science department to pass on the first part of Lüdtke's message. The men in the white coats reacted precisely as he'd anticipated, so then I gave them the second part, making it perfectly plain that they would be held to account if we had to let this serial killer back onto the streets. By the time I got back to the squad room Biene had an address for me.

The simplest way to describe Elise Kluge was that she was the sort of woman who would think that Paul Ogorzow, a low-level railway worker with an unimpressive physique, lifeless oyster eyes, a broken nose, and a sullen pout, was an attractive proposition for an extramarital affair. She admitted that she'd been seeing him and, after a little more persuasion on my part, that she'd been sleeping with him too. She could say that they'd been at it for several months, but she couldn't be specific about dates: "I don't exactly keep a lover's diary, if you know what I mean."

So Ogorzow's story checked out. For the rest of the day, Lüdtke had us all running around that same Rummelsburg-Friedrichsfelde-Karlshorst corner of Berlin, trying to get him something he could use in his next interrogation.

There wasn't much. I went to Rummelsburg and interviewed the stationmaster again. He repeated his assurances that Ogorzow had been an exemplary worker. But then, in a moment of vanity, he let slip that he was on very good terms with one of the senior managers at the Reichsbahn and had been kept fully up to date with all the police operations. I asked if he'd passed any of this information on to Paul

Ogorzow, and the stationmaster naturally denied it, but I was certain now that this was the means by which the killer had stayed ahead of all our plans.

A butcher called Schumann had another interesting story to tell me, albeit one with no value as evidence. Schumann's shop was at 25 Dorotheastrasse, right next door to Ogorzow's apartment building. Schumann had been putting up a police poster asking for information about the S-Bahn murderer when Ogorzow had walked by.

"Maybe he lives next door," Schumann had said, lightheartedly.

Ogorzow had laughed. "Maybe you're right," he replied.

24

By midmorning on July 13, more than twenty-four hours had passed since Ogorzow had last been interrogated and we were still no nearer to unearthing any evidence to incriminate him. Then one of the forensics boys called. They'd found blood on Ogorzow's S-Bahn uniform: a microscopic amount on the sleeve of his jacket and enough on the crotch of the pants to be visible to the human eye. "There's not enough to tell the blood-type," he said. "But it's definitely human."

The news hit the murder squad like a dose of smelling salts. Men who were depressed, exhausted, and devoid of all energy suddenly sprang to life. Lüdtke had Ogorzow summoned from his cell, and questioned him once again.

Naturally, Ogorzow had a story to explain it all away. He'd had sex with his wife just a few days before he'd been arrested. "I reckon the blood came from her," Ogorzow said. "She was on the rag, know what I mean?"

We got back to work again. The first news was not good. When asked about her husband's claims, Gertrude Ogorzow confirmed that they had indeed made love when she was menstruating. Frau Kluge, on the other hand, said that she didn't believe a word of it. "Paul hates it when it's that time of the month. He says it disgusts him. Scares him, more like, if you ask me."

Forensics took another look at the pants. There was no way of telling whether the blood came from Frau Ogorzow or not, they said, but the pattern was not consistent with the description Ogorzow had given. The type of contact he'd described would lead to a smear of blood, but the pattern on his pants was more of a spatter. That was much more consistent with blood spurting or splashing from a wound.

"A wound like a blow to the skull with a blunt object?" Lüdtke asked.

"Yes," said the man from forensics, "exactly like that."

I was sent to question Gertrude Ogorzow yet again. This time she admitted that there was no truth to her husband's story. They hadn't had sex in the way he'd claimed. I got the feeling her faith in him was starting to crack. He must have told her so many stories over the years, given so many explanations for his strange moods and late-night absences. Perhaps she'd assumed that he was having an affair. If he was a good provider and treated her well, that was something she might forgive. Rape and murder were another story. As I left her I wondered just how well he really had treated her. Whatever the friends and neighbors might say, no outsiders ever really knew what went on in a marriage. I found it hard to believe that a man who could brutalize women the way that Ogorzow did would be sweetness and light with his wife.

By now there was no one in the murder squad who doubted that Lüdtke had got the right man. After work, the talk in the late-night bar was all about the old man's incredible instinct for sniffing out killers, no matter how unlikely they seemed.

"You wouldn't think Ogorzow had it in him, to look at him," Baum said. "He's such a scrawny little creep. I reckon a decent-size woman is probably stronger than he is."

And then it came to me, the common denominator that linked all the women he'd attacked: women of different ages, classes, and professions, who seemed to have so little in common. "That's it!" I exclaimed. "The victims—they're all small!"

"You sure?" Richter asked. "I don't remember that."

"That's because you weren't looking for it, none of us were. But trust me. Those files are engraved into my brain. All his victims are a meter fifty-five or less. I'm sure of it."

I went back to Alex, got out the victims' files, and looked up all their heights. Sure enough, they were all, without exception, petite. Lüdtke had gone home for the night, but first thing next morning I informed him of my discovery. To my disappointment he didn't seem as excited as I was. "It's interesting," he said. "Once we've gotten him to confess, it's a handy piece of information to throw at him. Maybe it will help explain why he does it. But right now, there are other avenues I want to explore with Herr Ogorzow."

It would soon become apparent that the Commissar was speaking the literal truth. But when we sat down again with Ogorzow, Lüdtke began by informing him that his story about the menstrual blood was in tatters. "The scientists say it's the wrong kind of blood, and your wife's admitted you never had sex when she was having a period."

"She never," Ogorzow insisted. "She wouldn't say nothing against me."

"Wouldn't, or wouldn't dare?" Lüdtke asked.

Ogorzow didn't reply.

"Well, that's all done with anyway," said Lüdtke. "There's blood on your clothes. It came from someone you battered to death. We'll find out who it was soon enough. But that's not what I want to talk about now. No, I want to know how you get to work."

That surprised Ogorzow. He looked distinctly unsettled and ill-at-ease. "Sorry, I'm not with you," he said, presumably trying to buy some time to work out what he needed to say.

"It's a simple question. You live in Karlshorst. You work at Rummelsburg. That's about four kilometers away. So how do you get from home to work and back again every day?"

"I dunno. Depends, really. Lots of different ways."

I leaned over to Lüdtke and whispered: "He had a man's bicycle in the hall of his apartment."

"Do you walk?" Lüdtke asked.

"Yeah, maybe, sometimes."

"I'm not surprised. It's a very nice area. Walking through all the allotments, past the gardens and orchards on a nice summer's morning. Who could ask for anything more pleasant?"

Ogorzow nodded enthusiastically. "Oh yeah, very pleasant. Absolutely."

"But still, it's a fair way to walk every day, four kilometers. I dare say you probably cycle a lot of the time too."

Again Ogorzow nodded. "Yeah, yeah . . . I do that and all."

Lüdtke had a map, folded up beside him. Now he opened it up and spread it on the table between him and Ogorzow. It covered those oh-so-familiar areas of eastern Berlin, showing every road and track, down to the smallest footpath.

"Here's Dorotheastrasse, where you live," Lüdtke said, placing his forefinger on the map. "And over . . . ah . . . here is Rummelsburg station. Now, how do you get between those two places?"

"I couldn't rightly say. I'm not very good with maps, me."

"Oh, I'm sure you're not that bad," Lüdtke said, encouragingly. "A man like you, working on the railways—don't tell me you can't look at a map and work out exactly where you're supposed to place one of those signal lamps you were talking about."

"Well, yeah, a railway map, maybe. But this is different, isn't it?"

"No it isn't," said Lüdtke, suddenly as cold as ice. "It's a map, just the same as any other map. It shows an area you know like the back of your hand. You're very well aware of the paths you walk along, or cycle along, when you go to work. So stop jerking me around and tell me which ones they are."

Ogorzow gave in. "Oh all right, then. Here . . ." He gave a desultory wave of his hand that just about traced a route along the map. "I go that way some of the time. Or this way here."

Now Lüdtke and I were the ones who had to play poker, for we had just been dealt a winning hand if only we could use it. Women had been attacked on both the routes Ogorzow had described: women who had survived and might just be able to identify Ogorzow as their assailant.

"That's very interesting," Lüdtke said to him. "Very interesting indeed. Now, tell me, what else have you done when you've been going along these paths?"

"I've not done nothing. I walk. Or I go on my bike. That's it."

"Really. So when you happen to meet a woman, out by herself at night, you just raise your cap and wish her good evening. Is that it?"

"Yeah, well, something like that."

"Bullshit. You're lying to me, Ogorzow, and you know it as well as I do. You attack women on those paths. You hit them. You stab them . . ."

He looked blankly back at Lüdtke. "No, I never."

"You raped them . . ."

"No."

"You killed at least two of them . . ."

"No, I didn't kill no one."

"So what did you do? All these women that you met along the way . . . what did you do to the women?"

Silence had fallen on the interview room, but it felt as though Lüdtke's words were still vibrating, unheard, in the air all around us. Ogorzow sat dumbly, yet his face was once again telling us exactly how much trouble he knew he was in. He was chewing and twitching his lips. His eyes were blinking. Now he flopped forward and rested his head in his hands as if the weight of all his guilt had become insupportable. Finally, he raised his head again and said: "All right, maybe I was a bit cheeky. But that was all."

"Cheeky? What's that supposed to mean?" Lüdtke asked.

"Well, maybe I'd light them up, you know, with my flashlight. Shine it in their faces. Maybe I said a few things, like, dirty things. Just to give them a bit of a thrill. But that was all, I swear."

"That's what you were doing, was it? Giving these women a bit of a thrill? I see . . . Tell me, did they look to you as if they were thrilled? Did they shriek like girls on a fairground ride? You know, a little bit scared, but having a wonderful time underneath."

Ogorzow was dumb enough to think that he was being given a way out. "Yeah, yeah, that was it. They was scared, but they was happy. I mean, one of them shouted at me. They get like that, women, don't they? But nothing serious, just mouthing off a bit."

"Very well then, tomorrow, you and I will take a little walk along the same paths that you use to get to work. And as we walk along, you can show me some of the places where you shone your flashlight at these women. Maybe you could point out the place where that woman shouted back at you too. How does that sound to you?"

Ogorzow shrugged. "All right."

"Excellent," said Lüdtke. "Then that is what we will do."

Ogorzow was led away again. Lüdtke turned to me, and this time he wasn't slumped against walls, or closing his eyes in exhaustion. He was filled with energy and conviction.

"Get hold of all the women from the first attacks," he said. "Budzinski, Jablinski, Nieswandt, and Schumacher. I want them all close at hand tomorrow. Keep them out of sight, but close, always close."

"Yes, Commissar."

"And see if you can find any record of this woman who shouted back at him. If she was angry enough to shout, she might have made a complaint as well."

"I'll see to it immediately."

"And there's one last thing . . ."

Lüdtke gave me a final, very strange order. "Weimann will sort it out for you," he assured me when I looked a little unnerved by what he'd just requested. Then he held up a hand in front of my face with his thumb and forefinger just a couple of centimeters apart, and said: "We're close—this close! But this is the trickiest moment of all. We've gone fishing. We've hooked our fish. He's on the line. But now we have to bring him in . . . slowly . . . delicately . . . knowing that at any time the line may break." He slapped his hand against my upper arm and gripped my biceps. "But it won't break, Heuser. Believe me, it will not break."

Lüdtke grinned with a predatory glee I'd never seen in him before. "We're going to land this damn fish. Just you wait and see."

25

Lüdtke was right. Ogorzow was almost in our grasp. By midafternoon we'd found a record of a complaint from a woman who'd had a flashlight shone in her face in a way that exactly matched the description he'd given. So now we called up every similar incident reported in that leafy corner of Berlin, and a pattern emerged that precisely matched Ogorzow's steady escalation from low-level encounters that might frighten or humiliate a woman, through the first physical assaults, to full-blown rape and eventually murder. He'd been at it for at least three years, and though the women who had survived his attacks had no desire ever to encounter him again, they were soon persuaded to help us if that meant saving other women from the ordeals they had been forced to endure.

Gertrude Ogorzow was also changing her tune. I spent another hour with her and she revealed a very different Paul Ogorzow from the decent family man that the neighbors saw. "He's a jealous man," she said, "jealous like you wouldn't believe. I never cheated on him, not once, though I had my opportunities all right. You might not think it to look at me now, but there was a time when plenty of men were chasing after me. But I never said yes. I'd made my vows and I was sticking to them. Paul just wouldn't believe it, though. I don't know if it's his mother's fault—she was always off with other men, that one, though she's been good to us and I shouldn't speak ill of her. But I'm only telling the truth. All the time he was a boy, there was one man after another. So maybe that's why he's the way he is."

"How did it show, your husband's jealousy? Was he angry with you? Was he ever violent?"

"Not really violent, no—I mean, no more than any other husband getting angry with his wife. He could shout a bit, I suppose, when he thought I'd been looking at a man, which was often. I only had to say 'excuse me' to someone on the street and Paul would think I was flirting with him. But it was mostly him trying to control me. He had all these rules about how I was supposed to behave when he was off at work: places I could or couldn't go; people I was allowed to speak to, all that sort of thing."

I thought of Ogorzow in his working hours and the things he was doing to other women, and the hypocritical injustice of his attitude toward his wife filled me with a greater determination than ever to rid the world of this menace.

The following day, Lüdtke took Ogorzow out for his tour of the leafy neighborhoods between Karlshorst and Rummelsburg. It was a perfect day for a stroll among the gardens. The sun was shining and the temperature was in the high twenties, with just enough of a breeze to keep it from feeling too hot. The allotments were lush with vegetables coming into their prime. The beds were filled with potato plants, lettuces and cabbages, marrow plants, and ripening ears of sweet corn, while tomato vines and runner beans climbed up trellised frames, bamboo poles, and slender hazel branches bound with twine. There were even a few strawberry beds with their scarlet fruit clustered beneath the clumps of dark green leaves.

Such an abundance of life was a strange setting for our pursuit of violent death. As Lüdtke and Ogorzow walked along the dusty, shade-dappled paths, I was close by to handle any tasks Lüdtke might require, and there were uniformed constables all around us to deter Ogorzow from even thinking of escape. Ogorzow pointed out four places where he said that he'd flashed his flashlight at women and made obscene suggestions. Now his stupidity came to our aid, for two of them were actually locations at which he'd attempted murder. I fetched both his victims from the car that was slowly shadowing Ogorzow's movements, out of his sight and hearing. One of the women was unable to identify him as her assailant. The other, however, needed just one look before she said: "That's him. I'd know him anywhere," and then burst into tears.

The net was drawing tighter around Paul Ogorzow. We had enough now to convict him as an aggressive, violent sexual predator, but the murders were another matter.

Lüdtke and I took Ogorzow back to Alex and straight to the interview room. Before we could begin our questions, however, Ogorzow approached Lüdtke and in a quiet, confidential, man-to-man tone said: "Can you and me talk alone?" He glanced knowingly at me. "Without him."

"Of course," Lüdtke said. "I'll get rid of him immediately."

He turned to me and made a great show of insisting that I leave the room so that he and "Herr Ogorzow" could have a private conversation. While his back was turned, he tapped his Party badge and whispered: "I've been expecting this."

The Party was a form of Freemasonry, a brotherhood in which one member was expected to help out another. Ogorzow hoped to use his considerable status as a Nazi loyalist and SA sergeant as a means of extracting himself from the unfortunate situation in which he now found himself.

It didn't work. Within a few minutes, Lüdtke was opening the door to the corridor and ushering me back into the interview room. "Ah, Heuser, do come in. I was just explaining to Ogorzow that I am sadly unable to help him. On the contrary, I am determined to make sure that our movement is purged of elements whose behavior would besmirch the good name of National Socialism. In any case, my orders come direct from General Heydrich himself, and I don't recall him asking me to exclude Party members from my inquiries. You were there, Heuser. Do you remember Heydrich saying I should go easy on anyone with a Party badge?"

"No, Commissar. Absolutely not."

"Good, I'm glad that's settled. So you see, Ogorzow, you've had it. We're going to get you. It's all over. Why don't you save us all some time and maybe do yourself a little good, eh? Courts always look kindly on criminals who've confessed to their crimes. If you show the judges genuine regret and remorse for what you've done, they may show you a little mercy."

Ogorzow was a deflated, diminished figure. The flicker of hope that had perked him up when he believed he could use his Party status to get himself an easy ride had been crushed. Now he just sat there, slumped and wordless.

"Let's start at the beginning," Lüdtke said, undeterred by Ogorzow's lack of response. "It's pointless even trying to deny the sex crimes. We've got you for sexual assault, rape, attempted murder—that's enough to put you away for life right there."

"I didn't do it," he said, but the denial lacked any conviction.

"Come on, we all know you did. And we know you killed Gerda Ditter, too, in her little shack in Friedrichsfelde. You stabbed her, just like you'd stabbed the other ladies: Budzinski, Jablinski, and Nieswandt. Only this time you killed her. Didn't you, Ogorzow? You killed her."

"I didn't mean to," he blurted, without thinking.

Slowly it dawned on Ogorzow that he'd just given the game away. After all these months, we had him. But it was one thing solving the Friedrichsfelde cases—even the Ditter murder—and quite another tying Ogorzow definitively to the S-Bahn killings. Those were the ones that the Party and the public alike wanted solved, and Lüdtke intended to get the job done while Ogorzow was still in a mood to confess.

He turned to me and asked: "Do you have that package from Dr. Weimann?"

"Yes, Commissar."

"Get it for me, please."

I left the room and returned a minute or two later carrying a white cardboard box, about forty centimeters square and thirty deep. I placed it on the table, just to Lüdtke's right.

"I want to talk to you about the S-Bahn murders," Lüdtke said.

"What about them?" Ogorzow asked.

"Well, you went on escort duty with the SA, keeping women safe."

"Yeah, that's right."

"Which is ironic, really, since you're the man who committed the murders. Aren't you?"

"No, that's not me."

"You're sure about that? Six women killed on the S-Bahn: two strangled, four battered to death. That wasn't you?"

"No, definitely not."

"Open the box, please, Heuser."

"Yes, Commissar."

I lifted the lid of the box. Ogorzow leaned forward to see what was inside. He was greeted with the sight of four skulls, each one of them severely damaged, even with holes in a couple of cases.

If that white box had been full of deadly cobras, Ogorzow could not have recoiled any more sharply, nor borne a more vivid expression of mortal terror on his face. He shuffled backward on his chair, away from the table, as Lüdtke very calmly removed the skulls one by one.

"Do you recognize these, Ogorzow? You should. They're only here because of you. Look, here's Elfriede Franke. She was doing valuable work as a nurse until you threw her off that train outside Karlshorst. And here's young Irmgard Frese, just nineteen, her whole life ahead of her, until you put an end to it on Prinz-Heinrich-Strasse."

Ogorzow pulled his arm across his face to hide the sight of the two cracked white skulls. It struck me that he'd never before considered the reality or the consequences of what he'd done. His ability to keep killing was in that sense dependent on being able to dissociate himself from any consideration of his victims as people who had emotions or rights, including the right to life itself. Now he was confronted with the truth and he couldn't stand it.

"Stop it! Please stop it!" he begged.

But Lüdtke did not stop. He took out the skulls of Gertrud Siewert and Johanna Voigt, so that now there were four of them in a line across the table, all staring at Ogorzow with their wide-eyed empty sockets and manic, grinning teeth.

He started weeping. "I'll tell you everything, I swear, everything. Just take them away from me. For God's sake have some mercy, I'm begging you."

Lüdtke was implacable. "Mercy? Did you show these women any mercy?"

"I'll talk!" Ogorzow wailed. "I'll talk! Just take them away!"

Lüdtke nodded at me, and I packed the skulls away and put the lid back on the box. Ogorzow calmed down a little, though he still kept darting terrified glances at the box as though he feared that the skulls might at any moment burst out of their own accord.

And then, at last, he told us everything.

There had, he admitted, been at least twenty rapes, as well as the eight murders and six attempted murders. At first he tried to pretend that he'd merely punched the women about the head. But then he admitted to using a length of heavy telephone cable, hidden up his jacket sleeve, as his weapon.

Ogorzow was consumed by a hatred for women and a desire for revenge for the harm the female sex had done him. It began, he said, when he caught gonorrhea from a Berlin stripper. He claimed that a Jewish doctor had then made the problem worse. "That filthy Yid knew I was a Party member and he hated the Nazis, so obviously when he's treated me he's made sure I'm left with side effects, and it's them side effects that influenced my mental state. You know, made me the way I am."

My wild guess that the killer might be afflicted with a sexual disease had been right, but I derived little satisfaction from it. That he blamed a Jew for his evil actions rather than accepting responsibility for them himself, only lowered my opinion of this vile little man still further. The mythical creature that had terrorized Berlin for so many months turned out to be a weakling and a coward. He only ever attacked small women, he added pathetically, because he was afraid of bigger ones.

As Dr. Weimann had hypothesized, Ogorzow had shared with Peter Kürten the discovery that the act of killing was the ultimate sexual stimulation. Touching his victims, overcoming their resistance, and then watching their bodies fall helplessly from the train were all powerfully erotic, even orgasmic experiences for him. But the most horrendous revelation of all concerned his activities on the night of December 3, 1940. He had, he said, raped and killed Irmgard Frese first. Then he'd attacked Elfriede Franke and thrown her from the train. After that, he went to work on the night shift at Rummelsburg as though nothing had happened. While out on his rounds, checking the signal lanterns, he realized that he was close to the spot where he'd killed Frese. So he went back to the scene of the crime and had sex again, this time with her dead body.

When he'd finished his account I sat there, busying myself with my notes, trying to come to terms with the experience of encountering a genuinely evil human being. To be given a glimpse into the mind of a man like Paul Ogorzow was to enter a world of violence, degradation, and filth, a world without pity, morality, or any feeling whatsoever for his fellow human beings—a world with which I had nothing in common at all.

26

Paul Ogorzow's final act as he was led away from the interview room was to beg one last time for his Party status to be taken into account. That soon became an irrelevance. He was expelled from the National Socialist Party two days after making his confession. On July 24, in a special hearing at the Third District Court of Berlin, he pleaded guilty to all the charges against him. He was declared a public enemy and sentenced to death. The execution—beheading by the guillotine at Plötzensee Prison—was set for the following day.

The entire murder squad celebrated the closing of the case at a bar near Alex. All our old arguments and personal conflicts were forgotten as we drank toasts, slapped backs, and cheerfully agreed that we were all the most splendid fellows. Toward the end of the evening, Lüdtke got to his feet amid a chorus of cheers, whistles, and shouts of encouragement and made a brief speech. "Ladies and gentlemen," he began, "this is a great day in the history of our squad, and of the Criminal Police across our entire Fatherland." There were more cheers, accompanied by a thunder of applause, slammed tabletops, and boots stamping on the floor.

"We all know how hard this case has been. We all remember the times when it seemed as though we would never catch the S-Bahn murderer. We remember the thousands of interviews we had to conduct, the statements that had to be checked again and again, and the constant grind of patrolling the S-Bahn, night after night, without the slightest respite." There was a murmur of grim agreement from the audience.

Lüdtke paused and grinned. "Some of you men even remember the dresses you had to wear while you sat on the train, waiting to see if the killer would attack you." Now there was an explosion of laughter, combined with a barrage of more or less obscene suggestions aimed at the men who had played those decoy roles. Lüdtke held up his hand to silence them and then continued more gravely: "But now you know that your effort was worthwhile. We kept going. We stuck to our principles and did our job in the proper manner. And in the end, we tracked down that filthy bastard Paul Ogorzow and tomorrow we will rid the world of his evil!"

The whole bar seemed to shake at the applause that greeted those words. By now, Lüdtke's audience included not only the murder squad, but all the other drinkers in the bar. Even the staff had set their duties aside to listen to what he had to say. For that one night, we were the city's heroes, and the next day everyone in the bar would boast to their friends and coworkers that they had been there to see us. But Lüdtke had one more dramatic coup up his sleeve. He waited until the room fell silent, then said, "I have here a message from General Heydrich himself . . ." There was a collective gasp of surprise, followed by a tense expectancy as we waited to hear what the great man had written. "It goes as follows: 'My dear Commissar Lüdtke, please accept my warmest congratulations to you and your men on your great success. Your conduct as police officers represents the highest standards of our National Socialist community. A guilty man has been caught and punished, and decent German women may go about their lives in peace and security once again. *Heil Hitler!* Heydrich.'"

Lüdtke put the letter away, stood to attention, and saluted: "*Heil Hitler!*" The whole bar roared out its reply. Someone broke into "The

Horst Wessel Song," the anthem of the National Socialist movement, and we all joined in, whether Party members or not, waving our beer glasses in time to the music. It may sound appalling to say so now, but my memory of our singing is one of innocence. We knew for certain that we had done something good. We truly believed that our country was great and our cause was just.

For my part, when I'd sufficiently recovered from the night's celebration to be able to form a coherent thought, I felt certain that my decision to become a policeman had been the correct one. The principles with which my father had raised me had also been thoroughly vindicated. Hard work, a perfectionist approach to detail, and a determination to carry out my orders to the letter had brought me everything a young detective could possibly desire. I must have persuaded Lüdtke that I could obey his personal rules, too, for he invited me to join him in writing the official account of the solving of the S-Bahn murders, to be published in the national *Journal of Criminology*, thereby forever linking my name with his in the annals of the Berlin murder squad's greatest triumphs. As a result of the interest in the case paid by the likes of Heydrich and Nebe, I had been noticed and marked as a young man to watch by the most powerful men in the SS and police establishments. Within days of Ogorzow's execution I was informed that I could expect to receive both promotion and a career-enhancing transfer within a matter of months.

Until I did, I was more than happy settling down to the regular work of a police homicide department: domestic murders in which one had to look no further than the surviving spouse for the prime suspect, or underworld killings in which one antisocial leech of a black-market profiteer rid the world of another. My hours were regular, and free time guaranteed. Much, much more significantly, Biene and I now had the time and freedom to enjoy the glorious sensation of being young and in love.

We spent evenings together seeing films and plays, walking arm-in-arm through the city or dancing cheek-to-cheek around my living room floor while the gramophone played recordings of our favorite dance bands. For all the perils of the age, life was still rich with opportunity and great hopes for the future. Biene and I made love with the passion that comes when animal desire is combined with heartfelt emotion. On weekends we would go out to the Wannsee beach and bask in the sunshine. I took a picture of Biene there one Sunday afternoon, looking like a movie star with her huge smile, her round sunglasses, and her two-piece bathing costume, and it kept me warm for many months in the freezing winter that followed. The beach showed off Biene to her very best advantage, and that sporty, coltish body of hers looked equally splendid stretched out on the sand or cutting through the waters of the lake in a front crawl worthy of an Olympian.

At the end of July, my friend and comrade Frank Baum was posted to join Einsatzkommando 9, part of Einsatzgruppe A, which had followed Army Group North into the Baltic states and on to the gates of Leningrad. The former Latvian capital of Riga was now the administrative center of a new German province called the Reich Commissariat Ostland, or "East Land." On the Central Front, our forces had stormed into Smolensk and were heading east, and by August they were within striking distance of Moscow. Arthur Nebe, who was still the nominal commander of the Criminal Police, had established his headquarters in Minsk as leader of Einsatzgruppe B. In the south we had driven the Red Army out of Kiev and were advancing toward the oil fields of the Caucasus. A second Reich Commissariat of the Ukraine had been established and was now being administered from the city of Rivne.

As hard as it may be to believe, those of us still working at our normal jobs had no idea of what was really happening in Russia. So far as I was concerned, Baum was lucky to be going there. Ostland was one of the foundries where our vast new empire would be forged, and where a young man of ability and determination could make a name for himself. I longed for such an opportunity myself. And not long afterward, I got it.

In the early autumn of 1941 my promotion to Criminal Police Commissar and SS-First Lieutenant was duly confirmed. It came with a pay raise and, best of all, the elevation to *Beamter* status. From now on my position as an officer of the state was secure for life, and, as if that were not enough, I was informed that so far as the SS was concerned I could now refer to myself as "Dr. Heuser." It was felt that my studies at the Leaders' School more than compensated for not taking the final exams of my legal doctorate.

In October I received orders to transfer to Riga to join a unit within Einsatzgruppe A known as Sonderkommando 1b, under the command of SS-Lieutenant-Colonel Erich Ehrlinger. I was promised a special hardship bonus and extra annual leave, but those incentives were of far less interest to me than the prospects that this new posting would surely bring with it.

Of course, Biene and I were a little downcast as we spent our last night together. She cried as we danced, our bodies pressed close together to the sound of Rina Ketty singing that most melancholy but beautiful song of wartime parting, *"J'attendrai."* The title meant "I will wait," and Biene swore that she would wait for me, no matter how long it might be before I returned home. Yet as sad as we both were to be parting, we had no doubt that—like a young Roman tribune being sent to the wilds of Britannia—I was embarking on the vital task of bringing civilization and the rule of law to a distant province still mired in barbarism. I was safe from the perils of the front line itself, and I was building a career that we both believed would bring us security for the rest of our days.

For her part, Biene planned to return home to her family in Hamburg. "I won't miss you so much if I have my parents to comfort me," she said. "And I can't stay here. It would be too painful to work in the same old office, but without you there. Every building, every street, every blade of grass in the Tiergarten reminds me of you. But I promise you, the day you come back I'll be here, waiting for you."

On our final morning together, after we had said our last farewells on the station platform, kissed with the longing of those who fear they may never be able to kiss one another again, and sworn our undying love for the thousandth time, I turned to step up onto the train. Biene caught my arm. "There's one last thing I want you to know," she said. "I'm proud of you, my darling. I'm so very, very proud."

27

KOBLENZ, WEST GERMANY: OCTOBER 22, 1961

From her seat in the Koblenz District Court, Paula Siebert had a view through a window across the treetops toward the facade of the old Electoral Palace. With its magnificent portico of eight huge Ionic columns, its arcaded ground floor, and the calm, symmetrical march of its windows and skylights, the palace was a temple to the classical, rational values of its late-eighteenth-century creators. There was a similar appeal to reason in the courtroom itself, where a large mosaic on one wall depicted the parable of the wise and foolish virgins. It happened to stand in the direct eyeline of the defendants: a not-so-subtle reminder of the consequences of their own foolishness. Even before the proceedings had properly got under way, many of the accused were already staring at that mosaic so intently that they seemed to be counting every single one of the innumerable marble tesserae involved in its making. It took Paula a moment or two to register that this was just a means by which they could avoid any eye contact whatsoever with anyone else in the court, or any acknowledgment of its proceedings.

She happened to have been walking up to the court just after Heuser arrived. He'd been driven there in a prison bus, and though he raised a file of documents to his face to hide himself from the handful of photographers waiting by the entrance, she'd recognized his profile and caught sight of a single nervous bloodshot eye peering around the side of the pale brown cardboard file. He'd managed to compose himself since then, and from the way the others had greeted him it was evident that he was the leader of the group. Of the others, nine were instantly forgettable middle-aged men whose absolute lack of physical presence felt like a plea of innocence in itself. "Look at me," they each seemed to be saying. "Can you really believe that anyone so insignificant could possibly have been a killer? Can you honestly imagine me in an SS uniform? Do I look like a devil to you?"

And the truth was they didn't, for these were an essentially random collection of individuals who happened, by chance, to have been given a posting to a particular place at a specific time. When the war broke out, Feder, Dalheimer, and Wilke were all policemen, though none had shown anything like the promise Heuser displayed as a detective. Wilke, for example, had been a student of theology and classics who had only joined the force after a brief, unfulfilling career as a primary-school teacher. Kaul also worked for the police service, but as an office administrator: he was always happiest checking accounts and ticking boxes, and that had still applied in Minsk, too.

The rest had been civilians. Harder was a shopkeeper in Paula's own hometown of Frankfurt—she'd never dared ask her mother if she'd ever bought goods from his store. Merbach was a car mechanic by trade, whose chief role in Minsk had been to supervise the SS motor pool. Oswald was an electrical technician and engineer. Schlegel was an academic. His prewar ambition had been to teach business studies. Von Toll had been managing a country estate in East Prussia when the conflict began.

The three judges presiding over the case would be well used to the idea that apparently meek and harmless individuals could be capable of the most heinous crimes. But how could the six lay jurors alongside them not think to themselves that these men looked just like their neighbors; that they were simply ordinary, law-abiding Germans forced to obey disgusting orders?

Only one of the accused seemed in any way to conform to the stereotypical image of an unrepentant Nazi killer. While all his old comrades were dressed in suits and ties, doing their best to look respectable, Franz Stark wore an old leather jacket and a rough plaid shirt. His pinched face glowered at the courtroom in brazen defiance. The others seemed to shy away from him a little, repelled by both snobbery and fear. Of all the defendants, Stark had by far the roughest background, the most meager education, and the least professional prestige. He'd been a committed Nazi since the very earliest days of the Party, but even senior Reich officials had been appalled by his brutal behavior in Minsk.

Paula herself had no legal standing in the trial. She wouldn't be allowed to examine witnesses, let alone the accused. Her role was simply to observe the progress of the case and be ready to provide additional evidence or undertake further inquiries, should the need arise. She'd expected to find herself amid a horde of reporters and members of the public, all gathering to see the wicked war criminals in the flesh. Less than five months had passed, after all, since the Israelis had hanged Adolf Eichmann, the principal organizer of the Holocaust. His trial and execution had attracted huge headlines all over the world. But here they were, about to start by far the biggest trial ever conducted by Germans of their own war criminals, and the press seats and public gallery were less than half full. Of the reporters who were present, the majority were talking to one another in English: foreign correspondents from the American and British press.

Perhaps the German press had other fish to fry. Two weeks earlier, *Der Spiegel* had printed a cover story claiming that the West German armed forces had performed so poorly in a multinational training exercise called Fallex 62 that they had been officially described as "prepared for defense to a limited extent"—the lowest possible rating that any NATO force could receive. Franz Josef Strauss, the Federal Minister of Defense, responded to this public humiliation by accusing the magazine of treason and threatening the strongest possible retaliation against its owner, Rudolf Augstein, and his journalists. The *Spiegel* Affair, as it was now being called, had become the topic of every conversation and many an argument as believers in free speech clashed with government supporters. That was one good enough reason why the Heuser case had slipped off the radar, but there might have been only limited interest in the trial no matter what. Paula's fellow countrymen and women really did seem to be sending a very clear message that they had no desire to rake over the ashes of the past. Or perhaps they just couldn't face the truth of what lay among those ashes.

When the initial formalities of the trial had been concluded, with all the defendants pleading not guilty to every one of the charges in front of them, the prosecution began to lay out the basic facts of the case. A series of place names were read out, each with its own number . . . Rakow, 100 . . . Minsk/Koidanov, 3,000 . . . Trostinets, 16,500 . . . Slutsk, 1,600 . . . On and on went these names and numbers, each pair representing the site and death toll of a mass execution. And these insignificant gray men had helped carry them out. Not that they ever used any term as vulgar as "execution," for theirs had been a world of euphemism and evasion in which "actions" consisted of the "resettlement" of men, women, and children to "settlement areas" where they were "processed." But they had known exactly what they were doing, which was why they were always drunk out of their minds on the vodka stacked in crates right next to the bullets as they did it. Ah yes, the vodka . . . The prosecutor had already stated that a conservative estimate of 31,970 people had been killed.

Paula was curious to know when he would reveal something she'd learned while interviewing a quartermaster who had supplied the killers with their food and drink. He reckoned that he'd delivered around thirty thousand bottles of vodka to the various killing sites: a bottle, in other words, for every single person that had died.

How hard those killers had tried to obliterate their consciousness along with their consciences. And that was not all, for in addition to the other indictments against them, two of the defendants were charged with a variety of individual killings. Stark had killed three innocent, defenseless men while enraged by a perceived humiliation for which they had been in no way responsible. The other lone murderer was Heuser. He had been directly, personally responsible for the deaths of at least eight other people. He'd ordered the death of one woman with the writing of a single letter "L," for "liquidation," on her case file. Her crime had been to have sex with a Luftwaffe pilot, an unforgivable sin for someone classed as less than fully human (the pilot, of course, had not been punished at all). One, possibly two other men had been shot either by him or on his direct instructions for the capital crime of writing letters. Like the serial killer he once hunted, Heuser had dragged two women out into wastelands in the dead of night, murdered them, and left their bodies where they lay. He'd shot a Catholic priest and then ordered the execution of three suspected saboteurs in circumstances so hellish that Hieronymus Bosch would have struggled to invent anything more grotesque. One of the trio had made a bid to escape. Heuser had shot him, too.

Paula knew, beyond any doubt, that these events had happened. She knew that Heuser had been responsible for them. Yet his transformation from the fine, principled detective who had helped track down the infamous S-Bahn murderer to the blood-drenched fiend that the case against him described was impossible to comprehend. How could a human soul be corrupted so totally, so fast? And how, knowing all that he'd done, could Heuser then return to civilian life, reestablish himself in the police, and present himself once again as an admirable, honorable pillar of law and order? It was not just that he'd deceived the police force for which he worked, or the public that he served. He had somehow managed to persuade himself of his own essential blamelessness, his moral superiority to the criminals he hunted with such exemplary energy and rigor.

What in God's name had happened to make him the way he was?

Paula was suddenly aware that Heuser profoundly scared her. It was not that she feared him in any physical sense. There had never been any suggestion that he'd hurt anyone before or after his time in Minsk, nor had he been remotely threatening in any of his interviews with her. No, what chilled her to the bone was that she, Kraus—absolutely anyone—might have within them the same capacity for evil and the same ability to numb themselves to its consequences.

She looked at Heuser now, impassively taking notes as the prosecutor set out the case against him. He seemed as normal and innocuous as the men on either side of him: just a run-down middle-aged man of the sort one might find sitting alone in a city café, or watching the world go by from a lonely park bench. From time to time, when the crimes being described were particularly egregious, he fiddled nervously with his spectacles. When the evidence against him seemed exceptionally telling, he would dab his face with his fingers to wipe away the sweat glistening on his forehead or beading his upper lip.

That sweat seemed to Paula like the shame and guilt seeping from Heuser's body. His attempts at self-deception were breaking down. His physical reactions were giving him away. She thought of the effort, the years of concentration and self-discipline, that he must have expended in building the wall he'd put between himself and his memories of Minsk. The identity photo that had troubled her so much now seemed to her like the picture of a mask beneath which a maggot-infested head was being eaten away from within. It was almost enough to make her feel a shred, not of sympathy, but perhaps of compassion for Georg Heuser. He had arrived in the Reich Commissariat Ostland as a decent enough young man. But he had left it a monster.

28

RIGA AND MINSK, REICH COMMISSARIAT OSTLAND: OCTOBER 1941–FEBRUARY 1942

In October 1941 I reported to Sonderkommando 1b in Riga. My new commander, Ehrlinger, and his men had undertaken a number of what they called "actions" on their march into Russia and the Baltic states, but I knew almost nothing about these events, for my new comrades were oddly unwilling to talk about their experiences to date. I therefore had no idea what I was letting myself in for. It took an accidental encounter to give me a hint of what was to come.

One night I was walking down a narrow side street in the old part of Riga, not far from the cathedral, when I heard someone call my name from the far side of the street. It was Frank Baum. He'd been given a forty-eight-hour leave from Einsatzkommando 9 and was hell-bent on spending every minute of it blind drunk.

I have to admit, I didn't at first recognize my old murder squad colleague. The last time I'd seen Baum, he was still a cheerful soul who could bring a smile to my face on the gloomiest of days. Now he was a stumbling, ill-kempt wreck, and it was apparent from his hollow eyes and drawn face that his condition was more than just a matter of a few too many drinks. But what the real problem was, I did not immediately discover.

Only when we had found a restaurant whose sole available dinner dish was a tasteless horse-meat stew, washed down by vinegary red wine and vodka, did Baum slowly begin to open up, though his story was so rambling and his speech so indistinct that I found it hard to keep track of what he was trying to say. I managed to establish that something had happened at a place called Ponary in Lithuania. Baum said the site had been chosen because the Russians had been planning a military airfield there and had dug a series of huge holes in the ground, where they planned to put aviation-fuel storage tanks: "Saved my men from having to dig pits of our own."

I tried to get Baum to explain what kind of pits he meant and describe what had happened there, but words failed him. He struggled, he stammered, but nothing came out. I don't think that alcohol was the problem. It was more that he was still in a state of shock. Eventually he reached into his uniform jacket and with some difficulty pulled out a tatty envelope, grimy with drink stains and oily fingerprints.

Baum's hands were shaking like a man with the palsy, so it took him a while to remove the half dozen black-and-white photographs the envelope contained and hand them over to me. At first it was hard to make sense of the images: men cradling guns while behind them twenty or more women undressed in the open air; two men at the edge of one of the holes he'd described, pointing guns at a shapeless white object; the bottom of another hole, as big and deep as a quarry, half filled with people standing in front of uniformed men with guns; dead bodies lying in rows along a shallow, grassy slope; more bodies; and more again.

"What exactly is happening here?" I asked.

Baum shrugged helplessly. All he could say was: "That is what we do."

Poor Baum. He'd dreamed of the easy life in Paris, but there was no resemblance whatsoever between life in our Western territories and those in the East. We may have conquered Denmark, Norway, Holland, Belgium, and France, but that didn't prevent us from seeing them as cultured, civilized nations, whose people were really little different from ourselves. The East was different, a vast, barren landscape in which there were no boundaries to behavior and all conventional standards of legality and morality had been cast aside as a matter of basic principle: a land whose inhabitants were officially considered to be less than human.

Even so, there was still a need for proper administration. The security, law and order, and political control of the Minsk area had initially been Arthur Nebe's responsibility, but he and his men had moved on to Smolensk, some three hundred kilometers to the east. Ehrlinger had then been ordered to take over from Nebe in Minsk and establish a permanent Criminal Police, Gestapo, and SD intelligence presence. This was formally titled the Office of the Commander of the Security Police and SD. We, however, always referred to it by the abbreviation KdS.

The region around Minsk, which we called White Russia, was quite unlike Germany in terms of its Jewish population. At home, Jews constituted a very small percentage of the people as a whole. Berlin, for example, had a much greater Jewish presence than many other German cities, yet they numbered only about sixty thousand, out of some four million Berliners. In the shtetls, the small towns and villages that surrounded Minsk, however, as much as half the total population was Jewish. And in Minsk itself there were tens of thousands of Jews, who had been confined to a small ghetto immediately after our forces had occupied the city.

Their numbers had been somewhat reduced by various executions during the late summer and early autumn, but then came orders from Berlin: Minsk was to take a further twenty-five thousand so-called "Reich Jews" currently living in the cities of Hamburg, Frankfurt,

Düsseldorf, Berlin, Bremen, Vienna, and Brno. Seven trains, each containing roughly a thousand Reich Jews, reached Minsk before winter set in. Only the final transport from Vienna was still due when I arrived in the city.

In order to make room for these newcomers, almost twelve thousand of the Russian Jews already in the ghetto had been liquidated in the first weeks of November. I wasn't present in the city for either of these massacres, so I had no sense of what the killing of so many people actually entailed. They were just more casualty figures: more of those endless numbers that the Russian campaign seemed to generate.

The realization of what was really happening only dawned on me very slowly, over a period of weeks and months, like a great red sun that rose within me, centimeter by centimeter, until it flooded my entire being with its bloody radiance. And what was true for me was true for us all. For it was only in those last months of 1941 and early '42 that what people now call the Holocaust gradually emerged from countless more or less random acts of violence to become something very different: a coherent program of extermination, planned with extraordinary precision and detail.

In those last days of November, however, I still believed that I'd come to Minsk to bring law, not slaughter, to its people. Filled by the conviction that I'd been granted the privilege of seeing an empire being built before my eyes, I decided to keep a war diary. It was intended as an objective, almost academic account of my experiences and observations. Very swiftly, however, it took on a rather different role—as a sort of release valve for the intense emotions stirred up by the incomprehensible universe into which I soon found myself flung. I'd work on it late into the night, writing in an abbreviated shorthand of my own devising that I'd first used to take notes in university law lectures, and that only I could possibly decode.

I'd not opened those diaries in more than forty years before I began work on this memoir, but when I read the opening pages I thought: "You poor boy. You have no idea what you are about to experience. No idea at all."

29

I wrote to Biene in the final week of November 1941. It was just one of countless millions of letters sent by men at war to the women they'd left at home, but it said a lot, I think, about my state of mind at the time—not just in what I wrote, but in what I chose to exclude as well.

My darling Biene,

I'm writing this looking at your picture—the one we took that day by the Wannsee—thinking how beautiful you are and wishing you were here. When I lie alone in bed at night I ache for the feel of your body next to mine, the scent of your hair, the smile on your face, and the sound of your voice. I am proud to be doing my duty for the Fatherland now and am determined to carry out my orders to the very maximum of my abilities, but I long for the day when the war is won and we can be together again.

You wouldn't believe the place where I am based now. We all thought Alex was a huge building, but I swear this one makes it look like a small, provincial police station. It's called the Lenin House, and although the Ivans did their best to destroy the whole of Minsk before we took it in July, this one building remained untouched. It was the headquarters of the local Communist Party and no Bolshie dared be the one who so much as scratched the bright white paint on that! The Lenin House looms over the rest of the city like a giant's castle over a peasant village. So far I cannot seem to take more than two steps past the front door without becoming hopelessly lost. I expect I'll soon become familiar enough with it, though.

I have made one good friend here in Minsk. His name is Eberhard von Toll and he is working in the same unit as I am. By military rank von Toll is only a common conscript, yet he can claim to be a genuine aristocrat. His father is the Baron von Toll—very grand!—and the family have lived for centuries in Estonia. But when Ribbentrop signed the pact with Stalin in '39 and the Baltic Germans were repatriated back to the Reich, the family lost all their land. So von Toll was working as a farm manager in East Prussia when he was called up. Since he can speak Russian, Estonian, and a little Latvian as well as German, he was assigned to work as an interpreter, and now he's my right-hand man. He's even been trying to pick up a few words of Yiddish so that he can help me communicate with all the Jews who live here.

Von Toll is a very decent fellow with a handsome Nordic appearance. He is devoted to his wife Karin, who is another member of the Estonian-German aristocracy. He proudly showed me her picture, so I showed him my one of you, and we both agreed that we were very lucky men. Although his family have been cruelly and unjustly stripped of all their possessions, von Toll does not have the slightest bitterness and he carries himself with a natural confidence and self-assurance that I can only envy. When we are not on duty we talk as one man to another, rather than as an officer and an enlisted man—we in the SS are always told to think of one another as comrades, no matter what our ranks—and I always look forward to our conversations.

Tomorrow von Toll and I are both being given a tour of Minsk by another comrade, Rudolf Schlegel, who has been here almost from the moment the city was captured, so he knows his way around. Schlegel is a few months younger than me, but has the SS rank of captain, making him senior to me. On the other hand, I possess a police rank and he does not, so we treat one another as equals. Schlegel had an academic interest in anthropology before the war, and has informed views on the social, biological, and facial characteristics of lesser races, which I'm sure will be of great interest when we visit the Jewish ghetto.

All this talk of comrades has just reminded me—I met Frank Baum a few weeks ago in Riga. We toasted one another—several times!—the way soldiers do and got a little bit drunk. This is what happens when we do not have the civilizing company of women! Frank was in fine form and remembered you very fondly. He asked me to send you his very best wishes.

And I, of course, send all my love and longing to you, my darling.

I love you so much,

Georg

Ah, the lies we tell to the ones we love . . . But how could I tell her the truth about poor Baum? Even if I'd tried, the censors would have cut it out. And how could I reveal what I really felt about my SS officer comrades? It was absolutely true that we were supposed to see one another as members of the same Aryan brotherhood, but I was still motivated by ambition above all else, and we were all competitive young men fighting for status within a vast organization. The fact that Schlegel had a captain's rank—and greatly increased salary—burned my guts, and the feelings would only get worse as the months and even years went by. My frustrated desire for promotion would eat away at me like a running sore throughout my time in Minsk.

As for the truth of what my work there would entail—well, I'd no more idea of that than Biene did. Not when I wrote that first letter. But the next few days would begin the process of opening my eyes.

The following morning, as we were walking from the Lenin House to his car, Schlegel gave us a little lecture, almost as if we were his pupils rather than his comrades. "Minsk is an unusual place," he began. "The local White Russians don't hate the Jews. That's totally unlike the Latvians or Lithuanians. Putting a bullet in the back of a Jew's head is a pleasure to them, which is why so many of them are happy to do it on our behalf. The Ukrainians are just the same, but not the White Russians. Not only do they not appear to feel any hostility toward the Jews, they do everything they can to help them. I suspect this has something to do with Bolshevism. For some reason a great many natives here really believe in Stalin—Jews and non-Jews alike—and that common loyalty overrides any racial divide. My point is, Heuser, that the Jews and the partisans here are working hand-in-glove. Our enemies are united against us."

I couldn't quite believe what I'd just heard: the casual, matter-of-fact way that the shooting of Jews was discussed, as if we were a gang of murderers comparing notes on how to carry out our crimes. I still hadn't quite understood that that was precisely what we were. On that disturbing note, we began our tour of inspection.

A vast area behind the Lenin House was just a featureless plain, dotted with occasional scraps of old buildings, through which ran roads going nowhere, passing nothing. It was hard to believe that anyone had lived here in centuries, yet it had been a thriving area of the city just a few months before. Elsewhere, we had been busy since June, using Soviet prisoners-of-war as forced labor to clear the streets and rebuild those structures that were not beyond repair. But Schlegel's car still drove down roads lined on either side by great piles of rubble, wooden beams, and twisted, buckled steel girders. A large open space, known as Freedom Square, had once been one of the finest sights in the city, but was now just another wasteland, with a gibbet in the center from which, Schlegel proudly told us, partisans were regularly hanged.

A little further on, we came to one of the buildings that were large enough and sufficiently well-preserved to act as local headquarters for our various military and civilian agencies. Along one entire wall was a gigantic pile of personal luggage, well over two meters high and extending several meters from the side of the building. It seemed to cover every stratum of society, from the fine steamer trunks of the wealthy to leather and cardboard suitcases, large wicker hampers, and simple canvas sacks at the bottom of the scale.

"That's Jew baggage," said Schlegel. "Came in on a recent transport and we haven't had time yet to go through it all."

We drove on and stopped outside what must once have been a very beautiful church, with two fine bell-towers either side of a fine classical facade. It was looking a little tatty now. The white stucco with which it had been covered had fallen off in patches, and what remained was smoke-stained and pockmarked with bullet holes. By the standards of the rest of Minsk, however, it was remarkably well preserved.

"This is the Catholic Cathedral of the Virgin Mary," said Schlegel. "It is now holding regular services as any other cathedral would. But I'll give you five guesses as to what it was when we arrived here in July."

"I don't know," I said. "What would the Bolshies do with a cathedral? Was it some sort of shrine to heroes of the revolution, perhaps?"

"A good guess, but wrong. Come inside and try again."

We got out of the warm, snug car and into the freezing air—only November, and already the temperature there was as cold as any I'd ever known, a grim portent of the winter to come. Inside, the cathedral wasn't much warmer and the walls were stripped of all decoration. There were no statues anywhere: no plaques or paintings, no stained glass in the windows, just grubby, peeling paintwork that was a reddish-brown color up to head height and a dirty white from there to the ceiling. The floorboards were rough and quite bare of any covering. The pews had all been removed and the altar was little more than a folding table with a simple wrought-iron cross placed upon it.

"Look," said Schlegel, pointing to what must once have been a small side chapel. I stared into the gloomy recess and tried to make sense of what looked like a workbench with a vice clamped to its side, and next to that some sort of manually operated lathe. "Got it yet?" he asked. "Take a smell, why don't you?"

I sniffed and detected not the usual cathedral scents of candles and incense but something totally improbable: motor oil and exhaust fumes. "This place smells like a garage," I said.

Schlegel clapped. "Correct! That's exactly what it was. The Bolsheviks stripped every single religious symbol from the place and made it the city's main motor-repair center. Come over here, I'll show you, they smashed through one of the walls to make an entrance for cars and trucks."

I was quite speechless. I'd never come across anything like it. "They really are savages!" snapped von Toll, bitterly. Doubtless he could imagine similar indignities being inflicted on his old family home.

"Quite so," agreed Schlegel. "Still, it's gradually being restored to its intended purpose now. It gives us a chance to show the locals that we're more civilized than the brutes they've had to put up with for the past twenty years. It wouldn't be difficult!"

We continued with our drive, entering a residential area. Most of the Russian population lived in houses that reminded me strongly of the hut in Friedrichsfelde where Ogorzow killed Gerda Ditter.

These single-story structures, some made of brick but the great majority wooden, lined streets that were often little more than dirt tracks. "It's so primitive," I said, as we passed along yet another poverty-stricken street.

Schlegel grinned. "Ha! This is luxurious compared to what's next."

We drove a little further and then came to a barbed-wire fence, stretching away on either side of the road ahead of us. There was an opening in the fence, across which a simple wooden barrier had been placed, guarded by a pair of SS men. Beyond it the street seemed no different from the ones we had just driven down, except that it was incomparably more crowded with people.

"Welcome to the ghetto," said Schlegel.

30

The Minsk ghetto occupied about twenty blocks, most of them sub-divided by narrow winding alleys. The fence in front of us ran right around it. The main thoroughfare cut through the ghetto from one side to the other, with a gate guarded by SS men at either end. Every ghetto building had a number, and all Jews were obliged to wear a white badge on their chest, clearly showing the number of their building. They also had to wear their yellow badges—some in the shape of Stars of David, but most just plain, roughly cut circles—on both the front and back of their clothes, so that coming or going, they could always be seen to be Jews.

Here and there I could see groups of our people, both Wehrmacht and SS, standing around. Some were laughingly mocking passing Jews, telling them what filthy Yids they were, lashing out at them with boots or sticks, or knocking the skullcaps off their heads. Another group had set up a race. Four very small Jewish men were crawling along the road. Each was carrying a much larger Jew on his back, and there were loud shouts of encouragement and even the odd kick of the backside to make them go as quickly as possible toward the finishing line. Of course I found it all distasteful—I have never been anti-Semitic, either then or now—but in truth this was little differ-ent from the kind of Jew-baiting that SA storm troopers had been indulging in for years on the streets of Berlin, and many other German cities besides. We had all become numb to it over time.

Elsewhere the shouts were angrier. We passed one young soldier—he could not have reached his twentieth birthday—waving his rifle at a group of Jewish women, ordering them to move. They didn't seem to understand what he was saying and I could hear him becoming more frustrated, a note of anger and even anxiety entering his voice. We drove past without stopping and turned into another block. We were halfway along it when the sound of shots echoed down the street, followed by the wail of a woman crying out in anguish. Now I was much more concerned. It was one thing to mock Jews, quite another to shoot them out of hand in broad daylight. Schlegel, however, didn't appear to have noticed. I tapped him on the shoulder and said: "We need to turn back."

"Forget it," he said. "That's just one less mouth to feed."

I was shocked by his attitude, but there was little I could do. Like it or not, Schlegel was senior to me and I was a newcomer. I had no right to contradict him. And so I began the process of moral compromise: I made the first excuse for doing nothing, turning a blind eye, justifying the unjustifiable.

Deeper into the ghetto we went. It had been in existence for a little over four months and the overcrowding was almost indescribable. The official allocation of space was 1.4 square meters per adult Jew—nothing for children.

"Would you like to see inside one of their houses?" Schlegel asked. He stopped the car. We got out and he led us up to one of the wooden buildings. Almost without breaking stride, he kicked the door open and in we went, our boots clattering like hammers on the floorboards. The house had two rooms both packed tight with old folk, women, and children. They cowered away, crowding themselves together in the corners of the rooms so that we were left on our own in the middle. Some looked terrified at our arrival. Others seemed too sick,

starved, or exhausted to care. A few stared at us with silent but uncon-
cealed hatred. One or two muttered under their breath in a language I
took to be Russian, and I saw von Toll struggling to disguise his shock
at what he'd heard.

The smell of filthy, unwashed humanity was overpowering. "My
God," I said, disgusted by the spectacle. "They live like rats in a sewer."

Schlegel gave a casual shrug. "Ach, this is nothing. Half of them
are out at work. In the evening they will be crammed together much
more closely. How else do you think they keep warm?"

The house was no warmer than the cathedral had been, which is
to say, perishing cold. There was a crude heating-stove in one of the
rooms, but nothing to put in it and no electrical power anywhere in
the ghetto. So Schlegel's question wasn't rhetorical: all the Jews had
to prevent them from freezing was the heat of their own bodies,
and they made precious little of that.

They were given one meal a day, consisting of a thin gruel of
five grams of buckwheat cooked in thirty centiliters of water, plus a
hundred and fifty grams of buckwheat bread. There were only two
kitchens in the ghetto, so the inmates had to distribute their gruel
to all the inhabitants in fifty-liter containers, dragged on wooden
sledges. The men who supervised this process were the elite of the
ghetto, and on the rare occasions when there was anything left over
at the end of the day, they were allowed to consume it. Workers were
given extra rations—a little bit more of the same diet—at their places
of work. Some of the Jews also tried to barter for food, but this was
both illegal and futile. A diamond watch, smuggled into the ghetto in
the lining of a coat, would be exchanged for a single small loaf of black
bread. It seemed like a poor exchange. But then, a loaf might keep a
man alive for an extra day, and one cannot eat diamonds.

Thus far, all the Jews we had seen were of a type to gratify the most
rabid Party propagandists. The old men in particular seemed hunched,

hook-nosed, heavily bearded, and shifty-eyed, with skullcaps on their heads and prayer shawls around their shoulders. But then we passed through an entrance in a second fence, which enclosed a tiny fraction of the ghetto as a whole. Above the entrance was a sign that read *sonderghetto*—"Special Ghetto." Within, the people looked quite different from the rest: much more like normal Europeans. Though their clothes were dirty there were some, at least, who wore suits, coats, and dresses of much better quality.

"Who are these people?" I asked.

"Listen," said Schlegel.

It took me a second, but then I realized that all around me I could hear German being spoken.

"This is what they call the Hamburg ghetto," Schlegel said. "We've put all the Reich Jews here. When the first lot arrived there were still dead Russian Jews everywhere, so the new ones had to clear up the mess in order to have somewhere to sleep." He gave me a hard, confrontational look, like a drunk in a bar, looking for a fight. "You look shocked, Heuser. Believe me, when you've spent a few months in this shit-hole, a few thousand dead Jews here or there will seem like nothing at all."

We drove back to our base in silence. When we arrived, I thanked Schlegel for giving us such an educational tour. He went back to the SD office while von Toll and I walked on to mine. On the way we passed a lavatory. "Please excuse me, First Lieutenant," said von Toll, stopping by the door and reaching for the handle, "but I think I'm going to be sick."

31

On the following morning I woke at 04:00. The final trainload of Vienna Jews had arrived overnight, and unloading was due to begin at 05:00. By that time they had been in transit for four days and nights, but the conditions in which they were transported were not quite as insufferable as they would later become. The Reichsbahn had set aside redundant Czech and Austrian rolling stock for the resettlement of Reich Jews, all of whom had to pay for their tickets. They traveled in third-class passenger carriages. There was no heating or water supply on the trains, but at least there were seats for half the transportees, and compartment floors and corridors for the rest. There was a large kitchen wagon and the Jews were even allowed to write postcards and letters, which were collected at the various stops along the way and posted to their families and friends at home. Just as I'd done my best to paint the happiest possible picture for Biene in my letter to her, so the writers of these communications strove to reassure those they had left behind with upbeat descriptions of the journey as a great adventure, making light of any discomforts on the way. In this, of course, they were doing us a great favor, perpetuating the myth that the process of "resettlement" was really what it purported to be, rather than something else entirely.

Why else would the Jews have kept buying their tickets and getting on their trains in all the weeks, months, and years that followed?

This particular consignment of Viennese Jews had been guarded on their journey by a detachment from a Police Reserve Battalion: former uniformed police officers, now too old for active front-line duty, who served as guards and sentries, thereby releasing younger, fitter men for the front line. They traveled in a second-class compartment at the back of the train. There were also five goods wagons, containing the baggage. I now understood why I'd seen such a giant pile of cases, for each adult Jew had a baggage allowance of fifty kilograms. This generous quantity served two purposes. First, it provided yet more reassurance to the Jews that they were true settlers, who would be allowed to start a new life in Ostland. But far more significantly, the baggage was an attempt to make the destruction of the Jews a self-financing program. The transportees naturally packed their most precious possessions, including valuables such as gold, silver, jewels, clothes, food, wine, and, of course, their money. In theory, all of it was supposed to be returned to the Reich. The cash, precious metals, and jewels were earmarked for the Reichsbank's vaults, while the clothes and foodstuffs would be redistributed to the people. Theory and practice, however, turned out to be very different things.

I reached the goods depot at approximately 04:30 and conferred with my colleague SS-First Lieutenant Kurt Burkhardt, who was in charge of Jewish affairs. He'd already received a report from the officer in charge of the guard. Eight Jews had been shot while trying to escape at various points on the journey. The officer was more concerned, however, that his men had been given nothing to eat since reaching Bialystok, many hours earlier, except for bread and margarine. They were also worried that they would now be called to join in a mass execution of the Jews. The officer claimed that they had undertaken such tasks in Poland and morale had suffered considerably as a result.

I suppose there was some excuse for my inability—or was it willful refusal?—to acknowledge the truth of what Frank Baum was showing me in his vile photographs. But here was yet more evidence, as if everything I'd heard and seen the previous day were not proof enough of what had been happening to Jews in the Eastern Territories. Yet I still couldn't bring myself to face that truth, and was as relieved as that police battalion officer when Burkhardt told him that we would supply sausages for his men's return journey and gave a solemn assurance that these Jews were not about to be shot, but were on the contrary being taken to a special ghetto, set aside for their use. The officer and his men were then escorted to a nearby barracks where they were given food and a place to rest before their journey back home that evening.

At precisely 05:00 the unloading of the Jews began. The officer in charge of this phase of the operation was SS-Captain Stark. He too had come here to Minsk as part of Sonderkommando 1b, though even then I hesitated to call him a comrade. Stark was a crude, ignorant bully, who did not look on our work as a necessary, sometimes burdensome duty, but as a welcome opportunity to indulge the most sadistic aspects of his personality. This was evident from the moment the first Jews emerged from the train, still expecting to be given the opportunity to start a new life. The men were dressed in their best suits and winter coats, and almost all wore hats. The women, too, were smartly dressed—many in furs—and the mothers could be heard giving words of encouragement to their children, telling them to stand up straight and be of good cheer. There was a pathetic eagerness in their smiles, a determination to make the best of things and even, it seemed to me, a belief that they might be treated a little better in Minsk than they had been in Vienna. I even heard one woman tell her children: "I am sure they'll send a bus to take us all to our new homes."

Each train was required to nominate a leader to act as its representative with the Reich authorities. The Viennese had chosen a once-prominent lawyer, Dr. Friedman, a distinguished-looking gentleman with a fur-trimmed coat, a gray homburg hat, gold pince-nez, and a neat silver beard. He stepped forward to greet Captain Stark, who was standing on the platform holding a leather horsewhip, which he tapped against the side of his leg. Friedman held his hand out to Stark and, in a rich, mellifluous voice, which I could just imagine him using to mesmerize the judges and jurors in a courtroom, began to introduce himself. But no sooner had he begun to say, "Good day, my name is . . ." than Stark shouted, "Shut your filthy Jew mouth!" in a crude, lower-class Bavarian accent that presented a sorry contrast to Friedman's impeccable diction. The latter struggled to compose himself, and I could see the shocked, appalled looks on the faces of the other transportees as Stark stepped forward and used his whip to flick the hat off Friedman's head so that it fell to the ground.

Stark stamped on the hat repeatedly until it was filthy, crumpled, and devoid of all shape. Then he turned back to Friedman and shouted in his face: "Always remove your hat in the presence of a German officer! Never speak unless you are spoken to! Do you understand me, Jew?"

Friedman was clearly determined to maintain some vestige of dignity. He straightened himself, pulled back his shoulders, and calmly replied: "Yes."

Without the slightest warning, Stark struck Friedman with his whip, a hard blow to the side of the old man's face that made him stagger backward, trip over his heels, and fall to the ground. Stark stood motionless watching the old man as he rubbed his face, across which a savage red welt was forming, and then struggled back to his feet.

When Friedman was finally able to stand up opposite him again, Stark repeated: "Yes what?"

An absolute silence fell across the goods depot. In the distance I could hear the whistle of a passing train. The breeze sent a few scraps of paper scurrying across the platform. But seconds passed without any further noise before Friedman finally managed to force out the words "Yes, sir."

I was very disturbed to see this kind of behavior. I still retained the belief that no German officer should act with such callous contempt for the dignity of others, whatever their status. But I must surely have known that I was being unrealistic. I'd seen the ghetto. I knew what awaited the Jews. Stark's behavior was all of a piece with that.

Certainly it had an effect on the new arrivals from Vienna. They were cowed and silent as Stark and his men ordered them to place all their hand baggage on waiting trucks, then form into a column, five abreast. If any dawdled, Stark lashed out at them with his whip: women, old people, and children alike. When all one thousand were standing in line, Stark announced that they were now to be marched to the ghetto. If any of them even tried to escape, one hundred of their Jew brethren would be shot. With that, they were herded away, through the city. Only the most elderly or infirm were loaded on trucks and driven to their destination.

Burkhardt later told me that the Vienna Jews had all been taken to an old, red-painted schoolhouse that housed all new arrivals in the ghetto, until places could be found for them in other buildings. Several hundred men, women, and children from the previous transport, which had come in from Hamburg and Bremen on the 19th, were still in the schoolhouse, there being nowhere for them to go. "It's not my problem," he said when I asked him whether this situation could be tolerated. "Stark has been given the task of keeping order in the ghetto. Let him sort it out."

32

The Vienna Jews were installed in the ghetto. They were starved. They were frozen. They were worked till they dropped. The old, the weak, and the sick began to die, a few more every day. Others fell victim to the combination of instant summary justice and sheer sadism by which the tiny number of armed guards kept the tens of thousands of ghetto dwellers in order. But there were as yet no concerted actions taken against them, and much of my time was occupied with conventional police and counterespionage work. All the while, though, the subplots of our terrible drama kept spreading beneath the surface of our lives, like the roots and tendrils of weeds and brambles that see the open air only when springtime comes again.

I was lucky enough to have my own office. This enabled me to conduct professional interviews and even low-level interrogations, and it also meant that I could have private conversations. Early one evening, when our work for the day was done, I poured a glass of brandy for von Toll and another for myself. He told me that he'd just heard a very interesting rumor. Apparently, Stark wasn't a true German. He'd been born in America, most likely to an American father. I asked von Toll how he'd come by this information and he replied that it was one benefit of being an enlisted man, rather than an officer. "As my grandmother used to say, all the best gossip comes from the servants' quarters."

We talked about this and that, and then von Toll said: "You know, my family can trace their German roots back for centuries, but being here makes me feel like a foreigner . . ." He gave me one of his characteristically wry half-smiles before he added: "Even more of a foreigner than Stark. I've not grown up in the same country as you. No one's told me all the reasons why I should hate the Jews. Now I find myself unable to do so. And I cannot understand why they must be treated so much worse than I would treat any farm animal—even one destined for the slaughterhouse."

"What has hating the Jews got to do with it?" I replied. "I don't hate them."

"Really?" said von Toll, sounding genuinely puzzled.

"Absolutely. I don't have feelings about them one way or another."

"Well surely you must know some."

"Actually, I don't. There were some Jewish shopkeepers my mother used to go to in the old days, but there weren't any Jewish boys in my year at school—none that I knew, anyway. And by the time I got to university, they'd all left. They weren't allowed to go there anymore."

"But if you have nothing against them, how can you just stand there and do nothing when you see them treated the way they are here?"

That simple question was the one that tormented all of us who were posted to Minsk and still possessed any shred of conscience or decency. It ate away at us, a nagging voice in the back of all our minds. Yet von Toll was the only one who dared ask it out loud, for there was surely only one answer: one couldn't "just stand there." But none of us could face that truth, and so I gave von Toll the answer, or rather the excuse, that I told myself, too, as we all have ever since: "Because everyone who is treating the Jews in that way is acting under orders, and it is not my place, or theirs, to question those orders. My sworn duty, like yours, is to obey whatever orders are given to me on the Führer's behalf."

"No matter what those orders might be?" von Toll asked.

"Well, yes . . . surely the whole point about an order is that it is not a request to be questioned or debated. It has to be obeyed."

"But surely the way we are treating the Jews is different. This is absolutely a matter of right and wrong."

There are times when it helps to have been trained as a lawyer. It enables one to pretend that there is something a little primitive, unsophisticated even, about thinking in terms of good and evil. "Perhaps, but we aren't the ones making those moral decisions. We are simply servants of the Reich—the agents, as it were, acting for those people, so the moral responsibility is theirs, not ours."

Von Toll said nothing, but I could see that he wasn't convinced by my sophistry. I poured him some more brandy. The bottle had come from the baggage seized from the Vienna transport. It occurred to me that if we treated the Jews any better we wouldn't be drinking this cognac, but I thought it best not to point that out.

Ah yes, the baggage: now there was another institutional falsehood. I'd been looking into the subject of the possessions and valuables seized from the Jews. SS regulations were absolutely clear that the unauthorized taking of so much as a pfennig in cash or a single item of property constituted looting, for which the penalty was death. In practice, however, matters appeared to be much more ambiguous. All perishable foodstuffs, including alcohol, were consumed by SS personnel in Minsk, on the premise that it would be impractical to transport them elsewhere. That was reasonable enough. The money, meanwhile, was taken to the finance department of the KdS, where it was sorted into different currencies: not just Reichsmarks, but also Russian rubles, French and Swiss francs, British sterling, U.S. dollars, Spanish and even Mexican pesos. From there it was shipped to Riga and then on to Berlin, but just as a gang works on a hierarchical basis, with money flowing from all the petty criminals and hooligans on the street up toward the boss at the top, with each layer taking a little cut on the way, so there were many deductions from the appropriated money on its journey from Minsk, or anywhere else where Jewish transports were processed, all the way to the Reich Finance Ministry.

There was another source of gold, one that I could hardly credit when I first heard of it: gold teeth and fillings, removed from the mouths of liquidated Jews, shortly before they were killed.

"Don't look so fucking squeamish, Heuser," Stark said contemptuously, when the look on my face too clearly gave away the disgust I felt on being given this information. "Or are you just worried you won't get your share?"

Ten months had passed since I'd been troubled by the thought of drinking contraband coffee. Now I was being cut in on the gold-tooth racket. I got a piece of the rings and watches. And somehow I came to terms with that, too. Little by little I was making all the necessary adjustments that we all employed simply to hold on to our sanity. The crucial thing was to distract oneself from the truth of what was really going on: to try, as far as possible, to live in denial. One way of doing that was to look inward instead of out, and immerse oneself in the professional conflicts and power struggles of the KdS.

Thanks to my joint Kripo-Gestapo role, I had access to personnel files, so I took the opportunity to look at Stark's record. It turned out that those American rumors were true. Franz Stark was born in St. Louis, Missouri, on October 27, 1901. Mother: Christiane Stark; father: unknown. Fräulein Stark had immigrated to America in 1890, but she returned home to Germany in 1903, bringing her son with her. She was not a good mother. She beat the boy, inflicting such serious injuries to his head that in 1905 he was taken from her and given to foster parents. His schooling ended at the age of thirteen. He subsequently trained as a mechanic without gaining any formal qualifications.

It was like reading the life stories of Kürten or Ogorzow: a poorly educated child of an unstable family and an unsuitable mother, and the subject of violent abuse. I was working alongside a psychopath, one whose lust for violence was evident from the start of his adult life.

In 1919, age eighteen, Stark had moved to Munich. He joined the National Socialist movement on January 1, 1920, in its absolute infancy, when it was still the German Workers' Party and Drexler, not Hitler, was its leader. In 1921 he signed up with the Brownshirts on the very day they were formed. Two years later he fought alongside Hitler at the Beer Hall Putsch and later won the Party's Blood Medal for his participation in this and countless other acts of violence. After a few years of menial employment, he found work in 1933 as a handyman on Heydrich's personal domestic staff. From there he became a clerk in the SS. His rise from clerk to officer class was swift.

It was clear I was dealing with a very dangerous man indeed. Stark had free rein in Minsk to act out his most wicked urges without restraint, indeed with the approval of his superiors, while his Party history and his personal connection to Heydrich made him untouchable. Stark's problem, however, was that, like Paul Ogorzow, he was handicapped by his stupidity. He had just enough intelligence to realize the strength of his position, but not quite enough to appreciate its limitations. In the end he would be brought down by a lowly Jewish barber, a man called Steiner, whom I was just about to meet.

I'd been allotted the services of a stenographer/typist to assist with the writing of memos. Her name was Fräulein Krankl, and she was one of the many women who had come to Minsk in the hope of finding a husband among the thousands of single men, far from the comforts of home, who were stationed in the city. A man would have to have been sexually deprived for a very long time, however, before he turned to Fräulein Krankl. She had the plain face and shapeless physique of a woman doomed to spend her life as a spinster. Yet even the dowdiest wallflower can dream of being a rose, and one day, not long before Christmas, she arrived to take dictation looking as though she'd just put on a bright yellow wig.

I was foolish enough to comment on the fact that she appeared to have had her hair done, and Krankl started simpering coyly and batting her eyelashes at me in her idea of an alluring, coquettish manner. I then received a long account of her session with some Viennese Jew called Steiner. He and his two sons were barbers by profession.

"Steiner cuts Gauleiter Kube's hair, and gives him his morning shave every day," Krankl told me. "Now he and his sons are looking after us girls as well. Such a charming man . . ." I looked at her pointedly and she became very flustered. I could see her trying to find a way to rectify her error. "For a Jew, I mean," she said.

It struck me then that I'd not had my hair cut for some while, and it was in danger of looking unkempt. So I told Krankl: "In that case, please arrange an appointment for me with this Steiner man. He can see me tomorrow morning at nine."

That evening, nursing a glass of schnapps in the officers' mess, I thought how Steiner's role illustrated a strange contradiction about our life in Minsk. On the one hand, we were told to regard the Jews as little more than subhuman vermin. Yet at the very same time, we relied on them to do all our dirty work. They were orderlies, cleaners, and porters in the military hospitals. They took out the garbage. They cleaned our offices, our living quarters, and even the cells in our prisons. They mended our shoes and clothes. They sorted through captured Russian weapons and the appropriated possessions of their own people. They staffed army and Luftwaffe warehouses and typed letters for the few German businessmen brave enough to come here in search of their fortunes. They provided sexual services too, since some of the men had pretty Jewish girlfriends, though such behavior was strictly forbidden. And now, apparently, they cut our hair too.

So it was that the following morning I found myself sitting back in the barber's chair: an SS officer allowing a Jew to run a razor blade over his neck. Having trimmed my hair, Steiner had asked if I would like him to give me a shave and hot towel treatment as well. None of this was costing me any money, and my morning schedule was comparatively light, so there was no reason to decline the offer. And I could hardly say: "I don't think so. I'm worried that you might slit my throat."

Steiner and I made inconsequential conversation, just as if I were a customer in his shop in Vienna. The haircut was perfectly satisfactory and the shave a very smooth one. The hot towel treatment afterward was particularly relaxing. Only one thing puzzled me: he wore no yellow badges on his coat. Either he had a death wish, coming to SS headquarters improperly dressed, or someone very powerful indeed had given him permission to do it.

"Ah yes, sir, that was Gauleiter Kube's idea," Steiner said, when I raised the subject with him. "It was the ladies, you see. They didn't like seeing the Stars of David—upset them, apparently. So I've got an exemption"—and then he paused for a fraction—"although Captain Stark does not seem to approve of it."

"No, I shouldn't think he does," I said.

"He was—how can I put this?—somewhat upset when he saw that the badges had been removed from my coat."

"Ah well, if the Gauleiter has given the order, that's all that matters, eh?"

I thought no more about Steiner and his coat. There were other far more pressing matters to concern us all. But Stark hadn't forgotten. He regarded all the ghetto Jews as his property. He took Steiner's coat as a personal insult, delivered by the barber and the Gauleiter alike. And in time he would have his revenge.

33

December 1941 marked both the furthest limits of Germany's wartime conquests and the moment at which our fortunes turned irrevocably for the worse. The retreat that wouldn't end until Berlin itself was an occupied city began when the Russians launched a counteroffensive across a broad front either side of Moscow, and a second assault down in the Ukraine, advancing on Kharkov. Days later I happened to be talking to an officer in military intelligence. He told me in strict confidence that Stalin had shipped his entire Siberian army, forty divisions, all the way from the far Pacific coast to Moscow. They were crack troops, apparently, fully equipped for winter, and their T-34 tanks were a class above anything we had. Meanwhile our armored divisions were stuck and our guns wouldn't fire because we didn't have any lubricating oil that worked in extreme cold. "We've lost the best part of three hundred thousand men already and the whole campaign is going to shit," the officer said. "Of course we'll turn it around. But even so, it's a shock."

A day later came the news that the Japanese had bombed the U.S. Navy base at Pearl Harbor, in the Hawaiian islands.

That was a sensational enough event in itself. But what followed was even more significant, for Hitler used the attack as a pretext to declare war on the United States of America. It was a moment of pure, self-destructive folly on the Führer's part. We were stretched to the very limit fighting the Russians in the east. If the Americans now joined the British in the west, how could we possibly keep them at bay?

To these human enemies could be added another foe, even mightier and more pitiless than the rest: Old Father Frost. The winter of '41–'42 was brutally cold and we were utterly unprepared for its rigors. One morning my work took me to the main railway station. A troop transport had just come in, bringing the wounded back from the front. There were men walking around the platform with crazed, staring eyes. It took me a moment to realize that they had no eyelids. I asked a medical orderly what had happened to them and he just said: "The cold."

He went on to explain that the frost singed skin and flesh, like a sort of cold fire, so that it simply died and fell from men's bodies. Eyelids, ears, noses, and lips were stripped from faces; hands lost their fingers; bodies their arms and legs. Even sexual organs had been known to freeze like icicles and snap off.

For the Jews, of course, it was even worse. They died by the hundred and their frozen corpses piled up in the streets because they couldn't be buried in the rock-hard soil. Finally matters got so bad that Burkhardt had to organize a detachment of men to go into the Jewish cemetery and use dynamite to blast a hole big enough to be used as a mass grave.

When those Jewish bodies were finally buried, almost all were naked: their clothes had long since been stripped to provide some tiny scrap of warmth to those still living. Our people were no different, taking any clothes or blankets they could find just to stay warm. I spotted an army corporal on the street one day wearing a real banker's coat: dove-gray cashmere down almost to his ankles, with a collar of soft black mink. When he passed me I saw there was a hole in the back. Someone had crudely tried to darn it, but after my months in the murder squad I hardly needed to be told the significance of the blood spatter that still stained the fabric. I didn't do anything. The soldier belonged to the Wehrmacht, so whom he chose to shoot was their business, not mine.

Among the women, there was no more fashionable item of clothing than a fur coat from the Jewish baggage, and a man who could provide such a thing was never short of company. There were Jewesses working in menial roles at the KdS, and it struck me that any one of them might see a German girl walking around in what had once been her coat and know that there was no possible hope of recovering her property. Were she to be so crazy as to report the theft to a policeman, she would most likely be shot. So the Jews kept their mouths shut and shivered in silence. Never, not for a single instant, was there any relief from their degradation.

Yet they were not the only victims of our presence in Minsk. Another day, word reached the KdS office that there were thousands of Russian prisoners-of-war lying dead on the outskirts of the city, lined up on either side of the Smolensk road. They had been sent on a work detail in the middle of a blizzard with no coats, gloves, or even in some cases boots, and were simply left outside until they were all dead. A party of Jewish workers had seen the Russians and one of them, a young woman, tried to offer one of the freezing men a small scrap of bread: her ration for the day. Both she and the prisoner were shot dead on the spot.

The army liked to look down on the SS, seeing themselves as honorable warriors who fought for their Fatherland, while we were just thugs and murderers in the service of the Nazi Party. Yet for every Jew that ever died at the hands of the SS in Minsk, those chivalrous gentlemen of the Wehrmacht killed a Russian prisoner. I wrote in my diary:

This miserable country makes barbarians of us all. No matter where one turns, it is impossible to escape the presence of death. Some of us may continue to exist, but who is truly living? And where, apart from the vodka bottle, can one find the slightest warmth or comfort amid the ice and snow and frozen flesh? One day, perhaps, Minsk will be a thriving provincial center within a mighty German empire. For now, however, it is just a vastly magnified version of Dr. Weimann's chilly mortuary.

That winter destroyed us. Though our retreat from Moscow was not yet as calamitous as Napoleon's had been, the notion of our invincibility was stripped from us. And as our physical might began to fray, so did the qualities that had provided our inner strength: our discipline, our determination, even our dignity. Stark, for example, celebrated Christmas in his own special way. He and a small troop of men went to the Novinki lunatic asylum, not far from the city, and selected twenty-five inmates, apparently at random. They then took them, still wearing their asylum uniforms, to one of the many small natural sandpits, formed by deposits from ancient rivers, that littered the region. These were too small to be used for large-scale operations, but Stark demonstrated that they sufficed perfectly well for smaller actions, for all twenty-five inmates were shot and then dumped in the pit. Stark killed at least seven of the loonies personally. "I emptied a whole magazine into them," he boasted when I saw him at the mess, later in the day.

On New Year's Day, a group of KdS men went into the ghetto and shot almost five hundred of its inhabitants, without any authorization from a senior officer, let alone any actual orders. It was astonishing, frankly, that anyone had the strength to carry out a mass liquidation after the debauchery that had occurred the previous night. Fräulein Krankl, who was outraged by our behavior, took to describing the

KdS as a pigsty, and it was hard to argue with her. Of course the Ogor-zow case had shown me the effect that overwork, stress, and fatigue can have on even the most conscientious people. But this was something more. There was a wantonness, a willful spitting in the face of conventional morality. As if to prove the point, Stark shot a drunken Russian dead for the crime of singing a patriotic song as he staggered down the street, waving his empty vodka bottle in the air.

"It's very simple," said von Toll when I mentioned my impressions to him. "We are all damned and we know it. So now we have nothing to lose."

He was right. Yet we hadn't even begun to scratch the surface of our sins. The real evil, however, wouldn't be long in coming.

In January, my original commanding officer, Ehrlinger, was transferred out of Minsk and replaced by SS-Major Dr. Walter Hofmann. Within days of taking over, Hofmann was summoned to Riga by SS-General Jeckeln, the overall commander of all police forces in the Reich Commissariat of Ostland. While we were shivering in Minsk, Heydrich had summoned representatives from various arms of the Reich's military and civil administration to a daylong meeting at a villa on the Wannsee in Berlin. There he outlined the precise nature and extent of the "final solution to the Jewish question." Jeckeln then passed Heydrich's orders on to Hofmann, who flew back to Minsk, summoned all us KdS officers, and told us that in the future, our policy toward all the Jews of Europe, including German Jews, would be one of total liquidation, although neither that, nor any other word suggesting mass extermination, was ever to be used in public. The approved term for the transportation of Jews to their places of execution would continue to be "resettlement." What happened to them on their arrival was now to be referred to as "processing."

Between ourselves, of course, we could be more frank. Thus Hofmann felt free to inform us that we would soon engage in "a vigorous schedule of executions in the spring." As soon as the snow disappeared, so, he assured me, would the Jews. In the meantime, Hofmann was keen to show Berlin that, in his words, "We're not just sitting here in Minsk with our fingers up our asses." To that end Stark was dispatched with a unit of twenty men to Rakov, a small village about thirty-five kilometers to the west of the city, chosen because there was a natural depression there that alleviated the need to dig a pit. Stark and his people killed a hundred Jews.

I, however, still possessed enough common humanity to be deeply troubled by what we were about to do. As a policeman I'd been trained to obey orders without question: even Lüdtke, so cavalier with the rules in some respects, had been adamant about that. Yet I'd also been trained to protect the innocent and punish those who killed. I was finding it very hard indeed to resolve those two contradictory imperatives. And for all my arguments to the contrary, I knew deep down that it was quite simply wrong.

Von Toll, needless to say, felt even more strongly than I. He insisted that this new policy of extermination was nothing more or less than "criminal insanity," and made no secret of the fact that he was desperate to be transferred away from Minsk. Anywhere would do, he said, including the front line. "I'd far rather be shooting at armed Russians than defenseless Jews. For one thing, I actually hate the damn Russians."

I replied that it was not in my power to get him sent somewhere else. This wasn't entirely true. Hofmann would probably have done it for me had I insisted. The fact was, I needed von Toll as an interpreter and I hated the thought of losing the one person with whom I could talk openly about the truth of our task in Minsk. I might argue with the things he said, but that didn't mean that I wasn't thinking them too. I simply lacked the courage to express those thoughts out loud. Still, at least I'd one good thing to look forward to. After a full year of service I was due for three weeks' leave, from February 10 to March 3, and I intended to spend it in Berlin. Biene was trying to get some time off too, so that we could be together again. Barely three months had passed since I'd last seen her, but it seemed more like three years, such was the chasm, of experience as much as distance, that now seemed to separate us.

Yet my leave was almost ruined before I'd even left Minsk. Just days before I was due to set off on the long train journey to Berlin, Hofmann told me that he'd been given orders to carry out a major action against the ghetto Jews between the first and third of March. Five thousand men, women, and children were to be rounded up in Minsk and then transported by train forty kilometers to Koidanov, where the soil was soft enough for pits to be dug. There they would all be exterminated.

"I am determined to fill my entire quota," Hofmann said. "So it's essential that every one of my men, and in particular the officers, makes a personal contribution to our effort. I regard you as a key member of the staff here, Heuser, and I must insist on your presence. To be frank, you're the best man I've got. So when we get down to work, before dawn on the first of March, you must be here, assisting our efforts."

I attempted politely to remind Hofmann that I wasn't planning to arrive back until the third, and that he'd approved my travel plans, but he was having none of it: "If you do not report for duty at dawn on the first, I will consider you absent without leave." That effectively meant returning to Minsk by the evening of the previous day. To make matters worse, Biene had just written to tell me that she might not be able to leave Hamburg until the last week in February, at the earliest. If I was to take a train from Berlin and be back in Minsk by the 28th, our time together would be drastically curtailed.

And what kind of mood would I be in when we met? After all the months of pretense and self-deception I was now to be confronted by the reality of mass slaughter. The prospect of my first action against the Jews made me feel sick with trepidation. I'd be facing no physical danger whatsoever, yet I couldn't have been more troubled if I were having to confront an entire Soviet division single-handed. Soon I would be called upon to fire my gun at a defenseless human being. What in God's name was I going to do?

34

KOBLENZ:
NOVEMBER 18, 1961

Paula and Kraus were fugitive lovers in Ludwigsburg, never showing any signs of intimacy at work, rarely going out together in public
unless they went into the center of Stuttgart, twenty minutes down the
road. But whenever Kraus came to Koblenz to drop in on the trial and
get a feel for how things were going, it gave them a chance to be a little
less circumspect. They were colleagues, working on the same project
more than four hundred kilometers from home. Of course they would
have a coffee together in the morning, grab a quick lunch during the
midday recess, or dine at the same restaurant in the evening. Paula
even felt able to take his hand and give it a discreet squeeze as they
stood in line one morning at a self-service café near the courthouse,
both of them needing a cup of coffee before the day's proceedings
began. Heuser was due to give evidence about events in the autumn of
1943, and Kraus wanted to hear what the man who considered himself such a good policeman had to say about the months in which he
had committed some of his most terrible crimes.

For now, though, Kraus was more interested in the *Spiegel* Affair,
which had expanded and deepened with every passing day. The
magazine's offices had been raided by the police, who had occupied
them ever since. Augstein, the proprietor, had been arrested and
jailed, along with his two main editors. Conrad Ahlers, the reporter

responsible for the controversial story detailing the army's failings, had been seized in his hotel while on vacation in Spain. Meanwhile, as riots and demonstrations against the arrests broke out across the country, Chancellor Adenauer had given a speech describing revelations of military weakness as "an abyss of treason."

"This is only the start of it," Kraus said, removing a sticky pastry from a display on the counter and putting it on his tray. "I was talking to some fellows at the prosecutors' office yesterday and the word is Strauss is in serious trouble. Apparently, he called our military attaché in Madrid and ordered him to have Ahlers arrested. Of course, our old friend Generalissimo Franco was only too happy to oblige, but it was completely illegal and now Strauss is under huge pressure to admit the whole thing to Parliament. Did you know Stammberger wasn't even consulted before any of the arrests took place? The Minister of Defense throwing people in prison without even letting the Minister of Justice know what was going on? It's outrageous! There's word Stammberger's planning to resign within the next forty-eight hours and he's taking another four cabinet ministers with him."

They were ordering their coffees now. As the girl behind the counter went to make them, Paula said, "Well that's a good sign, don't you think?"

Kraus looked surprised. "A good sign?" he repeated, collecting the coffees and reaching into his trouser pocket for some change. "How can it possibly be good? Apart from bringing the Old Man's ultimate downfall one day closer, I suppose . . ."

They made their way between the crowded tables, through an atmosphere pungent with the smells of coffee and cigarette smoke to an empty space in the far corner of the café. Paula sat down, sorted out her coat and bag, and had a sip of coffee before she replied: "It's good because we know about it all and we can talk about it without being afraid that anyone will hear us and report us. It's good because the moment Strauss admits what he did he'll have to resign, and the police will have to give the *Spiegel* offices back to the staff. And it's good because five ministers are defying the Chancellor and I'm almost certain that none of them will be shot."

Kraus chuckled. "Well, when you put it like that . . ."

"Don't you see that this is the proof that what we do, you and I, really matters? We have to expose the crimes the Nazis committed so that it is unthinkable that they, or anyone like them, can ever return to power. Of course there will always be scandals. Of course arrogant politicians will throw their weight around. But as long as no one dies, and voters can kick them out of office when the next elections come around, then we are making progress."

"Well said, Paula . . . well said." Kraus tapped his hand against the table three times—a traditional sign of support for a speaker. As Paula drank some more coffee he polished off his pastry in a couple of bites, and emptied his own cup in one draft. Then he lit up a cigarette and let out the first lungful of smoke with a sigh. "OK . . . back to the days of jackboots and death's heads. I've read most of the transcripts. Now tell me what's really happening."

Paula thought for a moment and said: "Well, the first thing to say that won't be obvious from the transcripts is that Heuser is running the entire defense, for all of them, not just himself."

"That makes sense. He may not be a qualified lawyer, but he knows his way around a criminal case as well as anyone in the court."

"Exactly. I think the others look on him as their secret weapon: the man who can make it all go away. You see them in recesses, all gathered around him in the corridor behind the courtroom, like schoolchildren around a teacher. He'll give one of them advice about what to say when he's cross-examined, or tell another one what he did right or wrong the last time he was in the witness box. When there are technicalities the others don't understand, he explains what's going on."

"Sounds impressive. Is it working?"

"Up to a point, yes. Stark has already changed his testimony. He told us he carried out two actions—killing a hundred Jews at Rakow and a family of gypsies in Minsk—on Heuser's say-so. Now he's suddenly not sure that he can actually remember getting any specific orders."

"So that's the only witness removed—cunning little shit, isn't he?"

"Very . . . but it's not always to his advantage. I get the feeling Kaul—"

"That's the office administrator who was always trying to get out of the actions, right?"

"Exactly . . . Well, I think he's harboring a private grudge against Heuser. He knows Heuser despised him for not having the guts to take his place on the shooting lines like a man. Now he's getting his own back. Nothing too blatantly hostile, but put it this way: if Heuser ever told Kaul to shoot someone, Kaul will certainly not have forgotten it."

Kraus grinned. "Don't you love it when gangsters start falling out? Still, I'll tell you what I see from the transcripts . . . Triage."

Paula frowned. "I'm sorry, I don't understand."

"It's a basic element in battlefield medicine. The doctors at the field hospitals divide the patients into three: the ones whose wounds are so serious they're going to die, no matter what; the ones whose wounds are so light they don't need immediate treatment; and the ones whose wounds are survivable, but only if they're dealt with immediately. The last group get all the attention."

"All right . . . so what's the connection to Heuser?"

"Simply that he and his lawyer, Geis, are doing precisely the same thing with the charges against him. Wherever the evidence is over-whelming, they don't really try to mount a factual defense. Heuser says, 'Yes, I did it. But I had no choice. I was obeying orders and I feared for my life if I dared to go against them.' Or he does his whole penitent sinner routine: 'I was wrong, I know. I can't tell you why I did it. I was like an automaton . . . No, wait! I was a schizophrenic, doing things that I knew to be terribly wrong . . . I hated it, actually. Yes! That's true! Just ask all these witnesses who remember me saying how sickened I was . . . And anyway it wasn't my fault because I was so damn drunk—no, really, completely sloshed, practically every minute of the day . . . Maybe that's why I was sick all the time? . . . But seriously. I didn't even know what I was doing!'"

By the end of the recital, Paula had her hand over her mouth trying to stifle her laughter. "Stop! Stop!" she begged. "Everyone's looking at us. They must think we're insane."

"I don't know what you think is so funny," replied Kraus, with heavy mock indignation. "I'm taking it all practically verbatim from the court reports."

"I know . . . That's what's so funny. I mean, I shouldn't laugh. It isn't really very funny at all. But—"

"No, it's all right. Sometimes we have to laugh in the face of evil. But now I'll be serious again. I want to finish my triage. OK?"

"Yes, I'm fine now."

"Good. So, the first tactic is: when you know you're beaten, just try to cut your losses. The second tactic, which has been depressingly successful, is to go the exact opposite way: force the court to drop any case which is demonstrably flawed, and do so as quickly as possible. Geis has already had two charges dropped because there's a fifteen-year statute of limitations. That ran out for war crimes on May 8, 1960, fifteen years after the Nazis surrendered, but we didn't even know about the two crimes in question until we went to Moscow in '61, so they're out, irrespective of all the evidence we found. Then when Stark changed his evidence, for example—Geis was on to that right away, demanding that the charges be dismissed. Bang! Another two charges dropped. A few more were excluded on other procedural grounds. Suddenly that's at least a quarter of all the charges vanished as if they'd never been there at all."

"And the third part of the triage?" Paula asked.

"Ah, those are the interesting ones—all those occasions where you know he did it, and I know he did it, but there are just enough holes for Heuser to wriggle through. Perhaps the date isn't specific, or the documents are ambiguous, or two witnesses have given slightly contradictory evidence—which of course they do, because they're describing events twenty years ago, when they were off their heads with alcohol, or fear, or both—but it's just enough to create doubt. That's where Heuser and Geis get to work. They're hoping to find the tiniest little hole in the fabric and then they pull at it and tear at it a little more and loosen the thread until the whole damn thing falls to pieces. And that's really why I decided to come to see the proceedings today."

"What, because you want to see what Heuser's doing firsthand?"

"Partly that . . . but also because I have a terrible suspicion that he's going to succeed."

35

BERLIN AND MINSK: FEBRUARY–JUNE 1942

It took almost three days to reach Berlin from Minsk. Partisans had blown the line about fifty kilometers southwest of Baranovichi, and a mechanical problem in Warsaw held us up another few hours. It was plain to see that our new empire was not as secure as our propagandists were suggesting, but I gave little thought to such strategic considerations. I was too busy asking myself how on earth I could possibly avoid the mass executions that awaited me on my return to the KdS. But no matter how I considered the problem, my conclusion was always the same: I couldn't.

As everyone in those days used to say, there was a war on. A man in uniform didn't pick and choose his duties. If a soldier was told to attack a machine-gun nest, he didn't tell his commanding officer that on the whole he'd rather not run into a hail of bullets. He attacked, like it or not.

I, of course, had no fear of being shot or blown up. My enemy, if that was what I could call them, would be not be armed combatants, but helpless, naked civilians, quite unable to fight back. And that, of course, was the problem. As I contemplated my duty, I could hear von Toll insisting that this killing of the innocent and defenseless, whatever their race, was madness and an unforgivable crime against humanity. I told myself what had I told him, that it was our duty and we had to obey it without question. Yet I could not rid myself of von Toll's protestations.

Most of my first few days in Berlin were spent with my family and those friends who were still in town, even an old girlfriend or two, but I found it almost impossible to make normal, polite conversation with the people around me. I could hardly bear to listen to their petty domestic problems, or their opinions on the progress of the war. All they knew of the Russian Front was what they'd seen on the news-reels, with martial music blaring and pictures of burning Russian tanks and our boys grinning at the camera. They had no idea of the frozen corpses by the side of the road; the haunted faces of the Jews, crammed into their ghetto like matches in a box; the constant killings and the drunken nights.

Wanting to remind myself of better times, I paid a visit to the homicide department. Most of my old colleagues were now scattered across Europe, filling SS posts just as I was, but Lüdtke was still there and Papa Schmidt, too. Schmidt told me that General von dem Bach-Zelewski, the Higher SS and Police Leader who had overseen all the actions undertaken by Einsatzgruppe B throughout Ostland, had gone on an extended sick leave. "They've sent him off to Hohenly-chen," said Schmidt, referring to the SS sanatorium north of Berlin. "He's being given regular doses of pretty-blond-nurse."

"What's the matter with him?" I asked.

"Officially, a stomach complaint," Schmidt replied. Then he brought his head close to mine and lowered his voice: "But I've been told that he's actually been suffering from 'hallucinations connected with the shooting of Jews,' whatever that might mean."

"God only knows," I said, though of course I knew very well. Bach-Zelewski couldn't get the killings out of his head, and he was one of the hard men, a member of the Party since 1930 and of the SS since '31. If he couldn't take it, who could?

In the end I sought advice from Commissar Lüdtke. I called him up to ask if he could spare me some time for a private conversation. "Of course," he replied. "Let's meet at that place where we ate the balcony pig stew. You remember the one?"

"How could I forget?"

Lüdtke gave a gentle chuckle. "Indeed, that was a meal to remember. They have a private room there. I'll make sure that we are not disturbed."

And so I made my way once again to Frau Meissner's restaurant. She insisted on telling us about her son Franz's latest exploits. He was, she said, fighting somewhere on the Eastern Front. "Of course, he can't tell me where. But he tells me it's all going very well. I sent him some nice thick woolly socks to keep him warm. He was ever so grateful to get them."

I assured her that she had done her boy a great favor. "I am on leave from Russia myself, and nothing makes a soldier there happier than the arrival of nice warm clothes."

Her face lit up. "You've been in Russia too. Oh, perhaps you've met my Franzi."

"Well, Russia is a very big place," I said, in as kind a voice as I could muster. "But if I come across your son I'll be sure to remember you to him."

"Oh thank you, sir. It would mean so much to me to think that Franzi has a friend out there, looking out for him."

Frau Meissner led us through to a little room with a single table at the back of her establishment. We ordered beers and a bowl of soup each. "We don't have much on the menu these days, I'm afraid," she told us. "But we make the best of what we've got."

Lüdtke lit a cigarette and looked at me thoughtfully. "So, what's the problem?"

I thought for a moment. There was no way to explain my situation without describing the action that awaited me in Minsk, and that could be considered a breach of security. Still, Lüdtke was a senior officer in the Criminal Police, with contacts at the highest levels of the Reich Security Main Office. Surely he was cleared for even the most sensitive information.

"It involves an upcoming operation," I said. "Do I have your permission to inform you of its nature?"

"Ah, Heuser," he smiled, "always so careful to protect your back. All right, then, let me protect mine, too. Is this operation conducted under the auspices of the Security Police?"

"Yes."

"Then I see no reason why you, as a junior officer, should not ask for professional advice from a former commander."

"Thank you."

"Ah, here comes Frau Meissner with our soup. Why don't you mull over what you need to talk about while we deal with it. The hotter the better, eh?"

This was indeed a soup that was greatly improved by being too hot to taste. We chatted inconsequentially about old times in the murder squad. Lüdtke mentioned that he'd received a Christmas card from Biene, and I said I'd bumped into Frank Baum.

Lüdtke grinned at the mention of his name. "How was he?"

"He's changed a great deal."

"War does that. No one gets out unmarked."

"It wasn't war that changed him—at least, not in the sense of fighting. It was something else . . . Baum's unit was shooting Jews, thousands of them. It's what we call an 'action.' The thing is, I've got my first action when I get back to Minsk next week: five thousand ghetto Jews. . . . And I don't know what to do."

Lüdtke stuck a cigarette in his mouth and used the time it took to light it, draw the first smoke, into his lungs, and then blow it slowly, contemplatively back out again, to collect his thoughts.

"I've heard about this sort of thing. There've been rumors ever since we went into Poland, back in '39. But one always hopes the stories are exaggerated, or simply invented. I assume you know for certain that they're not."

"Oh yes, they're true all right."

"So what will your part in this be?"

"I'm working on the initial roundup and then I'll be included in the actual shooting, too. Hofmann says that it's a matter of principle. Everyone knows that this is a terrible business, and the men can't be expected to participate unless the officers are seen to be doing it too."

"Well that's true enough."

"It feels as though I'm being asked to commit murder. How can a police detective, of all people, possibly consent to that? But equally, I'm an officer; I'm supposed to obey orders and set an example to my men."

Lüdtke stubbed out his cigarette and immediately lit another. "I can see your dilemma. But you're not the first man and you certainly won't be the last to face this kind of choice. War is always filled with cruelty and suffering. That's the nature of it."

"But not toward defenseless civilians, surely?"

"On the contrary, it has always been cruelest of all toward them . . . You surely remember your classical history: 'Carthago delenda est.'"

"Carthage must be destroyed . . ."

"That's it. Carthage was a massive city. When the Romans finally seized it they killed more than four hundred thousand people and sold the survivors into slavery. Then they razed the city to the ground, obliterating it forever. Scipio Africanus gave the orders for that 'action.'

I daresay there were officers under his command who balked at them. But they obeyed all the same."

"But the Romans and the Carthaginians were at war with one another. Are we at war with the Jews?"

"We're at war with whomever our leaders care to choose. Look, Heuser, I know how you feel. I was called up in 1916 and I ended up on the Italian front, in the 12th Infantry Division under Lequis. In October '17 we came down out of the Carinthian Alps, smashed through the Italian lines, and didn't stop moving till we reached the Adriatic. The Italians were routed. Their entire army just evaporated. Six hundred thousand men either deserted or surrendered. A splendid result, wouldn't you agree?"

I said, "Absolutely," with enthusiasm, but I felt a degree of envy, too. Lüdtke's war service had been an uncomplicated matter of one fighting man against another. I envied that simplicity. I soon discovered, however, that it wasn't as simple as I had imagined.

"Well, let me tell you why we won so easily." Lüdtke said. "We gassed them. The Italians had useless gas masks, much worse than the French or the Tommies, so they had no chance. They'd lost thousands, dead and wounded, before we even reached their lines. The rest took one look and ran away. It was amazing. We walked right up to their lines and they hardly fired a shot. If anyone did have the nerve to fight back, we showed them our latest toy—flamethrowers. Most of them were burned to death in their trenches and bunkers, but a few ran down the hill in flames, screaming and tumbling over like human pinwheels. It was terrible to see and it was also wrong. After all, the whole world agrees that the use of gas was criminal. So, should the artillery officers who commanded the guns that were loaded with gas shells have obeyed the order to fire?"

"I don't know," I said, feeling that my chances of finding a right answer were diminishing even further.

"No, you don't know," he said. "That's the whole point. Soldiers almost never know the true purpose, let alone the outcome, of what they're ordered to do—not at the time. But looking back now, I'm certain that the use of poison gas saved many more lives than it took. After all, we didn't have to spend weeks trying to fight our way through the Italian lines. Tens of thousands of men on both sides made it to the end of the war because of that—me included. So you'll never find me apologizing for what we did."

"I suppose not, but—"

"But nothing. Look, Heuser, I don't know what's happening out there in the wilds of Russia. But I cannot believe that you, or anyone else, would be asked to slaughter your fellow human beings, whatever race or religion they are, for no strategic purpose at all. For God's sake, man, we're Germans. We're the most cultured, scientifically advanced people on earth. We believe in laws, in order, in correct procedures. So whatever you're ordered to do, there will be a reason for it. You must simply trust that the reason is good. And if any of your men come to you and say, 'I can't do this, I don't believe it's right,' just tell them what I have told you. It is not our business to think. It is our business to obey. Trust me, my boy, once you think like that, everything becomes much easier."

So Lüdtke concluded by telling me almost exactly what I had told von Toll. His endorsement of my opinion lifted a huge weight of doubt off my shoulders.

"Thank you, sir, that's been a great help," I said.

Lüdtke reached across the table and patted me on the shoulder. "Think nothing of it. Tell you what, it's bitter cold outside. Why don't we have a quick glass of schnapps to warm us up before we go?"

From that moment on, my leave seemed to get better with every passing day. I went for a drink with Uli Schneider, an old friend who'd been a Luftwaffe reservist with me together back in '35 and

'36. Schneider was on the administrative staff at Tempelhof Airport, coordinating transport for senior officers, politicians, even the Führer himself. He told me there was a flight leaving Berlin on the morning of the 28th, bound for Minsk: some bigwig from the Reich Ministry for the Occupied Eastern Territories. So if I wanted to fly back to Minsk in a few hours, instead of spending two days on a train, I only had to ask. "And he's taking one of the Führer's personal Condors," Uli added. "So you'd really be flying in style."

Naturally, I leapt at his invitation. Now I could spend all of my birthday—and all night—with Biene. I called her in Hamburg and she was thrilled by the news. A day later her train was pulling into Berlin's Lehrter Station, and from the moment Biene and I set eyes upon one another it was as though it had been minutes rather than months since we were last together. For three days and nights we hardly left my apartment, except for occasional expeditions to buy food and champagne, and one trip to the movies. We saw something called *Women Are Better Diplomats* because everyone I'd met in Berlin said Biene would love it. But it made no impression on me at all, since she and I spent the entire time in the back row, kissing like a pair of lovesick students. It was wonderful just for once to forget about the war, the Russians, and the damn Jews; to think of nothing more than her skin, her lips, her breasts, and her hot, wet pussy; to fuck and fuck . . . My God, I have never in my life done it so often or so excitingly.

It wasn't just the physical release after all the months away, nor even the passion between us, that made our lovemaking so exciting. It was the glorious sensation that having lived so long in the shadow of death, I was plunging into the ultimate celebration of life. The warmth of Biene's body, the sparkle in her eyes, the dazzling joy of her smile, were the very opposite of the cold, dark barrenness by which I'd been surrounded. Her love was like a magic potion spreading through me, reviving my spirits and leading me back from the underworld up to the light of the sun.

On our second night, as we were lying together in a state of drowsy bliss, Biene laid her head on my shoulder and wrapped her legs around my thigh. As her fingers toyed with the hair on my chest she whispered: "Do you know what the time is? Just past midnight . . . which means it is now February 27th." She looked up at me with the sweetest, most gentle expression, and said, "Happy birthday, my darling. I love you."

I replied: "I love you too," and the relief I felt was as great as the joy, for I knew then that my heart was still intact. I was now twenty-nine years old. I had seen shocking things, and feared that I would soon be called upon to commit acts of violence that went far beyond anything I had ever experienced. But I was still, for now at least, a functioning human being.

The following morning, when the time came to leave, Biene insisted on coming with me to the airport to see me off. She said it would be romantic, standing on the tarmac, watching "my handsome man in his smart uniform" climbing the steps up to the airplane that was taking him away to war. Of course, she started crying when the time came to say goodbye, but when I took pity on her she insisted that, on the contrary, crying was an essential part of romance. Only a man, apparently, would fail to understand that.

It makes me smile, even now, just thinking of the look on her face as she said those words, and even my tired old manhood stirs a little thinking of how she pressed her body against mine to give me one last farewell kiss. Darling Biene, my beautiful flower, surrounded by bloodstained snow.

The Condor was a magnificent aircraft. From the outside it looked like a bomber, with its four mighty engines and bristling machine guns. But inside it was decked out like the most luxurious airliner in the skies. There was even a steward to serve us coffee from a silver pot into the finest bone-china cups.

The "bigwig" on the trip with me was Dr. Alfred Meyer, deputy to the Minister for the Occupied Eastern Territories, Alfred Rosenberg. Meyer was a stern-looking man who did not seem to relax throughout the entire flight. He insisted on asking me about every detail of life in Minsk. Keenly aware of the influence that a man of such eminence could have on my career, I was very careful to describe it all in terms that he would appreciate. I told him that we were experiencing a satisfactory rate of natural wastage among the Jewish settlers, and were shortly to move into a more active phase of operations, now that the coming spring enabled us to pursue a vigorous resettlement policy.

"Yes," said Meyer. "I am hoping to examine one such action against the Jews for myself, starting tomorrow, I believe."

Having explained that I had been away for a number of days and had not taken part in the detailed planning for the upcoming action, I did my best to paint the best possible picture of our general approach to the task. Meyer seemed satisfied with what he heard—naturally I gave no indication whatever of the uncertainties that had plagued me—and I could tell that I had made a favorable impression. It had taken me three days by train to get from Minsk to Berlin. The return journey, however, occupied fewer than four hours.

36

And so our action began. While I was en route from Berlin, the elders of the Jewish Council had been informed that we would require five thousand people for resettlement, but when our men arrived at the ghetto to collect them, no one was there. They had all gone into hiding, gathering in cellars, holes they had dug in the ground, roof spaces—anywhere that a human body might be concealed.

We were then ordered to surround the entire Russian ghetto and comb the place, street by street, house by house. It was well after midday before we had about fifteen hundred victims ready to be marched down to the freight yard, by which time the entire operation was running behind schedule. It was exhausting work and one was constantly in a state of nervous tension, playing a deadly game of hide-and-seek, never knowing when or where the next person would be found, or how they might resist.

Many of the Jews tried to escape, and a considerable number were shot. Their bodies were left where they fell as a reminder to the rest of what would happen to anyone who tried to defy us. I wasn't personally responsible for killing anyone, but this was the first time that I had observed the process in person, and simply to witness it was bad enough.

Stark, meanwhile, had been in a foul mood, even by his standards. He was down at the freight yard at around 16:30, loading Jews onto the trains to be taken off to Koidanov, where the actual processing was due to take place, when Gauleiter Kube came by with a couple of his people. Kube didn't say anything to Stark at first. He was too busy laying into Burkhardt for the "outrageous" methods he and his men had used to clear the ghetto. Kube, who was regarded by many of the senior SS officers in Ostland as being unacceptably soft on Jews, complained that small children had been killed, and called it "an obscenity."

Kube shouted at Burkhardt until he couldn't think of anything more to say; muttered, "We'll talk again"; and was just about to go away when he caught sight of Stark, who was using his trusted personal methods to make sure that the Jews were herded into the cattle cars as quickly as possible. Stark was really laying into them with his whip. Kube marched across to him, shouting: "You don't hit people with whips!"

Kube tried to grab the whip and take it away from Stark, but it was attached by a leather loop to Stark's wrist, so it wouldn't come off. The two men wrestled over it for a moment, then Kube let go, stood up straight, dusted himself down, and told Stark precisely what kind of an animal he thought he was, right in front of Stark's men.

For the next few hours, Stark stormed around in a rage, swearing he'd get back at Kube. The following morning we discovered what form his revenge had taken.

It emerged that sometime around midnight, Stark had summoned one of his cronies and the two of them went off into the ghetto and tracked down his old bugbear, Steiner the barber, and his two sons at the hovel where they lived. Of course it was filled to the rafters with people and pitch-black. But Stark's man had a flashlight with him, so they shone it around until the Steiners had been identified and then dragged them out into the street at gunpoint. What happened next, neither Stark nor his sidekick would say. But whatever the precise circumstances, the outcome was not in doubt. The Steiners were dead.

Some of the female workers in the office were actually in tears at the news, which struck both their vanity and sentimentality with equal force. They couldn't decide whether they were more upset that three men were dead, or that they'd no longer be able to find a decent hairdresser in Minsk. I felt sorry for Steiner, of course. He had been an excellent barber and a perfectly agreeable man. But the cruel fact was that Stark had only brought forward an execution that was bound to happen eventually. The question, therefore, was how the authorities would react.

Stark had carried out a private, entirely unauthorized act, in the middle of an official operation, specifically targeted at Russian, not German, Jews. If von Toll was right that the extermination of the Jews was an act of pure insanity, then part of that madness was the very pretense that this was all a perfectly rational, orderly activity, conducted according to rules. Seen from that perspective, it was unacceptable, even illegal, to kill people on a whim, even if they were all marked for eventual death. It was perfectly possible that Stark might find himself in the perverse situation of being an SS officer who was punished for killing the wrong kind of Jew.

Meanwhile all hell was breaking loose at Koidanov because the shooting squads there weren't killing the other kind fast enough. As darkness fell on the second day of the action, they had to cease firing with well over a thousand people still waiting to be dealt with. I was ordered to take charge at the pit on the following day. "I need someone I can count on to finish off the job," said Hofmann, paying me the least-wanted compliment of my life.

No sooner had word got around that I was running tomorrow's show than one of the men assigned to the shooting squad sidled up and begged me to relieve him from his duty.

"I'm sorry, Lieutenant, but I just can't bear the idea of killing defenseless human beings, I don't care what race they are."

I didn't threaten to have him shot for disobedience. Whatever anyone may say, no SS man was ever shot for refusing to kill Jews. We all knew it was an intolerable duty. Of course, that didn't stop me insisting that it had to be done, but the man wouldn't budge. In the end I was the one who gave in. "You can be my loader," I said. "Stand right by me and make sure I've always got a loaded gun. Even if you don't have the guts to shoot, you can damn well see what the rest of us are having to put up with."

Not surprisingly, von Toll also looked for a way out of the shooting squad. "I'm sorry," I told him, "you've got to shoot. People know we're friends. If I'm seen letting you off, it'll look bad for both of us."

Once again, though, I allowed him a compromise that I was denied myself. "You will be issued with a pistol. The magazine holds eleven rounds. Fill it, with another round in the chamber. When you have fired all twelve rounds you can spend the rest of the day on guard duty, keeping the perimeter of the pit secure. Fair enough?"

"Thanks," he said.

"You're welcome. I just wish I could give myself the same orders."

The following morning, I awoke at dawn. It was bitterly cold, with a brisk wind driving and snow still on the ground. As I got dressed I made a particular effort to ensure that my uniform was neat and tidy, for I was going to have exalted company as I went about my duties. Deputy Reichsminister Meyer had spent the previous day in meetings with Hofmann and Kube. He now wanted to observe the disposal process itself, and following our meeting on the plane had requested me as his guide. Merbach, the officer in charge of the motor pool, drove Meyer and me out to Koidanov personally, making inane, supposedly humorous conversation like an overexcited taxi driver, until I politely requested that he remain quiet so that I could answer any questions Dr. Meyer might have about today's events. I got the impression Merbach was desperately trying to cover up the fact that he was not at all looking forward to what he was about to do. But then, who was?

37

Koidanov itself was a modest little town, scarcely more than a village, that sat in the lee of a steep, tree-covered hill. We arrived just as the first wagonloads of Jews were being unloaded. Their train had been parked in a siding since the previous afternoon, and they had been kept without water, food, or sanitation throughout that time, so they were very weak and their clothes were rank with human waste. Even in the cold air, the smell was quite noticeable, and I could see Meyer's mouth curl with distaste.

The Jews were ordered to strip, and their clothes were taken away to be searched for valuables—it was remarkable how many of them, still hoping that they might not be doomed, sewed gold coins, paper money, or even diamonds into their garments. Then they were lined up and one by one ordered to open their mouths, and any gold teeth or fillings they possessed were extracted by the Jewish dentists from the ghetto who were used for this task.

Barefoot, reduced to their underclothes, and in some cases entirely naked, the shivering Jews clasped their arms against their chests, desperately trying to retain the slightest bit of warmth. Many of them had blood smeared around their mouths as a result of the dental work. By now they could have no doubt as to their fate. One or two tried to run away, more in panic than in any serious resistance, and were immediately shot. Others shouted curses or cried out in anguish: women were wailing and weeping, tearing at their faces and their bare blue-white skin with their fingernails. And of course there were considerable numbers of distressed children. But most of the adults—male and female alike—were astonishingly calm.

I cannot say whether they were resigned to their fate or just too hungry and exhausted to care anymore. But just as I had seen mothers fussing over their children on that day in late November when the Vienna transport arrived, so now I observed them stroking their little ones' hair and whispering calming words in their ears.

We walked past the Jews, taking the route that they would soon be using as they were led to their execution. On the way, we passed the pit that had been filled yesterday. It had been covered only with a thin layer of earth, and blood was still oozing from one corner of the grave. I heard Meyer whisper, *"Mein Gott!"* to himself. The distaste of the Berlin hierarchy for the physical consequences of the orders they so blithely gave was a topic of much bitter discussion in the KdS officers' mess. Himmler himself had famously visited Minsk back in August '41, ordered a shooting to be arranged for his benefit, and damn near fainted when blood and bits of brain had splashed onto his greatcoat. It was only thanks to his adjutant grabbing his sleeve that the mighty Reichsführer, his complexion almost as pale and waxy as a corpse, had not fallen into the mass grave himself. Meyer was no less squeamish.

A fresh pit had been dug. It was approximately twenty-five meters long, ten wide, and three deep: the size of a modest public swimming pool. As Meyer stepped to one side together with Hofmann to watch the proceedings, I summoned my loader, told him to grab a box of ammunition, and made my way to the killing line.

Roughly twenty of us shooters were arrayed along one side of the pit, approximately one meter from the edge. I could see Schlegel two men down from me. Merbach and Stark were beyond him, and von Toll beyond them.

Once we had all been assembled, the first load of Jews were marched toward the pit in single file and told to walk along the narrow rim between the shooters and the edge of the pit, until each of us had a Jew standing directly in front of him. The Jews were ordered to turn to face the pit. We all then placed our pistols against the back of the neck of the person in front of us and fired a single shot. The impact of the bullet simultaneously killed them and sent them flopping forward down into the pit. Then the next twenty Jews, who had been standing just a few meters away, watching their brethren be slaughtered, stepped forward and took their place in the line.

From the point of view of the shooter, there was a terrible intimacy to the whole thing. One was standing so close to the Jews that every hair on their head, every blemish or vein on their skin, was visible; close enough to smell them; close enough to hear them breathe. My first was a middle-aged woman. She must once have been much heavier, for the skin was loose around her belly and thighs, and her breasts hung on her chest like deflated balloons. When she stood in front of me I could see the marks on her shoulders left by the brassiere she had only recently removed. She was hanging her head, and my hand was shaking so that I did not manage a clean shot through her neck. The bullet went too high and took off part of her skull, and her death could not have been instantaneous because I can still to this day hear her crying out in pain.

As she fell into the pit I could see the open wound at the back of her head, and an image came to me of the skulls on the table when Lüdtke interrogated Ogorzow. I wanted very much to be sick, but there was no time. I had to swallow the vomit back down into my stomach and ready myself to kill the next one. We all fired again . . . and so it continued. The trucks kept rolling in from the railway siding. The clothes were stripped. The teeth were pulled. The Jews walked to the pit. Men, women, children, and old folk took their place before the muzzles of our guns. Most of the time they were still. At others times, we had to reach out and grab them to hold them in place.

The children were the worst, wanting to run to their mothers, crying and kicking out as we clenched our fists ever tighter around their arms. They had to be still, you see. If they were moving it was much harder to get a good shot. But we got them anyway.

We shot. They died. The pit got fuller. Again and again, the exact same events being repeated with barely any discernible difference, like a factory production line—more and more Jews coming to the end of the conveyor belt, dying and falling into the pit.

From time to time there were pauses: holdups in the system as we waited for more trucks to arrive, or more Jews to be stripped and searched. After we had been going for a while—I honestly couldn't say how long, for one loses all sense of time in a situation like that—one of the men broke down and started screaming, even more hysterically than the most crazed of the Jewish women. He worked in the motor pool, and my God, how I envied the look of relief on Merbach's face as he saw that he now had a perfect excuse to leave the shooting line and take his man back to Minsk.

Von Toll, too, emptied his magazine, left a dozen Jews dead in the pit in front of his position, and went off to join the guards. Someone else, of course, had to take his place, and there was quite an argument among the guards until a Latvian could be found to volunteer.

We were working in two-hour shifts. When my group's was over we were given paper bags filled with sandwiches for our lunch. I tried to force one down, but no sooner had I swallowed the last bite than it all came back up again and I was horribly sick. And so history repeated itself: I vomited when I first saw a murder victim, and I vomited when I first committed murder too. This time there was no hip flask of schnapps to steady my stomach, but several cases of vodka were piled beside the ammunition boxes. I took a bottle with me. It was empty soon enough.

By the afternoon, the shooting had just become a blur of noise and sound, and the smell of cordite, blood, and shit filled the air. At one point Schlegel shouted out in shocked surprise, "No! That's our damn waitress!" as he realized that one of the Jews in the line being marched toward our pistols worked at the KdS mess. We were killing our own staff, like Saturn devouring his sons; and that, more than anything else, seemed to sum up the lunacy of it all. We would rather have Frau Levy lying dead in a hole in the ground than bringing us our evening bowls of soup.

The atmosphere at dinner that night was terrible. The men were sweating vodka and festering with resentment at what we were having to do. A few muttered curses at the bastards in Berlin: some of the things that were said verged on the mutinous. Others insisted that the Führer would never condone such mindless slaughter and couldn't have been informed about what was happening out here, so far from his headquarters.

"Wait till Adolf hears about this—he'll put a stop to it, just mark my words!" Merbach insisted, and there were plenty of men who were desperate enough to agree with him. Schlegel didn't join in the argument. He was too busy staring at his dinner plate and rambling on about the dead waitress.

Dr. Meyer, I later discovered, had left early in the afternoon, while it was still light. He had a meeting in Riga the following day and wanted to be sure of getting to his destination before night fell. I, meanwhile, had killed my first human beings. I'd crossed that Rubicon of blood and, like Caesar, could never go back to the other side.

38

There was a secure area around the Lenin House that was fenced and guarded to keep us secure from partisan saboteurs. I had a room in a large house within this compound that had been requisitioned as officers' quarters. It was run like a boarding house, with a breakfast room downstairs that doubled as a sitting room in the evening. There were a couple of round tables with four simple wooden chairs, a colorful rug on the parquet floor, a small dresser filled with decorative china, and paintings of Russian country life on the wall; also a small portrait of the Führer. At the far end of the room stood a small table with a radio on top, and a baby grand piano covered with a white cloth on which a jug of fake flowers had been placed; our landlady, Frau Aranski, assured us that she would place real flowers there once the warm weather came. All in all it was a nice enough place, and I had no complaint about the cleanliness of my room, or the comfort of my bed.

Night after night, however, I was woken from my sleep by the sound of men shouting and screaming as they were seized by nightmares and the fear of death that can overcome even the strongest man in the earliest hours of the morning. One time, soon after the Koidanov shootings, I woke at about 02:30, hearing a man's raised voice disturb the stillness of the night, but when I sat up in bed and listened, trying to work out who it might be, the house was absolutely quiet. There wasn't a sound from any of the other rooms. I realized then that I had woken myself. The screaming man was me.

It was no real surprise. I'd been having bad dreams ever since I'd arrived in Minsk. Ogorzow had stalked me through the ghetto, while the Jews packed like sardines in their wooden huts yelled garbled words of abuse in a language I could not understand, or reached out to grab me so that I could not escape the killer. The frozen bodies on the Smolensk road split open like ripe figs to reveal their guts, then laughed at my nausea and weakness at the sight.

Since Koidanov, these dreams had grown even worse. The terrible images from the killing-pit swirled around my mind in a kaleidoscope of savagery. I felt as though my brain had been indelibly branded with the sights, sounds, and smells of that terrible scene. They haunted me day and night. There was always vodka to dull my senses, but the alcohol that numbed me in my waking hours only seemed to fuel the flames of my torment at night. The other men felt exactly as I did, I was sure of it. But no one ever spoke of these things. How could any of us have gone on if we did?

And so we all carried on as if our lives bore some faint resemblance to normality. In mid-March, Hofmann, who had only ever been a temporary appointment, moved on to another post, and a new commander of the KdS, SS-Lieutenant-Colonel Strauch, took his place. Strauch arrived bearing the dubious honor that Bach-Zelewski was said to have called him "the worst human I have ever met in my life," though whether the general had made that remark before or after he'd gone crazy no one was sure. All we knew was that Strauch was thirty-five years old, came from Münster, and was a lawyer by profession. He'd joined the Party in October '31 and the SS two months later. On first acquaintance it was hard to tell just how bad a human he was, but he was certainly passionate about the business of extermination.

In November '41 he'd taken part in an action at Rumbula in Latvia: 10,600 people "processed" in a single day. On that occasion he'd been a direct subordinate of Jeckeln. Now that he had his own command, it seemed obvious that he would want to prove himself just as effective as his former master.

Since he was now my boss, I had no option but to find a way of getting on with Strauch. But that task was complicated by another change in personnel. Burkhardt, the former head of Jewish Affairs, was sent off to run operations against saboteurs, economic criminals, and partisans. His replacement was a new arrival at the KdS, SS-First Lieutenant Erich Lütkenhus. Like me, he was a Criminal Police Commissar. Of course, that shared professional status placed us in direct competition, and this is where the *Beamter* system had its drawbacks. For a person of no ambition, total job security encouraged laziness and complacency. On the other hand, those of us who were determined to do as well as possible were confronted by a very large group of people chasing a quantity of jobs that would inevitably decrease the higher up the scale we went. War, of course, was easing this problem to some extent, since many potential job applicants were removed from the field. But even so, it was clear from the outset that Lütkenhus and I would be competing for the same positions and the same promotions.

I could see at once that he was highly intelligent, competent, and ambitious. He'd have noted the same of me. We were both perfectly polite to one another. In a social context he might have made agreeable company. But professionally we were rivals, just as much as we were also comrades, and almost everything that either of us did in Minsk over the months that followed was influenced as much as anything by the need we both felt to excel and, above all, to exceed the other's performance. One should never underestimate the competitive instincts of young men as a factor in the conduct of war.

I scored the first points in the contest when General Heydrich paid a flying visit to Minsk at the beginning of April. He stayed overnight at Gauleiter Kube's quarters, since they were the most luxurious in the city. But virtually all his working time was spent with us at the KdS. Heydrich confirmed in person that we were embarking upon the complete elimination of all the Jews in Europe and French North Africa. The entire continent would be combed from one end to the other so that not a single Jew could escape. "There are eleven million of these vermin," Heydrich told us. "And we will have them all."

Our contribution to the process would continue with the processing of a series of transports of Reich Jews, beginning in the spring. Heydrich made it absolutely clear that they were not to be held in the ghetto, but killed immediately upon arrival. He assured us that this was the personal wish of the Führer. We could therefore be certain that we were carrying out a true Führer order. It was some reassurance, I suppose, to be confident that we were all acting in the best interests of our leader and our country; but for every one of us who looked forward to the arrival of the first transport with eager anticipation, there were more who regarded it with dread.

Over lunch, Heydrich painted a dramatic picture of the planning required for the gigantic task he had set in motion. "Consider this, gentlemen," he said. "We have a program, planned down to the last detail, that will tell our comrades throughout Europe the exact quotas they have to round up for trains leaving their particular territories on a series of specific dates. We will know the destination of every one of these trains, and the route they will take to get there. The commandants and staffs of camps in the General Government area of Poland, and here in the Reich Commissariat of Ostland, will know precisely how many people they will need to deal with, and when.

"Even now, designers, scientists and engineers are working on remarkable innovations that will greatly increase the rates of killing and disposal. We are just beginning operations at a facility in Poland that will be able to process ten thousand individuals a day. And thanks to the ingenious mind of SS-General Nebe—a man whose great talents Heuser here knows very well—we are producing gas vans that can deal with twenty-five people, just by driving down the road. I promise you, gentlemen: you will not have to worry about bullets and grave-pits for long!"

A toast was called. Every other man might have been drinking to the successful outcome of the Final Solution, but I was raising my glass in triumph at the totally unexpected honor Heydrich had paid me, one that I knew would have cut Lütkenhus to the bone. The general continued: "Be proud, gentlemen, be very proud. Only the men of the SS possess the mental discipline, the determination, and the courage to execute a project such as this. You must be as hard as granite to carry out your allotted task. And I know that you will succeed!"

Later, Heydrich sought me out to ask how I was doing. I assured him that I was immensely proud of the trust he had placed in me. I might have considered my duties repugnant, they might be tormenting me every night in my dreams, but I was still determined to do them to the very best of my abilities, just as my father and Lüdtke, too, had always insisted.

"I won't let you down, General," I said.

Heydrich gave me the friendliest of smiles. "Of course you won't," he replied.

39

Within a matter of weeks the first transports would be arriving from the Reich. Now we needed to find somewhere reasonably close to Minsk where the people in them could be processed. It had to be easily accessible, yet sufficiently far from any prying ears and eyes that our activities could be carried out with appropriate discretion. Heydrich might have described the extermination of European Jewry as though it were a great and noble enterprise, but it was impossible not to notice that it was conducted as much as possible away from potential witnesses, very much like the kind of criminal enterprises we policemen had once been used to investigating. Not that one voiced this observation out loud, of course, nor even allowed one's mind to dwell too much upon it. The key to remaining mentally intact was to consider what one had to do as a series of technical problems to be solved. One at all costs avoided any consideration of what they actually involved in human terms. And when reality became inescapable, well, that was what the vodka was for.

Strauch found the site he was looking for on an estate covering several square kilometers near a village called Maly Trostinets. The Stalinists had run it as a collective farm, but since our arrival it had housed a small-scale concentration camp, where a few hundred inmates worked the land, as well as operating a sawmill, joinery, locksmith's workshop, and various other light-industrial activities. When the weather was agreeable, Trostinets was used as a recreation area where the men and women of the Lenin House could go to spend a few hours in the country. There were stables for the use of KdS officers and their guests, and some of the estate's old farm buildings had been converted into storehouses for all the possessions seized from Jews arriving in Minsk. The women greatly enjoyed being taken there to pick out new clothes, cosmetics, and other knickknacks for themselves. They'd spend hours picking and choosing, just as if they were on a shopping expedition to the KaDeWe, and then on Monday mornings they'd bring their new trophies in for inspection by the other females. This seemed to do wonders for the women's morale, and since they could not gain access to the storehouse without an officer's authorization, the men could exact a service for their cooperation that made them happy, too.

About three kilometers to the east of the camp there was a small wood that the locals called Blagovshchina. It was very quiet and peaceful, and the slender trunks of the tall pines grew so close together that one could easily reach out one's hands and touch a tree on either side. Strauch, Lütkenhus, and I drove out there one morning soon after Heydrich's visit. The sun was out and the hint of springtime warmth in the air was enough to have begun to melt the snow beneath our feet and on the branches of the trees. For a few moments, as we made our way into the woods from the track where our car was parked, I could even picture myself coming here with Biene, strolling hand in hand, imagining we were the only two people in the world as we stopped to kiss in the dappled shade beneath the feathery pines.

My reverie was broken by Strauch. "There," he said, pointing to a glimpse of bright sunlight up ahead. "That looks like a clearing." He picked up speed so that Lütkenhus and I had to scurry after him to catch up.

Sure enough, we soon emerged into an open space roughly a hundred meters in diameter. "What do you think?" Strauch said, with a beaming smile that indicated he felt personally responsible for the existence of this bright, welcoming glade. I'd never seen him so cheerful.

Lütkenhus looked around pensively, then said: "There certainly seems to be enough space for a good number of pits, with room around them to establish a cordon of armed guards. We would need to cut a path up from the track, but once that is accomplished, I agree, Lieutenant-Colonel: this is an ideal location."

"Do you have any objection, Heuser?" Strauch asked.

It took me a second or two to reply. As I looked at the peaceful, unspoiled woodland around me, my mind was filled with a picture of the obscene violation we would soon visit upon it, and a feeling of nausea almost as intense as that I'd felt beside the death-pits of Koidanov surged within me.

"Heuser! I asked if you had any objection," Strauch repeated.

I swallowed hard. "None at all. I concur entirely with Lütkenhus."

Strauch pursed his lips and gave a nod of deep satisfaction. "Excellent . . . excellent . . . Then it is decided. We will kill them here."

Once the site of the executions had been established, Strauch ordered Lütkenhus to put together an agreed protocol for processing the transports, so that every man would know exactly what was required of him. As a first step the three of us, along with Burkhardt, whose experience as the previous officer in charge of Jewish Affairs was felt to be useful, met at the Lenin House to discuss the key issues affecting the efficiency and smooth running of the operation. Lütkenhus began the meeting by describing the basics of the operation, using a map spread out on the table between us.

"I'll discuss the logistical requirements facing us in terms of men, ammunition, rations, and so forth in a moment," he said. "But with your permission, Lieutenant-Colonel, I would like to begin by considering the fundamental process that we must undertake."

There was an indifferent shrug of assent from Strauch, and Lütkenhus continued: "The transports will arrive at the goods depot here. Let us assume for the sake of argument that all one thousand individuals on board have survived the journey, and that we select approximately forty to work either here or at Maly Trostinets. That leaves us with nine hundred and sixty to dispose of."

"Do you expect me to be impressed by your grasp of mathematics?" sneered Strauch. It was becoming clearer by the day that Bach-Zelewski had been right: he really could be a deeply unpleasant man when the mood took him.

I could see that Lütkenhus was angered by the boss's sarcasm. He took a sip of water to calm himself, then went on: "Once the Jews have been unloaded, they will hand over all their baggage to us, ostensibly for safekeeping, followed by their money, jewelry, watches, and any other valuables. This will also be the point at which we select those individuals who are best suited to work, either because of their physical strength or any special skills they may have.

"The remainder will now be loaded onto trucks and driven to Blagovshchina, which is approximately eighteen kilometers from the goods depot. At the far end of their journey they will be unloaded, stripped of their clothes, inspected for gold teeth and fillings, and then led to the pit for liquidation and disposal. My two most important considerations are first, to establish the smooth and efficient operation of the entire procedure, and second, to ensure that the Jews do not have the motivation, the means, or the weight of numbers to put up any meaningful resistance at any one of these stages."

"Agreed," said Strauch, meaning it this time. "Continue."

Lütkenhus leaned over the map and tapped his finger on the Bla-govshchina woods: "The point of maximum risk is here at the pit. From the moment they are unloaded from the trucks, the Jews will be able to hear the sound of the guns at the pit, even if it is somewhat muffled by the trees. It will be obvious to them that they are about to be shot. Since they are going to die anyway, they have nothing to lose by attempting some form of resistance. Of course, they cannot suc-ceed. We are all fully armed and they have no weapons at all. Never-theless, if there were enough of them, they might cause considerable disruption and even a few casualties before they were put down. It is therefore crucial that the number of live Jews at the processing site at any one time is kept to an absolute minimum."

The flaw in his position was obvious. "But if there is not a concen-tration at the site," I observed, "it follows that—"

Lütkenhus interrupted me. "Yes, there must be a concentration somewhere else. And clearly that will be at the goods depot, especially at the start of the day. I had, of course, already deduced that that is where trouble is most likely to occur."

He flashed a smug little smile in my direction, as if to say: "You walked into that."

"Not if the Jews still think they are going to live," said Strauch, ignoring the game being played by Lütkenhus and me. "The key is to keep their spirits up and to maintain their belief that this really is a matter of resettlement."

"Then we must treat them well," I said, wanting to reestablish my position. "There is nothing to gain from being abusive. We don't want any of the Stark style of control."

Burkhardt didn't like that. "Stark is a good man. His methods may not be to your taste, Heuser, but he gets results."

"Not the result we desire here," I said.

The room fell silent for a second as we three junior officers waited to see whose side Strauch would take.

"Heuser is right," he declared, "even if he does sound worryingly like that gutless bureaucrat Kube. We need to keep our visitors sweet. I want them to be told all about the farms we have waiting for them and the houses where they will live. Get something written up, Lütkenhus, then have it distributed among the most persuasive, believable men we have—the real charmers. The Jews think they know how to sell goods to us Gentiles. Well, let us sell this imaginary new world to them."

"I believe that postcards have proved very effective elsewhere," I said. "New arrivals are encouraged to write to their loved ones at home about their safe arrival. This gives them something enjoyable to do and reassures the people they write to. Thus they are less alarmed when the time for their resettlement comes."

"That makes sense," agreed Strauch.

"And I think we should give them receipts," I added.

"Receipts for what?" asked Strauch. "Our bullets?"

Lütkenhus and Burkhardt both laughed a little too loudly at that. But this time it was I who was a move ahead. "No, for their luggage," I said. "We should tag their bags and give them a receipt."

"What on earth is the point of giving a man a receipt for his baggage when he'll soon be too dead to collect it?" asked Burkhardt derisively. If he was expecting any appreciation for his remark, he was immediately disappointed. Strauch had seen my point at once. He gave an exaggerated sigh, rolled his eyes to the ceiling, and answered: "Because, you thickhead, a man with a receipt is a man who thinks he'll live long enough to see his possessions again."

"That's really very clever, Heuser," said Lütkenhus, much like a tennis player applauding his opponent's good shot: acknowledging my merit as an adversary, while retaining his determination to beat me.

In the wake of the meeting, Lütkenhus was ordered to write up the final plan, which therefore bore his imprimatur, but I came away feeling that my contribution had been noted and that a detail as small as the issuing of receipts could have a disproportionately beneficial effect. We had just conducted a meeting that might have taken place in any company or government department. The office politics were just the same. One's contributions were noted, approved of, or dismissed, and one's career took a tiny step forward or back. That was the only way to approach it, and the corporate analogy was about to be taken a step further with another staple of working life: a massive interdepartmental row.

40

At the beginning of May we received Reichsbahn Timetable No. 40, listing the seventeen weekly transports of around a thousand "settlers" at a time that would arrive in Minsk between May 16 and September 5. There was just one problem: every single one of the transports was planned to reach us on a Saturday. Strauch was furious. He started stamping up and down the floor, his face puce with rage, the veins bulging on his forehead as he yelled: "I'm not going to have my lads spending every weekend from now to the end of the summer shooting filthy fucking Jews!"

He stopped dead in the middle of the office, pointed at Lütkenhus, and shouted: "You! You're in charge of Jewish matters. Call up those shitheads down at the Reichsbahn office, arrange a meeting and tell them they can take their shitty trains and shove them up their ass!"

Lütkenhus rang the Reichsbahn's area manager, a man called Reichardt, who made it very clear that he wasn't going to let the SS interfere with the nice new timetable. Not without a fight. He told Lütkenhus that his schedule was very busy. The first day he had free for a meeting was May 22—the Friday after the first transport was due in and a day before the second. Reichardt obviously thought he could bounce us into taking the first two trainloads, but he didn't know Strauch, who then spoke directly to Berlin, telling them that he absolutely would not accept delivery of the May 16 transport. Then he told Lütkenhus to make it clear to Reichardt and his people that we were not going to open any trains on any weekend, ever. "The Jews can sit in a siding and rot, for all I care. They can drown in their own shit. But they're not getting off those trains."

Lütkenhus had a look of absolute horror on his face. I could see he was trying to work out how he could possibly convey Strauch's feelings on the matter without making an enemy of every single train official in Minsk. I couldn't help but smile. Strauch saw me. "Don't you sit there simpering like a schoolgirl," he said. "I'm off on my annual leave. I won't be here on May twenty-second, and as of now I'm making you my deputy in my absence, with particular responsibility for transport matters. So that means you're the one who has to make sure this shit storm gets sorted out. And if it doesn't, you'll be the one standing up in front of the men, telling them why all their damn weekends have been canceled."

So then it was Lütkenhus's turn to smile.

That was an irritation. On the other hand, as Lütkenhus had just heard firsthand, I'd suddenly become Strauch's appointed deputy. This was just the sort of opportunity I'd been craving. It also put me in charge of a number of officers who held a rank senior to me. Surely I could expect a promotion to captain in order to regularize the situation. Wasn't that the logical next step?

Evidently not. I didn't get my promotion: not then, or at any point in my time in Minsk. I was given more power, more responsibility, and even the odd medal, but no promotion and none of the extra pay that would have come with it. At the time, the fact that my career had apparently stalled as absolutely as a frozen tank in the Russian winter ate away at me with every month that passed and every other colleague who received preferment—even von Toll rose up the ranks from enlisted man to master sergeant, for God's sake. Looking back, it seems an absolute irrelevance. But perhaps that was just another way in which I was trying to distract myself. And God only knows I was about to require distraction.

On May 11, 1942, a trainload of Jews from Vienna, not previously listed on any timetable, arrived in Minsk with virtually no advance warning. Strauch was convinced it was the Reichsbahn's way of firing a shot across his bow. "They seem to forget that these fucking trains belong to the SS," he ranted. "We've chartered them. We're paying for them. We should be able to say when they arrive."

It had never before occurred to me that someone, somewhere, was sending out invoices for all the rolling-stock required for the Final Solution. But I asked around and quickly discovered that the Reichsbahn charged four pfennigs per Jew, per kilometer. If there were one thousand Jews on each train, it therefore cost the SS forty Reichsmarks per kilometer to transport them. The distance between Vienna and Minsk was almost exactly 1,250 kilometers, so that incoming train represented an expenditure of fifty thousand Reichsmarks, which was roughly as much as the annual pay of all the officers in the KdS put together. And there were thousands of these trains, packed with Jews, crisscrossing Europe. My mind spun at the cost of the whole enterprise, and that was without taking into account all the men involved; plus our support staff and equipment, the ammunition we used, the trucks we drove, and the food and drink we consumed. No wonder Himmler wanted us to seize all the Jews' valuables and send them back to Berlin. How else could he fund their extermination?

These musings were all very intriguing, but however much it had cost, the train was pulling into the sidings at Minsk. And that meant we had to deal with its cargo.

Lütkenhus, thinking purely of his own advancement, was thrilled by the chance to put his great plan into effect. At Strauch's suggestion, he'd recruited Schlegel, the reassuring teacher, to give the Jews their welcoming speech. He'd given Merbach an exact specification for precisely how many vehicles would be needed for every aspect of the operation, with how many drivers and guards. He'd liaised with me to organize men from both the police battalion and Latvian units to act as guards at the station and around the pit itself. I'd also ordered a squad of men under my command to take some of the Russian prisoners of war off the army's hands and employ them as diggers to prepare the pit itself.

We requisitioned some workers from Maly Trostinets to collect and sort through all the discarded clothes, and the usual dentists were present to remove the gold teeth. The food, water, and vodka had been ordered. Each man in the shooting squad was issued with twenty-five rounds of ammunition, with more in boxes a short way from the pit, if needed.

I arrived slightly late at the pit and collected the standard allowance of twenty-five rounds handed out to every man in the shooting squad. After that I took my place in the line and soon discovered that, difficult as it was to steel oneself to kill Russian Jews, it was far, far harder to deal with those from the Reich. Goebbels could churn out endless propaganda films that showed Jews as hook-nosed vermin, less than fully human. But Goebbels never had to place the hot muzzle of his pistol on the golden-blond hair of a girl's neck, smell the burning of her skin beneath the metal, and hear a voice that was just as German as his own crying out in pain. He never had to look into clear blue eyes and pretend that their owner had to be murdered because they belonged to an inferior race.

One of the men I killed was an old boy who pleaded for mercy because he'd won the Iron Cross fighting for the Fatherland in the last war. I shot him just to shut him up, but it didn't do any good. I still couldn't rid my mind of the sound of his words, or the look of disbelief in his eyes—the incredulity that any fellow member of the human race could actually mean everything that had ever been said about the need to remove the Jew from Europe forever.

It was as though the whole grotesque business were a gigantic experiment, conducted by an insane, all-powerful psychiatrist who sought to establish just what terrible sins once-decent men might be capable of if correctly manipulated. "We have established that you can bring yourself to kill people who look and sound alien. Very well then, what if they look and sound just like you? What if they come from the same cities, even the same neighborhoods—how will you manage then?"

The only way to cope was to clamp my heart, deafen my ears, and stare blankly ahead of me so that I could barely distinguish between a small boy and an elderly woman and a man of my own age and size. They were all just faceless, shapeless targets, and I an automaton. I shot, I grabbed, I shot, I pushed, I shot again and again. Then I reloaded, put the vodka bottle to my mouth and swallowed as much of the raw, caustic spirit as I could manage before I started to choke, and went back to add more bodies to that overflowing pit. That night, when I closed my eyes to sleep, all the bodies came back to haunt me in nightmares that grew ever more extreme.

Now I started to consider the cost of it all in terms other than the purely financial. For every death, a bottle of vodka was drunk, a dream endured, a memo written. The great game of "let's pretend this is normal" continued with a structural reorganization of the KdS. This, we were all informed, would now be modeled on that of the Reich Security Main Office itself. That meant creating five separate departments. Personnel and finance were Departments I and II, respectively. The SD were Department III, the Gestapo Department IV, and the Criminal Police Department V.

I was appointed the director of Department IV, making me the chief of the Gestapo in Minsk and all its surrounding areas. The department had four subdivisions, including one dealing with sabotage, economic crimes, and intelligence about partisan activities, which was commanded by Burkhardt, and another for Jewish and Polish affairs, commanded by Lütkenhus. That meant that although both men had the same rank as me, I was in practice their immediate superior. So Lütkenhus was no longer my competitor, but my subordinate. It was all very gratifying, as far as it went. But they still didn't make me a captain.

Just to add to my frustration, there was even a vacancy at that rank, for Stark was told to pack his bag at once and make his way to Paris, where he would be seconded to the SD for just three weeks. Thereafter he would be transferred to a permanent new post in the administrative department of the local SS in Munich. This was his punishment for killing the Steiners, and somewhere within the bowels of the Main Office a bureaucrat was congratulating himself on its elegance. Given Stark's closeness to Heydrich, he had to be handled with care, and a nice vacation among the whores of Paris, before a cushy posting in the Bavarian capital, could hardly be described as the severest of censures. In reality, though, Stark was being buried as deeply and safely as possible, left to rot in the back of a dusty office and given meaningless tasks so unimportant that even his absolute ignorance and stupidity could do no damage. I wondered, should I advise someone at the Munich Kripo to keep a discreet eye on SS-Captain Franz Stark? He had many characteristics of a psychopathic killer and he'd developed a taste for blood in Minsk. I doubted he would be able to go too long without wanting to try again.

I never made that call to Munich. I had other, more important things to deal with. Lütkenhus was sent off to the Reichsbahn offices to negotiate with Reichardt and his people. He did a very good job of it, a fact that might once have concerned me. Now, though, I was his superior and could afford to be far more relaxed. His success reflected well on me, and it was my name on the correspondence that was sent confirming the new transport arrangements Lütkenhus had managed to establish. Therefore, as far as the personnel files were concerned, it was I who had sorted out the problem. My letter summarized the situation very neatly, I thought, and to the great advantage of the KdS.

Under the subject heading "Agreement of the Transport of Jews from the Reich," reference "Meeting with SS-First Lieutenant Lütkenhus 22.5.42," I wrote:

Following today's meeting between Reichsbahn Superintendent Reichardt and SS-First Lieutenant Lütkenhus, I will briefly summarize the results of the negotiations as follows:

1. *The train originally expected on the Saturday before Whitsun will be held at Koidanov and will only be sent on to Minsk in the early hours of Tuesday morning: the exact time to be confirmed with me later.*

2. *As the appropriate state authority, the Reichsbahn office here in Minsk will ensure that the departure times of future transports are adjusted correspondingly.*

3. *Until the timetable is adjusted, transports of Jews will be held at Koidanov on weekends, so that they arrive in Minsk on any day except for Friday, Saturday, or Sunday.*

4. *The Reichsbahn will ensure that transports will arrive in Minsk on a track that allows our trucks to get as close to them as possible.*

With my special thanks for your consideration and understanding in this matter,

Dr. Georg Heuser

The letter was sent on the morning of Saturday, May 23: the train's official arrival date. As I sent the messenger on his way to the Reichsbahn office, I knew that Strauch would be happy when he returned from leave: the men would get their weekend off, plus a Whitsun holiday on Monday; and the train would arrive when we wanted it, on Tuesday. For my own part, I had planned an agreeable series of weekend activities, which revolved around a party Gauleiter Kube and his wife, Anita, held at an estate in Loshytsa to the south of the city. A number of the girls from the office were there, all taking the opportunity to put on summer dresses for the first time that year. Some even changed into swimming costumes, for there was a small lake just in front of the main house, but although some of the men stripped off and dived in, the water was still icy cold that early in the season and none of the girls could quite summon up the courage to join them. A band from the Ukrainian Auxiliary Police battalion provided musical accompaniment and there was an impressive open-air luncheon, served by members of the Kubes' domestic staff, all of whom were local White Russians.

Anita Kube was an attractive, gregarious blonde some twenty-five years younger than her short, bald husband. We'd been introduced at a cocktail party a few weeks earlier when she was delighted to discover that we were exactly the same age. "From now on I shall think of you as my twin!" she'd exclaimed. Then she laid her hand, with its long scarlet fingernails, on my arm and said: "It is such a relief to have someone else young to talk to. All the people my husband brings back to the residence are so ancient. I know we shall be the greatest friends!"

We bumped into one another again at Loshytsa and I congratulated her on the hard work and discipline of her servants. "Thank you, Dr. Heuser," she replied, evidently delighted by this compliment. "As I always say, twelve Russian swine are cheaper than one good German maid."

She laughed at her own witticism and it seemed rude not to join in. Neither of us could know just what a high price would later be paid for Anita Kube's cut-rate employment policy.

The following morning I was woken before dawn to be told that the Reichsbahn office at Koidanov had just released the transport that had been held there since Friday night. The train consisted of freight cars—or "cattle cars," as people refer to them now—rather than old passenger cars. Owing to the rudimentary nature of the train and the length of time spent in the siding at Koidanov, the Jews were in considerably worse condition than usual. We dealt with them, however, in the usual way.

41

GOETHE UNIVERSITY, FRANKFURT, WEST GERMANY: DECEMBER 11, 1962

There had been two significant mentors in Paula Siebert's life as a lawyer. One was Max Kraus, who had given her both the opportunity to begin her career and the support to make the best of that opportunity. The other was Professor Albrecht Mauritz of Frankfurt's Goethe University, who had taken her under his wing when she was the lone female law student amid an army of men. "I spent six months in a concentration camp because I refused to distinguish between students on the grounds of religion or race," he'd told her. "Why should I now discriminate on the grounds of sex?"

Whenever the pressure of her situation had become too much for her, she had gone to him and he had sat her down in one of the old armchairs in his book-lined study, poured coffee for them both, and listened to her troubles. She had valued him all the more because his kindness had not been unconditional. "Please understand, Fräulein Siebert, that I do not devote my valuable time to your company, however delightful it may be, out of sentimentality. I do it because I think you are an exceptional student who has the potential to become an equally exceptional lawyer. You will therefore repay me best by proving me right."

Ever since, whenever she had felt herself flagging, or been tempted to cut a corner or do less work than she knew a particular task really required, Paula had only to think of Mauritz's shrewd eyes looking at her through the smoke from the pipe without which, he always claimed, he couldn't think clearly, and she would knuckle down with her determination fully restored.

Now, though, the thought of him was not enough. In the months since her conversation with Kraus that morning at the cafeteria, she had been unable to rid herself of the growing fear that the trial was going to go horribly wrong. All lawyers doubt the outcome of long and complex proceedings, all the more so when there are multiple charges and defendants involved. But in this instance Paula felt that she had good reason to be concerned. Heuser and Geis had become disconcertingly effective at creating doubt, undermining evidence, and weakening the prosecution. And the court had seemed happy to let them do it. Stark, for example, had been treated with near contempt, as though he were nothing but a crude thug who required neither respect nor special consideration. But Heuser was a man who knew how to play the legal game. She could see that the judges, and even to an extent the prosecution team, saw him as a man like them, who understood the finer points of the law and deserved to be granted a degree of respect. She couldn't believe that he would entirely get away with his crimes: he'd admitted too much guilt for that. But she could see him escaping with a greatly reduced number of convictions, and punishments that were little more than a slap on the wrist. And she needed someone to whom she could pour out her worries: someone who would understand her and the law alike.

So here she was again, back in the same armchair with coffee from the same cup, watching the professor tamp down the tobacco in the same old pipe. She'd been delighted by the genuine pleasure with which Mauritz had greeted her, but was now struck by the slight but undeniable shift that had taken place in the balance of their relationship. When she had first come to this room, she was a girl of nineteen, and he an academic of international renown, still in the prime of his professional life as he entered his early sixties. Now, a dozen years later, she was a grown woman and he an elderly gentleman of seventy-four, his back a little bent and his movements betraying the caution of a man who cannot quite trust his body to obey his instructions anymore. His mind, however, was as bright as ever and his gaze had lost none of its disconcertingly direct perception.

"So, you said you wanted to talk to me about this Heuser war-crimes trial. My congratulations, by the way, for getting them to court at all. I cannot imagine that it was an easy case to build. Now, how can I help?"

"The same way as you always did in the past, by listening to my woes."

Mauritz smiled. "Ah, my dear Doctor, you have a splendid legal mind, but you are still a woman. You think that talking in itself is a solution. As a mere man, I prefer actually to solve things."

Had another man said those words, Paula would have been infuriated. But Mauritz had earned the right to patronize her a little.

"All right, then," she replied. "I'll give you a problem to solve, or at the very least to dissect."

"Much better! I'm all ears."

"Well, the problem is this. We have eleven defendants, ten of them relatively insignificant, but one who matters a great deal. That's Heuser, of course. And I am concerned that the court is letting him get away with crimes that we all know he has committed."

"Hmm . . . do you think that this is a political matter? We all know that there are still plenty of judges out there who remain, if not supporters of the Nazi cause, then sympathetic to those who acted on its behalf."

"I don't think so. The supervising judge is Randenbrock, the director of the district court. We've not heard anything to suggest that he's biased in that way at all. It's more a case of, I don't know . . . being unduly sensitive to the legal niceties. If there's any flaw in the evidence at all, Randenbrock makes it obvious that he won't even ask the jury to reach a verdict."

Mauritz raised a quizzical eyebrow and gave another one of those thoughtful hums that Paula knew were his way of suggesting she had just walked headfirst into a very large hole.

"Give me an example," he said.

She thought for a moment and then said: "Thirty Jews were killed on the very last day before the Russians recaptured Minsk. Heuser was the last officer left in the KdS. We have witnesses who say that he was given orders to kill the Jews. We also know that when the Russians arrived they found thirty dead Jews. There'd actually been thirty-one in the cellar, but one escaped. He dug a hole in the floor and got out through the sewer beneath the building."

"Is he still alive?"

"I don't know . . . Not that I'm aware of."

"So he's not a witness in the case?"

"No."

"So you have no witnesses who actually saw Heuser, or men acting under his orders, carrying out the killing."

"No, but—"

"Were there still other German forces in the city, who might have killed the Jews?"

"Yes, but—"

"But nothing. There is no proof that it was Heuser, rather than some other man, who carried out the execution. Case dismissed. Next . . ."

Paula took a deep breath, restraining the overwhelming temptation to argue the point. Mauritz expected his students, past or present, to be able to keep their cool under pressure. If one line of attack failed, there was no point wasting time on complaints. You just had to find another way forward.

She thought fast, flicking through the charges in her mind until she came to the strongest of the ones that Randenbrock had kicked out. "All right . . . Heuser's also accused of killing a Jew on the Maly Trostinets estate—that was the place outside Minsk where they carried out most of the mass executions, but there was also a small camp there, with Jewish and Russian prisoners. And this time there are two witnesses. One is the former SS captain who ran the camp and the other is Kaul, another one of the defendants. The captain remembers Heuser coming to the camp, brandishing a handful of letters, written by one of the inmates, that his men had intercepted. Smuggling letters from the camp was strictly forbidden, on pain of death."

"Yes," said Mauritz. "I know."

Paula felt herself blushing: "Of course, I'm sorry, I did not mean . . ."

"It's quite all right. Continue with your story."

"Well, according to the captain, Heuser insisted on having all the Jews who worked in the camp rounded up, and then had the man he suspected of sending the letters shot. So that's one piece of testimony. Meanwhile Kaul says he remembers going down to Trostinets on a day off—it's unbelievable, but the countryside around the estate was also a recreation area for the SS. Anyway, Kaul says he bumped into Heuser twice on this particular day. On the first occasion he was walking along a path with a single Jew, who was in his custody. Then Kaul met Heuser again a little later and asked him what had happened to the Jew and Heuser put up two fingers, like a little boy pretending to fire a gun, and said: 'Bang! And it was over.'"

"I see," said Mauritz. "So both these witnesses are describing the events of the same day, from two different perspectives."

"Exactly."

"So what was the date?"

"Well, we don't have a precise date. For these more or less random incidents it's almost impossible to pin them down to a particular day.

But the period during which both the captain and Kaul were in Minsk ran from July 1942 until April 1943, so it had to be in that time frame."

"Very well, so you don't have a date. How about a name? Was the victim—or victims—identified?"

"No, but that's impossible . . ."

"Of course . . . And I assume that there are no former prisoners from the camp who can testify to this event."

"They were all killed."

"And you can't produce the victim's body, because how could one possibly find just one set of remains among so many? And there's no murder weapon, no bullet, no forensic evidence at all."

"Of course not." Paula found herself becoming increasingly indignant. Mauritz was treating her like a lazy student who hadn't done enough work. "Look, we did our very best to gather every single scrap of evidence available. Just getting two witnesses, both former SS officers, to testify was a miracle. You have no idea how hard it was to do that."

"Please, don't take offense . . . I wasn't casting aspersions on you or your colleagues. I've already congratulated you on putting together any case at all in these exceedingly difficult circumstances. All I am doing is asking you to consider this as if it were any other homicide."

"But it isn't!"

"Why not? When all is said and done, one man has killed another. I'm perfectly willing to believe that Heuser either shot a man or ordered him to be shot. But equally, were I Heuser's lawyer I'd have been appalled if Randenbrock hadn't slung the charge out."

Siebert was about to speak, but Mauritz raised a hand to stop her. "Wait . . . think . . . Where is the proof? How can you or anyone else possibly say that Heuser is guilty in this particular case beyond any reasonable doubt? And what would it say if we were to find men guilty merely on the strong suspicion that they had committed a crime?"

"It would say that we are serious about dealing with the evil done by the Nazis in our name."

"Would it? I don't think so, and I experienced that evil at first hand. Personally, I am glad that these animals are being allowed all the rights and due process that they denied to their own victims. If we ever resorted to summary justice, we would be no better than them. So when you tell me that Randenbrock is looking at the evidence that has been presented to the court and concluding that it's insufficient, I applaud him. In fact, I am delighted. It tells me that all my work, all my faith in justice, everything that I suffered, was not in vain, because in the end we have created a country in which even war criminals are treated fairly under law."

Mauritz finished making the point with the assertiveness of a man who is expecting a counterargument, but Paula's response surprised him. She sipped her coffee reflectively and then said: "It's funny, I was saying something just like that to a friend a few weeks ago. He was complaining about Strauss—the way he'd handled the whole *Spiegel* thing— and I said yes, but at least we live in a country in which we can complain without being arrested. And if we don't like our leaders we can vote them out. So if that's a step forward, then how can I complain if criminals aren't found guilty unless there's actual proof of their crimes?"

"And a country in which Nazis face trial in a German court. That's true progress! Let me ask you another question. Are there any charges on which you are reasonably confident of getting guilty verdicts?"

"I think so. We have a mass of documentary evidence for the major actions. Many of the defendants have confessed to taking part in mass killings."

"Have any of them tried to pretend that the killings as a whole did not take place?"

"Heavens no! That would be impossible. They know as well as we do what went on."

"Well then, you've done a fine job. The court is considering everything with scrupulous care and absolute regard for the law. It's subjecting evidence to stringent tests. In cases of doubt, it's always erring on the side of the defendants. Yet despite all this, it is still undeniable that acts of great evil were done. That, my dear, is a triumph for justice and freedom, and I salute you for your part in it. Now just trust in the court and it will reach the correct conclusions."

"Thank you, that means a great deal to me . . . I just hope you're right."

Mauritz smiled. "Of course I'm right. I'm your professor. I'm always right. Now . . . more coffee?"

42

MINSK: JUNE 1942–OCTOBER 1943

The longer I spent in Minsk, the harder I found it to recognize myself. I became a completely different man, one capable of doing things he could not previously even have imagined. Every time I took part in one of the transport actions I killed more people by the time I'd emptied my first magazine than Paul Ogorzow had in all his assaults in the gardens of Friedrichsfelde and the carriages of the No. 3 line. But perhaps this had always been my true self. Had the killer been lurking in me all the time, just waiting to be let out? He was, of course, a secret self, an identity I could not admit to anyone outside the closed circle of the Minsk KdS, and so the sense of alienation from the people I'd known in my other life, already strong when I went back to Berlin on leave, became overpowering. Back then, my love for Biene and her faith in me had broken down the wall between me and the rest of the world, but now that rampart of skulls and bones had grown taller, stronger, infinitely more impervious to other people's emotions and entreaties.

Biene wrote to me every week, and my only replies were occasional paltry jottings that said nothing of any worth whatsoever. In the end even these meager responses were beyond me. I started several letters, but found myself becoming as wordless as Baum had been that night we met in Riga. I wasn't allowed to tell Biene what was happening in

Minsk, nor what my duties entailed, and even if I had been, it would have made no difference. Who could possibly inflict the violence, the filth, the lies, and the self-delusion of a life like mine on anyone they cared about at all?

Meanwhile, Biene tried as hard as she could to be happy and positive for my sake. She told funny little stories about her mother's dachshund, which she insisted was the silliest dog in all the world; or the crazy things people were doing at the Kripo department in Hamburg where she'd gone to work. She sent photographs of herself smiling and blowing me kisses. There was never any talk of poor rations or bombing raids, though I knew the city had suffered them; never any self-pity or weakness. She was as brave as she was beautiful and I knew that I did not deserve her. Even worse, I felt ashamed by her love.

One morning, when my guts were heaving, my nose still filled with the pit-stench of blood, shit, and cordite, and my head feeling ready to crack open with the battering it had received from all the vodka it had taken me to get through the day before, and with a hand that shook as it lifted the first cigarette of the day to my lips—for I'd become a smoker as well as a murderer—I wrote to Biene and told her not to wait for me any longer. I lied and said that perhaps when this war was over we would meet as friends and I would be able to explain. I can't remember what other self-serving garbage I spewed at her: probably the standard nonsense about how I didn't believe I could give her what she wanted, and how my decision wasn't a reflection upon her, but on me. But I can still recall the emptiness that opened up inside of me when I put the letter in the mail and threw away my darling Biene, the finest woman I ever knew, who truly loved me and would certainly have married me if I'd asked. And I remember reaching for another bottle after I'd done it, too.

By midsummer we were well into the schedule of weekly transports. We now had gas vans intended to save our men from the onerous, distressing business of shooting all our victims, though the vans kept breaking down and were, in any case, too few to do the whole job even when they worked. We persuaded the Reichsbahn to restore an old Russian branch-line so that the trains could be taken almost all the way to Blagovshchina, making the job of processing the passengers very much less complicated. And while all this was going on, General Heydrich's own body lay rotting in a grave at the Invaliden Cemetery in Berlin, for the man I'd once so foolishly idolized had been assassinated by Czech partisans in Prague. But really, who cared about one more body here or there when the whole world had just become one gigantic charnel house?

At the end of July we carried out the single bloodiest action undertaken in all my time at the Minsk KdS. More than nine thousand Jews were shot and gassed at Blagovshchina, another pit to the west of the city, and in the houses and streets of the ghetto itself. I was involved on all three days: it all felt horribly familiar, tedious even. As I was coming away from my two-hour shift at the shooting pit I bumped into Kaul, who continued to pull every string he could to avoid these actions.

"It's all right for you, Heuser," he said as we walked away from the pit. "You're used to it all."

"Trust me," I told him, "I've had enough of this shit too."

I wasn't the only one. Lütkenhus, who had initially taken up his responsibility for Jewish Affairs with such enthusiasm and determination, proved to be even more badly scarred than the rest of us by the ghastliness of it all. That he was now a chain-smoking drunk was nothing unusual: it would have been more of a shock to find a man who wasn't. It wasn't even remarkable that he'd lost the will to live. To exist in a world so devoid of any redemption, to have proved as conclusively as we had done that the God of love and mercy had either died or simply lost interest in his creations, was enough to deaden the

strongest soul. But what marked out Lütkenhus was his active determination to perish as violently as possible. His stated ambition was
to get himself a transfer to the front, to a unit guaranteed to be in the
thick of the fiercest fighting, so that he could take a bullet in his brain,
to go along with all the bullets he'd shot into the Jews.

He confessed this to me one night in late September. We'd gassed
and shot another trainload that day. After all the hundreds of people
he'd killed, there was one who'd finally broken him.

"You know how it is, Heuser," he said, having armed himself with
what we used to call the Minsk Cure: a cigarette in one hand and a
vodka bottle in the other. "It's always the damn kids that are the worst.
Don't you find that when they're standing in front of you, hardly
more than chest-high some of them, you just want to ruffle their hair?
Well I do, anyway. That's what I want to do, not shoot the poor little
bastards."

"Don't think like that. It won't do you any good," I replied, trying as
ever to put it all at a distance.

"I can't help it. I can't stop thinking. Like this afternoon, for
example . . . There was a line of them coming toward us and I was
doing the usual thing, trying to work out which one I was going to
get. I always hope it'll be a really ugly one, or one that's so old you feel
you might be doing them a favor, putting an end to their suffering."

"I know, I do the same thing," I admitted. We all did. We all wanted
the vilest possible caricature of a conniving Jew in front of our gun.

"But then you never seem to get them, do you? I looked at the
Jews and there was a mother and her little boy and they . . . they . . ."
Lütkenhus dragged a hand across his face to wipe tears from his eyes
and watery snot from his nose. "They were beautiful, Heuser, really
beautiful. I mean, you or I would be proud to have a wife and son like
these two. And she was talking to him, the way they do, and by now
it was obvious that I was going to get one or the other of them. It was

the boy. He was, I don't know, eight or nine I suppose, something like that, thin as a rake of course, with a mop of brown hair. Do you know, she was tidying it as they got near us. She wanted her little boy to look his best as . . . as . . . Oh Christ . . ."

Lütkenhus was sobbing now. No one paid too much attention. We'd all broken down at one time or another.

"It's all right," I said, rubbing his bowed shoulders and trying to comfort him. "Just try to forget it . . ."

Lütkenhus shook his head. "No, no," he said, straightening up. "I don't want to forget. I want to tell you about the boy."

I wished he'd just shut up, but there was nothing to be done but hear him out. "Of course," I assured him. "I understand."

"The boy came up to me and stood with his back to me and I . . . I couldn't shoot. I just couldn't do it. And then he turned around to look at me with these huge, dark eyes and he said: 'Wasn't I standing still enough, sir? My mother told me I had to stand still.' So I said: 'No, you were standing very still. You did well.' And then he smiled, Heuser. This little boy smiled at me and he turned his back to me again and . . ." He took another desperate swig from his bottle, "and he stood to attention like a good little soldier. And so I . . . I shot him."

Lütkenhus got his transfer by the end of the year, though he never managed to find a way of getting himself killed: not in wartime, at any rate. I, meanwhile, carried on exactly as I always had done: obeying my orders, doing my best, and trying not to think too hard, too often about the consequences. But something must have been going on inside me, some sort of unspoken, subconscious rebellion against what we were doing. For why else was my next move so precipitous, so foolhardy, and so totally contrary to my apparent best interests?

43

The final transport on the Reichsbahn timetable arrived at the new railway siding by Maly Trostinets at the very beginning of October: just over five hundred Vienna Jews, all to be gassed on arrival. I was in charge of disembarking them from the transport and then loading them into the vans. I had a small detachment of our men with me and also von Toll, who was acting as an interpreter with a platoon of Ukrainian police auxiliaries assigned to the job. The men were in a good mood. This was the last major action of the year, the load was only half as big as usual, and all the vans were actually working for once, so they wouldn't have to do any shooting.

The train arrived and we started the usual routine of unloading the Jews and their baggage, handing out the receipts and postcards, and all the rest of it. There were probably three or four hundred people already on the siding when I saw a woman getting off one of the wagons. All the other transportees looked as exhausted, hungry, and filthy as usual, but this one was different. She seemed to have been completely untouched by her experience, a blond angel who couldn't be sullied by anything earthly. Even the sun came out from behind a cloud after days of incessant rain, just for the pleasure of shining on her.

I was dumbstruck. People talk about love at first sight, of men who catch sight of a beautiful woman across a crowded room, or in the stalls of the opera house, and in that single instant they are lost in desire. This was exactly like that, except that my first sight of this beauty took place on a dirty siding in the middle of Russia, amid a crowd of people who were all condemned to death, the very last place where one would ever expect such a thing.

I walked toward the point where my angel had come to ground, drawn to her as helplessly as an iron filing toward a magnet. I'd seen countless beautiful women going to their deaths at the pits of Koidanov and Blagovshchina, some even more lovely than this one. But for some reason, she was the one who touched me. I felt impelled to save her. I couldn't let her die. And so, without any clear plan in my mind, I went to her.

As I drew closer I could see that she was a slender creature in her early twenties. She had short blond hair and bright blue eyes, and the smile that she was directing at the girl next to her—a brunette in her teens—was filled with cheek and mischief, as if they had embarked on a daring adventure made all the more exciting by their parents' disapproval. She reminded me a little of Biene, maybe that was what had attracted me. In any case I stopped before the two of them, held out my hand, and, trying to hide any trace of what I was really feeling, brusquely demanded: "Papers!"

The two of them reached into their coats and produced their identity documentation. They were sisters: surname Lang, place of birth Vienna, age twenty-two and seventeen. The older, blond one was called Hannah. Her younger sister was Liselotte.

"Are there other members of your family with you?" I asked.

"Our brother Gottfried," Hannah Lang answered, without any trace of nervousness or intimidation.

"Where is he?"

She looked around, darting her eyes across the crowd, then called out: "Friedl! Friedl!" Her voice sounded confident, clear, and beautiful.

A tall, strapping lad appeared and gave his sisters a smile that was, like his eyes, the spitting image of Hannah's.

"Give the officer your papers," she instructed him.

"There you are, sir," he said as he handed them over: Gottfried Lang, age nineteen, also born in Vienna.

I handed all three sets of papers back to their owners and looked at the three Langs. It was just possible to believe that young Liselotte might conceivably be Jewish, but the other two looked as Aryan as it was possible to imagine. That at least gave me a plausible excuse for what I planned to do next.

"A word, please, Fräulein Lang," I said summoning her, like a waitress, with my finger. "You other two, stay exactly where you are."

I led Hannah a few meters away, so that we could no longer be overheard, and, keeping my voice as low as possible, told her: "I am SS-First Lieutenant Dr. Georg Heuser, the head of the Gestapo here in Minsk." I saw the first stab of fear in her eyes at the mention of the word "Gestapo." Good. I needed her to believe in the seriousness of her situation. "I have the power of life and death. There is no one in this city so mighty that he would not fear my knock on his door. Nor is there anyone so low that I cannot save him, if it suits my purpose. Do you understand?"

She nodded, and now her voice was a small, frightened thing as she barely whispered: "Yes."

"Now I'll present you with a choice. You can follow the other people on this train into one of those black vans over there. In that case you, your brother, and your sister will die very horribly, very soon."

The blood was draining from her face and I could see the first tears welling in her eyes. "Or you can trust me, do exactly what I say, without a word to anyone of our conversation, and the three of you will live."

"What do you want me to do?"

"Go to your brother and sister and tell them to obey my instructions to the letter. Are you sure they will follow your lead?"

"Of course, but what about my parents? When will we see them?"

I was about to walk away, but those last words stopped me in my tracks. "What do you mean? Are your parents on this transport too?"

"No. They came here about a month ago, at the beginning of September. Look, I have a postcard from them."

She put her hand in her pocket again and pulled out one of the cards we handed out to the Jews to occupy them while they waited to be taken to the pit. *"My darling Hannah, Lisl, and Friedl,"* it read. *"Papa and I have arrived safe and sound in Russia. We are in the countryside, just outside Minsk. Soon we will be driven to our new home. I hope we will see you all here very soon. Papa sends his love. With all kisses to you, my beloved children, Mama."*

Now it was my turn to feel my skin go pale. I looked at the date on the postcard: I'd been at the pit that day. My God, maybe I'd killed this woman or her husband. It was all I could do to remain impassive as I told their daughter: "I have to tell you, Fräulein Lang, that your parents are dead. Everyone who comes here on these trains dies. Everyone you see around you will soon be dead. That is why you must do as I say."

She looked around her in bewilderment. "You don't mean it. You cannot mean it!"

"I repeat, they all die."

"Then I don't want to live," she said, her voice rising. "I'll die too!"

There was now a very real possibility that she would try to warn the other Jews. If she did that, I would have no choice but to shoot her dead, and the thought of that was insupportable. I reached out and grabbed her arm, squeezing it so hard she winced in pain. "No you won't. You will live so that your brother and sister can live."

She was still wavering on the edge. "Think of your parents," I insisted. "Would they want you dead? Stay alive for them. Please."

In that one last word I somehow let some fraction of my true emotion show. I could see a change in her, some recognition that I was desperate for her to survive. Perhaps she saw me as a fellow human being then, not a machine in a uniform, I don't know.

She snatched her arm away from me, took a few seconds to pull herself back together, and then said: "I'll go and tell my brother and sister to do as you say."

"But nothing else, you understand? Not a word to anyone of anything I have said. Your lives depend upon it."

"I understand."

"Good."

We walked back to the other two Langs. One of the men from the German detachment was gingerly clambering down from one of the transport cars, ten meters or so away, trying not to jar his fifty-year-old bones. I recognized him as Fassbender, a police Watch Master from Mannheim. I called him over and told him to stand guard over the three young people. "They're to remain here," I said. "If any of those Ukrainian apes tries to take them off to the vans, tell him these are my personal prisoners, whom I am holding on Gestapo business, and I'll shoot anyone who so much as lays a finger on them."

The siding had all the hubbub of a busy marketplace, with the Jews as both customers and cattle. Some of them were lining up to collect their baggage receipts or handing over their valuables. Others were already climbing up into the vans. I should by now have been giving them all the prepared speech about the joys of their new life in the wide-open spaces of Ostland, but I could see that some of my men were so familiar with the patter that they were spontaneously using it to encourage their passengers.

"Up you get, ladies and gentlemen," another middle-aged policeman was saying. "All aboard for the Farmhouse Express, just waiting to take you to your fine new homes!"

"Everything going well here?" I asked the policeman.

He gave me a broad grin, "Oh yes, First Lieutenant, going aboard like little lambs they are this morning!"

"Excellent, carry on."

Finally I found von Toll. "Take charge here for a while," I told him. "There's something I need to do back at the office."

"Is it anything to do with that girl I saw you talking to?" he asked.

"When we are having a drink tonight and talking man-to-man, then maybe I'll answer that question. For now, however, I'm giving you an order, Squad Leader, and I expect it to be obeyed."

Von Toll stood up straight. "Yes, First Lieutenant!"

"Then go about your business."

I returned to where the Langs were waiting, watched over by Fassbender. He stood to attention as I approached. "I'll take these three off your hands now," I said. "But I need you to do something for me. Their name is Lang. Their luggage will have been labeled and numbered on departure. Make sure that it's brought to my office at the KdS, unopened and with nothing missing. I intend to search it personally."

"Yes, First Lieutenant."

"Very good, then, get on with it."

When he'd gone, I told the Langs to follow me and led them to my car. "Both my driver and I are armed," I told them. "If you make the slightest hostile or rebellious move against either of us, you will be shot. Now get in the back, sit on your hands, and do not move until you are specifically told to do so."

The youngest one, Lisl, hesitated, too frightened to do as I'd told her. Gottfried, too, was looking at the car with sullen suspicion.

"It's all right," Hannah told them. "Do what Dr. Heuser has told you. Look, I'm not afraid to get in!"

Once Hannah had led the way, the others soon followed. We drove back to the Lenin House in silence. The place was half empty, as was normal on a transport day. I took the Langs to an interrogation room, sat them down on one side of the table, and took my place at the other. "You will speak for the family," I said to Hannah. "You other two keep quiet. First question: What kind of Jews are you? You don't look like Jews. You do not have a Jewish family name and only one of you has a Jewish first name. Yet your papers say that you are Jews and there you were on that transport. Do you have an explanation?"

"Yes," said Hannah. "The explanation is that we are not Jews. My father is . . ." She hesitated for a moment, and I waited for her to correct herself.

"Hannah?" asked her sister, nervously.

"Is," said Hannah, with a particular emphasis, "a Roman Catholic by birth and upbringing. Both his parents are Catholic. My mother had a Catholic father, but her mother was Jewish."

"I see. So were you raised as Catholics or Jews?"

"Neither. My parents are not religious. We celebrate Christmas and have Easter egg hunts in the garden, if that is what you mean. But that's just a matter of tradition. We hardly ever go to church."

"But you were not raised as Jews?"

"No!" There was a tone of exasperation in her voice, as if she couldn't believe I was making such a fuss over something that seemed so unimportant to her. Yet her survival was hanging in the balance with every answer she gave. "I told you. My parents do not believe that people should be divided by religion."

"Were they Bolsheviks, then?" That would have been as fatal as Judaism to the Langs' chances of survival. Far from being alarmed by the question, however, all three of them burst out laughing.

"What's so amusing?"

"You'd know if you met my father," the boy interrupted. "He has no time for Bolshies. He likes his nice house and his large cars and his bottles of first-class Tokay too much for that!"

The girls laughed again, even Hannah. For that moment she'd forgotten what I'd told her. Her parents were still alive to her and they came alive to me, too, a happy, loving family, used to prosperity and status. So how had they ended up in Minsk?

I waited for the laughter to subside. "Let me sum up the situation, as I see it," I said. "As I'm sure you know, in Jewish lore, Judaism is passed on through the maternal line. So to a Jew, you're Jewish. To a German, however, you are not. Your precise legal status is that of '*Mischlings* of the second degree,' which is to say mixed-race with one Jewish grandparent. You are not classified as Jewish unless you are married to Jews, or you have an especially undesirable appearance that marks you outwardly as a Jew, or you have a political record to show that you feel and behave as a Jew—that you are Bolsheviks, in other words. I am satisfied that none of those conditions applies. I am thus puzzled as to why you find yourself here, all the more so since you were evidently being raised as Germans rather than Jews. In a case such as this, even your Jewish parent should not have been deported, nor your German one, of course. And yet here you are. Do you know why?"

"Yes!" said Hannah, forcefully. "It was that horrid man Pichler."

"And what did he do?"

"Betrayed my parents!" blurted Gottfried Lang. "When all Papa did was point out the mistakes he was making."

"Please, one at a time . . . Fräulein Lang, tell me what happened as simply as possible, without any interruptions."

"My father's a surgeon, a very fine surgeon," she said. "As well as having a private practice, he works at the General Hospital in Vienna and teaches students from the Medical University there. As a young man, he was in the army medical corps, on the Italian Front. My mother was a nurse at the field hospital. That was how they met."

I held up a hand to stop her. "So both your parents served our allies in the Great War?" I was by now used to seeing Jewish war veterans at the pits, but it was most irregular to have a half-Jewish woman who had served as a military nurse and her Aryan husband both sent for resettlement. I was even more curious now to discover what had happened. "Please carry on, Fräulein Lang."

"A couple of years ago, just after the war began, Papa had problems with a student called Pichler," she said. "He was entering the last year of his studies, but he wasn't any good. Papa tried to help him, but Pichler wouldn't listen. He was too lazy, and too arrogant. So Papa told him that unless he improved his standards, he would fail the course and therefore not qualify as a doctor.

"Pichler was furious. He went to his father, who was high up in the Party in Vienna, with lots of influential friends. Everyone knows that Papa's married to a woman who has a Jewish parent. So Herr Pichler used that against him. They said that unless he personally made sure that his son passed his medical exams with flying colors, he'd make sure that Mama was exposed as a Jew and Papa's medical career was destroyed. Papa said: 'No.' It wasn't in his power to pass a student whose work was not up to standard, and even if it were, he'd never put the lives of patients at risk by letting loose an incompetent doctor upon them. Mama begged him to divorce her and make the problem go away. She was willing to sacrifice herself for the family, but Papa absolutely refused. And he said the same thing you did, that they could not do anything to a Jew married to a German with German children."

"Your father was very brave, but I'm afraid to say very foolish, too," I said. "Tell me, was there any Jewish paraphernalia at your house?"

"Yes," said Hannah. "We have a menorah that Mama inherited. We light the candles for Hanukkah, just like we sing Christmas carols and have a Christmas tree. It's something nice to do every year and it looks very pretty with all the other decorations."

"I see . . ." That complicated matters somewhat, just when everything had been looking so hopeful. But all was not lost. It all depended on the boy. "Tell me, young man, are you circumcised?"

The boy shook his head, blushing to the roots of his hair.

"Well then, you weren't brought up as a Jew. And if you weren't, nor were your sisters. I'm sure I'll be able to resolve this unfortunate situation, but for now I must return to my work. You will stay here until I return. I'll ask Fräulein Krankl, my assistant, to bring you something to eat and drink."

I drove straight back to the railway siding. Things were not going well. Because of all the rain we'd had over the previous few weeks, the wheels of the gas vans were churning up the earth and turning it into thick, impassable mud. As a result the vans couldn't get close enough to the pit to enable the bodies to be dumped into it. There was nothing to be done but shoot the Jews instead. So the day was longer and a great deal more unpleasant than the men had anticipated, which had a very damaging effect on their morale and thus their efficiency. The Jews were treated with even more brutality than usual. I had at least saved the Langs from that; but keeping them alive might well be a great deal more difficult.

44

There was a cellar beneath the Lenin House that was sometimes used for storage. There wasn't much down there at the time and it was out of the way, so that was where I installed the Langs and their baggage. Whenever anyone asked who they were or what they were doing down there, I simply replied that they were Germans who appeared to have been misclassified as Jews. If anyone showed any signs of disapproval, and few dared do that to my face, I pointed out that no one in Minsk had done more than I in the service of our national mission to eliminate the scourge of world Jewry. And it was precisely because I was so determined to rid Europe of the Jews that I did not wish to see good Germans suffer the fate reserved for subhumans. Of course, I had no personal interest whatsoever in the scourge of world Jewry, even assuming there was such a thing. I was just doing my job. But over the months I had acquired a reputation in Minsk as a hard, unflinching perfectionist, so no one dared question my motives.

No one, that is, apart from von Toll: "Are we talking man-to-man now?" he asked, as we sat over a bottle of vodka.

"Of course—we're talking as friends."

"Then you won't mind me saying that I think you're crazy, bringing that blonde and her family back here. For God's sake, man, you of all people can't be seen screwing Jews."

"I don't intend to."

Von Toll gave a laugh of mocking disbelief. "You don't intend to screw a woman who looks like that? Then you won't be shot for fucking Jews. You'll be shot for being a pansy!"

"You know I'm not a pansy. And I know she's not a Jew. I've checked her bloodline and her family history and it is quite clear that she and her siblings have been wrongly classified. They are categorically not Jews."

Von Toll slapped me on the back. "Well, if you can prove that, you deserve to screw her. And she should be damn grateful, too."

For his part, Strauch didn't waste any time when I informed him that there were three transportees from Vienna currently installed in the cellar. He'd heard about Hannah Lang and immediately jumped straight to the same conclusion as von Toll: "You know that if you fuck her it could be a court-martial offense?"

I repeated what I'd told von Toll: "She's not a Jew. She's a *Mischling* of the second degree." But then I added something new that had occurred to me overnight: "The situation of the Langs is actually a very interesting one. To the Jews they are Jews, since the religion is passed on through the maternal line. To us Germans, however, they are, or rather should be, German, since we are principally interested in the father. One might describe them as racial double-agents. I can see that proving useful."

"Oh really? And where, precisely, do you intend to use them . . . other than your bed?"

"I don't know. But in the meantime, I shall find something for them to do. Jew or Gentile, they should be working for their living."

"We could just kill them, you know."

"Not if they are German we can't."

"They came here with papers that say they are Jews. You may file, for the record, your argument stating that they've been wrongly designated. You may do whatever you want with any of them: work them, screw them, kill them, it's all the same to me. But they eat Jews' rations and they keep the yellow stars on their coats."

"I don't want them in the ghetto, though. Not yet."

Strauch thought for a second and said: "Fine. But if you file your arguments for reclassifying the Langs as German, then I'll note my concerns in writing too. Berlin can decide who was right, if it ever comes to that. I'm too tired to bother with it now. I'm not sleeping well at the moment. Do you find that too—that it's hard to sleep?"

"Sometimes."

Strauch took off his glasses, rubbed a hand over his face, and then looked at me with screwed-up eyes, trying to get me in focus. "I must say, Heuser, you are the last person on earth I'd have expected to do something like this," he said, putting the glasses back on. He blinked a couple of times and then examined me more directly. "You don't normally so much as take a shit without making sure that it'll be to your advantage. You must know what a risk you are taking with this. I have no reason to wish you ill. You've always been a good officer. But I won't be here forever. My replacement might well take a different view."

"That's why I'm going to make sure that all the Langs' paperwork, along with my accompanying legal arguments, are perfectly in order. I haven't completely lost track of my senses."

Strauch gave me an uncharacteristic grimace that might almost have passed for a friendly smile. "Oh, I think you have. And it's really quite fascinating, like watching a lion fall in love with a gazelle: one can't help wondering when it'll rediscover its true nature and eat."

It turned out that Hannah Lang could type and take dictation, so I added her to the secretarial pool at the KdS. Gottfried had been in his first year at the Medical University before being deported, and

Liselotte wanted to be a nurse like her late mother. Very well—there was always a need for more workers at the army hospital.

I told all three of them to keep their eyes and ears open. I wanted to know what people were saying—our own soldiers and KdS staff, just as much as the other Jews, or the Russians. If asked, they were to tell the truth about their situation: they were in limbo, neither Jewish enough to be killed, nor German enough to be safe. I assumed that the Jews would try to exploit the Langs, just as I had done. So I warned them they should remember where their interests lay. I possessed absolute power over them; the Jews had none whatsoever. I was therefore the better friend.

For now at least they were safe, but the whole business was proving to be a monumental distraction. And the most absurd aspect of it all was that I had not yet laid or even attempted to lay so much as a finger on Hannah Lang.

We were now well into October. Sometimes, even in Minsk, there came a beautiful day, and it was possible to imagine what life would be like if the city were not half ruined and the woods still unsullied. One particular morning, the air was cold and refreshing. The sun shone down from a clear blue sky through trees already beginning to shed their red and golden leaves. I thought of Hannah Lang. Perhaps it was just the joy of a perfect day making me giddily optimistic, but it seemed to me that when I was with her I was just a little bit more like my old self again, and I wanted to show her that there was still a decent, thoughtful man beneath my forbidding SS uniform. I knew it might take some time to win her around, but I was willing to be patient. It would also be difficult to be seen together in public, at least at first, so I might have to take her back to my private quarters. I very much hoped she would not jump to the wrong conclusion as to my intentions. I desired her, of course I did. But my feelings were far deeper and more worthy than the animal lust that Strauch and von Toll had described when they spoke of her. "Maybe I'm a fool," I said to myself, "but I want Hannah and I to be lovers."

In the meantime, I still had work to do. I ran a string of spies in the ghetto and one of them, a light-fingered young thief called Mishkin, had come to me two days earlier with letters he'd discovered, written anonymously from someone in Maly Trostinets. They must have been passed by hand, via a labor detail, to someone in the ghetto. They described the guard routines at the camp—sentry shift-times, patrol details, everything—invaluable information for the partisans who were surely intended to be its eventual recipients.

Jews were forbidden from corresponding in any way at all with anyone outside their camp or ghetto—aside, of course, from the postcards written from the railhead upon their arrival here. The penalty for anyone found writing a letter was death.

I went to the camp that morning with a couple of men and my driver. On my arrival I found the commandant, explained the situation, and told him that I wanted all the Jews working at the camp to be rounded up and assembled in the central square. He objected, pointing out that some of them were out plowing the fields, while the others were distributed among the various workshops at the camp. I replied that I was very sorry to disturb the busy schedule at his camp, but this was an urgent security matter, and if he had any doubts about its importance he was welcome to discuss the matter with Lieutenant-Colonel Strauch. He grudgingly offered me his cooperation and told a squad of his men to assist us in gathering and herding the Jews into place.

I was walking toward the square when I came across a Jew in mechanic's overalls. I ordered him to come with me and pointed my gun at him to emphasize the point. Then, about a hundred meters further on, we bumped into that gutless filing clerk Kaul.

"Hello, Heuser. What are you doing here?" he asked.

I was feeling playful—perhaps because of Hannah's arrival in my life, perhaps because it was such a beautiful day. So I twirled the gun on my finger, cowboy-style, just to unnerve him and said, "Tracking down an offender. You?"

"The employee pay slips at the camp do not tally with the monies paid out. I'm dealing with the discrepancy."

"Then that makes two of us. I too have a discrepancy to sort out."

We made our farewells and I carried on to the square. "Join the rest of them," I said to the mechanic, and he made his way to the other Jews, around two hundred of them, gathered in the square, all seated on the ground. While my men and those from the camp covered me with their guns, I stood before the Jews and held the letters up.

"You all know the rules on writing letters and the penalty for disobeying them. Yet here I have letters, clearly sent from this camp, recovered in the Special Ghetto at Minsk. I'm not interested in conducting a general investigation, nor do I wish to mount mass reprisals. I simply want to know who wrote these letters and deal with that person alone, so that those who are innocent can be left unharmed. However, if the guilty party does not step forward, I'll be obliged to kill inmates at random until the culprit either makes his confession or is named by someone else.

"You all know me. I am a stickler for the rules. I would much rather that only one of you were punished. But you also know that I do not make idle threats. I'll order the shootings to begin if no one comes forward. You have two minutes to decide, starting now."

It took ninety seconds. Then a man stood up, gave his name as Yakov Loeb, and said that he was the writer.

"Come here, Loeb," I said.

He stepped forward, a small, wiry man with close-cropped receding hair and a short gray beard. I must say I admired the forthright way he approached me, with his head up and not a trace of fear.

"If you wrote these letters, you'll be able to tell me their contents. So . . . ?"

"They describe the dispositions of the guards at the Maly Trostinets camp," he said, looking me right in the eye. "And if you think I only sent one copy, then you're more of a fool than I took you for."

"I see. Well, thank you for being so frank, Loeb." I summoned the nearest of my men. "Shoot him."

Loeb stood straight and made no attempt whatsoever to beg for mercy or escape his fate. My man fired a single shot with his rifle, and then another when Loeb was on the ground, just to make sure.

I addressed the Jews, feeling the silent hatred rising from their ranks and facing it down, just as Loeb had done to me. "Go back to your work," I said. "Remember what happens to those who break the rules. And just to concentrate your minds, there will be no food ration today."

It was 11:30 and the pots of gruel were already cooking in the camp kitchen. I told my men to kick them over and watched as the weak, tasteless liquid seeped into the kitchen's bare-earth floor.

"I'm afraid you'll have to drive your people a little harder this afternoon, since there is even less food in their bellies than usual," I told the commandant when I got back to his office.

"Maybe they should just eat Loeb," he replied.

I gave him a tight smile in acknowledgment of his witticism, then went on: "The rules are there for a reason. There's no harm in reminding them of that from time to time."

"Quite so."

"By the way," I said, "I need to get some provisions from the stores. Has the baggage from the last transport been sorted yet?"

"Of course—by all means help yourself."

"How much gold did we get this time?"

The commandant smiled. "Plenty. Those Vienna Jews can afford the best and most expensive dentistry. Lots of married couples with nice gold rings, too."

I went to the storeroom and helped myself to my standard share of the gold, various tins of meat and fish, a couple of jars of pickles, and a decent bottle of Riesling. I let the men take a bottle of brandy each, and they returned to Minsk in a fine mood.

Back at the Lenin House I bumped into Kaul again.

"Did you deal with your problem?" he asked.

"Oh yes, it was easy," I replied. I made a little gun out of my first two fingers, placed it against Kaul's skull, and said: "Bang! And it was over."

Kaul looked appalled. I laughed. And then, having had a man killed, deprived his starving companions of their meager rations, and appropriated foodstuffs stolen from people I had then helped to murder, I went back to my quarters hoping to persuade a captive woman that I was quite a nice fellow, really, once you got to know me. I was, of course, unable to see the hopeless tangle of contradictions and misperceptions I had become. But then, among the many lessons I learned in Minsk was that one can become all but totally deranged while still functioning very efficiently at work and remaining confident that one's personal behavior is perfectly normal, one's thoughts completely rational. Or to put it another way, one of the symptoms of madness is the conviction that one is sane.

45

My work for the day was completed by about 20:00. I went down to the cellar where the Langs had been installed. They had no beds, just thin straw mattresses laid directly on the stone floor. Their baggage, however, must have included blankets, for the mattresses were all covered. By Jewish standards this was luxury. Hannah was there with the other two. "Put your coat on," I said. "You're coming with me."

Lisl gasped and looked at Hannah with anxious, fearful eyes. "There's no cause to be alarmed," I reassured her. "Your sister will be back soon, safe and sound."

We walked the short distance to my quarters making stilted conversation. "I hope your living quarters are satisfactory?"

"Yes, quite comfortable, thank you."

"Good . . ." And so on.

I let her in through the back door and up the servants' staircase. From the living room came the sound of someone playing the Radetzky March on the piano very loudly and very badly, accompanied by the voices of my fellow officers drunkenly singing along as they clapped and stamped their feet. Hannah stopped on the stairs when she realized what the music was. "It reminds me of home," she said. "The last dance of the night at the New Year Concert . . ."

I thought of her in her favorite party dress at a Viennese ball, dancing to Strauss without a care in the world, and wondered if there would ever again come a time when people could possess such simple, unfettered contentment. I'd never known it in my life. Perhaps I never would.

We got to my room. Frau Aranski had laid a table for us with a clean white cloth and a feast of food and wine. I thought of my first dinner with Biene in Berlin. The circumstances now were very different, but perhaps, just possibly, I might be able to re-create some of the magic of that night.

"Would you like a glass of wine?"

She said, "Yes," but there was a nervous edge to her voice and I saw her cast a glance at the bed just beyond the table.

"Please, sit down. And help yourself to whatever you'd like to eat."

She must have been starving. There would have been very little food on the train, and she'd only been on Jew rations since her arrival in Minsk. Yet she made no attempt to eat. She just sat silently, watching me suspiciously, waiting to see what I would do next. This was not at all how I'd hoped we'd start the evening.

I tried again to make conversation. "So, why didn't you come here at the same time as your parents?"

She shrugged. "The people in Vienna had the same problem as you. They couldn't decide whether we were Jews."

"Oh, I see . . ."

I could think of nothing further to say. Hannah glanced around the room, taking it all in: the carefully prepared dinner; my family picture on the mantelpiece above the fireplace; a selection of favorite books on a shelf. Then she focused directly on me and said, "So this is where you're going to rape me."

That took me completely by surprise. I was baffled by how she could possibly have got such an idea. "Rape you? What on earth do you mean?"

She gave an exasperated sigh. "Oh please, Dr. Heuser, I'm not completely naïve. You get my body and we stay alive. That's the deal, isn't it?"

When she put it like that, I realized that she was half right. That was the deal, when put at its crudest. But I'd never thought of it in those terms before. I tried to explain: "I would never force you. I . . . I . . ."

Hannah had been glaring at me in tight-mouthed defiance, but now her mouth literally dropped open. "God in heaven! You can't possibly think . . . But you do, don't you? You want to make me say yes. You want my consent!"

That was precisely what I'd been hoping for, even dreaming of, but her voice was rising and her eyes were filled with disgust. "Are you out of your mind? I'd rather you rape me than make me betray myself. Anything but that."

I couldn't believe what I was hearing. How could her vision of me be so different from mine of her?

"But I saved your life!" I pleaded. "I saw you get down from that train and I couldn't bear the idea that you were going to die. So I saved you. Doesn't that count for anything? This city is full of young women looking for a man. But I haven't gone with any of them. I've risked my career, my reputation, maybe even my life, to save you! I've fought with my commanding officer for the right to keep you alive. I've argued with my closest friend over you. Does that sound as if I'm a rapist?"

"Why not? You're a murderer, aren't you?"

I could have had her killed for calling me a murderer. But I was in no state to enjoy that irony. Forget her yellow star or my uniform. I was just another man trying to explain himself to a woman who wouldn't have him. And I didn't make a very good job of it. "No, no, I'm not," I insisted. "I take no pleasure in any of this . . . Yes, I have killed people. From the moment we set foot in this shitty country, no one has done anything but kill. But I've never killed anyone that I wasn't ordered to kill."

Hannah laughed in my face at that. "Listen to yourself! Did you hear what you just said?"

Now I felt as though I, not she, were the one pleading for their life. "I know what a real murderer is like. I've looked into the eyes of a man who loved death so much it made him come in his pants. I'm not like him. You have to believe that . . . I am not like him . . ."

For the first time I held out some hope that Hannah might be able to see the man I was, not the system I represented. She leaned back, letting herself calm down a little.

"I think I'll have some wine now, please," she said.

I poured some into her glass. She drank it in one swallow and then held her glass out again to be refilled. This time she sipped with more restraint and I let her be, not saying anything, just waiting for her to make the next move. She put her glass down on the table and played with the stem, pushing it around in small circles on the tablecloth. Then she spoke once again.

"All right then, you say you kill but you do not murder. So tell me how my parents died. How did you kill but not murder them?"

My spirits fell: not that, please, anything but that. What chance could I possibly have with her once she knew what happened in the woods of Blagovshchina?

"No, I can't do that. It's . . . it's a matter of operational security."

She practically sneered at me: "Oh come on . . . 'Operational security'? That's the most pathetic thing you've said all night. Tell me how they died."

Whatever tiny shred of hope I had of persuading her that I wasn't the base animal she imagined depended on my being honest with her now.

"You say they arrived here about a month ago?" I asked.

"Yes."

"Then that would have been Da 225 from Vienna."

"What do you mean, 'Da 225'?"

"Every transport taking Jews from one part of the Reich to another is numbered. The Reichsbahn people planned them all, months in advance. They're very proud of it."

"So there are hundreds of trains like the ones we were on?" She asked the question with a note of disbelief. Any civilian in the Reich would have sounded the same if they were confronted with the sheer scale of the operation.

"Yes, many hundreds."

"Taking people to die?"

"Not always. Some of the people are used as workers."

Hannah's face lit up. "So maybe my parents are alive!"

"No. We only keep the youngest, strongest men and those with special skills."

"But my father has a skill. He's a surgeon—a brilliant one."

"I mean a manual skill," I said. "A surgeon is considered an intellectual and thus too dangerous to survive. A dentist we might keep, but not a surgeon."

Her face fell. "I see . . ." She swallowed a mouthful of wine, perhaps hoping that it might be some kind of anesthetic. "So what happened to Da 225?"

I paused, trying to gather my memories. "Well, that was the September 4th transport, and it would have arrived in the early morning, just as yours did. That way we have the most time to process everyone."

"'Process'?"

"That's the approved term, yes." If she was going to know the truth about how we killed people, she might as well know how we tried to hide it, too. "It was hot that morning, I remember it very well, one of the last really baking days of summer. There is a place called Blagovshchina where we dig pits that . . ." I stopped, trying to find any words to soften the truth. But there were no words to sweeten the stench of Blagovshchina. "Pits that are used as mass graves. I was the officer in charge down there that day, so . . . You know, I swear this has only just occurred to me, but it's true: I wasn't shooting that day. So I couldn't possibly have shot them . . . Oh, thank God for that at least . . ."

Hannah wasn't in the slightest bit interested in how I felt. She simply asked: "They're all shot, then. Is that what you mean by processing?"

"On that day, yes."

"Tell me what it was like, this shooting. Tell me about my mother and father's last minutes on this earth. And tell me all of it, every detail. I want to know it all."

"No really, please, you don't . . ."

"Tell me it all!"

So I told her everything. I recounted how her parents were driven from the railhead down into the woods, then stripped and searched for gold teeth and fillings. I watched Hannah's mounting distress as she began to understand the degradation they had suffered. She brought her hand to her mouth when I described the search for gold and whispered: "Papa!"

I told her how those waiting to die stood in a line, stark naked, and watched the ones ahead of them being shot and falling into the pit before they themselves took their turn in front of the guns. And as I talked I felt something inside me give way. Maybe this is what Catholics feel in the confessional, this release that comes with admitting one's sins. But suddenly there were tears streaming down my face as well as hers, and I had to get the words out between sobs.

I finished, and for a second the only sounds were our noses sniffing and breaths being caught at the back of our throats. And then Hannah howled, a screaming wail of agony and rage too deep for any words, and she jumped out of her chair and threw herself at me with her hands out in front of her like claws, aiming straight for my face. I put up my arms to defend myself and though I caught one of her wrists, the other got through my defenses and I had to close my eyes as her fingernails tore at the skin of my temple and cheek. The shock of pain sent a surge of energy through me, blowing away my maudlin self-pity. I roared like a wounded lion and grabbed that other wrist too. Forcing her arms up and away from me, I struggled to my feet as she lunged at me with her teeth, kicked at my legs, and then when I was upright aimed a kneecap at my groin.

I shoved her away and she crashed backward into the table, sending it to the floor in an explosion of breaking plates, bottles, and glasses. I pushed her again, sending her further across the floor.

All the while, Hannah was screaming obscenities at me, calling me every foul name in the dictionary, saying how much she hated me. Then her legs hit the bed and she fell back onto it and my momentum carried me onward, on top of her, and we were lying half on and half off the mattress and my face was directly above hers. I wanted to make her stop screaming such terrible things so I placed my lips on hers and kissed her, just to shut her up, forcing my tongue between her teeth and driving it deep into her mouth.

She smelled so sweet and tasted so good and I was as hard as a rock. I pulled her arms up over her head and gathered both her wrists in my left hand. Then I pushed down with all my strength so that her hands were trapped against the mattress. With my right hand I reached down and pulled her skirt up over her thighs. She was writhing and bucking, but the weight of my body was on her so she could not stop me pulling her panties down to her knees. My mouth was still over hers, silencing her, though she was tossing her head this way and that trying to shake me off. I placed my legs between hers and forced her thighs apart as far as they would go. I fumbled with the buttons of my fly. Then I took her.

The moment I entered her she stopped moving entirely and her resistance gave way to a cold, almost deathly passivity. She just lay there until I'd emptied myself into her. It didn't take long and there was no real pleasure in it at all. In fact, as I felt myself shrinking within her, the overwhelming sensation was one of abject failure.

I rolled off her and we lay side by side on top of the bed, silent and motionless. Finally she just said: "You got what you wanted. Now what are you going to do?"

I got up off the bed and did up my pants. "Get dressed. If you leave now you can get back to the Lenin House before the curfew for Jews. If you're out after that, they'll shoot you."

"What if they do? You'll have us shot anyway."

The gulf between us was unbridgeable. To me, Hannah would always be the girl I saw getting off the train, looking golden in the sunlight. To her I was a killer and rapist, no better than any other psychopath. And now I'd proved her right. But I would not lower myself any deeper into the mire. There had to be some shred of decency left in me.

"No . . . no I won't. Here, take some of this food with you. I've got no need of it."

She was straightening her clothes, trying to give herself the appearance of dignity before she had to face the outside world. "Do you have a hairbrush?" she said, flatly.

"On the table over there."

She looked in my mirror and gave her hair a cursory tidying. Wordlessly she put the brush back precisely where she'd found it, then picked up her coat and put it on. The yellow star seemed to glare at me in silent reproach. She turned toward the door.

"Take the food," I repeated.

Hannah said nothing. She was turning the handle of the door. Suddenly the food seemed tremendously important to me. I took three quick strides toward her and held her arm to stop her leaving. She flinched as if I'd hit her. "Take your hands off me," she hissed. Her breath was coming in quick, shallow gasps and I could see she was on the verge of hysteria.

"Please," I said, as calmly as I could. "Take the food. It is going to be a long, cold, hungry winter and your brother and sister will be grateful for this, even if you are not. It could be the difference between life and death."

She relaxed a fraction and I let go of her.

"Wait here just one moment," I said. I had a three-week-old copy of the *Volkischer Beobachter*, the official Party newspaper. The headline read VICTORY IN SIGHT AT STALINGRAD!

"I'll wrap the food in this," I said, pulling out double sheets of paper with which to make parcels. She stood watching me without the slightest trace of expression or animation on her face. I held up the bread. "People in the ghetto would trade you everything they have just for this loaf," I said. "As for the rest of it . . . they've forgotten such things even exist."

Within a few minutes I had five loosely wrapped little parcels: meat, fish, pickles, bread, and margarine, each one of them worth its weight in gold in that madhouse of a city. Hannah had no bag, but her coat had two large patch pockets on the front. While she stood quite motionless, neither helping nor preventing me, I stuffed two little parcels into each pocket. I was left with one, the meat: the most valuable of all.

"Do you have another pocket?" I asked.

Wordlessly, she held out a hand and I gave her the little bundle of newsprint. She stuffed it into an inside pocket, then turned and walked out of the door without even a backward glance. I followed her out onto the landing. "Do you want me to walk you home?" I called out as she walked toward the stairs.

She ignored me: her turned back was all the answer she was ever going to give me. As I walked back to my room I could hear the music from downstairs. They had moved on to "The Horst Wessel Song." I listened for a moment to that stirring tune and then went back to my room.

The following day I informed Strauch that he need not worry about any inappropriate liaison between me and Hannah Lang. "I'm very glad to hear it," he said. "I was worried I might lose my most valuable officer over a piece of Jew trash. Out of curiosity, did you fuck it?"

"Yes, once."

"And?"

"She was frigid."

"I see. So tell me about those marks on your face. Did you cut yourself shaving by any chance?"

"She put up some resistance."

"So you'll be disposing of her and that gaggle of hers?"

"Not yet. The ambiguity of their status could make them useful informants. They know their survival depends on me. I can count on their loyalty."

"You're not letting the Lang woman work here any longer, surely."

"No. I've found another job for her with that oil distributor, Schinkel. He has a number of Jews and Russians working for him. The usual thing: he can get a dozen of them for the cost of a single German."

"Like Frau Kube and those maids she's always boasting about."

"Quite so. My concern, however, is that some of his employees may have links with the partisans. The Soviets would be very keen to know the state of our supplies, not to mention the precise details of our transport and storage operations. If Fräulein Lang wants to live, she can damn well find out precisely what information, if any, is being passed to the enemy. And then she can help me in making sure that any future information is false and comes directly from us."

Strauch steepled his fingers, rested his face on them, and looked at me over the top of his glasses. "How much of this have you told Schinkel?"

"I've told him that the commander of the security police and SD would very much appreciate his cooperation in finding work for a valued Jew, just as he would doubtless appreciate our continued friendship."

Strauch agreed. "The man is a fat, corrupt profiteer, no better than a damn Jew himself. It won't do him any harm to think that we have our eyes on him."

As I got up to leave I said: "You see? I knew those *Mischlings* would come in handy."

46

Winter set in, and with it the inevitable slowdown in our activities. There was really no sense from Berlin's point of view in sending Jews all the way to deepest Ostland to be processed in what was by now a very old-fashioned arrangement of shooting squads, gas vans, and burial pits. There were far more efficient, year-round death camps much closer at hand. Meanwhile the population of the ghetto had dropped to a little less than ten thousand, and virtually all of them were required as workers, for the time being at least.

We carried out the occasional action in the surrounding towns and villages. Other than that, however, our chief concern was simply getting through another bitterly cold winter. And we could count ourselves lucky. The defeat of General von Paulus and his Sixth Army at Stalingrad came as a terrible blow. For many of us, that was the moment when defeat became more than just a theoretical possibility. It's remarkable, however, how human beings carry on with their day-to-day lives in the face of impending disaster. Perhaps it is an essential trick of the mind: after all, we all know we're going to die, yet we strive and struggle to survive nonetheless.

I still supervised Gestapo operations in Minsk, liaising with the heads of my various sections and running my own operations against spies, saboteurs, and dissenters. Hannah Lang proved herself very useful. She gave me the names of a couple of Russian girls who had been acting suspiciously, and one of them turned out to be a partisan sympathizer. Hannah did not ask what had happened to the two of them—neither, of course, returned to work—and I did not volunteer the information.

Early in the New Year of 1943 I received a telephone call from Schinkel. "I'd like to discuss Fräulein Lang," he said.

"Is her work proving unsatisfactory?" I asked.

"Oh no, she's not at all unsatisfactory, not in the slightest . . ." Schinkel began a meandering recitation, listing Hannah's qualities, particularly the physical ones, and commenting that she really didn't look or act much like a Jew at all: in fact, one might almost take her for a proper German. I now realized the reason Schinkel was calling. He wanted to screw Hannah Lang, but he didn't want to make a move on a woman who was SS property without ensuring that it wouldn't get him into trouble. I told him to get to the point.

"Well," said Schinkel, "speaking man to man, if it's all right by you, I'd like to give the dirty little bitch a good seeing-to, if you catch my meaning."

So I was right about what he wanted. But how was I going to answer him?

Schinkel was a truly gross individual, as porcine in his manners as in his appearance. I was sickened to think of him hoisting his grossly fat body on to Hannah, or placing his blubbery lips, topped by a little mustache that looked like a parody of the Führer's, on her mouth. But it would sicken her even more. That, I now realized, was the key point.

"I have no objection at all," I said. "Do whatever you like. But I should point out that there are others here in Minsk who share your appreciation of Fräulein Lang's qualities. Should they ever choose to act upon their interest, their demands would of course take priority over yours."

"Oh yes, of course."

"And they would be very annoyed indeed if she came to them in anything other than prime condition. Think of Fräulein Lang as a very fine thoroughbred mare. You are the stable boy. From time to time you may take her out for a ride, to keep her in fine fettle. But when the master comes, he'll expect to find her looking glossy and well-fed. And if he sees even the slightest mark upon her, he'll be very displeased."

"I quite understand, absolutely, yes. Thank you, Dr. Heuser. Thank you very much indeed."

By putting it that way I made it impossible for Schinkel to take Hannah by force. In the end it would be up to her to decide whether the food that he'd doubtless offer her, since I'd made that specific suggestion, would be enough to counteract the disgust and self-loathing she would feel at accepting his invitation. She'd be forced to choose her own degradation. It might teach her a little humility.

Two weeks later I discovered her decision. During one of our routine meetings Hannah volunteered the information that Schinkel had offered to make her his mistress. The way she said it sounded vaguely provocative. She was woman enough to want to manipulate my emotions. I had no intention of allowing that to happen. "He told me he was planning to do that," I said, as casually as possible. "He even asked my permission."

That surprised her. "What did you say?"

"Evidently I said yes. And you?"

"I said yes too."

She looked me right in the eye, challenging me, wanting to provoke a reaction. I looked right back, without the slightest change to my expression. And then, when the meeting was over and she'd left the building, I grabbed a fine hand-cut lead crystal tumbler, booty from a recent train, and filled it almost to the brim with vodka. I downed it in one and then, letting out a bellow of rage, hurled that precious glass straight at the wall and watched as it exploded in a thousand sparkling shards.

Hannah's status as Schinkel's mistress soon became a matter of public knowledge. He felt free to show her off, and so I'd bump into the pair of them at concerts, cocktail parties, or screenings of films from home. For a while, of course, it hurt me to see Hannah on the arm of this vile individual, all the more so since Schinkel made vast profits from his oil trading and was happy to spend a great deal on clothes and jewels to show off his pretty new toy. It also troubled me to think that she would surely feel obliged to respond to him with greater passion—however fake it might be—than she'd shown me. It wasn't easy to think of her moaning and crying out in an imitation of ecstasy.

I spent the night of my thirtieth birthday alone, trying to keep those images of Hannah from my mind. I'd always assumed that at thirty I would be settled, with a secure job, a nice apartment in Berlin, a pretty wife to bring me dinner, and strong, healthy children. Instead I was stuck in Russia, in a single room, dreaming of a woman with a yellow star on her coat, whom I could never now possess. I am not often prone to self-pity, but that was one night when I wallowed in it.

Thank goodness that those melancholy feelings did not last for long. In the morning I reminded myself that Hannah no longer had any right to consider herself morally superior to me. If I was a rapist, she was a whore. We had both been dragged down to the same level. But then, who didn't become corrupted during those years in Minsk? Luckily there was always someone to whom one could point and say: "At least he is even lower than me."

For me that someone was an SS sergeant called Rübe, who appeared in Minsk early in 1943 like the second coming of Captain Franz Stark. He even carried a whip, just as Stark himself had done. Rübe was given the job of administering discipline in the ghetto and did so in ways that raised eyebrows at the KdS, even among those of us who imagined that there was no depravity that we had not already witnessed. He killed thirty pregnant women in the Jewish hospital. He shot an orphan boy putting flowers on his parents' grave. He slaughtered other ghetto dwellers on a whim, for no reason at all.

I despised Rübe, we all did, but what right did I have to feel in any way superior? By this point, I must personally have killed two or three hundred people, maybe more, all shot at point-blank range. I found this fact almost impossible to accept, and even harder to understand. I had never in all my life wanted or desired to kill anyone. Yet now I was a serial killer in uniform, operating on a scale far beyond any conventional murderer.

And what had it all been for? That summer saw a second defeat on the scale of Stalingrad when our armored divisions were broken in a failed attack on the Kursk salient. From that moment on we would not take a forward step on the Eastern Front—or anywhere else, come to that.

Even so, my first real intimation of impending Armageddon did not come from anything that happened on the battlefields of the Russian Front, but from events at home.

In early August I received a letter informing me that Biene was dead. The RAF had bombed Hamburg at the end of July and she was one of the casualties. Her mother wrote to tell me the news. She said that Sabine had always spoken very fondly of me and would have wanted me to know. Frau Tietmeyer explained that she had moved out of the city, specifically to escape the bombs, but Biene refused to join her because she didn't want to let the people at the Kripo down. So that magnificent bravery killed her in the end.

I ought now to be recounting how I cried as if my heart would break, and howled and drank myself insensible, but the appalling truth is that the news had no immediate effect on me at all. I should have been distraught, but I had grown so hardened to slaughter that the tragedy of Biene's death bounced off my heart like a pistol bullet off a Tiger tank. Her mother had also sent a sad little bundle, tied together with a pale blue silk ribbon that was crumpled and twisted from all the times it had been knotted and untied: letters that I'd sent Biene, and photographs of the two of us together. They'd been entrusted to her for safekeeping, Frau Tietmeyer said, when Biene had decided to stay in the city. Any normal man would have wept to see those images of happier times, filled with such love and hope for the future, but I remained completely numb. Minsk had done that to me.

A few days later, however, Karlo List, a KdS man from Hamburg who had just returned from his leave, told me what happened there the night that Biene died.

The English sent more than seven hundred heavy bombers to attack the city. The weather had been hot for weeks, not a drop of rain, and they dropped incendiaries. It was like putting a match to a giant tinderbox. Fires broke out everywhere and the blazing buildings merged together to create a single giant firestorm. The flames consumed all the oxygen in the atmosphere, so that all the people huddling together in their shelters had nothing to breathe but carbon monoxide. So they died—forty thousand innocent civilians in a single night. And once they had died, their bodies were consumed in the flames.

"You can't imagine the horror of it," List said. "It was so hot in the shelters that the people down there began to bake—literally bake. And they couldn't breathe, so they went insane, screaming and shouting and fighting to get out. But a lot of the air-raid wardens wouldn't open the doors. They had their orders: in a raid, everyone has to stay under cover. So the shelters became death-traps. A few people were strong enough to force their way out, but it was no better on the streets. They were roasted up there, too.

"The next day there were bodies everywhere, lying on the pavements, in the gutters, even in the middle of the road. It was like the ghetto last summer, you remember, after the July action? Except these bodies were all blackened and burned from the fire. And people were walking or cycling right by them, trying to pretend the bodies weren't really there. It was simply terrible. If I live to be a hundred years old, I'll never forgive those English bastards."

List's news made me very, very angry, and that rage somehow freed all the emotions that I'd been unable to feel up to that point: my sadness, my loss, my bereavement all became real to me. I broke down and wept for Biene, and that seemed to take a great weight off my shoulders, as though the tears were washing away a burden that I'd been carrying without even knowing it. And when those tears subsided, I was suddenly able to think with great clarity, and an idea came to me like a kind of revelation.

I thought of the day Heydrich had come to Minsk and boasted of a new camp that could dispose of ten thousand Jews in a single day by gassing them and then cremating their bodies. And it struck me that this was exactly what the British had done in Hamburg. First they had gassed their victims, using carbon monoxide, just as we did in our gas vans here. And then they had cremated them. But the British had made Heydrich's great camp look puny, for they had not processed ten thousand innocent people, but forty thousand.

Then I considered all the planning that must have gone into the raids. Just putting seven hundred bombers into the air at once, and getting them to the same place at exactly the right intervals so that they didn't collide with one another—why, that would require a timetable that even the Reichsbahn boys would be proud of. I imagined all the meetings that must have taken place, all the memos that must have been written to make sure that there was enough aviation fuel at the airfields, and all the correct bombs for each plane, and plenty of bullets for the gunners.

It all seemed very familiar to me, so then I realized what the British were really up to. "This," I decided, "is their final solution to the German question."

Summer gave way to autumn, the season of decay—an apt metaphor, perhaps, for the overwhelming sense of entropy that now engulfed us. At every level, from the lowliest individual to the entire state of the Reich itself, there was a sense of things fraying at the edges, crumbling from within, heading inexorably toward a point of total collapse. The Russians could sense it. The partisans became ever more bold in their attacks on us, placing bombs in one German installation after another, even killing twenty people when they left an explosive device in the dining hall of the Lenin House itself. Of course, reprisals were ordered, local civilians rounded up and shot, but it made no difference, the attacks kept coming.

By now, most of my professional life was focused on anti-partisan activities. It was my job to catch spies and saboteurs. But the business of occupying a hostile nation and suppressing its population depends upon maintaining the balance of terror. As long as one can convince the mass of the population that one has the power and will to find, capture, torture, and kill wrongdoers, then fear will inhibit the vast majority from hostile action. But the very second that one loses one's grip, the people sense it and rise up, and once they do that, their sheer numbers become terrifying to their oppressors, for no matter how many you kill there are always many more to take their place. We were on the very point of that balance now. So both sides kept raising the stakes, making the wantonness and brutality of their actions ever more severe, waiting to see who would crack first.

On September 21 the partisans assassinated Gauleiter Kube. I was summoned from my bed to go to the scene. It wasn't difficult to piece together what had happened. The culprit was one of Frau Kube's "twelve Russian swine"—an attractive twenty-two-year-old house-maid called Yelena Mazanik. That evening, shortly before the Kubes retired to bed, Mazanik approached the guard on duty at the door to the Kubes' private quarters and said: "I bet you haven't had a drop of coffee today, Officer." Under questioning, he admitted that she was looking at him in a seductive fashion as she said these words.

The guard agreed that he'd not had any coffee and was thirsty, at which point Mazanik said that if he went downstairs to the kitchen, Domna the cook would give him a cup. Sure enough, this Domna woman confirmed that Mazanik had previously asked her to make coffee for the guard, saying that he was her boyfriend.

While the guard was in the kitchen, Mazanik entered the Kubes' quarters, went directly to the main bedroom, and placed a bomb between the mattress and the springs of Kube's bed. She remained in the building until the bomb went off but then left immediately, telling the guards at the main entrance that she was going to find a doctor. Shortly afterward, a car was heard in the distance, starting up and then accelerating at high speed.

Two things then happened. For our part, we rounded up three hundred men, women, and children from the area of Minsk where Mazanik lived, and shot the lot of them. The Russians, meanwhile, declared Mazanik a Hero of the Soviet Union and broadcast a radio interview in which she described how she had carried out the bombing, in the kind of detail that only the actual assassin could have known. So Mazanik had not only killed one of the most senior German officials in Russia, she had managed to get back behind Russian lines without our being able to lay a finger on her. We could have killed three hundred thousand people, it would have made no difference. Everyone knew that the Russians were winning.

Within days of Kube's death, Smolensk fell. The Red Army was now just two hundred kilometers away. Our old commander Ehrlinger was forced to retreat from Smolensk, ended up in Minsk, and made the best of a bad situation by taking charge. There were yet more organizational changes: the kind that beset an organization when its leaders try to pretend they can reshuffle their way out of imminent disaster. I was placed in charge of an entire new Department N, dealing exclusively with counterespionage and anti-partisan activities. There was, of course, no promotion to go with my new role, but it did have a very significant effect on me as a person. For now I was no longer obliged to take part in mass actions against huge numbers of people. Instead I frequently acted as an individual, dealing with solitary perpetrators. And so I found myself behaving in a way that must have made the ghost of Paul Ogorzow look on in admiration and even envy. For I became his brother-in-arms. Cloaked in the respectability of my uniform, I went out into the battered streets of Minsk to hunt my prey: a stalker and killer of women in the night.

47

LUDWIGSBURG: DECEMBER 22, 1962

Kraus was going back to his family for Christmas, "for the children's sake," he said. They had one more night together before Paula drove up to Frankfurt to spend ten days with her mother being ferried around to endless social events to meet the few remotely suitable men who were still unmarried and whom she had not already rejected. They should have been making wild, unfettered love, the kind that had come so naturally a year earlier, but as Paula lay in Kraus's arms she was consumed not by passion, but with the searing barbarity of the evidence she had been hearing in Koblenz.

"We had a witness last week talking about the gas vans," she said. Her eyes weren't looking up at Kraus, just staring into the darkness. "It was ghastly. They looked just like ordinary furniture vans, but the insides were lined with sheet metal, so they were airtight and impossible to escape. They put the Jews in there and then they ran a hose from the van's exhaust up into the back of the van, where all the people were, and started driving. The exhaust fumes would go into the compartment, people would start to choke, and the van would just keep driving. Of course by now all the people were banging on the side of the van, screaming and begging to be let out, but they were just ignored. When they got to the burial pit, they let the engine run until there was no more sound or movement from the back of the van, and then they would open up the door..."

"Paula, darling . . ." said Kraus, squeezing her tighter, but she ignored him. She was lost in the world she now inhabited, telling this vile story because she simply could not keep it inside her any longer. She had to let the poison out of her mind.

"All the bodies would be carried out and then the inside of the van was hosed down. I can't even begin to tell you what was in there. Blood, shit, hair, false teeth ... Even the judges were going pale ..."

"Paula ..." his voice was less patient now, but still she hardly even heard him, carrying on regardless.

"But that wasn't the thing that really got to me. The vans were actually converted from regular trucks by mechanics at the Criminal Police headquarters in Berlin. It was Nebe, the old police chief, who thought of running a hose from the exhaust, you see. So the van drivers would bring their vehicles all the way from Berlin to Minsk, and one of the men brought his fourteen-year-old son with him. Can you imagine, bringing a boy into that hell? The man must have been crazy. The witness was quite indignant when it was suggested to him that there was something profoundly wrong about it all. He said: 'Oh no, the lad never saw anything nasty. They gave him a job as an office boy for the SS.'"

"Paula! That's enough!"

"I'm sorry, it's just that I have to talk about it. I have to tell someone. And if I can't tell you, of all people . . ."

"Of course you can tell me. But not here, not now . . ."

"When, then? I'm not going to see you for a week, maybe more. Am I just supposed to keep it all inside, just stick a fake smile on my face and pretend that Christmas with my mother means anything at all to me? Well? Come on, tell me! What do you want me to do?"

"You could calm down. That would be a start."

Paula couldn't believe it. Kraus, the man who always had time for her, who was always ready to listen, implying she was just being a hysterical female. How could he do that, be exactly like all the other, lesser men? Then it struck her that he might be right: maybe she really was being hysterical. And that realization only made her even angrier—at herself now as well as at him—and she had to get away from him. She sat on the edge of the bed, her back to Kraus, her head in her hands, and suddenly her shoulders were shaking and the tears were flooding down her face.

Kraus reached over to the bedside table where she kept a box of tissues, pulled out a bundle, and then shuffled back across the bed. He sat on the edge beside her and handed her a couple of tissues.

"Thanks," she said.

"It's all right," he said, wrapping an arm around her. "Everything's going to be all right."

Paula gave a sad little shake of the head. "No it isn't."

Kraus didn't say anything right away. He let her cry herself out, blow her nose, dry her face, and compose herself before he asked her: "What's really the matter?"

She shrugged. "Everything."

Kraus chuckled affectionately. "Could you be more specific?"

Paula managed a forlorn smile. "I'll try."

"I'm all ears."

"The case is killing me . . ."

"Hmm, I think I'd worked that out for myself."

"I'm sorry. . . . I know it wasn't what you wanted to hear tonight."

"But it was what you had to say, so . . ." He pulled her closer to him. "It is all right. Really."

Now she turned her head to look up at him. "I don't think so . . . Barbara wants you back, it's obvious."

"That's not what it feels like to me. As far as I'm concerned she's just decided that the kids deserve to have a proper family Christmas and it's up to us to be grown-up enough to behave properly and give it to them."

Paula sighed, amazed that even a man as intelligent and perceptive as Kraus could be so deaf, dumb, and blind to the intentions of a woman he had known for almost all his adult life. "Is that what you think?" she asked.

"Why shouldn't I?"

"Because that's not what's happening." It all seemed very clear to Paula now, and she found herself able to talk as calmly as if she were analyzing the tactics of an opposing lawyer. "Can't you see? She's changed her mind. Either she's discovered how much she misses you, or she just doesn't want to raise two children by herself, worrying about money, knowing the neighbors are looking down on her."

"My God! You make Barbara sound like some cynical, calculating Machiavelli! She's not like that at all."

"She's a woman who's fighting to rescue her marriage, and honestly I don't blame her, because it's just what I would do if I were in her shoes. She'll be waiting at the door to greet you with the biggest smile you've seen from her in years and a kiss—just a little kiss on the cheek. And you'll smell her perfume and it'll bring back memories of all the good times, and she'll know it because it brought back the same memories when she put it on, too."

"My God! I had no idea you had such a vivid imagination!"

"She'll be five kilos lighter than the last time you saw her," Paula continued, barely pausing while Kraus spoke. "She'll have had her hair done, and even if you don't notice that, you'll certainly notice that it's roast pork for dinner . . ."

"My favorite, as everyone knows," said Kraus wryly.

"Exactly . . . and a Pilsner to go with it . . . and everything arranged just the way you like it."

"If you ask me, it's just as likely she'll be ice cold, polite at best, maybe with one of those fake smiles you were talking about, just to make the children think we're getting on."

"Well, if she's like that, then I'm wrong. But she won't be, I know she won't."

Kraus looked at her with something close to alarm on his face. "Do you think it would make any difference to me . . . to us? For God's sake, I love you."

"I know you do," she said, with a sadness that cut Kraus to the heart, for she sounded like a woman who'd already written them off.

"And you love me too!" he insisted.

"Yes . . . I do. But don't you see? It makes no difference. In the end, Barbara has everything: your children, your house, all your years together. I can't compete with that."

"You don't have to compete with her . . . or anyone. I'm here. I'm not going anywhere else. You've got me."

She kissed his chest.

"You silly thing," Kraus murmured. "I love you. I want you . . . I want you right now."

And so they made love, just as the occasion demanded. But even as they did, Paula was overwhelmed by a sense that the foundations of her life were crumbling beneath her. Her relationship with Kraus was bound so closely to the Heuser trial. And it seemed to her that both were entering their final stages.

48

MINSK:
OCTOBER 1943–JULY 1944

Yelena Mazanik wasn't the only attractive young woman recruited by the Soviets to infiltrate our ranks. One day in October my men discovered sketch plans of various areas of the Lenin House being carried by a suspected partisan. There were notes written alongside the sketches detailing the senior officers who worked in various offices, and the security procedures for their protection. Under interrogation the partisan confessed that he had received them from a fellow bandit called Lydia Ivanova. I was familiar with this woman, since she had worked for us for some time in a menial capacity and was the lover of a KdS sergeant by the name of Schranz. On being informed of her treachery, Ehrlinger ordered her execution and assigned me to carry it out.

This was perfectly normal procedure. We were fighting a war to the death against an opponent at least as ruthless as ourselves. There was neither the time nor the necessity for any form of trial, and to this day I defy anyone to tell me that the Russians, or anyone else, would have been any more interested in legal niceties. To that extent, at least, I still plead "not guilty." As for the rest, well, that's more open to debate.

I went around to Ivanova's apartment, knocked on the door, and was greeted by the sound of Schranz's voice telling me to come in, accompanied by the suppressed, high-pitched giggle of a playful young woman. I entered the apartment, which consisted of a single large room containing a couple of cheap armchairs, covered in tatty fabric. An SS uniform with SD flashes was thrown across one of the chairs; women's clothes were draped more tidily on the other. The rest of the furniture consisted of an old wardrobe, a dressing table scattered with the usual female paraphernalia, a basin up against one wall with a grimy mirror above it, and, directly opposite the door, a large double bed.

Schranz grinned when he saw me enter the room. He was evidently not expecting any trouble. Ivanova, too, was more amused than fearful at the interruption. She was a pretty thing, age twenty-four, with a slim, pert figure. Pulling a blanket over her breasts, she sat up and, speaking German with a strong White Russian accent, said: "Hello, Doctor."

I ignored her for now. Instead I told Schranz: "Get back to the Lenin House, right now." He did as he was told without question, getting up out of bed and walking across the room to get his uniform. Ivanova, however, frowned, uncertain what to do next.

"It's all right," I said. "You can stay here for now."

She gave me a grateful smile, assuming that she would be left alone to dress in private. Schranz pulled on his boots and walked across to get his winter coat from a hook on the back of the door. His uniform jacket was still undone as he opened the door. He paused for a moment, as if expecting me to come with him—I think he imagined that the purpose of my visit was to summon him back to work—but all he got was a jerk of my head, clearly indicating that he should get out at once. "See you later, darling," he said to the girl, and then, with a puzzled parting look at me, he departed.

I closed the door and strode back into the middle of the room. Then I grabbed Ivanova's clothes off the back of the chair, carried them toward the bed, and threw them down on the pulled-back sheets where Schranz had been lying. "Put them on," I said. "You're coming with me."

For the first time Ivanova appeared to be worried. "Why?" she asked. "I don't understand."

"You'll find out in due course. Hurry up. I don't have all day."

Ivanova must have known now beyond any possible doubt that this wasn't a social call. She chewed her lip, her eyes wide with fear.

"Get dressed," I repeated. "Or would you rather I dragged you out of here stark naked?"

I watched her as she dressed, but purely to make sure that she did not try to conceal a weapon about her person or make any bid to get away. Suspects would sometimes risk death by throwing themselves from windows rather than face certain destruction at our hands. But Ivanova wasn't quite that desperate: not yet. She was still at the stage of disbelief, still thinking of means by which she could persuade me to change my mind. But that wasn't going to happen. I was too old a hand at the game, too used to switching off my natural responses, both sexual and protective, to the sight of an attractive woman who was marked for death. The more that one could reduce one's victim to the status of a thing, just another job to be accomplished with the minimum possible fuss, the easier that job became.

Ivanova put on her underwear, her dress, and her shoes, and took a look in the mirror, almost as if she were saying farewell to the sight of her own face.

"Will I need my coat?" she asked, with an evident attempt to mask the desperation that lay behind that simple question.

"Give it to me," I replied.

The coat was an ancient, mangy fur. I wondered whether she had inherited it from an aged relative. Or perhaps it was the property of a slaughtered Jew, given to her by Schranz. She handed it over and I felt the pockets and the linings, looking for anything that might be hidden there. The coat was clean. I handed it back.

"You may put it on," I said. "Now it's time to go."

I walked the young woman downstairs and out through the front door. I held her arm in a way that a passerby, unaware of the strength with which I was gripping her, might have interpreted as affectionate. A sergeant called Rumstein was working for me at the time. He was waiting by the car. "Get in the back and keep an eye on her," I told him. "I'll drive."

We all got in the car, me in the front seat, the other two in the back, and set off through the city in the late afternoon gloom. It wasn't long before the young woman realized where we were going. "Why?" she asked again. "Why?"

I ignored her and remained silent as we drove up to the entrance to the Jewish ghetto. Once overcrowded to the point of inhumanity, it was now all but empty. Virtually everyone who had ever lived there was dead. I drove to the old cemetery, where Jews had been buried in the days when they still died of natural causes, and stopped the car fifty meters or so inside the entrance. Then I looked over my shoulder, toward the back of the car, and told Ivanova: "Get out."

To Rumstein I said: "You stay here."

"No, no!" she cried and clung to Rumstein. He tried to shove her away, but she would not be dislodged until I opened one of the rear passenger doors, leaned in, grabbed her roughly, and yanked her out. She fell onto the tarmac beside the car. Taking the pistol from my holster and pointing it down at Ivanova, I gave her a sharp kick in the stomach, winding her slightly. She made a hoarse retching sound as she struggled for air. "Get up," I said without the slightest shred of kindness, paying no mind to her pain, feeling no qualms whatsoever about treating a woman this way.

I could have killed her there and then, but I wanted a little more privacy when I did it.

Ivanova got to her feet, looking at me with tears in her eyes. I think she found it hard to comprehend how a man who had always been so pleasant to her in the past could possibly behave like this now. As her breathing came back to her she spoke again, asking a question that was also a plea: "Doctor, what are you doing?"

Without a word, I stepped behind her, grabbing her wrist with one hand while the other pressed the pistol to the side of her head. Then I wrenched at her wrist, pulling her arm up behind her back to prevent her from getting away. She gave a gasp of pain and I pushed her forward so that she almost stumbled. As she regained her footing she found herself walking away from the car, into the shadowy gloom of the cemetery.

I pushed her again, steering her to the right as we stepped off the path and moved between the gravestones toward an old monument, almost the height of a man, erected in honor of a prosperous family: all gone now, of course. Once we were behind it we were out of sight of any prying eyes. Desperately, Ivanova made one last attempt to wriggle from my grasp, so I cracked the barrel of my pistol hard against her skull. The sudden nauseating shock of pain seemed to knock the last resistance out of her. She knew she was done for now. Her body slackened and the only sound she made was a soft, sad weeping.

I took one final look around to see that I was unobserved. Then I let go of Ivanova's arm, grabbed the hair at the top of her head, and aimed a single fierce stamp of my boot at her calves, just below the knee. Her legs gave way and she dropped to her knees. Retaining my grip on her hair so as to keep her head still, I placed my pistol against the back of her neck, at the point where it joined the skull, and fired a single shot.

She died at once. I let go of her hair and she flopped forward onto the cold, damp grass that surrounded the monument. I did not bother to give her lifeless body a second glance. I just replaced the pistol in my holster and walked briskly back to the car. When I reached it I told Rumstein, "You drive," and settled down in the passenger seat. "Take me back to the office," I said.

49

Do I shock you? Are you disgusted by my behavior? I sincerely hope so, for what civilized person would not be? I certainly am. But I must confess that Ivanova wasn't the only one of my victims in those dying months of 1943. Soon after her death I put a bullet through another female spy and left her body on a patch of wasteland for the Russians to find. Ehrlinger felt it was important to remind them that we were still in business.

A Catholic priest called Godlevsky was suspected of political subversion. I took him out to Maly Trostinets and shot him behind a barn, having first gone to his church and taken a substantial amount of cash from the safe there: far more money than any church collection could ever have raised. Since we had not given it to him, the Russians must have done so: case closed.

Both of those executions, however, pale into insignificance beside the one that I am about to describe. For this marked the point at which my soul was irrevocably lost; when that imaginary evil psychiatrist would have looked on in delight, knowing that he had proved beyond doubt that even the most law-abiding of men could be transformed into depraved, inhuman beasts, given the right environment and stimuli.

In the wake of the September attack on the Lenin House, we had captured a number of suspected partisans. Of these, some died under interrogation, or were shot once their guilt had been established. But three of them, two men and a woman, were found to have had a particularly significant role to play in the planning and execution of the attacks. It was therefore felt that they should be killed in a special way, and it so happened that just such a way had recently presented itself. For while the number of Jews remaining to be processed was declining, and new, more efficient methods of execution and disposal were now in operation, the question of what to do with the bodies of those killed by more traditional means still remained.

For some months an operation known as Action 1005 had therefore been tasked with finding the most effective method for disposing of bodies, and then putting that method into practice across the Reich and its occupied territories. In the autumn of 1943 an Action 1005 team had arrived in Minsk to deal with the graves in the woods at Blagovshchina.

Its commander was Arthur Harder, an SS captain who had spent the previous few months going around Russia, opening up mass graves, removing the half-rotten corpses within, and then burning them. The dirty work at any given site was done by Russian POWs, who labored under heavy guard and were all shot when that particular operation was complete. They exhumed all the bodies and placed them on pyres comprising alternate layers of corpses and wooden logs. When the pyre was about five meters high it was doused in heating oil and set alight. It could take as long as two days for the bodies to burn through completely, but once the fire had finally died down, all that remained was ash.

Blagovshchina had been transformed from a delightful stretch of woodland into a foul, repugnant kingdom of the dead. Even before the exhumations, there were places where the ground itself used to shift, contort, and belch noxious fumes and vile liquids into the air as the gas from the decomposing bodies forced its way to the surface. Now the corpses were rising out of the ground as though the Day of Judgment had come. Yet Harder seemed relatively immune to the horror of it all. He told me that after a while it just became a job like any other.

We did not, of course, discuss the inescapable logic that underpinned Action 1005. A criminal suspect disposes of evidence that would prove his guilt because he fears that it may be found. In seeking to obliterate any trace of their Jewish victims, our leaders were effectively admitting two things. First, that the racial extermination policies of which they were so proud were terrible crimes; and second, that these crimes would otherwise be uncovered when the lands we had once conquered were recaptured by our enemies. Thus they had accepted their defeat and were merely trying to lessen their disgrace.

As long as the war was still going on, however, Action 1005 provided a perfect opportunity to give the captured partisans the send-off they deserved.

On the day of their execution, Harder was ordered to cease work early and to ensure that all the Russian POWs were returned to the bunker at Maly Trostinets, where they were being housed until the time came to dispose of them. Meanwhile, I put together a squad of Latvians and got Merbach to bring a couple of his trucks to transport us all to Maly Trostinets. Together we escorted the three partisans from the Minsk prison down to the site of Harder's most recent cleanup operation.

It took several pyres to deal with the contents of a single pit, and when we arrived a couple of them were fully ablaze, while two more were dying down. The atmosphere was cold and damp when we first got out of the car, but it became hotter with every step closer to the flames. This was the time of year, of course, when it was quite normal to see fires burning up the fallen leaves of autumn. Yet in Blagovsh-china the smoke that drifted over the air and disappeared between the trees was sweet with the pork-like smell of burning human flesh.

Looking around, I realized that this was the place where we'd processed the Vienna transport containing Hannah Lang's parents. Their bodies must have been somewhere close by: reduced to ashes, fueling the flames of the blazing pyres, or lying as death-cold skeletons, half draped in rotting flesh, waiting for the touch of a match.

A year earlier, such an idea would have been almost insupportable to me: my feelings for Hannah were still too raw. Two years earlier, it would have been inconceivable: I had no idea of the reality of our extermination campaign. Now, I just registered the thought and moved on.

We took the partisans from the sealed van in which they'd been brought down from Minsk, lined them up with guns trained upon them, and told them to strip. As they took off their clothes, one of the men started talking. I couldn't understand him, but one of the Latvians told me that he'd said: "Be brave, comrades, it will soon be over. We will not even feel the bullets that kill us. But when the Red Army catches these animals, then they will discover what it means to suffer."

My God, he had no idea of the irony of his words.

We all stopped for a moment to look at the naked woman. She was very thin after two months in prison and still bore the scars and bruises of her interrogation. Just then I heard a familiar voice: "Can we all just fuck her first, Doctor?"

It was Sergeant Rübe. He'd been at loose ends since the ghetto was liquidated and had consequently been reassigned to help Harder get rid of all the dead Jews. It was the sort of work that suited him.

"No time for fooling around," I replied. "It'll be dark if we don't get on with this."

Someone had placed a ladder by the side of the pyre. Harder sent two of his men up it and then three large stakes were passed up to them. They drove these down into the pyre until they were firmly in position: I dread to think what was holding them upright. Then ropes were passed up to the men.

It was now that the partisans realized that the stakes and ropes were intended for them. We were going to burn them to death. The woman started screaming hysterically and had to be physically restrained from trying to escape. The two men were given a few sound blows with rifle butts, hard enough to crack a rib or two, and all three of them were herded toward the pyre.

One by one the three partisans were forced up the ladder. The woman had to be carried up. Rübe happily volunteered for that task and then stayed up at the top of the pyre to help tie her and her comrades to the stakes. Then a large can of fuel oil was passed up the ladder and its contents were poured over the partisans. More cans were emptied over the lower levels of the pyre. Our men came down from the top and the ladder was removed. All was ready.

Up above us the woman was still crying. One of the men was shouting defiantly at us, while the other remained quite silent, looking around with fierce concentration. "You're trying to work out how to escape, aren't you?" I thought to myself, and made a mental note to keep an eye on him.

Another of Harder's team appeared with a long stick, at the end of which was a rag dripping in oil. A match was applied to the rag. Harder looked at me and asked: "Would you like the honor of lighting our fire?"

How could I refuse? I thanked him with a grim smile and took the flaming torch. I touched it to the pyre and the oil caught fire like the brandy around a crêpe suzette. Within seconds the whole pyre was ablaze and the writhing figures of the partisans were illuminated in a lurid orange glow, which became ever brighter until they were engulfed in dazzling, white-hot flame.

All that could be heard over the roaring blaze were the high-pitched death-cries of the woman. It was as if we were witnessing the burning of witches or heretics, centuries ago. I saw Rübe looking up at this scene of agony and suffering with a rapt expression on his face, as though he were yet another who found nothing so arousing as someone else's violent death.

Merbach crossed himself and turned away, unable to witness this terrible scene any longer. I watched him leave the immediate surroundings of the pyre.

It was then that Rübe shouted out: "Watch out! One of 'em's making a run for it!"

I looked back at the pyre. The fire was so dazzling that it was almost blinding, but in the darkness beyond it I could just see something moving. I raced around the pyre, pulling out my gun as I went. As my eyes gradually acclimated themselves to the dim, gray light of the dusk, I saw the outline of a naked man, one arm wrapped around his broken ribs, heading toward the trees. He could manage little more than a frantic, hobbling movement, so I had a second or two in which to raise my pistol, line it up, and fire three quick shots. He fell to the ground and I ordered two of my men to check whether he was dead. Guns at the ready, they raced up to where the partisan was lying. I thought I saw one of his legs give a feeble twitch. Then two more shots rang out and he lay still.

"Throw him on the flames!" I shouted and then returned to where Rübe was standing. "How are the other two doing?" I asked.

"Dead," he said, with something close to disappointment in his voice. "To be honest, I was hoping they'd survive a little longer."

Just then Merbach arrived in a state of great agitation. "Damn you, Heuser, you nearly killed me!" he shouted.

"What do you mean?"

"One of the bullets you fired just now missed the Russian and almost hit me. I swear I heard it go right past my face."

"Well that serves you right for running away," I replied. "If you'd been man enough to watch this little show, you'd have been quite safe."

Driving back to the city, I wondered what my old boss Lüdtke would have made of a killer with my modus operandi. I imagined him in the squad room, with a map pinned up on the wall, surrounded by pictures of the deceased and the crime scenes. I could hear him telling his men: "The killer appears to be indiscriminate in his choice of targets. The fact that he has killed women and a priest would suggest that he has no moral or religious scruples. That he can watch fellow humans burn to death is a mark of exceptional callousness. He is arrogant and supremely self-confident in his ability to avoid capture: why else does he leave the bodies where he killed them, without any attempt to disguise his activities? He is, in short, a cold-blooded, ruthless murderer."

And what if some eager young graduate of the Leaders' School should ask his boss: "Would you class him as a serial killer?" What would Lüdtke have said then?

50

I could no longer even claim that my apparently immoral acts had actually served a greater good. Any hope of that had long since disappeared. Whole areas of both Reich Commissariats, Ostland and Ukraine, were now under partisan control with their own farms, defense forces, and communist administrations. So far as most Russians were concerned it was not an act of courage to rebel against us, so much as a prudent investment for the future.

We Germans, meanwhile, lived in a strange state that I can only call fatalistic defiance. We knew that our armies were now engaged in a retreat that would surely take us all the way back to Berlin. But what could we do but fight on? Hitler would never surrender, and even if he did, we would then be left to the mercy of the Red Army, and better a swift bullet to the skull than a lingering death at their hands. So there was nothing to be done but prepare for a long, bloody, but ultimately futile struggle. In the meantime, our moral and spiritual collapse as individuals mirrored that of the Reich as a whole, as any principles we might once have held gave way to bitter cynicism, hope was replaced by fatalism, and moral standards collapsed into utter decadence. Our leaders continued to strut about and speechify as if we were still in the glory days of '41, but any admiration or even respect that we might once have had for them had given way to scorn.

In November we received a transcript of a speech given by Reichs-führer Himmler to a gathering of SS top brass in Posen. He told his audience: *"Most of you must know what it means when one hundred corpses are lying side by side, or five hundred or one thousand. To have stuck it out and at the same time—apart from some exceptions caused by human weakness—to have remained decent fellows, that is what has made us hard."*

Those words were read aloud in the mess to hoots of derisive laughter. How could Himmler of all people talk about being hard? And decent fellows: was that what we were? The officers of the KdS were slumped and sprawled around our dining table with our jackets thrown across the backs of chairs or simply fallen on the floor; our collars open and our suspenders off our shoulders, just hanging down beside our pants. Empty bottles rolled around the table and the air was rank with the stench of spilled alcohol, our sweaty, unwashed bodies, and the cigarette ends pressed into ash-trays or stamped beneath our heels. Several women had joined us at our table. They'd come here to Minsk as nice German girls, hoping to do their bit for the Fatherland and perhaps find a husband at the same time. Now they were drunken sluts in stolen clothes with dead women's lipstick smeared across their mouths, who sat on our laps with their breasts exposed, happy to let men stick their hands, or worse, up their skirts.

To one side a vodka-sweating sot, who not so long ago was a decent, well-mannered gentleman, grabbed a Russian waitress and dragged her toward him without the slightest momentary concern for her dignity. Another man had his tongue in a Jewess's mouth. The Jewess was Liselotte Lang, a sweet, innocent little girl who'd become a hard, calculating bitch in the year that she'd been here, selling her body for food and warm clothing. None of us thought worse of her for that. It was the only way to survive.

Someone picked up the transcript and read what Himmler had said about the treasure we had taken from the Jews. *"This wealth has been handed over to the Reich without reserve. We have taken none of it for ourselves."*

There was more laughter at this, and it grew stronger as another officer grabbed the text from the first one's hand and took up the recital: *"Whoever takes so much as a mark is a dead man. A number of SS men—there are not many of them—have fallen short and they will die without mercy."*

Suddenly the SS officers of Minsk, the supposed flowers of Aryan manhood, were pointing fingers at one another, like schoolboys in a playground, shouting "Bang!" and pretending to fall over dead. But Himmler had more rhetorical jewels in store for us: *"We had the moral right, we had the duty to our people to destroy this race which wanted to destroy us. But we have not the right to enrich ourselves with so much as a fur, a watch, a mark, or a cigarette, or anything else."*

Oh, we didn't? Why was there a bag of gold wedding rings, teeth, and fillings under the bed in my room? Why did every other man at this table have his own bag too, and a good thick wad of banknotes? How else was Lisl so smartly dressed and so prettily painted?

We'd become the twentieth-century citizens of Sodom and Gomorrah, and even if Himmler didn't know it, plenty of other people did. Official complaints were filed and a team from the Reich Security Main Office was sent to Minsk to investigate them. We managed to get a day's notice of their arrival, so the men desperately tried to sober up and kicked their mistresses out of their quarters. The women put their panties back on and came to work without any paint on their faces. We all behaved like good, clean, obedient SS officers and personnel. And then as soon as the inspection team had gone, the saturnalia commenced all over again.

I continued to have some contact with the Langs. Hannah was still Schinkel's mistress. She told me that she had to keep all the jewels and clothes he had supposedly given her at his apartment. "As soon as he is done with me, he'll simply pass them on to the next one."

"So what has he actually given you, after all this time?"

"Ten kilos," she said.

Well, better that weight in body fat than gold, and better the sweaty heat of Schinkel's bed than the icy chill of the grave. For all our complicated, bitter history, Hannah and I had come to some sort of unspoken accommodation. At least I had kept my word and done no harm to her or her siblings. I liked to think that she respected me a little bit for that, at least. Her most useful function now as an intelligence asset was to keep me apprised of all the orders placed by the local Wehrmacht and Luftwaffe units for various forms of fuel and lubricant oils, and Schinkel's success—or increasingly the lack of it—in supplying them. It was remarkable how much one could learn about military operations from data about supplies. In this case it was all too apparent that we were in very serious trouble, a fact that Hannah was bright enough to work out for herself as well. Under other circumstances she would have made a first-rate intelligence officer, for she was far more perceptive than most of the men under my command.

Come the spring of 1944, we mounted a series of operations against the partisans, fighting them all across White Russia throughout April and May. Our troops burned villages and slaughtered their inhabitants. The partisans sprang ambushes and either killed every German they found, or captured and tortured them in ways so bestial that even experienced Gestapo men such as myself were shocked. Meanwhile the Soviets came closer and closer to Minsk, advancing inexorably with every hour that passed.

By the last week of June, the Red Army was just a few kilometers away. The heat was stifling and the incessant air raids and partisan bombings filled the air with acrid smoke and rasping dust that left one red-eyed and choking. Minsk was being pulverized into dereliction. The entire city would soon be a barren wilderness, dotted with ruined buildings and pitted with the craters left by bombs and artillery shells. The roads were jammed with traffic: tanks and troops moving up to the front; trucks packed with wounded coming the other way; refugees fleeing the Russian advance.

Amid the noise, the chaos, and the overwhelming atmosphere of panic, the administration of the city had totally broken down. There were no police, not even secret ones. The only thing on the mind of any German was finding a way out of this hellhole. In the past few weeks we'd been evacuating the wives and children of German officials, followed by female workers. Plenty of men had found a way to barge into the queue ahead of the womenfolk: Schinkel, for example, scurried off without so much as a farewell to Hannah Lang—taking her jewels and clothes, of course. But there were still thousands of people desperate to get back to the Fatherland, and one by one the means of departure diminished until there was only one final train sitting at Minsk station. It had room for at most five hundred people, just a fraction of those who wished to get aboard.

The station was a seething mass of fear-stricken humanity. Between these frantic hordes and the safety of the passenger carriages stood a platoon of Waffen-SS soldiers. Their orders were very simple. The only people allowed to board were those with official travel passes, issued for this specific train. Anyone without a pass who attempted to stow away was to be shot. The soldiers felt very strongly about ensuring that the train got away safely with the correct number of people aboard, because they would be traveling on it too, as an armed guard. So they were fighting for their own escape as well.

I, however, could not be on that train. My work would not be done for two or three more days yet. My orders were to stay to the very end, destroy as much evidence as I could, and kill the tiny number of Jews, mostly workers for the KdS, who had somehow managed to stay alive until now. I'd therefore made my own travel arrangements. That just left the Langs to be dealt with.

51

First thing in the morning on June 28, I picked up my briefcase, walked through the empty, paper-strewn halls and corridors of the Lenin House, and went down to the cellar where the Langs had been living all this time. The three of them had not yet gotten up, but as soon as he heard the tap of my boot-heels on the concrete, Gottfried Lang sprang to his feet and watched me through hard, cynical eyes as I came ever closer.

Once a golden boy with a beaming smile and boisterous energy, Lang had become a shifty, conniving, ruthless seeker after the slightest advantage. I was quite certain that he had stolen, cheated, lied, and for all I knew killed, to stay alive. Now he looked as though he was ready to kill again. He was standing up against the wall, beside his filthy scrap of a mattress, a scrawny urchin glaring at me with the desperate intensity of a cornered animal.

"Have you come to finish us off?" he snarled.

"That's not why I'm here," I said.

"I don't believe you." Lang moved a fraction, and as he did so the light from the single bulb that illuminated the cellar glinted on something in his hand, a shard of glass he evidently intended to use as a homemade dagger. "You've been told to get rid of all the Jews," he said. "I know you have."

Very slowly, deliberately, I placed my briefcase on the floor, and then, without at any time taking my eyes off Lang, unbuttoned the flap of my holster and placed my right hand on the handle of my pistol. I raised my left, palm pointing toward Lang in a pacifying gesture. "I promise you that I mean no harm. I've always kept my word to you and your family in the past. You should believe me now. So just let go of whatever it is you've got in your hand, sit down nice and easy, and no one will get hurt."

"Do what he says," Hannah Lang said, very calmly. "Please, Friedl. Do what Dr. Heuser says."

Lang darted his eyes at his sister, then back at me. He tossed the piece of glass toward me and it cracked against the stone floor close to my feet, splitting in two. Then he sat down beside his sisters.

"Thank you, Hannah," I said. "Your brother should be very grateful to you. I came here to give you something. Look . . ." Pulling my hand away from my gun, I reached down, opened my briefcase, and extracted a large brown envelope.

"The last train for Germany leaves at 11:00 hours," I said, holding the envelope unopened in my right hand and tapping it against my left as I spoke. "It's quite impossible to board it without a numbered travel pass, properly stamped and authorized. Anyone attempting to board the train without the proper papers will be shot."

I gave another tap of the envelope to emphasize the word "shot." Then I looked around. I could see the first glimmers of curiosity and even hope entering the Langs' eyes, and I knew how hard they would be telling themselves not to be so foolish. There was no hope. There was only a constant, unrelenting struggle for survival. Minsk had taught them that—and that the struggle was bound to fail in the end.

I went on: "Luckily, I'm not without influence. I happen to know the officials responsible for issuing these travel documents. I've therefore been able to acquire three passes in your names. I've also spoken to my colleague Lieutenant Müller in the Jewish Affairs department. We had a very interesting conversation about the status of second-degree *Mischlings*. We both agreed that none of you had shown the slightest sign of any Jewish tendencies during your time at Minsk, and that you had all rendered valuable service to the Reich. We therefore felt entirely confident that we were acting within SS regulations to issue you with new identity papers, reassigning you as Germans. Even so, I advise you not to return to Vienna until the war is over. Go and stay with relatives elsewhere, if you have any. That is all."

I handed the envelope over to Hannah and the other two crowded around as she opened it. One by one the travel passes and identity papers emerged. The Langs gazed at them in amazement, unable to believe their eyes. Then Lisl looked up and threw herself at me, wrapping her arms around me and crying, "Thank you! Thank you!" in a voice that reminded me of the child she had been when I had first met her. I disentangled myself from her embrace, though not before she had planted a large, but quite innocent, kiss on my cheek.

Friedl cleared his throat, pulled back his shoulders, and walked over to me. He stuck out his hand. "Thank you, sir. I should have trusted you."

"That's all right," I said, shaking his hand.

Now only Hannah was left. We looked at one another silently. Those kilos that Schinkel's food had provided had kept her alive, but she was still painfully thin. Her face was drawn, her cheeks sunken, and her eyes looked unnaturally large. Yet she remained as fine-boned and elegant as ever. She was only twenty-four, but her experiences had given her the insight and understanding of someone much older. Still, there were times when she was simply a big sister, and this was one of them. She clapped her hands and said: "We're going to need food for the journey. You two, go and scavenge whatever you can. I want a word with Doctor Heuser."

The two younger Langs dashed off up the cellar stairs, and I was left alone with Hannah.

"Thank you," she said. "You didn't have to do that."

She looked me in the eye as she spoke, and there was no sense of inferiority or dependence on her part. In giving her papers that declared her a true German I'd inadvertently done more than provide her with a way out of Minsk. I'd restored her status as a human being.

"Yes I did."

We were standing very close together. Hannah sighed wordlessly and gave a sad, wistful shake of her head.

"Perhaps if we had met some other way," I said. "Maybe then . . ."

She shook her head again. "I fear for you," she said.

"Don't worry. I'll get out of here all right. I made a deal with Merbach. I've got two trucks packed with cans of gasoline. Von Toll's coming with me and we've got six of our best men for an escort. We're going nonstop all the way to East Prussia."

Hannah ignored the forced cheerfulness in my voice. "That's not what I meant. I'm sure you'll escape from Minsk. I'm sure you'll survive the whole war. I know you. Nothing touches you . . . That's not what I fear."

"So what is it, then?"

"I fear for your soul. You could have been a good person. But you'll be damned for the things you've done here. You must know that, don't you?"

"I've done my duty. I obeyed the orders given to me by my superiors to the best of my ability. That's all I've done."

Even as I made them, I knew how pathetic my excuses must have sounded.

Hannah implored me: "Dr. Heuser . . . please! You can't say that to me. I know you. I know what you've done." She looked me right in the eyes as if searching for a truth that remained frustratingly out of reach. "How could you?"

"I don't know . . ." I shrugged. "Maybe the same way you could do all the things you did to survive. No sane person could possibly have imagined the things that have happened here. They were utterly inconceivable. But then they happened and we all had to find a way to cope."

She looked at me aghast. "But that's grotesque! How can you possibly compare your situation to that of the people you killed and tormented? You . . . all of you . . . you're the Devil!"

"Maybe . . . but I'll tell you something about the Devil that I didn't previously understand. He's in Hell, just as much as the people he torments. He's the most damned of all."

"So you do know why I'm afraid for you, don't you? Will you promise me something?"

"Of course," I said, not meaning it. Our conversation was making me uncomfortable. I'd hoped for a few heartfelt words of thanks, and maybe even an admission by Hannah Lang that she'd misunderstood me. After all this time, I still wanted to hear her tell me that I was a much better man than she'd ever given me credit for, and that now she'd be forever in my debt. I hadn't anticipated that she would be talking to me with something close to pity.

"What is it you would like me to do?" I asked.

"Just try to lead a good life. Seek redemption. Make restitution for all the wrongs you have done. If you ever want to be at peace with yourself, this is your only hope."

She was right: of course she was. But I couldn't afford to think in those terms, not even for one second, as long as the war continued. Only the strongest and luckiest could hope to come through this alive. The moment I weakened, I'd be lost.

I didn't want to tell Hannah that, though. I was just wondering how to appease her when the two other Langs returned with some stale loaves of bread, a rusty can of soup, and two discarded vodka bottles that they had filled with water from a tap. They'd become a couple of cellar rats, able to sniff and scavenge scraps of food that fatter, sleeker animals would miss.

Hannah must have felt that she'd made her point, for she at once turned her attention to her siblings. In no time they collected their belongings and packed them in the same trunk they had put on the transport back in October '42. It had been with them in the cellar since the day they arrived, and even now I doubt that there was a single other Jew, anywhere in German territory, that could claim to have both survived a death transport and kept their baggage, to boot. But of course, the Langs weren't Jews anymore, even if they ever had been.

I escorted the three of them down to the station, forced my way through the crowd—even now, thank God, people made way for an SS uniform—and deposited them on the train. Hannah and I said our farewells on the platform. I wished her a safe journey, and she wished me a good life. Neither of us made any other reference to the future. We didn't promise to write to one another or to meet up again someday. We were both aware that could never happen. We'd known one another in Minsk, and that would be all. Neither of us would ever wish to be reminded of the people that we'd been there.

When the Langs were safely aboard the train, I returned to the Lenin House, where my men had made a large fire onto which they were throwing every document they could find. We cheered ourselves up with the thought that the Lenin House was by far the safest place in the city. The Soviets hadn't dared to destroy it when they left Minsk in defeat. They certainly wouldn't do so as they returned in triumph now.

Throughout the time that the SS and Security Police were in Minsk, we had a small concentration camp of our own, used to house the Jewish workers employed at the Lenin House. It consisted of little more than a single barrack building surrounded by a high barbed-wire fence, within one of the giant building's many courtyards. If I have not mentioned it up to now, it's just that one became so used to its presence that it simply wasn't noteworthy. The population of this camp had been declining over the past few months as our need for workers decreased and any surplus ones were disposed of, until there were just thirty-one left, and it was my responsibility to get rid of them. Once I'd done that, I'd be free to leave the city.

As always, we needed somewhere secure and reasonably discreet in which to do the job, and with so little territory left to work in, the obvious place was the cellar. Late on June 30, during a break in the endless task of document-burning, I took a squad of men to the camp. Some of the inmates had been working in the Lenin House as long as I had. I knew all of them by sight and many by name as well. One or two of them even said, "Good evening, Doctor." I didn't answer. As I knew from bitter experience, the more you acknowledged a man's existence, the harder it was to kill him. So I had them herded downstairs, letting the men kick or rifle-butt any who slackened their pace. Then they were locked in for the night, to be disposed of as easily as possible on the following morning.

This was, of course, the same cellar where the Langs had been kept, and as I woke up on July 1, soon after dawn, I couldn't help thinking about my final conversation with Hannah. She was right: I was damned, no matter what. I'd done too much to ever be forgiven. But maybe, just this time, I didn't have to kill these particular Jews. I was the only SS officer left in Minsk; there was nothing to stop me clearing out and leaving them to their fate. No one would give a damn. The city was falling. The war was lost. We hadn't managed to get rid of all the documents, either. What did any of it matter anymore?

I dragged myself out of bed and didn't bother with breakfast. There was no food to be had, anyway. All I could find was one last case of vodka, so I had half a bottle to steady my shaking hands and went to get my men, who were in no better state than I was. They stared at me through a dozen bleary, bloodshot eyes waiting for orders. I looked back at them, wondering what I would say, thinking all the times I'd done my duty, no matter what. My whole life had been dedicated to following orders and doing my best. How could I bring myself to stop now?

I decided to give the order to shoot.

But when I opened my mouth what I actually said was: "Load your machine pistols. Get your gear on the trucks. We're out of here in ten minutes, and we're not stopping for stragglers. If you're not on a truck, you stay here."

One of the men spoke up. "What about the Jews, sir? I thought we were supposed to get rid of them."

Good question: what about them? My answer, like my order seemed to come without thinking: "That's right, Maier, we were. But we're going to need every bullet we've got for shooting Ivans."

"But sir, we're leaving witnesses alive."

"Exactly. And if anyone ever accuses us of being killers, those witnesses can testify that we let them live. Trust me, Maier, I'm a lawyer and a policeman, I know about these things. And you've just used up one of your ten minutes."

The men raced away. Von Toll watched them go and said: "Why'd you do it . . . really?"

"It was a test. I wanted to see if I was still a human being. You know, see if there was anything left."

"I'm glad there is."

"Yeah, well, the Ivans'll probably shoot them anyway, just to make it look like we did it. They don't care. The Jews are just more Germans as far as they're concerned." I slapped him on the shoulder. "Let's get out of here. I'm sick of this fucking place."

We left the Lenin House with the Reds just a couple of hundred meters behind us. The trucks raced away down the street, dodging between bomb craters and falling shells, the men blazing away at the brown-coated figures chasing after us until we escaped the confines of the city and headed southwest toward the Polish border.

Three hours later we hit the tail-end of the main retreat. A line of trucks, tanks, artillery, and horse carts was crawling down the road ahead of us: the pride of the Wehrmacht going back home with its head bowed low and its tail between its legs. A rucksack lay in front of me on the floor of the truck. It contained a few personal belongings and my bag of gold rings and teeth. As long as I kept hold of that, I would not be poor. The day dragged on, the sun went down, and progress was painfully slow. The men were exhausted, the drivers half asleep at the wheel. But no matter how much they protested, I forbade them to stop on any account: we'd be continuing on through the night.

I wanted to be at least one hundred kilometers from Minsk by the time the sun came up.

52

KOBLENZ: MAY 22, 1963

The trees outside the courthouse were bright with blossoms and fresh new leaves. Kraus was already inside: he'd gone ahead, wanting a private word with the prosecutor. Paula was grateful for the chance to gather her thoughts in private as she walked from the hotel. As she had suspected, Barbara Kraus had decided that she wanted her husband after all. He hadn't moved back in yet, but he was spending more and more time at the family house or going on expeditions with Barbara and the children: trips to the zoo or the cinema, walks in the country, Sunday lunches, and so on. Paula and Kraus were still together, still telling one another "I love you," but both well aware that things couldn't go on the way they were. They'd talked many times and agreed that a decision of some kind had to be made. But nothing had been done.

It had always mattered a great deal to Paula that Kraus had already left home before she started going out with him. She had not stolen him from his wife, and if he went back to the marriage she had no desire to be his mistress: his little bit on the side. But she knew that Kraus would try to put off making a definitive decision for as long as possible. When she was feeling cynical she saw his procrastination as a simple matter of selfishness: why choose one woman as long as he could have both? But Kraus was fundamentally a decent man, and

Paula could also see that he was trying to find a way of resolving the situation without hurting either of the two women involved, however impossible that might be. Even so, she wasn't quite sure whether he was more bothered by causing pain to someone he loved, or having to cope with its consequences: an angry, tearful woman letting him know precisely how humiliated and deserted she felt. Well, Paula was going to save him that embarrassment.

Having waited in vain for Kraus to take action, she was doing so herself. She'd done her very best to come to terms with the idea of losing a man she still loved, and then she'd set about planning a new life for herself. She told herself that it was for the best, a change of seasons in her heart to match the one in the world around her. Kraus had changed her life, and all for the better, but he belonged to a different generation. He could only ever be a temporary lover, and now, while there was still time, she wanted to find someone closer to her own age to be the man for the rest of her life. But there was all the difference in the world between rationalizing something intellectually and coming to terms with it emotionally. That she still had to do. And in the meantime there was a trial to be finished: the last step on a four-year journey to which she still did not know the ultimate destination.

The Koblenz District Court was about to deliver the verdicts and sentences in the case of Georg Heuser and his ten codefendants.

The whole of the previous day had been given over to the reading of the judges' summing-up of the case. It ran to more than one hundred and fifty pages and included detailed biographies of all eleven defendants and authoritative summaries of Nazi policy against the Jews; the general activities of the SS in the occupied Eastern Territories from June 1941 onward; the structure and personnel of the KdS; the various genocidal "actions" that were the principal subjects of the case, and a charge-by-charge analysis of the case against each individual defendant. The evidence was described and its merits or failings assessed with absolute fairness and a scrupulous consideration for the rights of the accused.

Some of the men, notably von Toll, were dealt with in a matter of minutes, so straightforward and so relatively insignificant were the accusations against them. Heuser was another matter altogether. The sheer number of his alleged crimes, the complex and often contradictory nature of the evidence against him, and the extreme difficulty of meeting the proper standards of proof when dealing with events from so long ago, with so few surviving witnesses, had clearly taxed the judges to the limit.

That Heuser had organized, commanded, or participated in multiple mass executions and individual homicides was apparent to anyone who had followed the case. Having established beyond any doubt that almost thirty-two thousand people had died at the hands of the men of the KdS, the judges' only caveat was that this might be an underestimate: "It should be noted that the jury found that the victim counts of two major actions in March and July 1942 are minimum figures, which in reality may have been much higher."

But did any of that make Heuser guilty beyond a reasonable doubt?

As one prosecution case after another was analyzed and found wanting, Paula thought of herself sitting in Albrecht Mauritz's study while he pointed out that she could not provide a date, a victim's name, a body, or a murder weapon for the case of the letter-writing Jew allegedly shot at Maly Trostinets. She'd watched in dismay as Heuser, who had begun that penultimate day looking exhausted and fearful, relaxed with each passing hour. It was painfully obvious that he thought he'd gotten away with it.

Now, on the final morning, that impression was even stronger. Before the formal proceedings got under way, Heuser was chatting cheerfully to his lawyer, Geis, laughing like a man without a care in the world and telling the others not to worry. So it was Paula, her personal problems temporarily quite forgotten, whose guts were twisted with tension.

Having considered the events under review and the evidence pertaining to them on the first day, the court came to matters of the law as it related to the nature of guilt and the culpability for acts of homicide. After her session with Mauritz, Paula could accept the accused being given the same rights as any other criminal when considering the evidence against them, even if that policy made it much harder for the prosecution to secure convictions. But the court was bending over backward even when they were ruled guilty, and providing special dispensation when considering their possible sentences, too. The Federal Republic had done away with capital punishment from the moment of its birth, an understandable reaction after so much legalized, state-sanctioned murder during the Nazi years. But the judges were going further. They appeared to be ruling out life sentences, too.

Their verdict stated that: "The court is not dealing with the ordinary class of criminals." Paula's spirits sank as she heard the words being read out loud. "None of the accused committed these crimes of their own volition. Instead, they followed the orders of a government that no longer exists. Aside from the events dealt with in this trial, none had any conflicts with the law, and after the war, without exception, they regained reputable jobs and led a proper life in honorable circumstance. For this reason, they as well as their families are especially hard-hit by punishment so long after the event. Given the exceptional circumstances that made them criminals, their guilt does not seem so grave as to call for lifelong imprisonment as a means of expiation."

"I don't understand it," Paula whispered to Kraus, who was sitting next to her. "First they say that the estimated number of victims is probably too low, and then they decide that none of the accused will die in prison? It's just not logical."

In only one case did the court deem a life sentence appropriate: Stark's murder of the barber Steiner and his two sons. Paula could follow that legal reasoning easily enough. The Steiners had died because Stark had chosen, of his own free will, to kill them. In that case he had been acting entirely as an individual, rather than the agent of the state. Therefore it was murder, pure and simple. Kraus gave a bitter little snort at that. "Ironic, huh? The court took precisely the same view as the Nazi authorities in Minsk." His head was right by Paula's ear and he was speaking in a disturbingly intimate whisper. "They both thought shooting those three men without orders was more serious than wiping out three thousand ghetto-dwellers with them."

Stark aside, the other lesser defendants received sentences that struck Paula as derisory. Harder, the Frankfurt shopkeeper, got off with the lightest term: just three years and six months for his part in burning the three Russians. He was the only one who had never participated in the mass executions. Of those that had, Dalheimer and Oswald were sentenced to four years in jail; Feder, Kaul, and von Toll got four years and six months; Merbach seven years; Schlegel eight years; and Wilke ten years. These nine men had each already spent two or three years in prison. Obtaining parole would be a formality, since the court had already stated that none of them presented a continuing threat to society. All things considered, some could expect to be back on the street within little more than a year.

But what of Heuser?

As all the charges that Geis had managed to undermine were excluded, Max Kraus hissed, "You see? Triage . . . it worked," loudly enough for a few people nearby to hear and turn around with a mixture of puzzlement and disapproval on their faces. Even so, for all the skill with which Geis had mounted his client's defense, Heuser was found guilty on a total of ten counts, of which four related to individual transport actions. Taking all the mass executions of Jews in which he had been proven to have participated, the court deemed him to have had a hand in the deaths of 11,100 Jews.

"Of all the defendants, Heuser was involved in the most acts of extermination against the Jews," the judgment read. "He repeatedly played an active part and exercised a supervisory role. His education, his study of law, and his professional rank of Commissar imposed a particular requirement on him not to take part in these crimes. Thanks to his intelligence, his energy, and his esteemed and respected place among the members of the Security Police and SD Minsk, he, more than anyone, was in a position to avoid killing Jews if he had wanted to. It is to his credit that he recognizes this himself. He has made no excuses, but frankly admitted his guilt. He also shows genuine remorse and an inner readiness to atone for his deeds."

"Or he's a very good actor," commented Kraus.

The judgment continued: "Regarding the shooting of the Russian agent in the ghetto cemetery, the court accepted that the war in the East was carried out with merciless harshness on both sides. Heuser believed that by neutralizing the agent he was preventing harm to German soldiers on the front line. However, it was extremely reprehensible and inhuman to kill her without a fair hearing and without giving her the opportunity to arrange her affairs, and then to let her corpse lie unburied."

"That has to be murder, surely," Paula whispered.

But apparently not: Heuser was deemed a mere accessory to manslaughter in the female agent's case. In every other instance of guilt he was an accessory to murder. The court ruled that the element of murder in the mass executions lay not in the actions of the men who fired guns or drove gas vans, but in the minds and intentions of the men who had devised the Holocaust and given them their orders. Bearing that in mind, Heuser was sentenced as follows:

For the mass execution of Jews from the Minsk ghetto, March 1–3, 1942: six years in prison.

For the transport actions of May 11, May 26, September 4, September 25, and October 9, 1942: four years for each offense.

For the mass execution of Jews from the Minsk ghetto on July 28–30, 1942: ten years.

For the mass execution of Jews during the liquidation of the Minsk ghetto in October 1943: four years.

For the burning to death of three prisoners in November 1943: three years.

For killing a female Russian agent, autumn 1943: five years.

Even these sentences were little more than notional, for the jury mandated a maximum of fifteen years' total prison time. The years Heuser had already spent on remand would be counted toward that, and he had the chance of parole for good behavior.

Paula did the sums: Heuser would be out of jail in six or seven years, maybe less. He knew it too. She was watching him being led away to the cells, and he wasn't acting like a man who'd been condemned, but one who'd literally gotten away with murder. Just as he reached the door, Heuser turned his head back to the courtroom and for a second their eyes met. A flicker of a smile crossed his face, and it felt to Paula as though he were laughing at her, his old arrogance fully restored. She couldn't bear to look at him and had to turn her eyes away. By the time she glanced up again, Heuser was gone.

As the judges rose and the proceedings came to a close, Paula was practically in tears of frustration and rage. "Mauritz was wrong. This isn't a triumph for any kind of justice. They might as well have had Eichmann, Heydrich, and Himmler sitting on the judges' bench!"

Those final words had been said loud enough for everyone in her immediate vicinity to hear, and thunderous faces were turning around to see who had uttered them. "Let's get you out of here and into a bar before someone decides to sling you into jail as well," Kraus said as he put one arm around her shoulder, held the other up to ward off the anger all around them, and hustled her out of the court.

53

"*Prost!*" said Kraus, downing a glass of schnapps in one toss.

"*Prost,*" Paula replied sullenly, swallowing the strong clear spirit and then coughing as it burned the back of her throat.

Kraus pushed a dewy glass of Königsbacher, the local beer of Koblenz, across the table toward her. "Now take some of this to cool you down."

She did as she was told and then Kraus took out two cigarettes, handed her one, and said: "And now the final part of the medicine."

Paula was only a very occasional smoker, so the first breath of the nicotine-laden smoke made her head spin. By the second, however, she had regained her senses, and the combination of all the various chemicals she had just ingested was enough to take the edge off the fury eating away at her insides. She had expected Kraus to launch straight into a discussion of the case, but instead he looked at her and said: "So, did you decide to quit? The job, I mean . . ."

She nodded. "Yes . . . I really need to get away."

"It's all right, I understand. You've given yourself heart and soul to this. It's natural to want a change. Do you know where you're going?"

"Switzerland."

That took Kraus by surprise. "My God, you're leaving the country. I wasn't aware . . ."

Paula watched the realization that she'd beaten him to the punch, that she was leaving him as well as the office, dawn in Kraus's eyes, but he was still doing his best to act as if this were nothing but a professional issue. "So, ah . . . what are you going to be doing there?"

"I've got a job in the legal department of the United Nations Refugee Agency in Geneva," Paula replied, going along with the charade. "I said I didn't even want to talk to you about it until this case was over. They understood. So there's no rush, they're keeping the job open for me. It's just, well, I've spent enough time trying to right the wrongs of the past. I'd like to do something that's about now, about making things better for the future."

"I'll miss you," he said.

"And I'll miss you, too," she said. "Of course I will."

"You're sure you want to do this?"

Paula nodded. "Yes . . ." She felt a sudden urge to make all the things that they were hinting at explicit: "This isn't just about work. I know how torn you are. I understand. Go back to her, Max, go back to your children. It's the right thing to do."

She wanted to reach out and hold his hand but decided against it. How could she tell the man who loved her that she was leaving and then cling to him? It wasn't fair.

They sat together, not knowing what to say. A couple of times Kraus opened his mouth as if to speak, but then slumped back, unable to find the words.

Paula tried to change the subject. "Did you see the way that bastard smiled at me? He knew he'd won and he wanted to let me know it."

Kraus frowned. He shook his head, as if trying to rid his mind of all the bad thoughts Paula's decision to leave had put there. "It didn't look like that to me . . . I don't know, maybe you're right."

"I'm sure I am. We lost. That verdict . . . it just felt like the worst kind of defeat."

"No, there are worse kinds," Kraus said. "Anyway, we have no reason to feel bad . . . professionally, I mean. We made our case. We provided the prosecution with evidence that was good enough to secure all eleven convictions. We did our job."

"But the sentences . . . and the reasons for them . . . My God, how can they fall for that 'only obeying orders' shit?"

"Well, maybe that's what those men were doing. Listen, I was as angry as you when I heard that sanctimonious crap about them not belonging to the normal class of criminal. But then I thought about it and I asked myself: how many of those men would have committed a serious crime if they'd just led normal lives, in a sane society?"

"Stark, for sure," Paula said.

"OK. But the others?"

"Probably not."

"Right, so the thing that made them criminal was the fact that they happened to be in a particular place at a particular time. Their criminality was dependent on circumstances. It wasn't part of who they were."

"Yes, but that doesn't alter the fact that they killed, and killed, and killed."

"Because they were ordered to."

Paula was genuinely shocked: "How can you say such a thing?"

"Because I've had to obey orders too, and I know how it works. You can't say no. It's got nothing to do with being afraid of the consequences of disobedience. It's a whole bunch of other things. You've taken an oath. We all did: Heuser, me, even your father. We all swore our loyalty to the Führer and the Fatherland, and I promise you, no matter what our political views might have been, we meant it—just like the Tommies meant the oath that they swore, and the Ivans, and the Yanks."

"An oath can be broken. Surely it has to be if it leads you into doing something profoundly wrong?"

"Possibly . . . But even that oath wasn't the real reason we obeyed. We did it because the one thing every fighting man fears more than anything else—even death—is his own cowardice. You want to do your duty when the time comes. You want to be shoulder to shoulder with your friends. You're terrified of letting them down, of being the one who runs, or curls up in a ball with his head in his hands, crapping himself at the sound of the first bullet."

Kraus was speaking with bitter intensity, channeling the emotion he felt about what they were going through, almost as if by winning the argument he could win her back too. "Maybe you're in a landing craft, heading toward a beach, with bullets flying all around you. Or you're in a bomber crew, sitting in a tin can, five thousand meters in the air, while the guns fire flak at you and the enemy fighter planes come at you from all sides. Or maybe you're a poor dumb bastard in the middle of the Russian steppes who has to stand in line and kill a thousand Jews in a single day. What do you do? You obey your orders."

"I don't believe you can say such things." Paula was feeling guilty, ashamed of the pain she had inflicted; and that, perversely, made her want to inflict more. "What happened to doing this because you want to take the shame of being German off your children? When did you suddenly start apologizing for Nazis?"

The moment she said it, Paula knew she had gone too far. She had only rarely seen even a hint of Kraus's anger, and never directed at her. Now, though, his face was reddening and his hand was shaking as he reached for his packet of cigarettes, lit up, and then sat there, wreathed in smoke, burning it down to the filter before he felt calm enough even to speak.

"Don't ever call me a Nazi sympathizer. Call me anything you like. Say I'm a bastard. Say you don't want me anymore. Say I'm a fucking idiot for letting you go without getting down on my knees and begging you to stay . . . But if you have any desire to be my friend, never, ever say that."

"I'm sorry . . . I didn't mean . . ."

"Yes you did . . . and for once in your life that clever brain of yours has let you down. I hate the Nazis. I'll hate them with all my heart until my dying day. And one of the many reasons that I hate them is that they took decent human beings and forced them to become vile, murdering scum, just like them. Don't you get it? The Holocaust was the greatest criminal conspiracy there has ever been. It had everything: murder, rape, theft, kidnap, extortion . . . everything! It was as if the entire state had become psychopathic and anyone who got caught up in it was destroyed. Please don't take this the wrong way. I know how much you love your father. I'm sure he was a fine, loving, wonderful man. But I absolutely guarantee you that he did things or saw things in Russia that would appall you if you were ever to find out about them."

"Don't you dare insult my father!"

"I'm not insulting him," Kraus said. "I'm just trying to explain that it was impossible to avoid the madness. I certainly didn't."

"What about that clean, honorable war you said the Afrika Korps fought?"

"Yes, but it was still war. I killed people—lots of people. I saw women and children being blown apart by our bullets and shells. I ordered villages to be razed to the ground, so they couldn't provide cover to the enemy."

"But you were trying to survive against people who were trying to kill you. Heuser wasn't like that. He was killing people who were defenseless. And look at how he went about it. That man enjoyed what he did."

"No, that man enjoyed doing things well—whatever they were. I don't think he took any pleasure at all in the actual executions. I'm sure he really did find it all sickening. But he had to be the best at whatever he did. If they told him to catch a killer, he'd catch that killer faster than anyone else. If they told him to kill people, he'd kill them more efficiently than anyone else. The real difference between him and any of the other defendants wasn't that he was worse than them, morally. It's that he was better than them, professionally."

"But how can anyone apply a talent like that to something so evil?"

"Because there wasn't the choice of applying it to anything else. Look, I'm not saying that Heuser didn't do terrible things, or excusing him, or making out that he shouldn't have been sent to prison for the rest of his godforsaken life. He should, and I'm furious that he'll be back walking the streets as a free man when all the people he killed are rotting in their graves . . . I'm just saying that anyone in the same position would have acted the same way those guys did."

"That's not true!" Paula insisted. "You wouldn't have, for a start."

"You really think so? I don't. Why would I be any better than anyone else? Remember that bit in Kaul's evidence to the court where he was boasting about how he'd been told to give two wounded Jews the coup de grâce, but he'd fired his bullets into the side of the pit instead?"

"Of course, I remember that very well."

"Do you know what I thought when I read that in the transcript? I thought: 'You gutless heap of shit. You didn't have the balls to do what you were told, so those poor damn Jews suffered in agony for longer and some other sorry bastard had to do the job of finishing them off instead.' I bet that's what Heuser thought too, and the other defendants. That's what any soldier would think about a guy who behaved like that. And that's why very few of them did. They got pissed out of their brains to try and blank out the unbearable horror of what they were doing. They used all sorts of disgusting euphemisms to avoid having to write or say the truth in public. Even now, they do everything they can to pretend that they didn't turn into mass murderers . . . But when they were told to do those things, they did them. And I defy anyone to say that they would have done any different."

"And now they've gotten away with it," said Paula, sadly.

"No they haven't," said Kraus, before waving a waitress over and ordering more drinks. "Let me tell you something else that you learn when you go to war. You know how they say people live on in the memories of those who've loved them?"

"Yes, of course."

"Well they live on even more in the memories of those who've killed them. I was an infantryman. And most of the people I killed were ten meters away from me or less when they died. Some were right up close, hand-to-hand stuff. One, I came up behind him in the middle of the night and slit his throat. Blood everywhere . . ."

"Stop it, for God's sake . . ." Paula pleaded.

"But that's how it is. That's why we old soldiers almost never talk about our battles, even when we get together. We talk about the stupid things people did. We talk about the bastard officers we had, or the tarts we all fucked. But we never talk about the look on an eighteen-year-old boy's face when you stab him right in the guts with your bayonet and he realizes he's going to die . . . We don't talk about all the people trapped in no-man's-land, screaming in pain and crying for their mothers . . . We don't . . ."

Now Paula did reach for his hand. "Max . . ."

He looked at her. "I'm sorry . . . I just wanted you to understand . . ."

"Understand what?"

"Everything . . . Ach, I wish to God you weren't going."

She looked at him and was shocked to see that he was on the brink of tears. Her rock, the cliff that had always been so strong, so resolute, was about to crumble before her eyes.

She squeezed his hand as hard as she could.

"This is the best thing for us. I know it hurts. It hurts me, too. But it is for the best. Your family need you. I couldn't live with myself, knowing I was the bitch who was keeping you from your children."

Kraus swallowed hard. "I would never think of you like that."

"No, but I would."

She thought of all the times he had calmed her, talked her down from some outburst or other and got her thinking straight again. So she did what Kraus did. She waited and then, after he had emptied his glass and burned a cigarette right down to the filter in just two or three drags, she said: "Finish your story, the one about you and Heuser. Tell me how it ends."

"Yes, that's good . . . let's get to the end. Well, what I was trying to say, you know, with all that stuff about bayonets and dead kids, is that if this is what it's like for me, think how much worse it is for Heuser. Think about Lütkenhus, who killed himself because the thought of being arrested and having to face up to the truth of what he had done was too much for him. There was a gas-van driver who hanged himself in jail before we could even interrogate him. What was his name?"

"I can't remember . . . it doesn't matter."

"No, well, take it from me, those SS men can spend all day fooling the world and themselves that they aren't really killers. But when they close their eyes to sleep, that's when the nightmares come, and the terrors, the sweating and the screaming. Just go ask Frau Heuser how often she used to be woken up by her Georg sitting bolt-upright in his bed with a look on his face like he just saw the hounds of hell. I bet she never had an undisturbed night until he was packed off to prison. And I bet he was having the same dreams in jail that he'd had at home. So we shouldn't be angry that he won't be in prison for life, because he's got a different life sentence—a nightmare that won't ever stop until his lights go out forever."

Paula didn't reply. What more was there to say? They just sat there for a while in silence, finishing their drinks. Kraus had another cigarette. Finally he looked at her and said: "It was good, wasn't it, what we had together?"

"The best," said Paula.

They got to their feet and gathered up their things. Outside the bar the light was starting to fade. People walked by, some alone, others in groups, others arm-in-arm with lovers or friends.

Paula said she had to go, and they kissed goodbye on the cheeks, like acquaintances rather than lovers. She held her lips on Kraus's skin for an extra second, wanting him to know that she still cared for him. As they stepped apart he said: "Goodbye, then."

Paula could feel the tears welling up in her, but she didn't want to shed them now. So she forced a smile to her face. Then she said, "I really have to go," and walked away into the dusk.

―――――――――

Georg Heuser was released from prison on December 12, 1969, freed by order of the same Koblenz District Court that had imprisoned him six and a half years earlier. From the time of his arrest in July 1959, he served a total of 3,795 days in captivity, or to put it another way, roughly eight hours for every one of the people who perished at his hands, or in actions at which he was present.

He died of natural causes in January 1989, shortly before his seventy-sixth birthday.

ACKNOWLEDGMENTS

I would never have had the idea for this book had I not read *Berlin at War*, by the British historian Roger Moorhouse, which contains an excellent summary of the S-Bahn murders and mentions that one of the officers involved was subsequently a war criminal. That passing reference caught my imagination and set in motion the train of thought that led to *Ostland*. *Berlin at War* became an invaluable and much-pillaged work of reference as I was writing, while Roger himself was extraordinarily generous in giving me the benefit of his time, his own research materials, and his tremendous insight into the nature of life in Nazi Germany. He not only corrected many of my historical mistakes, he also made extremely astute editorial comments. I cannot thank him enough.

Jürgen Matthäus, Director of Applied Research Scholars at the U.S. Holocaust Memorial Museum in Washington, D.C., was another historian who helped me both as a writer and an individual. His essay "No Ordinary Criminal," in the book *Atrocities on Trial: Historical Perspectives on the Politics of Prosecuting War Crimes*, is the definitive English-language account of the Heuser trial, and was both an invaluable source of information and a springboard for further research. Dr. Matthäus was also very kind in personally assisting my research, not least because he directed me to Ex Post Facto, the online service that was able to provide me with a digital copy of the full judgment against Heuser, et al.—that really was a life-saver!

I had by that point already acquired a photocopied version of the judgment thanks to Thomas Kues, whose two massive articles on the Maly Trostinets death camp, running to a total of thirty thousand words in the journal *Inconvenient History*, represent perhaps the single greatest accumulation of data on that subject currently available. Kues is a "revisionist"—to put it politely—who has compiled his mass of information with the purpose of demonstrating that the numbers don't add up and that far, far fewer people died at the camp than previously thought. I profoundly disagree with him on that score, not least because none of the defendants in the Heuser trial denied that mass executions had taken place in and around Minsk, nor disputed their scale: they just sought to minimize their personal involvement. Nevertheless, Mr. Kues helped me.

Not for the first time, I owe a debt of gratitude to my parents, David and Susan Thomas, who gave me an invaluable guide to Moscow in 1961 (they were living there at the time) and the security precautions Westerners visiting the Soviet Union had to take.

Last, but absolutely not least, my profound thanks go to Rebecca Darby, who translated huge chunks of the trial verdict for me, talked me through much of the rest, and was constantly on hand when my attempts at online translation failed to extract any coherent meaning from assorted German magazine and newspaper accounts of the S-Bahn murders and the Heuser trial. This book could not have been written without her help.

It would require a full chapter to list all the books, articles, websites, and DVDs that provided me with research material. But I would like to give particular credit to the factual information and insight I derived from the following books in particular: *Ordinary Men: Reserve Police Battalion 101 and the Final Solution in Poland* and *The*

Origins of the Final Solution: The Evolution of Nazi Jewish Policy September 1939–March 1942, both by Christopher Browning; *Into That Darkness: From Mercy Killing to Mass Murder*, by Gitta Sereny; *The Holocaust: The Jewish Tragedy*, by Martin Gilbert; and *The Field Men: The SS Officers Who Led the Einsatzkommandos*, by French Maclean. A series of articles on the S-Bahn murders, *"Das Spiel ist aus"* ("The Game Is Up"), printed in *Der Spiegel*, December 1949 and January 1950, and *"Die gehorsamen Mörder"* ("The Obedient Killers"), *Die Zeit*'s report on the Heuser trial, published June 7, 1963, provided vital near-contemporaneous testimony. The two BBC-TV series *The Nazis: A Warning from History* and *Auschwitz: The Nazis and the Final Solution*, both written and directed by Laurence Rees, and ITV's *The World at War*, along with its companion documentaries on the Holocaust and Hitler's Germany, were all invaluable sources of information, eyewitness testimony, and imagery. The photographs of Minsk collected by the Holocaust Research Project informed my descriptions of the city, its ghetto, and the Maly Trostinets camp. I would rather not give any publicity to the website where I found pictures of happy Nazis having fun in Minsk, though I confess they were equally useful and, in their own way, equally shocking.

D.T.

July 2013